MARY ROBERTS RINEHART'S

CRIME BOOK

Mary Roberts Rinehart's
CRIME BOOK

Containing

FOUR COMPLETE STORIES

THE AFTER HOUSE

THE BUCKLED BAG

LOCKED DOORS

THE RED LAMP

NEW YORK

GROSSET & DUNLAP, *Publishers*

By arrangement with Farrar & Rinehart

THE AFTER HOUSE

CONTENTS

I. I plan a Voyage 1
II. The Painted Ship 11
III. I unclench my Hands 19
IV. I receive a Warning 33
V. A Terrible Night 48
VI. In the After House 56
VII. We find the Axe 66
VIII. The Stewardess's Story . . . 77
IX. Prisoners 89
X. "That's Mutiny" 99
XI. "The Dead Line" 110
XII. The First Mate talks 121
XIII. The White Light 133
XIV. From the Crow's Nest 140
XV. A Knocking in the Hold . . . 151
XVI. Jones stumbles over Something . 162
XVII. The Axe is gone 173
XVIII. A Bad Combination 185
XIX. I take the Stand 193
XX. Oleson's Story 205
XXI. "A Bad Woman" 218
XXII. Turner's Story 235
XXIII. Free Again 252
XXIV. The Thing 262
XXV. The Sea Again 279

" A hodge-podge of characters, motives, passions, all working together toward that terrible night of August twelfth, nineteen hundred and eleven, when hell seemed loose on a painted sea."

THE AFTER HOUSE

CHAPTER I

I PLAN A VOYAGE

BY the bequest of an elder brother, I was left enough money to see me through a small college in Ohio, and to secure me four years in a medical school in the East. Why I chose medicine I hardly know. Possibly the career of a surgeon attracted the adventurous element in me. Perhaps, coming of a family of doctors, I merely followed the line of least resistance. It may be, indirectly but inevitably, that I might be on the yacht Ella on that terrible night of August 12, more than a year ago.

I got through somehow. I played quarterback on the football team, and made some money coaching. In summer I did whatever came to hand, from chartering a sail-boat at a summer resort and taking passengers, at so much a head, to checking up cucumbers in Indiana for a Western pickle house.

I was practically alone. Commencement left me with a diploma, a new dress-suit, an out-of-date medical library, a box of surgical instruments of the same date as the books, and an incipient case of typhoid fever.

I was twenty-four, six feet tall, and forty inches around the chest. Also, I had lived clean, and worked and played hard. I got over the fever finally, pretty much all bone and appetite, but — alive. Thanks to the college, my hospital care had cost nothing. It was a good thing: I had just seven dollars in the world.

The yacht Ella lay in the river not far from my hospital windows. She was not a yacht when I first saw her, nor at any time, technically, unless I use the word in the broad sense of a pleasure-boat. She was a two-master, and, when I saw her first, as dirty and disreputable as are most coasting-vessels. Her rejuvenation was the history of my convalescence. On the day she stood forth in her first coat of white paint, I exchanged my dressing-gown for clothing that, however loosely it hung, was still clothing. Her new sails marked my promotion to beefsteak, her brass rails and awnings my first independent excursion up and down the corridor outside my door, and, incidentally, my return to a collar and tie.

The river shipping appealed to me, to my imagination, clean washed by my illness and ready as a child's for new impressions: liners gliding down to the bay and the open sea; shrewish, scolding tugs; dirty but picturesque tramps. My enthusiasm amused the nurses, whose ideas of adventure consisted of little jaunts of exploration into the abdominal cavity, and whose aseptic minds revolted at the sight of dirty sails.

One day I pointed out to one of them an old schooner, red and brown, with patched canvas spread, moving swiftly down the river before a stiff breeze.

"Look at her!" I exclaimed. "There goes adventure, mystery, romance! I should like to be sailing on her."

"You would have to boil the drinking-water," she replied dryly. "And the ship is probably swarming with rats."

"Rats," I affirmed, "add to the local color.

3

Ships are their native habitat. Only sinking ships don't have them."

But her answer was to retort that rats carried bubonic plague, and to exit, carrying the sugar-bowl. I was ravenous, as are all convalescent typhoids, and one of the ways in which I eked out my still slender diet was by robbing the sugar-bowl at meals.

That day, I think it was, the deck furniture was put out on the Ella — numbers of white wicker chairs and tables, with bright cushions to match the awnings. I had a pair of ancient opera-glasses, as obsolete as my amputating knives, and, like them, a part of my heritage. By that time I felt a proprietary interest in the Ella, and through my glasses, carefully focused with a pair of scissors, watched the arrangement of the deck furnishings. A girl was directing the men. I judged, from the poise with which she carried herself, that she was attractive — and knew it. How beautiful she was, and how well she knew it, I was to find out before long. McWhirter to the contrary, she had nothing to do with my decision to sign as a sailor on the Ella.

I PLAN A VOYAGE

One of the bright spots of that long hot summer was McWhirter. We had graduated together in June, and in October he was to enter a hospital in Buffalo as a resident. But he was as indigent as I, and from June to October is four months.

"Four months," he said to me. "Even at two meals a day, boy, that's something over two hundred and forty. And I can eat four times a day, without a struggle! Would n't you think one of these overworked-for-the-good-of-humanity dubs would take a vacation and give me a chance to hold down his practice?"

Nothing of the sort developing, McWhirter went into a drug-store, and managed to pull through the summer with unimpaired cheerfulness, confiding to me that he secured his luncheons free at the soda counter. He came frequently to see me, bringing always a pocketful of chewing gum, which he assured me was excellent to allay the gnawings of hunger, and later, as my condition warranted it, small bags of gum-drops and other pharmacy confections.

McWhirter it was who got me my berth on

the Ella. It must have been about the 20th of July, for the Ella sailed on the 28th. I was strong enough to leave the hospital, but not yet physically able for any prolonged exertion. McWhirter, who was short and stout, had been alternately flirting with the nurse, as she moved in and out preparing my room for the night, and sizing me up through narrowed eyes.

"No," he said, evidently following a private line of thought; "you don't belong behind a counter, Leslie. I'm darned if I think you belong in the medical profession, either. The British army'd suit you."

"The — what?"

"You know — Kipling idea — riding horseback, head of a column — undress uniform — colonel's wife making eyes at you — leading last hopes and all that."

"The British army with Kipling trimmings being out of the question, the original issue is still before us. I'll have to work, Mac, and work like the devil, if I'm to feed myself."

There being no answer to this, McWhirter contented himself with eyeing me.

6

I PLAN A VOYAGE

"I'm thinking," I said, "of going to Europe. The sea is calling me, Mac."

"So was the grave a month ago, but it did n't get you. Don't be an ass, boy. How are you going to sea?"

"Before the mast." This apparently conveying no meaning to McWhirter, I supplemented — "as a common sailor."

He was indignant at first, offering me his room and a part of his small salary until I got my strength; then he became dubious; and finally, so well did I paint my picture of long, idle days on the ocean, of sweet, cool nights under the stars, with breezes that purred through the sails, rocking the ship to slumber — finally he waxed enthusiastic, and was even for giving up the pharmacy at once and sailing with me.

He had been fitting out the storeroom of a sailing-yacht with drugs, he informed me, and doing it under the personal direction of the owner's wife.

"I've made a hit with her," he confided. "Since she's learned I'm a graduate M.D., she's letting me do the whole thing. I've made up some lotions to prevent sunburn, and that sea-sick prescription of old Larimer's, and she thinks I'm the whole cheese. I'll suggest you as ship's doctor."

"How many men in the crew?"

"Eight, I think, or ten. It's a small boat, and carries a small crew."

"Then they don't want a ship's doctor. If I go, I'll go as a sailor," I said firmly. "And I want your word, Mac, not a word about me, except that I am honest."

"You'll have to wash decks, probably."

"I am filled with a wild longing to wash decks," I asserted, smiling at his disturbed face. "I should probably also have to polish brass. There's a great deal of brass on the boat."

"How do you know that?"

When I told him, he was much excited, and, although it was dark and the Ella consisted of three lights, he insisted on the opera-glasses, and was persuaded he saw her. Finally he put down the glasses and came over to me.

"Perhaps you are right, Leslie," he said soberly. "You don't want charity, any more than they want a ship's doctor. Wherever you go and whatever you do, whether you're swabbing decks in your bare feet or polishing brass railings with an old sock, you're a man."

He was more moved than I had ever seen him, and ate a gum-drop to cover his embarrassment. Soon after that he took his departure, and the following day he telephoned to say that, if the sea was still calling me, he could get a note to the captain recommending me. I asked him to get the note.

Good old Mac! The sea was calling me, true enough, but only dire necessity was driving me to ship before the mast — necessity and perhaps what, for want of a better name, we call destiny. For what is fate but inevitable law, inevitable consequence.

The stirring of my blood, generations removed from a seafaring ancestor; my illness, not a cause, but a result; McWhirter, filling prescriptions behind the glass screen of a pharmacy, and fitting out, in porcelain jars, the medicine-closet of the Ella; Turner and his wife, Schwartz, the mulatto Tom, Singleton, and Elsa Lee; all thrown together, a hodge-podge

9

THE AFTER HOUSE

of characters, motives, passions, and hereditary tendencies, through an inevitable law working together toward that terrible night of August 12, when hell seemed loose on a painted sea.

CHAPTER II

THE Ella had been a coasting-vessel, carrying dressed lumber to South America,
and on her return trip bringing a miscellaneous
cargo — hides and wool, sugar from Pernam-
buco, whatever offered. The firm of Turner
and Sons owned the line of which the Ella was
one of the smallest vessels.

The gradual elimination of sailing-ships and
the substitution of steamers in the coasting-
trade, left the Ella, with others, out of commission. She was still seaworthy, rather fast, as
such vessels go, and steady. Marshall Turner,
the oldest son of old Elias Turner, the founder
of the business, bought it in at a nominal sum,
with the intention of using it as a private yacht.
And, since it was a superstition of the house
never to change the name of one of its vessels,
the schooner Ella, odorous of fresh lumber or
raw rubber, as the case might be, dingy gray in
color, with slovenly decks on which lines of

seamen's clothing were generally hanging to dry, remained, in her metamorphosis, still the Ella.

Marshall Turner was a wealthy man, but he equipped his new pleasure-boat very modestly. As few changes as were possible were made. He increased the size of the forward house, adding quarters for the captain and the two mates, and thus kept the after house for himself and his friends. He fumigated the hold and the forecastle — a precaution that kept all the crew coughing for two days, and drove them out of the odor of formaldehyde to the deck to sleep. He installed an electric lighting and refrigerating plant, put a bath in the forecastle, to the bewilderment of the men, who were inclined to think it a reflection on their habits, and almost entirely rebuilt, inside, the old officers' quarters in the after house.

The wheel, replaced by a new one, white and gilt, remained in its old position behind the after house, the steersman standing on a raised iron grating above the wash of the deck. Thus from the chart-room, which had become a sort of lounge and card-room, through a small barred window it was possible to see the man at the wheel, who, in his turn, commanded a view of part of the chart-room, but not of the floor.

The craft was schooner-rigged, carried three lifeboats and a collapsible raft, and was navigated by a captain, first and second mates, and a crew of six able-bodied sailors and one gaunt youth whose sole knowledge of navigation had been gained on an Atlantic City cat-boat. Her destination was vague — Panama perhaps, possibly a South American port, depending on the weather and the whim of the owner.

I do not recall that I performed the nautical rite of signing articles. Armed with the note McWhirter had secured for me, and with what I fondly hoped was the rolling gait of the seafaring man, I approached the captain — a bearded and florid individual. I had dressed the part — old trousers, a cap, and a sweater from which I had removed my college letter. McWhirter, who had supervised my preparations, and who had accompanied me to the wharf, had suggested that I omit my morning shave. The result was, as I look back, a lean and cadaverous six-foot youth, with the hospital pallor still on him, his chin covered with a day's beard, his hair cropped short, and a cannibalistic gleam in his eyes. I remember that my wrists, thin and bony, annoyed me, and that the girl I had seen through the opera-glasses came on board, and stood off, detached and indifferent, but with her eyes on me, while the captain read my letter.

When he finished, he held it out to me.

"I've got my crew," he said curtly.

"There is n't — I suppose there's no chance of your needing another hand?"

"No." He turned away, then glanced back at the letter I was still holding, rather dazed. "You can leave your name and address with the mate over there. If anything turns up he'll let you know."

My address! The hospital?

I folded the useless letter and thrust it into my pocket. The captain had gone forward, and the girl with the cool eyes was leaning against the rail, watching me.

"You are the man Mr. McWhirter has been looking after, are n't you?"

"Yes." I pulled off my cap, and, recollecting myself — "Yes, miss."

"You are not a sailor?"

"I have had some experience — and I am willing."

"You have been ill, have n't you?"

"Yes — miss."

"Could you polish brass, and things like that?"

"I could try. My arms are strong enough. It is only when I walk —"

But she did not let me finish. She left the rail abruptly, and disappeared down the companionway into the after house. I waited uncertainly. The captain saw me still loitering, and scowled. A procession of men with trunks jostled me; a colored man, evidently a butler, ordered me out of his way while he carried down into the cabin, with almost reverent care, a basket of wine.

When the girl returned, she came to me, and stood for a moment, looking me over with cool, appraising eyes. I had been right about her appearance: she was charming — or no, hardly charming. She was too aloof for that. But she was beautiful, an Irish type, with blue-gray eyes and almost black hair. The tilt of her head was haughty. Later I came to know that her *hauteur* was indifference: but at first I was frankly afraid of her, afraid of her cool, mocking eyes and the upward thrust of her chin.

"My brother-in-law is not here," she said after a moment, "but my sister is below in the cabin. She will speak to the captain about you. Where are your things?"

I glanced toward the hospital, where my few worldly possessions, including my dress clothes, my amputating set, and such of my books as I had not been able to sell, were awaiting disposition. "Very near, miss," I said.

"Better bring them at once; we are sailing in the morning." She turned away as if to avoid my thanks, but stopped and came back.

"We are taking you as a sort of extra man," she explained. "You will work with the crew, but it is possible that we will need you — do you know anything about butler's work?"

I hesitated. If I said yes, and then failed —

"I could try."

"I thought, from your appearance, perhaps

16

you had done something of the sort." Oh,
shades of my medical forebears, who had be-
queathed me, along with the library, what I
had hoped was a professional manner! "The
butler is a poor sailor. If he fails us, you will
take his place."

She gave a curt little nod of dismissal, and I
went down the gangplank and along the wharf.
I had secured what I went for; my summer was
provided for, and I was still seven dollars to the
good. I was exultant, but with my exultation
was mixed a curious anger at McWhirter, that
he had advised me not to shave that morning.

My preparation took little time. Such of my
wardrobe as was worth saving, McWhirter took
charge of. I sold the remainder of my books,
and in a sailor's outfitting-shop I purchased
boots and slickers — the sailors' oil skins. With
my last money I bought a good revolver,
second-hand, and cartridges. I was glad later
that I had bought the revolver, and that I had
taken with me the surgical instruments, anti-
quated as they were, which, in their mahogany
case, had accompanied my grandfather through
the Civil War, and had done, as he was wont to

chuckle, as much damage as a three-pounder. McWhirter came to the wharf with me, and looked the Ella over with eyes of proprietorship.

"Pretty snappy-looking boat," he said. "If the nigger gets sick, give him some of my sea-sick remedy. And take care of yourself, boy." He shook hands, his open face flushed with emotion. "Darned shame to see you going like this. Don't eat too much, and don't fall in love with any of the women. Good-bye."

He started away, and I turned toward the ship; but a moment later I heard him calling me. He came back, rather breathless.

"Up in my neighborhood," he panted, "they say Turner is a devil. Whatever happens, it's not your mix-in. Better — better tuck your gun under your mattress and forget you've got it. You've got some disposition yourself."

The Ella sailed the following day at ten o'clock. She carried nineteen people, of whom five were the Turners and their guests. The cabin was full of flowers and steamer-baskets.

Thirty-one days later she came into port again, a lifeboat covered with canvas trailing at her stern.

CHAPTER III

I UNCLENCH MY HANDS

FROM the first the captain disclaimed responsibility for me. I was housed in the forecastle, and ate with the men. There, however, my connection with the crew and the navigation of the ship ended. Perhaps it was as well, although I resented it at first. I was weaker than I had thought, and dizzy at the mere thought of going aloft.

As a matter of fact, I found myself a sort of deck-steward, given the responsibility of looking after the shuffle-board and other deck games, the steamer-rugs, the cards, — for they played bridge steadily, — and answerable to George Williams, the colored butler, for the various liquors served on deck.

The work was easy, and the situation rather amused me. After an effort or two to bully me, one of which resulted in my holding him over the rail until he turned gray with fright, Williams treated me as an equal, which was gratifying.

The weather was good, the food fair. I had no reason to repent my bargain. Of the sailing qualities of the Ella there could be no question. The crew, selected by Captain Richardson from the best men of the Turner line, knew their business, and, especially after the Williams incident, made me one of themselves. Barring the odor of formaldehyde in the forecastle, which drove me to sleeping on deck for a night or two, everything was going smoothly, at least on the surface.

Smoothly as far as the crew was concerned. I was not so sure about the after house.

As I have said, owing to the small size of the vessel, and the fact that considerable of the space had been used for baths, there were, besides the family, only two guests, a Mrs. Johns, a *divorcée*, and a Mr. Vail. Mrs. Turner and Miss Lee shared the services of a maid, Karen Hansen, who, with a stewardess, Henrietta Sloane, occupied a double cabin. Vail had a small room, as had Turner, with a bath between which they used in common. Mrs. Turner's room was a large one, with its own bath, into which Elsa Lee's room also opened.

I UNCLENCH MY HANDS

Mrs. Johns had a room and bath. Roughly, and not drawn to scale, the living quarters of the family were arranged like the diagram on page 199.

I have said that things were not going smoothly in the after house. I felt it rather than saw it. The women rose late — except Miss Lee, who was frequently about when I washed the deck. They chatted and laughed together, read, played bridge when the men were so inclined, and now and then, when their attention was drawn to it, looked at the sea. They were always exquisitely and carefully dressed, and I looked at them as I would at any other masterpieces of creative art, with nothing of covetousness in my admiration.

The men were violently opposed types — Turner, tall, heavy-shouldered, morose by habit, with a prominent nose and rapidly thinning hair, and with strong, pale-blue eyes, congested from hard drinking; Vail, shorter by three inches, dark, good-looking, with that dusky flush under the skin which shows good red blood, and as temperate as Turner was dissipated.

Vail was strong, too. After I had held
Williams over the rail I turned to find him
looking on, amused. And when the frightened
darky had taken himself, muttering threats, to
the galley, Vail came over to me and ran his
hand down my arm.

"Where did you get it?" he asked.

"Oh, I've always had some muscle," I said.
"I'm in bad shape now; just getting over
fever."

"Fever, eh? I thought it was jail. Look
here."

He threw out his biceps for me to feel. It
was a ball of iron under my fingers. The man
was as strong as an ox. He smiled at my surprise, and, after looking to see that no one was
in sight, offered to mix me a highball from a
decanter and siphon on a table.

I refused.

It was his turn to be surprised.

"I gave it up when I was in train— in the
hospital," I corrected myself. "I find I don't
miss it."

He eyed me with some curiosity over his
glass, and, sauntering away, left me to my work

of folding rugs. But when I had finished, and was chalking the deck for shuffle-board, he joined me again, dropping his voice, for the women had come up by that time and were breakfasting on the lee side of the after house.

"Have you any idea, Leslie, how much whiskey there is on board?"

"Williams has considerable, I believe. I don't think there is any in the forward house. The captain is a teetotaler."

"I see. When these decanters go back, Williams takes charge of them?"

"Yes. He locks them away."

He dropped his voice still lower.

"Empty them, Leslie," he said. "Do you understand? Throw what is left overboard. And, if you get a chance at Williams's key, pitch a dozen or two quarts overboard."

"And be put in irons!"

"Not necessarily. I think you understand me. I don't trust Williams. In a week we could have this boat fairly dry."

"There is a great deal of wine."

He scowled. "Damn Williams, anyhow! His

instructions were — but never mind about that. Get rid of the whiskey."

Turner coming up the companionway at that moment, Vail left me. I had understood him perfectly. It was common talk in the forecastle that Turner was drinking hard, and that, in fact, the cruise had been arranged by his family in the hope that, away from his clubs, he would alter his habits — a fallacy, of course. Taken away from his customary daily round, given idle days on a summer sea, and aided by Williams, the butler, he was drinking his head off.

Early as it was, he was somewhat the worse for it that morning. He made directly for me. It was the first time he had noticed me, although it was the third day out. He stood in front of me, his red eyes flaming, and, although I am a tall man, he had an inch perhaps the advantage of me.

"What's this about Williams?" he demanded furiously. "What do you mean by a thing like that?"

"He was bullying me. I did n't intend to drop him."

I UNCLENCH MY HANDS

The ship was rolling gently; he made a pass at me with a magazine he carried, and almost lost his balance. The women had risen, and were watching from the corner of the after house. I caught him and steadied him until he could clutch a chair.

"You try any tricks like that again, and you'll go overboard," he stormed. "Who are you, anyhow? Not one of our men?"

I saw the quick look between Vail and Mrs. Turner, and saw her come forward. Mrs. Johns followed her, smiling.

"Marsh!" Mrs. Turner protested. "I told you about him — the man who had been ill."

"Oh, another of your friends!" he sneered, and looked from me to Vail with his ugly smile.

Vail went rather pale and threw up his head quickly. The next moment Mrs. Johns had saved the situation with an irrelevant remark, and the incident was over. They were playing bridge, not without dispute, but at least without insult. But I had had a glimpse beneath the surface of that luxurious cruise, one of many such in the next few days.

That was on Monday, the third day out. Up to that time Miss Lee had not noticed me, except once, when she found me scrubbing the deck, to comment on a corner that she thought might be cleaner, and another time in the evening, when she and Vail sat in chairs until late, when she had sent me below for a wrap. She looked past me rather than at me, gave me her orders quietly but briefly, and did not even take the trouble to ignore me. And yet, once or twice, I had found her eyes fixed on me with a cool, half-amused expression, as if she found something in my struggles to carry trays as if I had been accustomed to them, or to handle a mop as a mop should be handled and not like a hockey stick — something infinitely entertaining and not a little absurd.

But that morning, after they had settled to bridge, she followed me to the rail, out of earshot. I straightened and took off my cap, and she stood looking at me, unsmiling.

"Unclench your hands!" she said.

"I beg your pardon!" I straightened out my fingers, conscious for the first time of my clenched fists, and even opened and closed them once or twice to prove their relaxation.

"That 's better. Now — won't you try to remember that I am responsible for your being here, and be careful?"

"Then take me away from here and put me with the crew. I am stronger now. Ask the captain to give me a man's work. This — this is a housemaid's occupation."

"We prefer to have you here," she said coldly; and then, evidently repenting her manner: "We need a man here, Leslie. Better stay. Are you comfortable in the forecastle?"

"Yes, Miss Lee."

"And the food is all right?"

"The cook says I am eating two men's rations."

She turned to leave, smiling. It was the first time she had thrown even a fleeting smile my way, and it went to my head.

"And Williams? I am to submit to his insolence?"

She stopped and turned, and the smile faded.

"The next time," she said, "you are to *drop* him!"

But during the remainder of the day she neither spoke to me nor looked, as far as I could tell, in my direction. She flirted openly with Vail, rather, I thought, to the discomfort of Mrs. Johns, who had appropriated him to herself — sang to him in the cabin, and in the long hour before dinner, when the others were dressing, walked the deck with him, talking earnestly. They looked well together, and I believe he was in love with her. Poor Vail!

Turner had gone below, grimly good-humored, to dress for dinner; and I went aft to chat, as I often did, with the steersman. On this occasion it happened to be Charlie Jones. Jones was not his name, so far as I know. It was some inordinately long and different German inheritance, and so, with the facility of the average crew, he had been called Jones. He was a benevolent little man, highly religious, and something of a philosopher. And because I could understand German, and even essay it in a limited way, he was fond of me.

"*Setz du dich,*" he said, and moved over

I UNCLENCH MY HANDS

so that I could sit on the grating on which he stood. "The sky is fine to-night. *Wunderschön!*"

"It always looks good to me," I observed, filling my pipe and passing my tobacco-bag to him. "I may have my doubts now and then on land, Charlie; but here, between the sky and the sea, I'm a believer, right enough."

"'In the beginning He created the heaven and the earth,'" said Charlie reverently.

We were silent for a time. The ship rolled easily; now and then she dipped her bowsprit with a soft swish of spray; a school of dolphins played astern, and the last of the land birds that had followed us out flew in circles around the masts.

"Sometimes," said Charlie Jones, "I think the Good Man should have left it the way it was after the flood — just sky and water. What's the land, anyhow? Noise and confusion, wickedness and crime, robbing the widow and the orphan, eat or be et."

"Well," I argued, "the sea's that way. What are those fish out there flying for, but to get out of the way of bigger fish?"

Charlie Jones surveyed me over his pipe.

"True enough, youngster," he said; "but the Lord's given 'em wings to fly with. He ain't been so careful with the widow and the orphan."

This statement being incontrovertible, I let the argument lapse, and sat quiet, luxuriating in the warmth, in the fresh breeze, in the feeling of bodily well-being that came with my returning strength. I got up and stretched, and my eyes fell on the small window of the chart-room.

The door into the main cabin beyond was open. It was dark with the summer twilight, except for the four rose-shaded candles on the table, now laid for dinner. A curious effect it had — the white cloth and gleaming pink an island of cheer in a twilight sea; and to and from this rosy island, making short excursions, advancing, retreating, disappearing at times, the oval white ship that was Williams's shirt bosom.

Charlie Jones, bending to the right and raised to my own height by the grating on which he stood, looked over my shoulder. Dinner was about to be served. The women had come out. The table-lamps threw their rosy glow over white necks and uncovered arms, and revealed, higher in the shadows, the faces of the men, smug, clean-shaven, assured, rather heavy.

I had been the guest of honor on a steam-yacht a year or two before, after a game. There had been pink lights on the table, I remembered, and the place-cards at dinner the first night out had been caricatures of me in fighting trim. There had been a girl, too. For the three days of that week-end cruise I had been mad about her; before that first dinner, when I had known her two hours, I had kissed her hand and told her I loved her!

Vail and Miss Lee had left the others and come into the chart-room. As Charlie Jones and I looked, he bent over and kissed her hand.

The sun had gone down. My pipe was empty, and from the galley, forward, came the odor of the forecastle supper. Charlie was coughing, a racking paroxysm that shook his wiry body. He leaned over and caught my shoulder as I was moving away.

"New paint and new canvas don't make a new ship," he said, choking back the cough. "She's still the old Ella, the she-devil of the Turner line. Pink lights below, and not a rat in the hold! They left her before we sailed, boy. Every rope was crawling with 'em."

> "The very rats
> Instinctively had left it," —

I quoted. But Charlie, clutching the wheel, was coughing again, and cursing breathlessly as he coughed.

CHAPTER IV

I RECEIVE A WARNING

THE odor of formaldehyde in the forecastle
having abated, permission for the crew
to sleep on deck had been withdrawn. But the
weather as we turned south had grown insuffer-
ably hot. The reek of the forecastle sickened
me — the odor of fresh paint, hardly dry, of
musty clothing and sweaty bodies.

I asked Singleton, the first mate, for permission to sleep on deck, and was refused. I went
down, obediently enough, to be driven back
with nausea. And so, watching my chance, I
waited until the first mate, on watch, disappeared into the forward cabin to eat the night
lunch always prepared by the cook and left
there. Then, with a blanket and pillow, I
crawled into the starboard lifeboat, and settled
myself for the night. The lookout saw me, but
gave no sign.

It was not a bad berth. As the ship listed,

the stars seemed to sway above me, and my last recollection was of the Great Dipper, performing dignified gyrations in the sky.

I was aroused by one of the two lookouts, a young fellow named Burns. He was standing below, rapping on the side of the boat with his knuckles. I sat up and peered over at him, and was conscious for the first time that the weather had changed. A fine rain was falling; my hair and shirt were wet.

"Something doing in the chart-room," he said cautiously. "Thought you might not want to miss it."

He was in his bare feet, as was I. Together we hurried to the after house. The steersman, in oilskins, was at his post, but was peering through the barred window into the chart-room, which was brilliantly lighted. He stepped aside somewhat to let us look in. The loud and furious voices which had guided us had quieted, but the situation had not relaxed.

Singleton, the first mate, and Turner were sitting at a table littered with bottles and glasses, and standing over them, white with fury, was Captain Richardson. In the doorway to the main cabin, dressed in pajamas and a bathrobe, Vail was watching the scene.

"I told you last night, Mr. Turner," the captain said, banging the table with his fist, "I won't have you interfering with my officers, or with my ship. That man's on duty, and he's drunk."

"Your ship!" Turner sneered thickly. "It's my ship, and I — I discharge you."

He got to his feet, holding to the table. "Mr. Singleton — *hic* — from now on you're — captain. Captain Singleton! How — how d' ye like it?"

Mr. Vail came forward, the only cool one of the four.

"Don't be a fool, Marsh," he protested. "Come to bed. The captain's right."

Turner turned his pale-blue eyes on Vail, and they were as full of danger as a snake's. "You go to hell!" he said. "Singleton, you're the captain, d' ye hear? If Rich — if Richardson gets funny, put him — in irons."

Singleton stood up, with a sort of swagger. He was less intoxicated than Turner, but ugly enough. He faced the captain with a leer.

"Sorry, old fellow," he said, "but you heard what Turner said!"

The captain drew a deep breath. Then, without any warning, he leaned across the table and shot out his clenched fist. It took the mate on the point of the chin, and he folded up in a heap on the floor.

"Good old boy!" muttered Burns, beside me. "Good old boy!"

Turner picked up a bottle from the table, and made the same incoördinate pass with it at the captain as he had at me the morning before with his magazine. The captain did not move. He was a big man, and he folded his arms with their hairy wrists across his chest.

"Mr. Turner," he said, "while we are on the sea I am in command here. You know that well enough. You are drunk to-night; in the morning you will be sober, and I want you to remember what I am going to say. If you — interfere again — with — me — or — my — officers — I — shall — put — you — in — irons."

He started for the after companionway, and Burns and I hurried forward out of his way, Burns to the lookout, I to make the round of the after house and bring up, safe from detection, by the wheel again. The mate was in a chair, looking sick and dazed, and Turner and Vail were confronting each other.

"You know that is a lie," Vail was saying. "She is faithful to you, as far as I know, although I'm damned if I know why." He turned to the mate roughly: "Better get out in the air."

Once again I left my window to avoid discovery. The mate, walking slowly, made his way up the companionway to the rail. The man at the wheel reported in the forecastle, when he came down at the end of his watch, that Singleton had seemed dazed, and had stood leaning against the rail for some time, occasionally cursing to himself; that the second mate had come on deck, and had sent him to bed; and that the captain was shut in his cabin with the light going.

There was much discussion of the incident among the crew. Sympathy was with the captain, and there was a general feeling that the end had not come. Charlie Jones, reading his Bible on the edge of his bunk, voiced the general belief.

"Knowin' the Turners, hull and mast," he said, "and having sailed with Captain Richardson off and on for ten years, the chances is good of our having a hell of a time. It ain't natural, anyhow, this voyage with no rats in the hold, and all the insects killed with this here formaldehyde, and ice-cream sent to the fo'c'sle on Sundays!"

But at first the thing seemed smoothed over. It is true that the captain did not speak to the first mate except when compelled to, and that Turner and the captain ignored each other elaborately. The cruise went on without event. There was no attempt on Turner's part to carry out his threat of the night before; nor did he, as the crew had prophesied, order the Ella into the nearest port. He kept much to himself, spending whole days below, with Williams carrying him highballs, always appearing at dinner, however, sodden of face but immaculately dressed, and eating little or nothing.

A week went by in this fashion, luring us all to security. I was still lean but fairly strong again. Vail, left to himself or to the women of the party, took to talking with me now and

then. I thought he was uneasy. More than
once he expressed a regret that he had taken
the cruise, laying his discontent to the long
inaction. But the real reason was Turner's
jealousy of him, the obsession of the dipso-
maniac. I knew it, and Vail knew that I knew.

On the 8th we encountered bad weather,
the first wind of the cruise. All hands were
required for tacking, and I was stationed on the
forecastle-head with one other man. Williams,
the butler, succumbed to the weather, and at
five o'clock Miss Lee made her way forward
through the driving rain, and asked me if I
could take his place.

"If the captain needs you, we can manage,"
she said. "We have Henrietta and Karen, the
two maids. But Mr. Turner prefers a man to
serve."

I said that I was probably not so useful that
I could not be spared, and that I would try.
Vail's suggestion had come back to me, and this
was my chance to get Williams's keys. Miss
Lee having spoken to the captain, I was relieved
from duty, and went aft with her. What with
the plunging of the vessel and the slippery

decks, she almost fell twice, and each time I caught her.

The second time, she wrenched her ankle, and stood for a moment holding to the rail, while I waited beside her. She wore a heavy ulster of some rough material, and a small soft hat of the same material, pulled over her ears. Her soft hair lay wet across her forehead.

"How are you liking the sea, Leslie?" she said, after she had tested her ankle and found the damage inconsiderable.

"Very much, Miss Lee."

"Do you intend to remain a — a sailor?"

"I am not a sailor. I am a deck-steward, and I am about to become a butler."

"That was our agreement," she flashed at me.

"Certainly. And to know that I intend to fulfill it to the letter, I have only to show this."

It had been one of McWhirter's inspirations, on learning how I had been engaged, the small book called "The Perfect Butler." I took it from the pocket of my flannel shirt, under my oilskins, and held it out to her.

"I have not got very far," I said humbly. "It's not inspiring reading. I've got the wineglasses straightened out, but it seems a lot of fuss about nothing. Wine is wine, is n't it? What difference, after all, does a hollow stem or green glass make —"

The rain was beating down on us. The "Perfect Butler" was weeping tears, as its chart of choice vintages was mixed with water. Miss Lee looked up, smiling, from the book.

"You prefer 'a *jug* of wine,'" she said.

"Old Omar had the right idea; only I imagine, literally, it was a skin of wine. They did n't have jugs, did they?"

"You know the 'Rubaiyat'?" she asked slowly.

"I know the jug of wine and loaf of bread part," I admitted, irritated at the slip. "In my home city they're using it to advertise a particular sort of bread. You know — 'A book of verses underneath the bough, a loaf of Wiggin's home-made bread, and thou.'"

In spite of myself, in spite of the absurd verse, of the pouring rain, of the fact that I was shortly to place her dinner before her in the capacity of upper servant, I thrilled to the last two words.

" '*And thou*,' " I repeated.

She looked up at me, startled, and for a second our glances held. The next moment she was gone, and I was alone on a rain-swept deck, cursing my folly.

That night, in a white linen coat, I served dinner in the after house. The meal was unusually gay, rendered so by the pitching of the boat and the uncertainty of the dishes. In the general hilarity, my awkwardness went unnoticed. Miss Lee, sitting beside Vail, devoted herself to him. Mrs. Johns, young and blonde, tried to interest Turner, and, failing in that, took to watching me, to my discomfiture. Mrs. Turner, with apprehensive eyes on her husband, ate little and drank nothing.

Dinner over in the main cabin, they lounged into the chart-room — except Mrs. Johns, who, following them to the door, closed it behind them and came back. She held a lighted cigarette, and she stood just outside the zone of candlelight, watching me through narrowed eyes.

"You got along very well to-night," she observed. "Are you quite strong again?"

"Quite strong, Mrs. Johns."

"You have never done this sort of thing before, have you?"

"Butler's work? No; but it is rather simple."

"I thought perhaps you had," she said. "I seem to recall you, vaguely — that is, I seem to remember a crowd of people, and a noise — I dare say I did see you in a crowd somewhere. You know, you are rather an unforgettable type."

I was nonplussed as to how a butler would reply to such a statement, and took refuge in no reply at all. As it happened, none was needed. The ship gave a terrific roll at that moment, and I just saved the Chartreuse as it was leaving the table. Mrs. Johns was holding to a chair.

"Well caught," she smiled, and, taking a fresh cigarette, she bent over a table-lamp and lighted it herself. All the time her eyes were on me, I felt that she was studying me over her cigarette, with something in view.

"Is it still raining?"

"Yes, Mrs. Johns."

"Will you get a wrap from Karen and bring it to me on deck? I — I want air to-night."

The forward companionway led down into the main cabin. She moved toward it, her pale-green gown fading into the shadow. At the foot of the steps she turned and looked back at me. I had been stupid enough, but I knew then that she had something to say to me, something that she would not trust to the cabin walls. I got the wrap.

She was sitting in a deck-chair when I found her, on the lee side of the after house, a position carefully chosen, with only the storeroom windows behind. I gave her the wrap, and she flung it over her without rising.

"Sit down, Leslie," she said, pointing to the chair beside her. And, as I hesitated, "Don't be silly, boy. Elsa Lee and her sister may be as blind as they like. You are not a sailor, or a butler, either. I don't care what you are: I'm not going to ask any questions. Sit down; I have to talk to some one."

I sat on the edge of the chair, somewhat uneasy, to tell the truth. The crew were about on a night like that, and at any moment Elsa Lee might avail herself of the dummy hand, as she sometimes did, and run up for a breath of air or a glimpse of the sea.

"Just now, Mrs. Johns," I said, "I am one of the crew of the Ella, and if I am seen here —"

"Oh, fudge!" she retorted impatiently. "My reputation is n't going to be hurt, and the man's never is. Leslie, I am frightened — you know what I mean."

"Turner?"

"Yes."

"You mean — with the captain?"

"With any one who happens to be near. He is dangerous. It is Vail now. He thinks Mr. Vail is in love with his wife. The fact is that Vail — well, never mind about that. The point is this: This afternoon he had a dispute with Williams, and knocked him down. The other women don't know it. Vail told me. We have given out that Williams is seasick. It will be Vail next, and, if he puts a hand on him, Vail will kill him; I know him."

"We could stop this drinking."

"And have him shoot up the ship! I have been thinking all evening, and only one thing

45

occurs to me. We are five women and two men, and Vail refuses to be alarmed. I want you to sleep in the after house. Is n't there a store-room where you could put a cot?"

"Yes," I agreed, "and I'll do it, of course, if you are uneasy, but I really think —"

"Never mind what you really think. I have n't slept for three nights, and I'm showing it." She made a motion to rise, and I helped her up. She was a tall woman, and before I knew it she had put both her hands on my shoulders.

"You are a poor butler, and an indifferent sailor, I believe," she said, "but you are rather a dear. Thank you."

She left me, alternately uplifted and sheepish. But that night I took a blanket and a pillow into the storeroom, and spread my six feet of length along the greatest diameter of a four-by-seven pantry.

And that night, also, between six and seven bells, with the storm subsided and only a moderate sea, Schwartz, the second mate, went overboard — went without a cry, without a sound.

I RECEIVE A WARNING

Singleton, relieving him at four o'clock, found his cap lying near starboard, just forward of the after house. The helmsman and the two men in the lookout reported no sound of a struggle. The lookout had seen the light of his cigar on the forecastle-head at six bells (three o'clock). At seven bells he had walked back to the helmsman and commented cheerfully on the break in the weather. That was the last seen of him.

The alarm was raised when Singleton went on watch at four o'clock. The Ella was heaved to and the lee boat lowered. At the same time life-buoys were thrown out, and patent lights. But the early summer dawn revealed a calm ocean, and no sign of the missing mate.

At ten o'clock the order was reluctantly given to go on.

CHAPTER V

WITH the disappearance of Schwartz, the Ella was short-handed. I believe Captain Richardson made an attempt to secure me to take the place of Burns, now moved up into Schwartz's position. But the attempt met with a surly refusal from Turner.

The crew was plainly nervous and irritable. Sailors are simple-minded men, as a rule; their mental processes are elemental. They began to mutter that the devil-ship of the Turner line was at her tricks again.

That afternoon, going into the forecastle for some of my clothing, I found a curious group. Gathered about the table were Tom, the mulatto cook, a Swede named Oleson, Adams, and Burns of the crew. At the head of the table Charlie Jones was reading the service for the burial of the dead at sea. The men were standing, bareheaded. I took off my cap and stood,

48

just inside the door, until the simple service was over. I was strongly moved.

Schwartz disappeared in the early morning of August 9. And now I come, not without misgiving, to the night of August 12. I am wondering if, after all, I have made clear the picture that is before my eyes: the languid cruise, the slight relaxation of discipline, due to the leisure of a pleasure voyage, the Ella again rolling gently, with hardly a dash of spray to show that she was moving, the sun beating down on her white decks and white canvas, on the three women in summer attire, on unending bridge, with its accompaniment of tall glasses filled with ice, on Turner's morose face and Vail's watchful one. In the forecastle, much gossip and not a little fear, and in the forward house, where Captain Richardson and Singleton had their quarters, veiled hostility and sullen silence.

August 11 was Tuesday, a hot August day, with only enough air going to keep our sails filled. At five o'clock I served afternoon tea, and shortly after I went to Williams's cabin in the forward house to dress the wound in his head, a long cut, which was now healing. I passed the captain's cabin, and heard him quarreling with the first mate, who was replying, now and then, sullenly. Only the tones of their voices reached me.

When I had finished with Williams, and was returning, the quarrel was still going on. Their voices ceased as I passed the door, and there was a crash, as of a chair violently overturned. The next bit I heard.

"Put that down!" the captain roared.

I listened, uncertain whether to break in or not. The next moment, Singleton opened the door and saw me. I went on as if I had heard nothing.

Beyond that, the day was much as other days. Turner ate no dinner that night. He was pale, and twitching; even with my small experience, I knew he was on the verge of delirium tremens. He did not play cards, and spent much of the evening wandering restlessly about on deck. Mrs. Turner retired early. Mrs. Johns played accompaniments for Vail to sing to, in the chart-room, until something after eleven, when they, too, went to their rooms.

A TERRIBLE NIGHT

It being impracticable for me to go to my quarters in the storeroom until the after house was settled, I went up on deck. Miss Lee had her arm through Turner's and was talking to him. He seemed to be listening to her; but at last he stopped and freed his arm, not ungently.

"That all sounds very well, Elsa," he said, "but you don't know what you are talking about."

"I know *this*."

"I'm not a fool — or blind."

He lurched down the companionway and into the cabin. I heard her draw a long breath; then she turned and saw me.

"Is that you, Leslie?"

"Yes, Miss Lee."

She came toward me, the train of her soft white gown over her arm, and the light from a lantern setting some jewels on her neck to glittering.

"Mrs. Johns has told me where you are sleeping. You are very good to do it, although I think she is rather absurd."

"I am glad to do anything I can."

"I am sure of that. You are certain you are comfortable there?"

"Perfectly."

"Then — good-night. And thank you."

Unexpectedly she put out her hand, and I took it. It was the first time I had touched her, and it went to my head. I bent over her slim cold fingers and kissed them. She drew her breath in sharply in surprise, but as I dropped her hand our eyes met.

"You should not have done that," she said coolly. "I am sorry."

She left me utterly wretched. What a boor she must have thought me, to misconstrue her simple act of kindness! I loathed myself with a hatred that sent me groveling to my blanket in the pantry, and that kept me, once there, awake through all the early part of the summer night.

I wakened with a sense of oppression, of smothering heat. I had struggled slowly back to consciousness, to realize that the door of the pantry was closed, and that I was stewing in the moist heat of the August night. I got up, clad in my shirt and trousers, and felt my way to the door.

A TERRIBLE NIGHT

The storeroom and pantry of the after house had been built in during the rehabilitation of the boat, and consisted of a short passageway, with drawers for linens on either side, and beyond, lighted by a porthole, the small supply-room in which I had been sleeping.

Along this passageway, then, I groped my way to the door at the end, opening into the main cabin near the chart-room door and across from Mrs. Turner's room. This door I had been in the habit of leaving open, for two purposes — ventilation, and in case I might be, as Mrs. Johns had feared, required in the night.

The door was locked on the outside.

I was a moment or two in grasping the fact. I shook it carefully to see if it had merely caught, and then, incredulous, I put my weight to it. It refused to yield. The silence outside was absolute.

I felt my way back to the window. It was open, but was barred with iron, and, even without that, too small for my shoulders. I listened for the mate. It was still dark, and so not yet time for the watch to change. Singleton would be on duty, and he rarely came aft. There was no sound of footsteps.

I lit a match and examined the lock. It was a simple one, and as my idea now was to free myself without raising an alarm, I decided to unscrew it with my pocket-knife. I was still confused, but inclined to consider my imprisonment a jest, perhaps on the part of Charlie Jones, who tempered his religious fervor with a fondness for practical joking.

I accordingly knelt in front of the lock and opened my knife. I was in darkness and working by touch. I had extracted one screw, and, with a growing sense of satisfaction, was putting it in my pocket before loosening a second, when a board on which I knelt moved under my knee, lifted, as if the other end, beyond the door, had been stepped on. There was no sound, no creak. Merely that ominous lifting under my knee. There was some one just beyond the door.

A moment later the pressure was released. With a growing horror of I know not what, I set to work at the second screw, trying to be noiseless, but with hands shaking with excitement. The screw fell out into my palm. In my haste I dropped my knife, and had to grope for it on the floor. It was then that a woman screamed — a low, sobbing cry, broken off almost before it began. I had got my knife by that time, and in desperation I threw myself against the door. It gave way, and I fell full length on the main cabin floor. I was still in darkness. The silence in the cabin was absolute. I could hear the steersman beyond the chart-room scratching a match.

As I got up, six bells struck. It was three o'clock.

Vail's room was next to the pantry, and forward. I felt my way to it, and rapped.

"Vail," I called. "Vail!"

His door was open an inch or so. I went in and felt my way to his bunk. I could hear him breathing, a stertorous respiration like that of sleep, and yet unlike. The moment I touched him, the sound ceased, and did not commence again. I struck a match and bent over him.

He had been almost cut to pieces with an axe.

CHAPTER VI

IN THE AFTER HOUSE

THE match burnt out, and I dropped it. I remember mechanically extinguishing the glowing end with my heel, and then straightening to such a sense of horror as I have never felt before or since. I groped for the door; I wanted air, space, the freedom from lurking death of the open deck.

I had been sleeping with my revolver beside me on the pantry floor. Somehow or other I got back there and found it. I made an attempt to find the switch for the cabin lights, and, failing, revolver in hand, I ran into the chart-room and up the after companionway. Charlie Jones was at the wheel, and by the light of a lantern I saw that he was bending to the right, peering in at the chart-room window. He turned when he heard me.

"What's wrong?" he asked. "I heard a yell a minute ago. Turner on the rampage?" He saw my revolver then, and, letting go the wheel, threw up both his hands. "Turn that gun away, you fool!"

I could hardly speak. I lowered the revolver and gasped: "Call the captain! Vail's been murdered!"

"Good God!" he said. "Who did it?" He had taken the wheel again, and was bringing the ship back to her course. I was turning sick and dizzy, and I clutched at the railing of the companionway.

"I don't know. Where's the captain?"

"The mate's around." He raised his voice. "Mr. Singleton!" he called.

There was no time to lose, I felt. My nausea had left me. I ran forward to where I could dimly see Singleton looking in my direction.

"Singleton! Quick!" I called. "Bring your revolver."

He stopped and peered in my direction.

"Who is it?"

"Leslie. Come below, for God's sake!"

He came slowly toward me, and in a dozen words I told him what had happened. I saw then that he had been drinking. He reeled against me, and seemed at a loss to know what to do.

"Get your revolver," I said, "and wake the captain."

He disappeared into the forward house, to come back a moment later with a revolver. I had got a lantern in the mean time, and ran to the forward campanionway which led into the main cabin. Singleton followed me.

"Where's the captain?" I asked.

"I did n't call him," Singleton replied, and muttered something unintelligible under his breath.

Swinging the lantern ahead of me, I led the way down the companionway. Something lay huddled at the foot. I had to step over it to get down. Singleton stood above, on the steps. I stooped and held the lantern close, and we both saw that it was the captain, killed as Vail had been. He was fully dressed except for his coat, and as he lay on his back, his cap had been placed over his mutilated face.

I thought I heard something moving behind me in the cabin, and wheeled sharply, holding my revolver leveled. The idea had come to me that the crew had mutinied, and that every one in the after house had been killed. The idea made me frantic; I thought of the women, of Elsa Lee, and I was ready to kill.

"Where is the light switch?" I demanded of Singleton, who was still on the companion steps, swaying.

"I don't know," he said, and collapsed, sitting huddled just above the captain's body, with his face in his hands.

I saw I need not look to him for help, and I succeeded in turning on the light in the swinging lamp in the center of the cabin. There was no sign of any struggle, and the cabin was empty. I went back to the captain's body, and threw a rug over it. Then I reached over and shook Singleton by the arm.

"Do something!" I raved. "Call the crew. Get somebody here, you drunken fool!"

He rose and staggered up the companionway, and I ran to Miss Lee's door. It was closed and locked, as were all the others except Vail's and the one I had broken open. I reached Mr. Turner's door last. It was locked, and I got no response to my knock. I remembered that his room and Vail's connected through a bath, and, still holding my revolver leveled, I ran into Vail's room again, this time turning on the light.

A night light was burning in the bath-room, and the door beyond was unlocked. I flung it open and stepped in. Turner was lying on his bed, fully dressed, and at first I thought he too had been murdered. But he was in a drunken stupor. He sat up, dazed, when I shook him by the arm.

"Mr. Turner!" I cried. "Try to rouse yourself, man! The captain has been murdered, and Mr. Vail!"

He made an effort to sit up, swayed, and fell back again. His face was swollen and purplish, his eyes congested. He made an effort to speak, but failed to be intelligible. I had no time to waste. Somewhere on the Ella the murderer was loose. He must be found.

I flung out of Turner's cabin as the crew, gathered from the forecastle and from the decks, crowded down the forward companion-way. I ran my eye over them. Every man was there, Singleton below by the captain's body, the crew, silent and horror-struck, grouped on the steps: Clarke, McNamara, Burns, Oleson, and Adams. Behind the crew, Charlie Jones had left the wheel and stood peering down, until sharply ordered back. Williams, with a bandage on his head, and Tom, the mulatto cook, were in the group.

I stood, revolver in hand, staring at the men. Among them, I felt sure, was the murderer. But which one? All were equally pale, equally terrified.

"Boys," I said, "Mr. Vail and your captain have been murdered. The murderer must be on the ship — one of ourselves." There was a murmur at that. "Mr. Singleton, I suggest that these men stay together in a body, and that no one be allowed to go below until all have been searched and all weapons taken from them."

Singleton had dropped into a chair, and sat with his face buried in his hands, his back to the captain's body. He looked up without moving, and his face was gray.

"All right," he said. "Do as you like. I'm sick."

He looked sick. Burns, who had taken

Schwartz's place as second mate, left the group and came toward me.

"We'd better waken the women," he said. "If you'll tell them, Leslie, I'll take the crew on deck and keep them there."

Singleton seemed dazed, and when Burns spoke of taking the men on deck, he got up dizzily.

"I'm going too," he muttered. "I'll go crazy if I stay down here with *that*."

The rug had been drawn back to show the crew what had happened. I drew it reverently over the body again.

After the men had gone, I knocked at Mrs. Turner's door. It was some time before she roused; when she answered, her voice was startled.

"What is it?"

"It's Leslie, Mrs. Turner. Will you come to the door?"

"In a moment."

She threw on a dressing-gown, and opened the door.

"What is wrong?"

I told her, as gently as I could. I thought

she would faint; but she pulled herself together and looked past me into the cabin.

"*That* is —?"

"The captain, Mrs. Turner."

"And Mr. Vail?"

"In his cabin."

"Where is Mr. Turner?"

"In his cabin, asleep."

She looked at me strangely, and, leaving the door, went into her sister's room, next. I heard Miss Lee's low cry of horror, and almost immediately the two women came to the doorway.

"Have you seen Mr. Turner?" Miss Lee demanded.

"Just now."

"Has Mrs. Johns been told?"

"Not yet."

She went herself to Mrs. Johns's cabin, and knocked. She got an immediate answer, and Mrs. Johns, partly dressed, opened the door.

"What's the matter?" she demanded. "The whole crew is tramping outside my windows. I hope we have n't struck an iceberg."

"Adèle, don't faint, please. Something awful has happened."

"Turner! He has killed some one finally!"

"Hush, for Heaven's sake! Wilmer has been murdered, Adèle — and the captain."

Mrs. Johns had less control than the other women. She stood for an instant, with a sort of horrible grin on her face. Then she went down on the floor, full length, with a crash. Elsa Lee knelt beside her and slid a pillow under her head.

"Call the maids, Leslie," she said quietly. "Karen has something for this sort of thing. Tell her to bring it quickly."

I went the length of the cabin and into the chart-room. The maids' room was here, on the port-side, and thus aft of Mrs. Turner's and Miss Lee's rooms. It had one door only, and two small barred windows, one above each of the two bunks.

I turned on the chart-room lights. At the top of the after companionway the crew had been assembled, and Burns was haranguing them. I knocked at the maids' door, and, finding it unlocked, opened it an inch or so.

"Karen!" I called — and, receiving no answer: "Mrs. Sloane!" (the stewardess).

I opened the door wide and glanced in. Karen Hansen, the maid, was on the floor, dead. The stewardess, in collapse from terror, was in her bunk, uninjured.

CHAPTER VII

WE FIND THE AXE

I WENT to the after companionway and called up to the men to send the first mate down; but Burns came instead.

"Singleton's sick," he explained. "He's up there in a corner, with Oleson and McNamara holding him."

"Burns," I said cautiously — "I've found another!"

"God, not one of the women!"

"One of the maids — Karen."

Burns was a young fellow about my own age, and to this point he had stood up well. But he had been having a sort of flirtation with the girl, and I saw him go sick with horror. He wanted to see her, when he had got command of himself; but I would not let him enter the room. He stood outside, while I went in and carried out the stewardess, who was coming to and moaning. I took her forward, and told the three women there what I had found.

66

WE FIND THE AXE

Mrs. Johns was better, and I found them all huddled in her room. I put the stewardess on the bed, and locked the door into the next room. Then, after examining the window, I gave Elsa Lee my revolver.

"Don't let any one in," I said. "I'll put a guard at the two companionways, and we'll let no one down. But — keep the door locked also."

She took the revolver from me, and examined it with the air of one familiar with firearms. Then she looked up at me, her lips as white as her face.

"We are relying on you, Leslie," she said.

And, at her words, the storm of self-contempt and bitterness that I had been holding in abeyance for the last half hour swept over me like a flood. I could have wept for fury.

"Why should you trust me?" I demanded. "I slept through the time when I was needed. And when I wakened and found myself locked in the storeroom, I waited to take the lock off instead of breaking down the door! I ought to jump overboard."

"We are relying on you," she said again, sim-

ply; and I heard her fasten the door behind me
as I went out.

Dawn was coming as I joined the crew, huddled around the wheel. There were nine men,
counting Singleton. But Singleton hardly
counted. He was in a state of profound mental
and physical collapse. The Ella was without
an accredited officer, and, for lack of orders to
the contrary, the helmsman — McNamara now
— was holding her to her course. Burns had
taken Schwartz's place as second mate, but the
situation was clearly beyond him. Turner's
condition was known and frankly discussed.
It was clear that, for a time at least, we would
have to get along without him.

Charlie Jones, always an influence among the
men, voiced the situation as we all stood together in the chill morning air.

"What we want to do, boys," he said, "is to
make for the nearest port. This here is a
police matter."

"And a hanging matter," some one else put in.

"We've got to remember, boys, that this
ain't like a crime on land. We've got the fellow
that did it. He's on the boat all right."

WE FIND THE AXE

There was a stirring among the men, and some of them looked aft to where, guarded by the Swede Oleson, Singleton was sitting, his head in his hands.

"And, what's more," Charlie Jones went on, "I'm for putting Leslie here in charge — for now, anyhow. That's agreeable to you, is it, Burns?"

"But I don't know anything about a ship," I objected. "I'm willing enough, but I'm not competent."

I believe the thing had been discussed before I went up, for McNamara spoke up from the wheel.

"We'll manage that somehow or other, Leslie," he said. "We want somebody to take charge, somebody with a head, that's all. And since you ain't, in a manner of speaking, been one of us, nobody's feelings can't be hurt. Ain't that it, boys?"

"That, and a matter of brains," said Burns.

"But Singleton?" I glanced aft.

"Singleton is going in irons," was the reply I got.

The light was stronger now, and I could see their faces. It was clear that the crew, or a majority of the crew, believed him guilty, and that, as far as Singleton was concerned, my authority did not exist.

"All right," I said. "I'll do the best I can. First of all, I want every man to give up his weapons. Burns!"

"Aye, aye."

"Go over each man. Leave them their pocket-knives; take everything else."

The men lined up. The situation was tense, horrible, so that the miscellaneous articles from their pockets — knives, keys, plugs of chewing tobacco, and here and there, among the foreign ones, small combs for beard and mustache — unexpectedly brought to light, caused a smile of pure reaction. Two revolvers from Oleson and McNamara and one nicked razor from Adams completed the list of weapons we found. The crew submitted willingly. They seemed relieved to have some one to direct them, and the alacrity with which they obeyed my orders showed how they were suffering under the strain of inaction.

WE FIND THE AXE

I went over to Singleton and put my hand on his shoulder.

"I'm sorry, Mr. Singleton," I said, "but I'll have to ask you for your revolver."

Without looking at me, he drew it from his hip pocket and held it out. I took it. It was loaded.

"It's out of order," he said briefly. "If it had been working right, I would n't be here."

I reached down and touched his wrist. His pulse was slow and rather faint, his hands cold.

"Is there anything I can do for you?"

"Yes," he snarled. "You can get me a belaying-pin and let me at those fools over there. Turner did this, and you know it as well as I do!"

I slid his revolver into my pocket, and went back to the men. Counting Williams and the cook and myself, there were nine of us. The cook I counted out, ordering him to go to the galley and prepare breakfast. The eight that were left I divided into two watches, Burns taking one and I the other. On Burns's watch were Clarke, McNamara, and Williams; on mine, Oleson, Adams, and Charlie Jones.

It was two bells, or five o'clock. Burns struck
the gong sharply as an indication that order,
of a sort, had been restored. The rising sun
was gleaming on the sails; the gray surface of
the sea was ruffling under the morning breeze.
From the galley a thin stream of smoke was
rising. Some of the horror of the night went
with the darkness, but the thought of what
waited in the cabin below was on us all.

I suggested another attempt to rouse Mr.
Turner, and Burns and Clarke went below.
They came back in ten minutes, reporting no
change in Turner's condition. There was open
grumbling among the men at the situation,
but we were helpless. Burns and I decided to
go on as if Turner were not on board, until he
was in condition to take hold.

We thought it best to bring up the bodies
while all the crew was on duty, and then to take
up the watches. I arranged to have one man
constantly on guard in the after house — a
difficult matter where all were under suspicion.
Burns suggested Charlie Jones as probably the
most reliable, and I gave him the revolver
I had taken from Singleton. It was useless,

but it made at least a show of authority. The rest of the crew, except Oleson, on guard over the mate, was detailed to assist in carrying up the three bodies. Williams was taken along to get sheets from the linen room.

We brought the captain up first, laying him on a sheet on the deck and folding the edges over him. It was terrible work. Even I, fresh from a medical college, grew nauseated over it. He was heavy. It was slow work, getting him up. Vail we brought up in the sheets from his bunk. Of the three, he was the most mutilated. The maid Karen showed only one injury, a smashing blow on the head, probably from the head of the axe. For axe it had been, beyond a doubt.

I put Williams to work below to clear away every evidence of what had happened. He went down, ashy-faced, only to rush up again, refusing to stay alone. I sent Clarke with him, and instructed Charlie Jones to keep them there until the cabin was in order.

At three bells the cook brought coffee, and some of the men took it. I tried to swallow, but it choked me.

73

THE AFTER HOUSE

Burns had served as second mate on a sailing-vessel, and thought he could take us back, at least into more traveled waters. We decided to head back to New York. I got the code-book from the captain's cabin, and we agreed to run up the flag, union down, if any other vessel came in sight. I got the code word for "Mutiny — need assistance," and I asked the mate if he would signal if a vessel came near enough. But he turned sullen and refused to answer.

I find it hard to recall calmly the events of that morning: the three still and shrouded figures, prone on deck; the crew, bareheaded, standing around, eyeing each other stealthily, with panic ready to leap free and grip each of them by the throat; the grim determination, the reason for which I did not yet know, to put the first mate in irons; and, over all, the clear sunrise of an August morning on the ocean, rails and decks gleaming, an odor of coffee in the air, the joyous lift and splash of the bowsprit as the Ella, headed back on her course, seemed to make for home like a nag for the stable.

Surely none of these men, some weeping, all grieving, could be the fiend who had committed

the crimes. One by one, I looked in their faces
— at Burns, youngest member of the crew, a
blue-eyed, sandy-haired Scot; at Clarke and
Adams and Charlie Jones, old in the service of
the Turner line; at McNamara, a shrewd little
Irishman; at Oleson the Swede. And, in spite
of myself, I could not help comparing them with
the heavy-shouldered, sodden-faced man below
in his cabin, the owner of the ship.

One explanation came to me, and I leaped at
it — the possibility of a stowaway hidden in the
hold, some maniacal fugitive who had found
in the little cargo boat's empty hull ample room
to hide. The men, too, seized at the idea. One
and all volunteered for what might prove to be
a dangerous service.

I chose Charlie Jones and Clarke as being
most familiar with the ship, and we went down
into the hold. Clarke carried a lantern. Charlie
Jones held Singleton's broken revolver. I carried a belaying pin. But, although we searched
every foot of space, we found nothing. The
formaldehyde with which Turner had fumigated
the ship clung here tenaciously, and, mixed with
the odors of bilge water and the indescribable

heavy smells left by tropical cargoes, made me dizzy and ill.

We were stumbling along, Clarke with the lantern, I next, and Charlie Jones behind, on our way to the ladder again, when I received a stunning blow on the back of the head. I turned dizzy, expecting nothing less than sudden death, when it developed that Jones, having stumbled over a loose plank, had fallen forward, the revolver in his outstretched hand striking my head.

He picked himself up sheepishly, and we went on. But so unnerved was I by this fresh shock that it was a moment or two before I could essay the ladder.

Burns was waiting at the hatchway, peering down. Beside him on the deck lay a blood-stained axe.

Elsa Lee, on hearing the story of Henrietta Sloane, had gone to the maids' cabin, and had found it where it had been flung into the berth of the stewardess.

CHAPTER VIII

BUT, after all, the story of Henrietta Sloane only added to the mystery. She told it to me, sitting propped in a chair in Mrs. Johns's room, her face white, her lips dry and twitching. The crew were making such breakfast as they could on deck, and Mr. Turner was still in a stupor in his room across the main cabin. The four women, drawn together in their distress, were huddled in the center of the room, touching hands now and then, as if finding comfort in contact, and reassurance.

"I went to bed early," said the stewardess; "about ten o'clock, I think. Karen had not come down; I wakened when the watch changed. It was hot, and the window from our room to the deck was open. There is a curtain over it, to keep the helmsman from looking in — it is close to the wheel. The bell, striking every half-hour, does not waken me any more, although it did at first. It is just outside the

77

window. But I heard the watch change. I heard eight bells struck, and the lookout man on the forecastle-head call, 'All's well.'

"I sat up and turned on the lights. Karen had not come down, and I was alarmed. She had been — had been flirting a little with one of the sailors, and I had warned her that it would not do. She'd be found out and get into trouble.

"The only way to reach our cabin was through the chart-room, and when I opened the door an inch or two, I saw why Karen had not come down. Mr. Turner and Mr. Singleton were sitting there. They were —" She hesitated.

"Please go on," said Mrs. Turner. "They were drinking?"

"Yes, Mrs. Turner. And Mr. Vail was there, too. He was saying that the captain would come down and there would be more trouble. I shut the door and stood just inside, listening. Mr. Singleton said he hoped the captain would come — that he and Mr. Turner only wanted a chance to get at him."

Miss Lee leaned forward and searched the stewardess's face with strained eyes.

"You are sure that he mentioned Mr. Turner in that?"

"That was exactly what he said, Miss Lee. The captain came down just then, and ordered Mr. Singleton on deck. I think he went, for I did not hear his voice again. I thought, from the sounds, that Mr. Vail and the captain were trying to get Mr. Turner to his room."

Mrs. Johns had been sitting back, her eyes shut, holding a bottle of salts to her nose. Now she looked up.

"My dear woman," she said, "are you trying to tell us that we slept through all that?"

"If you did not hear it, you must have slept," the stewardess persisted obstinately. "The door into the main cabin was closed. Karen came down just after. She was frightened. She said the first mate was on deck, in a terrible humor; and that Charlie Jones, who was at the wheel, had appealed to Burns not to leave him there — that trouble was coming. That must have been at half-past twelve. The bell struck as she put out the light. We both went to sleep then, until Mrs. Turner's ringing for Karen roused us."

"But I did not ring for Karen."

The woman stared at Mrs. Turner.

"But the bell rang, Mrs. Turner. Karen got up at once and, turning on the light, looked at the clock. 'What do you think of that?' she said. 'Ten minutes to three, and I'd just got to sleep!' I growled about the light, and she put it out, after she had thrown on a wrapper. The room was dark when she opened the door. There was a little light in the chart-room, from the binnacle lantern. The door at the top of the companionway was always closed at night; the light came through the window near the wheel."

She had kept up very well to this point, telling her story calmly and keeping her voice down. But when she reached the actual killing of the Danish maid, she went to pieces. She took to shivering violently, and her pulse, under my fingers, was small and rapid. I mixed some aromatic spirits with water and gave it to her, and we waited until she could go on.

For the first time, then, I realized that I was clad only in shirt and trousers, with a handkerchief around my head where the acci-

dent in the hold had left me with a nasty cut.
My bare feet were thrust into down-at-the-heel
slippers. I saw Miss Lee's eyes on me, and
colored.

"I had forgotten," I said uncomfortably.
"I'll have time to find my coat while she is
recovering. I have been so occupied —"

"Don't be a fool," Mrs. Johns said brusquely.
"No one cares how you look. We only thank
Heaven you are alive to look after us. Do
you know what we have been doing, locked in
down here? We have been —"

"Please, Adèle!" said Elsa Lee. And Mrs.
Johns, shrugging her shoulders, went back to
her salts.

The rest of the story we got slowly. Briefly,
it was this. Karen, having made her protest
at being called at such an hour, had put on a
wrapper and pinned up her hair. The light was
on. The stewardess said she heard a curious
chopping sound in the main cabin, followed by a
fall, and called Karen's attention to it. The
maid, impatient and drowsy, had said it was
probably Mr. Turner falling over something,
and that she hoped she would not meet him.

Once or twice, when he had been drinking, he had made overtures to her, and she detested him.

The sound outside ceased. It was about five minutes since the bell had rung, and Karen yawned and sat down on the bed. "I'll let her ring again," she said. "If she gets in the habit of this sort of thing, I'm going to leave." The stewardess asked her to put out the light and let her sleep, and Karen did so. The two women were in darkness, and the stewardess dozed, for a minute only. She was awakened by Karen touching her on the shoulder and whispering close to her ear.

"That beast is out there," she said. "I peered out, and I think he is sitting on the companion steps. You listen, and if he tries to stop me I'll call you."

The stewardess was wide awake by that time. She thought perhaps the bell, instead of coming from Mrs. Turner's room, had come from the room adjoining Turner's, where Vail slept, and which had been originally designed for Mrs. Turner. She suggested turning on the light again and looking at the bell register; but Karen objected.

THE STEWARDESS'S STORY

The stewardess sat up in her bed, which was the one under the small window opening on the deck aft. She could not see through the door directly, but a faint light came through the doorway as Karen opened the door.

The girl stood there, looking out. Then suddenly she threw up her hands and screamed, and the next moment there was a blow struck. She staggered back a step or two, and fell into the room. The stewardess saw a white figure in the doorway as the girl fell. Almost instantly something whizzed by her, striking the end of a pillow and bruising her arm. She must have fainted. When she recovered, faint daylight was coming into the room, and the body of the Danish girl was lying as it had fallen.

She tried to get up, and fainted again.

That was her story, and it did not tell us much that we needed to know. She showed me her right arm, which was badly bruised and discolored at the shoulder.

"What do you mean by a white figure?"

"It looked white: it seemed to shine."

"When I went to call you, Mrs. Sloane, the door to your room was closed."

"I saw it closed!" she said positively. "I had forgotten that, but now I remember. The axe fell beside me, and I tried to scream, but I could not. I saw the door closed, very slowly and without a sound. Then I fainted."

The thing was quite possible. Owing to the small size of the cabin, and to the fact that it must accommodate two bunks, the door opened *out* into the chart-room. Probably the woman had fainted before I broke the lock of my door and fell into the main cabin. But a *white* figure!

"Karen exclaimed," Miss Lee said slowly, "that some one was sitting on the companion steps?"

"Yes, miss."

"And she thought that it was Mr. Turner?"

"Yes." The stewardess looked quickly at Mrs. Turner, and averted her eyes. "It may have been all talk, miss, about his — about his bothering her. She was a great one to fancy that men were following her about."

Miss Lee got up and came to the door where I was standing.

"Surely we need not be prisoners any longer!"

84

she said in an undertone. "It is daylight. If **I** stay here I shall go crazy."

"The murderer is still on the ship," I protested. "And just now the deck is — hardly a place for women. Wait until this afternoon, Miss Lee. By that time I shall have arranged for a guard for you. Although God knows, with every man under suspicion, where we will find any to trust."

"*You* will arrange a guard!"

"The men have asked me to take charge."

"But — I don't understand. The first mate —"

" — is a prisoner of the crew."

"They accuse him!"

"They have to accuse some one. There's a sort of hysteria among the men, and they've fixed on Singleton. They won't hurt him, — I'll see to that, — and it makes for order."

She considered for a moment. I had time then to see the havoc the night had wrought in her. She was pale, with deep hollows around her eyes. Her hands shook and her mouth drooped wearily. But, although her face was lined with grief, it was not the passionate sorrow of a loving girl. She had not loved Vail, I said to myself. She had not loved Vail! My heart beat faster.

"Will you allow me to leave this room for five minutes?"

"If I may go with you, and if you will come back without protest."

"You are arbitrary!" she said resentfully. "I only wish to speak to Mr. Turner."

"Then — if I may wait at the door."

"I shall not go, under those conditions."

"Miss Lee," I said desperately, "surely you must realize the state of affairs. We must trust no one — *no one*. Every shadowy corner, every closed door, may hold death in its most terrible form."

"You are right, of course. Will you wait outside? I can dress and be ready in five minutes."

I went into the main cabin, now bright with the morning sun, which streamed down the forward companionway. The door to Vail's room across was open, and Williams, working in nervous haste, was putting it in order. Walking up and down, his shrewd eyes keenly alert, Charlie Jones was on guard, revolver in hand. He came over to me at once.

"Turner is moving, in there," he said, jerking his thumb toward the forward cabin. "What are you going to do? Let a drunken sot like that give us orders, and bang us with a belaying pin when we don't please him?"

"He is the owner. But one thing we can do, Jones. We can keep him from more liquor. Williams!"

He came out, more dead than alive.

"Williams," I said sternly, "I give you an hour to get rid of every ounce of liquor on the Ella. Remember, not a bottle is to be saved."

"But Mistah Turner —"

"I'll answer to Mr. Turner. Get it overboard before he gets around. And, Williams!"

"Well?" — sullenly.

"I'm going around after you, and if I find so much as a pint, I'll put you in that room you have just left, and lock you in."

He turned even grayer, and went into the storeroom.

A day later, and the crew would probably have resented what they saw that morning. But that day they only looked up apathetically from their gruesome work of sewing into bags of canvas the sheeted bodies on the deck, while a gray-faced negro in a white coat flung over the rail cases of fine wines, baskets and boxes full of bottles, dozen after dozen of brandies and liquors, all sinking beyond salvage in the blue Atlantic.

CHAPTER IX

MY first thought had been for the women, and, unluckily, to save them a shock I had all evidences of the crime cleared away as quickly as possible. Stains that might have been of invaluable service in determining the murderer were washed away almost before they were dry. I realized this now, too late. But the axe remained, and I felt that its handle probably contained a record for more skilful eyes than mine to read, prints that under the microscope would reveal the murderer's identity as clearly as a photograph.

I sent for Burns, who reported that he had locked the axe in the captain's cabin. He gave me the key, which I fastened to a string and hung around my neck under my shirt. He also reported that, as I had suggested, the crew had gone, two at a time, into the forecastle, and had brought up what they needed to stay on deck. The forecastle had been closed and locked in the presence of the crew, and the key given to Burns, who fastened it to his watch-chain. The two hatchways leading to the hold had been fastened down also, and Oleson, who was ship's carpenter, had nailed them fast.

The crew had been instructed to stay aft of the wheel, except when on watch. Thus the helmsman need not be alone. As I have said, the door at the top of the companion steps, near the wheel, was closed and locked, and entrance to the after house was to be gained only by the forward companion. It was the intention of Burns and myself to keep watch here, amidships.

Burns had probably suffered more than any of us. Whatever his relation to the Hansen woman had been, he had been with her only three hours before her death, and she was wearing a ring of his, a silver rope tied in a sailor's knot, when she died. And Burns had been fond of Captain Richardson, in a crew where respect rather than affection toward the chief officer was the rule.

When Burns gave me the key to the captain's room Charlie Jones had reached the other end of the long cabin, and was staring through into the chart-room. It was a time to trust no one, and I assured myself that Jones was not looking before I thrust it into my shirt.

"They're — all ready, Leslie," Burns said, his face working. "What are we going to do with them?"

"We'll have to take them back."

"But we can't do that. It's a two weeks' matter, and in this weather —"

"We will take them back, Burns," I said shortly, and he assented mechanically: —

"Aye, aye, sir."

Just how it was to be done was a difficult thing to decide. Miss Lee had not appeared yet, and the three of us, Jones, Burns, and I, talked it over. Jones suggested that we put them in one of the life boats, and nail over it a canvas and tarpaulin cover.

"It ain't my own idea," he said modestly. "I seen it done once, on the Argentina. It worked all right for a while, and after a week or so we lowered the jolly-boat and towed it astern."

I shuddered; but the idea was a good one, and I asked Burns to go up and get the boat ready.

"We must let the women up this afternoon," I said, "and, if it is possible, try to keep them from learning where the bodies are. We can rope off a part of the deck for them, and ask them not to leave it."

Miss Lee came out then, and Burns went on deck.

The girl was looking better. The exertion of dressing had brought back her color, and her lips, although firmly set, were not drawn. She stood just outside the door and drew a deep breath.

"You must not keep us prisoners any longer, Leslie," she said. "Put a guard over us, if you must, but let us up in the air."

"This afternoon, Miss Lee," I said. "This morning you are better below."

She understood me, but she had no conception of the brutality of the crime, even then.

"I am not a child. I wish to see them. I shall have to testify —"

"You will not see them, Miss Lee."

She stood twisting her handkerchief in her hands. She saw Charlie Jones pacing the length of the cabin, revolver in hand. From the chart-room came the sound of hammering, where the after companion door, already locked, was being additionally secured with strips of wood nailed across.

"I understand," she said finally. "Will you take me to Karen's room?"

I could see no reason for objecting; but so thorough was the panic that had infected us all that I would not allow her in until I had preceded her, and had searched in the clothes-closet and under the two bunks. Williams had not reached this room yet, and there was a pool of blood on the floor.

She had a great deal of courage. She glanced at the stain, and looked away again quickly.

"I — think I shall not come in. Will you look at the bell register for me? What bell is registered?"

"Three."

"Three!" she said. "Are you sure?"

I looked again. "It is three."

93

"Then it was not my sister's bell that rang. It was Mr. Vail's!"

"It must be a mistake. Perhaps the wires—"

"Mrs. Turner's room is number one. Please go back and ask her to ring her bell, while I see how it registers."

But I would not leave her there alone. I went with her to her sister's door, and together we returned to the maids' cabin. Mrs. Turner had rung as we requested, and her bell had registered "One."

"He rang for help!" she cried, and broke down utterly. She dropped into a chair in the chart-room and cried softly, helplessly, while I stood by, unable to think of anything to do or say. I think now that it was the best thing she could have done, though at the time I was alarmed. I ventured, finally, to put my hand on her shoulder.

"Please!" I said.

Charlie Jones came to the door of the chart-room, and retreated with instinctive good taste. She stopped crying after a time, and I knew the exact instant when she realized my touch. I felt her stiffen; without looking up, she drew

94

away from my hand; and I stepped back, hurt and angry — the hurt for her, the anger that I could not remember that I was her hired servant.

When she got up, she did not look at me, nor I at her — at least not consciously. But when, in those days, was I not looking at her, seeing her, even when my eyes were averted, feeling her presence before any ordinary sense told me she was near? The sound of her voice in the early mornings, when I was washing down the deck, had been enough to set my blood pounding in my ears. The last thing I saw at night, when I took myself to the storeroom to sleep, was her door across the main cabin; and in the morning, stumbling out with my pillow and blanket, I gave it a foolish little sign of greeting.

What she would not see the men had seen, and, in their need, they had made me their leader. To her I was Leslie, the common sailor. I registered a vow, that morning, that I would be the common sailor until the end of the voyage.

"Mr. Turner is awake, I believe," I said stiffly.

"Very well."

She turned back into the main cabin; but she paused at the storeroom door.

"It is curious that you heard nothing," she said slowly. "You slept with this door open, did n't you?"

"I was locked in."

She stooped quickly and looked at the lock. "You broke it open?"

"Partly, at the last. I heard —" I stopped. I did not want to tell her what I had heard. But she knew.

"You heard — Karen, when she screamed?"

"Yes. I was aroused before that, — I do not know how, — and found I was locked in. I thought it might be a joke — forecastle hands are fond of joking, and they resented my being brought here to sleep. I took out some of the screws with my knife, and — then I broke the door."

"You saw no one?"

"It was dark; I saw and heard no one."

"But, surely — the man at the wheel —"

"Hush," I warned her; "he is there. He heard something, but the helmsman cannot leave the wheel."

96

She was stooping to the lock again.

"You are sure it was locked?"

"The bolt is still shot." I showed her.

"Then — where is the key?"

"The key!"

"Certainly. Find the key, and you will find the man who locked you in."

"Unless," I reminded her, "it flew out when I broke the lock."

"In that case, it will be on the floor."

But an exhaustive search of the cabin floor discovered no key. Jones, seeing us searching, helped, his revolver in one hand and a lighted match in the other, handling both with an abandon of ease that threatened us alternately with fire and a bullet. But there was no key.

"It stands to reason, miss," he said, when we had given up, "that, since the key is n't here, it is n't on the ship. That there key is a sort of red-hot give-away. No one is going to carry a thing like that around. Either it's here in this cabin — which it is n't — or it's overboard."

"Very likely, Jones. But I shall ask Mr. Turner to search the men."

She went toward Turner's door, and Jones leaned over me, putting a hand on my arm.

"She's right, boy," he said quickly. "Don't let 'em know what you're after, but go through their pockets. And their shoes!" he called after me. "A key slips into a shoe mighty easy."

But, after all, it was not necessary. The key was to be found, and very soon.

CHAPTER X

EXACTLY what occurred during Elsa Lee's visit to her brother-in-law's cabin I have never learned. He was sober, I know, and somewhat dazed, with no recollection whatever of the previous night, except a hazy idea that he had quarreled with Richardson.

Jones and I waited outside. He suggested that we have prayers over the bodies when we placed them in the boat, and I agreed to read the burial service from the Episcopal Prayer-Book. The voices from Turner's cabin came steadily, Miss Lee's low tones, Turner's heavy bass only now and then. Once I heard her give a startled exclamation, and both Jones and I leaped to the door. But the next moment she was talking again quietly.

Ten minutes — fifteen — passed. I grew restless and took to wandering about the cabin. Mrs. Johns came to the door opposite, and asked to have tea sent down to the stewardess.

I called the request up the companionway, unwilling to leave the cabin for a moment. When I came back, Jones was standing at the door of Vail's cabin, looking in. His face was pale.

"Look there!" he said hoarsely. "Look at the bell. He must have tried to push the button!"

I stared in. Williams had put the cabin to rights, as nearly as he could. The soaked mattress was gone, and a clean linen sheet was spread over the bunk. Poor Vail's clothing, as he had taken it off the night before, hung on a mahogany stand beside the bed, and above, almost concealed by his coat, was the bell. Jones's eyes were fixed on the darkish smear, over and around the bell, on the white paint.

I measured the height of the bell from the bed. It was well above, and to one side — a smear rather than a print, too indeterminate to be of any value, sinister, cruel.

"He did n't do that, Charlie," I said. "He could n't have got up to it after — That is the murderer's mark. He leaned there, one hand against the wall, to look down at his work.

And, without knowing it, he pressed the button that roused the two women."

He had not heard the story of Henrietta Sloane, and, as we waited, I told him. Some of the tension was relaxing. He tried, in his argumentative German way, to drag me into a discussion as to the foreordination of a death that resulted from an accidental ringing of a bell. But my ears were alert for the voices near by, and soon Miss Lee opened the door.

Turner was sitting on his bunk. He had made an attempt to shave, and had cut his chin severely. He was in a dressing-gown, and was holding a handkerchief to his face; he peered at me over it with red-rimmed eyes.

"This — this is horrible, Leslie," he said. "I can hardly believe it."

"It is true, Mr. Turner."

He took the handkerchief away and looked to see if the bleeding had stopped. I believe he intended to impress us both with his coolness, but it was an unfortunate attempt. His lips, relieved of the pressure, were twitching; his nerveless fingers could hardly refold the handkerchief.

"Wh-why was I not — called at once?" he demanded.

"I notified you. You were — you must have gone to sleep again."

"I don't believe you called me. You're — lying, are n't you?" He got up, steadying himself by the wall, and swaying dizzily to the motion of the ship. "You shut me off down here, and then run things your own damned way." He turned on Miss Lee. "Where's Helen?"

"In her room, Marsh. She has one of her headaches. Please don't disturb her."

"Where's Williams?" He turned to me.

"I can get him for you."

"Tell him to bring me a highball. My mouth's sticky." He ran his tongue over his dry lips. "And — take a message from me to Richardson —" He stopped, startled. Indeed, Miss Lee and I had both started. "To — who's running the boat, anyhow? Singleton?"

"Mr. Singleton is a prisoner in the forward house," I said gravely.

The effect of this was astonishing. He

stared at us both, and, finding corroboration in Miss Lee's face, his own took on an instant expression of relief. He dropped to the side of the bed, and his color came slowly back. He even smiled — a crafty grin that was inexpressibly horrible.

"Singleton!" he said. "Why do they — how do they know it was he?"

"He had quarreled with the captain last night, and he was on duty at the time of the — when the thing happened. The man at the wheel claims to have seen him in the chart-room just before, and there was other evidence, I believe. The lookout saw him forward, with something— possibly the axe. Not decisive, of course, but enough to justify putting him in irons. Somebody did it, and the murderer is on board, Mr. Turner."

His grin had faded, but the crafty look in his pale-blue eyes remained.

"The chart-room was dark. How could the steersman —" He checked himself abruptly, and looked at us both quickly. "Where are — they?" he asked in a different tone.

"On deck."

"We can't keep them in this weather."

"We *must*," I said. "We will have to get to the nearest port as quickly as we can, and surrender ourselves and the bodies. This thing will have to be sifted to the bottom, Mr. Turner. The innocent must not suffer for the guilty, and every one on the ship is under suspicion."

He fell into a passion at that, insisting that the bodies be buried at once, asserting his ownership of the vessel as his authority, demanding to know what I, a forecastle hand, had to say about it, flinging up and down the small room, showering me with invective and threats, and shoving Miss Lee aside when she laid a calming hand on his arm. The cut on his chin was bleeding again, adding to his wild and sinister expression. He ended by demanding Williams.

I opened the door and called to Charlie Jones to send the butler, and stood by, waiting for the fresh explosion that was coming. Williams shakily confessed that there was no whiskey on board.

"Where is it?" Turner thundered.

Williams looked at me. He was in a state of inarticulate fright.

"I ordered it overboard," I said.

Turner whirled on me, incredulity and rage in his face.

"You!"

I put the best face I could on the matter, and eyed him steadily. "There has been too much drinking on this ship," I said. "If you doubt it, go up and look at the three bodies on the deck."

"What have *you* to do about it?" His eyes were narrowed; there was menace in every line of his face.

"With Schwartz gone, Captain Richardson dead, and Singleton in irons, the crew had no officers. They asked me to take charge."

"So! And you used your authority to meddle with what does not concern you! The ship has an officer while I am on it. And there will be no mutiny."

He flung into the main cabin, and made for the forward companionway. I stepped back to allow Miss Lee to precede me. She was standing, her back to the dressing-stand, facing the door. She looked at me, and made a help-less gesture with her hands, as if the situation were beyond her. Then I saw her look down. She took a quick step or two toward the door, and, stooping, picked up some small object from almost under my foot. The incident would have passed without notice, had she not, in attempting to wrap it in her handkerchief, dropped it. I saw then that it was a key.

"Let me get it for you," I said. To my amazement, she put her foot over it.

"Please see what Mr. Turner is doing," she said. "It is the key to my jewel-case."

"Will you let me see it?"

"No."

"It is not the key to a jewel-case."

"It does not concern you what it is."

"It is the key to the storeroom door."

"You are stronger than I am. You look the brute. You can knock me away and get it."

I knew then, of course, that it was the store-room key. But I could not take it by force. And so defiantly she faced me, so valiant was every line of her slight figure, that I was ashamed of my impulse to push her aside and take it. I loved her with every inch of my overgrown body, and I did the thing she knew I would do. I bowed and left the cabin. But I had no intention of losing the key. I could not take it by force, but she knew as well as I did what finding it there in Turner's room meant. Turner had locked me in. But I must be able to prove it — my wits against hers, and the advantage mine. I had the women under guard.

I went up on deck.

A curious spectacle revealed itself. Turner, purple with anger, was haranguing the men, who stood amidships, huddled together, but grim and determined withal. Burns, a little apart from the rest, was standing, sullen, his arms folded. As Turner ceased, he took a step forward.

"You are right, Mr. Turner," he said. "It's your ship, and it's up to you to say where she goes and how she goes, sir. But some one will hang for this, Mr. Turner, — some one that's on this deck now; and the bodies are going back with us — likewise the axe. There ain't going to be a mistake — the right man is going to swing."

"That's mutiny!"

"Yes, sir," Burns acknowledged, his face paling a little. "I guess you could call it that."

Turner swung on his heel and went below, where Jones, relieved of guard duty by Burns, reported him locked in his room, refusing admission to his wife and Miss Lee, both of whom had knocked on the door.

The trouble with Turner added to the general misery of the situation. Burns got our position at noon with more or less exactness, and the general working of the Ella went on well enough. But the situation was indescribable. Men started if a penknife dropped, and swore if a sail flapped. The call of the boatswain's pipe rasped their ears, and the preparation for stowing the bodies in the jolly-boat left them unnerved and sick. Some sort of a meal was cooked, but no one could eat; Williams brought up, untasted, the luncheon he had carried down to the after house.

At two o'clock all hands gathered amidships, and the bodies were carried forward to where the boat, lowered in its davits and braced, lay on the deck. It had been lined with canvas and tarpaulin, and a cover of similar material lay ready to be nailed in place. All the men were bareheaded. Many were in tears. Miss Lee came forward with us, and it was from her prayer-book that I, too moved for self-consciousness, read the burial-service.

"I am the resurrection and the life," I read huskily.

The figures at my feet, in their canvas shrouds, rolled gently with the rocking of the ship; the sun beat down on the decks, on the bare heads of the men, on the gilt edges of the prayer-book, gleaming in the light, on the last of the land-birds, drooping in the heat on the main cross-trees.

". . . For man walketh in a vain shadow," I read, "and disquieteth himself in vain. . . .

"O spare me a little, that I may recover my strength: before I go hence, and be no more seen."

CHAPTER XI

MRS. JOHNS and the stewardess came up late in the afternoon. We had railed off a part of the deck around the forward companionway for them, and none of the crew except the man on guard was allowed inside the ropes. After a consultation, finding the ship very short-handed, and unwilling with the night coming on to trust any of the men, Burns and I decided to take over this duty ourselves, and, by stationing ourselves at the top of the companionway, to combine the duties of officer on watch and guard of the after house. To make the women doubly secure, we had Oleson nail all the windows closed, although they were merely portholes. Jones was no longer on guard below, and I had exchanged Singleton's worthless revolver for my own serviceable one.

Mrs. Johns, carefully dressed, surveyed the railed-off deck with raised eyebrows.

"For — us?" she asked, looking at me. The

110

men were gathered about the wheel aft, and were out of ear-shot. Mrs. Sloane had dropped into a steamer-chair, and was lying back with closed eyes.

"Yes, Mrs. Johns."

"Where have you put *them?*"

I pointed to where the jolly-boat, on the port side of the ship, swung on its davits.

"And the mate, Mr. Singleton?"

"He is in the forward house."

"What did you do with the — the weapon?"

"Why do you ask that?"

"Morbid curiosity," she said, with a lightness of tone that rang false to my ears. "And then — naturally, I should like to be sure that it is safely overboard, so it will not be" — she shivered — "used again."

"It is not overboard, Mrs. Johns," I said gravely. "It is locked in a safe place, where it will remain until the police come to take it."

"You are rather theatrical, are n't you?" she scoffed, and turned away. But a second later she came back to me, and put her hand on my arm. "Tell me where it is," she begged.

"You are making a mystery of it, and I detest mysteries."

I saw under her mask of lightness then: she wanted desperately to know where the axe was. Her eyes fell, under my gaze.

"I am sorry. There is no mystery. It is simply locked away for safe-keeping."

She bit her lip.

"Do you know what I think?" she said slowly. "I think you have hypnotized the crew, as you did me — at first. Why has no one remembered that *you* were in the after house last night, that *you* found poor Wilmer Vail, that *you* raised the alarm, that *you* discovered the captain and Karen? Why should I not call the men here and remind them of all that?"

"I do not believe you will. They know I was locked in the storeroom. The door — the lock —"

"You could have locked yourself in."

"You do not know what you are saying!"

But I had angered her, and she went on cruelly: —

"Who are you, anyhow? You are not a sailor. You came here and were taken on because you told a hard-luck story. How do we know that you came from a hospital? Men just out of prison look as you did. Do you know what we called you, the first two days out? We called you Elsa's jail-bird! And now, because you have dominated the crew, we are in your hands!"

"Do Mrs. Turner and Miss Lee think that?"

"They feel as I do. This is a picked crew — men the Turner line has employed for years."

"You are very brave, Mrs. Johns," I said. "If I were what you think I am, I would be a dangerous enemy."

"I am not afraid of you."

I thought fast. She was right. It had not occurred to me before, but it swept over me overwhelmingly.

"You are leaving me only one thing to do," I said. "I shall surrender myself to the men at once." I took out my revolver and held it out to her. "This rope is a dead-line. The crew know, and you will have no trouble; but you must stand guard here until some one else is sent."

She took the revolver without a word, and, somewhat dazed by this new turn of events, I went aft. The men were gathered there, and I surrendered myself. They listened in silence while I told them the situation. Burns, who had been trying to sleep, sat up and stared at me incredulously.

"It will leave you pretty short-handed, boys," I finished, "but you'd better fasten me up somewhere. But I want to be sure of one thing first: whatever happens, keep the guard for the women."

"We'd like to talk it over, Leslie," Burns said, after a word with the others.

I went forward a few feet, taking care to remain where they could see me, and very soon they called me. There had been a dispute, I believe. Adams and McNamara stood off from the others, their faces not unfriendly, but clearly differing from the decision. Charlie Jones, who, by reason of long service and a sort of pious control he had in the forecastle, was generally spokesman for the crew, took a step or two toward me.

"We'll not do it, boy," he said. "We think we know a man when we see one, as well as having occasion to know that you're white all through. And we're not inclined to set the talk of women against what we think best to do. So you stick to your job, and we're back of you."

In spite of myself, I choked up. I tried to tell them what their loyalty meant to me; but I could only hold out my hand, and, one by one, they came up and shook it solemnly.

"We think," McNamara said, when, last of all, he and Adams came up, "that it would be best, lad, if we put down in the log-book all that has happened last night and to-day, and this just now, too. It's fresh in our minds now, and it will be something to go by."

So Burns and I got the log-book from the captain's cabin. The axe was there, where we had placed it earlier in the day, lying on the white cover of the bed. The room was untouched, as the dead man had left it — a collar on the stand, brushes put down hastily, a half-smoked cigar which had burned a long scar on the wood before it had gone out. We went out silently, Burns carrying the book, I locking the door behind us.

Mrs. Johns, sitting near the companionway

with the revolver on her knee, looked up and eyed me coolly.

"So they would not do it!"

"I am sorry to disappoint you — they would not."

She held up my revolver to me, and smiled cynically.

"Remember," she said, "I only said you were a possibility."

"Thank you; I shall remember."

By unanimous consent, the task of putting down what had happened was given to me. I have a copy of the log-book before me now, the one that was used at the trial. The men read it through before they signed it.

August thirteenth.

This morning, between two-thirty and three o'clock, three murders were committed on the yacht Ella. At the request of Mrs. Johns, one of the party on board, I had moved to the after house to sleep, putting my blanket and pillow in the storeroom and sleeping on the floor there. Mrs. Johns gave, as her reason, a fear of something going wrong, as there was trouble between Mr. Turner and the captain. I slept with a revolver beside me and with the door of the storeroom open.

THE DEAD LINE

At some time shortly before three o'clock I wakened with a feeling of suffocation, and found that the door was closed and locked on the outside. I suspected a joke among the crew, and set to work with my pen-knife to unscrew the lock. When I had two screws out, a woman screamed, and I broke down the door.

As the main cabin was dark, I saw no one and could not tell where the cry came from. I ran into Mr. Vail's cabin, next the storeroom, and called him. His door was standing open. I heard him breathing heavily. Then the breathing stopped. I struck a match, and found him dead. His head had been crushed in with an axe, the left hand cut off, and there were gashes on the right shoulder and the abdomen.

I knew the helmsman would be at the wheel, and ran up the after companionway to him and told him. Then I ran forward and called the first mate, Mr. Singleton, who was on duty. He had been drinking. I asked him to call the captain, but he did not. He got his revolver, and we hurried down the forward companion. The body of the captain was lying at the foot of the steps, his head on the lowest stair. He had been killed like Mr. Vail. His cap had been placed over his face.

The mate collapsed on the steps. I found the light switch and turned it on. There was no one in the cabin or in the chart-room. I ran to Mr. Turner's room, going through Mr. Vail's and through the bathroom. Mr. Turner was in bed, fully dressed. I could not rouse him. Like the mate, he had been drinking.

The mate had roused the crew, and they gathered in the chart-room. I told them what had happened, and that the murderer must be among us. I suggested that they stay together, and that they submit to being searched for weapons.

They went on deck in a body, and I roused the women and told them. Mrs. Turner asked me to tell the two maids, who slept in a cabin off the chart-room. I found their door unlocked, and, receiving no answer, opened it. Karen Hansen, the lady's-maid, was on the floor, dead, with her skull crushed in. The stewardess, Henrietta Sloane, was fainting in her bunk. An axe had been hurled through the doorway as the Hansen woman fell, and was found in the stewardess's bunk.

Dawn coming by that time, I suggested a guard at the two companionways, and this was done. The men were searched and all weapons taken from them. Mr. Singleton was under suspicion, it being known that he had threatened the captain's life, and Oleson, a lookout, claiming to have seen him forward where the axe was kept.

The crew insisted that Singleton be put in irons. He made no objection, and we locked him in his own room in the forward house. Owing to the loss of Schwartz, the second mate, already recorded in this log-book (see entry for August

ninth), the death of the captain, and the imprisonment of the first mate, the ship was left without officers. Until Mr. Turner could make an
arrangement, the crew nominated Burns, one of
themselves, as mate, and asked me to assume
command. I protested that I knew nothing of
navigation, but agreed on its being represented
that, as I was not one of them, there could be
no ill feeling.

The ship was searched, on the possibility of
finding a stowaway in the hold. But nothing was
found. I divided the men into two watches,
Burns taking one and I the other. We nailed up
the after companionway, and forbade any member of the crew to enter the after house. The forecastle was also locked, the men bringing their
belongings on deck. The stewardess recovered
and told her story, which, in her own writing,
will be added to this record.

The bodies of the dead were brought on deck
and sewed into canvas, and later, with appropriate
services, placed in the jolly-boat, it being the
intention, later on, to tow the boat behind us.
Mr. Turner insisted that the bodies be buried at
sea, and, on the crew opposing this, retired to his
cabin, announcing that he considered the position
of the men a mutiny.

Some feeling having arisen among the women of
the party that I might know more of the crimes
than was generally supposed, having been in the
after house at the time they were committed,

and having no references, I this afternoon voluntarily surrendered myself to Burns, acting first mate. The men, however, refused to accept this surrender, only two, Adams and McNamara, favoring it. I expect to give myself up to the police at the nearest port, until the matter is thoroughly probed.

The axe is locked in the captain's cabin.

(*Signed*) RALPH LESLIE.

Witnesses
{
John Robert Burns
Charles Klineordlinger (Jones)
William McNamara
Carl L. Clarke
Joseph Q. Adams
John Oleson
Tom MacKenzie
Obadiah Williams
}

CHAPTER XII

THE FIRST MATE TALKS

WILLIAMS came up on deck late that afternoon, with a scared face, and announced that Mr. Turner had locked himself in his cabin, and was raving in delirium on the other side of the door. I sent Burns down — having decided, in view of Mrs. Johns's accusation, to keep away from the living quarters of the family. Burns's report corroborated what Williams had said. Turner was in the grip of delirium tremens, and the Ella was without owner or officers.

Turner refused to open either door for us. As well as we could make out, he was moving rapidly but almost noiselessly up and down the room, muttering to himself, now and then throwing himself on the bed, only to get up at once. He rang his bell a dozen times, and summoned Williams, only, in reply to the butler's palpitating knock, to stand beyond the door and refuse to open it or to voice any request.

The situation became so urgent that finally I was forced to go down, with no better success.

Mrs. Turner dragged herself across, on the state of affairs being reported to her, and, after two or three abortive attempts, succeeded in getting a reply from him.

"Marsh!" she called. "I want to talk to you. Let me in!"

"They'll get us," he said craftily.

"Us? Who is with you?"

"Vail," he replied promptly. "He's here talking. He won't let me sleep."

"Tell him to give you the key and you will keep it for him so no one can get him," I prompted. I had had some experience with such cases in the hospital.

She tried it without any particular hope, but it succeeded immediately. He pushed the key out under the door, and almost at once we heard him throw himself on the bed, as if satisfied that the problem of his security was solved.

Mrs. Turner held the key out to me, but I would not take it.

"Give it to Williams," I said. "You must

understand, Mrs. Turner, that I cannot take it."

She was a woman of few words, and after a glance at my determined face she turned to the butler.

"You will have to look after Mr. Turner, Williams. See that he is comfortable, and try to keep him in bed."

Williams put out a trembling hand, but, before he took the key, Turner's voice rose petulantly on the other side of the door.

"For God's sake, Wilmer," he cried plaintively, "get out and let me sleep! I have n' slept for a month."

Williams gave a whoop of fear, and ran out of the cabin, crying that the ship was haunted and that Vail had come back. From that moment, I believe, the after house was the safest spot on the ship. To my knowledge, no member of the crew so much as passed it on the starboard side, where Vail's and Turner's cabins were situated. It was the one good turn the owner of the Ella did us on that hideous return journey; for, during most of the sixteen days that it took us to get back, he lay in his cabin, alternating the wild frenzy of delirium tremens with quieter moments when he glared at us with crafty, murderous eyes, and picked incessantly at the bandages that tied him down. Not an instant did he sleep, that we could discover; and always, day or night, Vail was with him, and they were quarreling.

The four women took care of him as best they could. For a time they gave him the bromides I prepared, taking my medical knowledge without question. In the horror of the situation, curiosity had no place, and class distinctions were forgotten. That great leveler, a common trouble, put Henrietta Sloane, the stewardess, and the women of the party at the same table in the after house, where none ate, and placed the responsibility for the ship, although I was nominally in command, on the shoulders of all the men. And there sprang up among them a sort of *esprit de corps*, curious under the circumstances, and partly explained, perhaps, by the belief that in imprisoning Singleton they had the murderer safely in hand. What they thought of Turner's possible connection with the crime, I do not know.

THE FIRST MATE TALKS

Personally, I was convinced that Turner was guilty. Perhaps, lulled into a false security by the incarceration of the two men, we unconsciously relaxed our vigilance. But by the first night the crew were somewhat calmer. Here and there a pipe was lighted, and a plug of tobacco went the rounds. The forecastle supper, served on deck, was eaten; and Charlie Jones, securing a permission that I thought it best to grant, went forward and painted a large black cross on the side of the jolly-boat, and below it the date, August 13, 1911. The crew watched in respectful silence.

The weather was in our favor, the wind on our quarter, a blue sky heaped with white cloud masses, with the sunset fringed with the deepest rose. The Ella made no great way, but sailed easily. Burns and I alternated at the forward companionway, and, although the men were divided into watches, the entire crew was on duty virtually all the time.

I find, on consulting the book in which I recorded, beginning with that day, the incidents of the return voyage, that two things happened that evening. One was my interview with Singleton; the other was my curious and depressing clash with Elsa Lee, on the deck that night.

Turner being quiet and Burns on watch at the beginning of the second dog watch, six o'clock, I went forward to the room where Singleton was imprisoned. Burns gave me the key, and advised me to take a weapon. I did not, however, nor was it needed.

The first mate was sitting on the edge of his bunk, in his attitude of the morning, his head in his hands. As I entered, he looked up and nodded. His color was still bad; he looked ill and nervous, as might have been expected after his condition the night before.

"For God's sake, Leslie," he said, "tell them to open the window. I'm choking!"

He was right: the room was stifling. I opened the door behind me, and stood in the doorway, against a rush for freedom. But he did not move. He sank back into his dejected attitude.

"Will you eat some soup, if I send it?"

He shook his head.

"Is there anything you care for?"

THE FIRST MATE TALKS

"Better let me starve; I'm gone, anyhow."

"Singleton," I said, "I wish you would tell me about last night. If you did it, we've got you. If you did n't, you'd better let me take your own account of what happened, while it's fresh in your mind. Or, better still, write it yourself."

He held out his right hand. I saw that it was shaking violently.

"Could n't hold a pen," he said tersely. "Would n't be believed, anyhow."

The air being somewhat better, I closed and locked the door again, and, coming in, took out my notebook and pencil. He watched me craftily. "You can write it," he said, "if you'll give it to me to keep. I'm not going to put the rope around my own neck. If it's all right, my lawyers will use it. If it is n't —" He shrugged his shoulders.

I had never liked the man, and his tacit acknowledgment that he might incriminate himself made me eye him with shuddering distaste. But I took down his story, and reproduce it here, minus the technicalities and profanity with which it was interlarded.

Briefly, Singleton's watch began at midnight.
The captain, who had been complaining of
lumbago, had had the cook prepare him a mus-
tard poultice, and had retired early. Burns
was on watch from eight to twelve, and, on
coming into the forward house at a quarter
after eleven o'clock to eat his night lunch, reported to Singleton that the captain was in bed
and that Mr. Turner had been asking for him.
Singleton, therefore, took his cap and went on
deck. This was about twenty minutes after
eleven. He had had a drink or two earlier in
the evening, and he took another in his cabin
when he got his cap.

He found Turner in the chart-house, playing
solitaire and drinking. He was alone, and he
asked Singleton to join him. The first mate
looked at his watch and accepted the invitation, but decided to look around the forward
house to be sure the captain was asleep. He
went on deck. He could hear Burns and the
lookout talking. The forward house was dark.
He listened outside the captain's door, and
heard him breathing heavily, as if asleep. He
stood there for a moment. He had an uneasy

feeling that some one was watching him. He thought of Schwartz, and was uncomfortable. He did not feel the whiskey at all.

He struck a light and looked around. There was no one in sight. He could hear Charlie Jones in the forecastle drumming on his banjo, and Burns whistling the same tune as he went aft to strike the bell. (It was the duty of the officer on watch to strike the hour.) It was then half after eleven. As he passed the captain's door again, his foot struck something, and it fell to the floor. He was afraid the captain had been roused, and stood still until he heard him breathing regularly again. Then he stooped down. His foot had struck an axe upright against the captain's door, and had knocked it down.

The axe belonged on the outer wall of the forward house. It was a rule that it must not be removed from its place except in emergency, and the first mate carried it out and leaned it against the forward port corner of the after house when he went below. Later, on his watch, he carried it forward and put it where it belonged.

He found Turner waiting on deck, and together they descended to the chart-room. He was none too clear as to what followed. They drank together. Vail tried to get Turner to bed, and failed. He believed that Burns had called the captain. The captain had ordered him to the deck, and there had been a furious quarrel. He felt ill by that time, and, when he went on watch at midnight, Burns was uncertain about leaving him. He was not intoxicated, he maintained, until after half-past one. He was able to strike the bell without difficulty, and spoke, each time he went aft, to Charlie Jones, who was at the wheel.

After that, however, he suddenly felt strange. He thought he had been doped, and told the helmsman so. He asked Jones to strike the bell for him, and, going up on the forecastle head, lay down on the boards and fell asleep. He did not waken until he heard six bells struck — three o'clock. And, before he had fully roused, I had called him.

"Then," I said, "when the lookout saw you with the axe, you were replacing it?"

"Yes."

"The lookout says you were not on deck between two and three o'clock."

"How does he know? I was asleep."

"You had threatened to get the captain."

"I had a revolver; I did n't need to use an axe."

Much as I disliked the man, I was inclined to believe his story, although I thought he was keeping something back. I leaned forward.

"Singleton," I said, "if you did n't do it, — and I want to think you did not, — who did?"

He shrugged his shoulders.

"We have women aboard. We ought to know what precautions to take."

"I was n't the only man on deck that night. Burns was about, and he had a quarrel with the Hansen woman. Jones was at the wheel, too. Why don't you lock up Jones?"

"We are all under suspicion," I admitted. "But you had threatened the captain."

"I never threatened the girl, or Mr. Vail."

I had no answer to this, and we both fell silent. Singleton was the first to speak: —

"How are you going to get back? The men can sail a course, but who is to lay it out?

Turner? No Turner ever knew anything about a ship but what it made for him."

"Turner is sick. Look here, Singleton, you want to get back as much as we do, or more. Would n't you be willing to lay a course, if you were taken out once a day? Burns is doing it, but he does n't pretend to know much about it, and — we have the bodies."

But he turned ugly again, and refused to help unless he was given his freedom, and that I knew the crew would not agree to.

"You 'll be sick enough before you get back!" he snarled.

CHAPTER XIII

THE WHITE LIGHT

WITH the approach of night our vigilance was doubled. There was no thought of sleep among the crew, and, with the twilight, there was a distinct return of the terror of the morning.

Gathered around the wheel, the crew listened while Jones read evening prayer. Between the two houses, where the deck was roped off, Miss Lee was alone, pacing back and forward, her head bent, her arms dropped listlessly.

The wind had gone, and the sails hung loose over our heads. I stood by the port rail. Although my back was toward Miss Lee, I was conscious of her every movement; and so I knew when she stooped under the rope and moved lightly toward the starboard rail.

Quick as she was, I was quicker. There was still light enough to see her face as she turned when I called to her: —

"Miss Lee! You must not leave the rope."

"*Must* not?"

"I am sorry to seem arbitrary. It is for your own safety."

I was crossing the deck toward her as I spoke. I knew what she was going to do. I believe, when she saw my face, that she read my knowledge in it. She turned back from the rail and faced me.

"Surely I may go to the rail!"

"It would be unwise, if for no other reason than discipline."

"Discipline! Are *you* trying to discipline *me*?"

"Miss Lee, you do not seem to understand," I said, as patiently as I could. "Just now I am in charge of the Ella. It does not matter how unfit I am — the fact remains. Nor does it concern me that your brother-in-law owns the ship. I am in charge of it, and, God willing, there will be no more crimes on it. You will go back to the part of the deck that is reserved for you, or you will go below and stay there."

She flushed with anger, and stood there with her head thrown back, eyeing me with a contempt that cut me to the quick. The next moment she wheeled and, raising her hand, flung toward the rail the key to the storeroom door. I caught her hand — too late.

But fate was on my side, after all. As I stood, still gripping her wrist, the key fell ringing almost at my feet. It had struck one of the lower yard-braces. I stooped, and, picking it up, pocketed it.

She was dazed, I think. She made no effort to free her arm, but she put her other hand to her heart unexpectedly, and I saw that she was profoundly shocked. I led her, unprotesting, to a deck-chair, and put her down in it; and still she had not spoken. She lay back and closed her eyes. She was too strong to faint; she was superbly healthy. But she knew as well as I did what that key meant, and she had delivered it into my hands. As for me, I was driven hard that night; for, as I stood there looking down at her, she held out her hand to me, palm up.

"Please!" she said pleadingly. "What does it mean to you, Leslie? We were kind to you, were n't we? When you were ill, we took you on, my sister and I, and now you hate us. Please!"

"Hate you!"

"He did n't know what he was doing. He was n't sane. No sane man kills — that way. He had a revolver, if he had wanted — *Please* give me that key!"

"Some one will suffer. Would you have the innocent suffer with the guilty?"

"If they cannot prove it against any one —"

"They may prove it against me."

"You!"

"I was in the after house," I said doggedly. "I was the one to raise an alarm and to find the bodies. You do not know anything about me. I am — 'Elsa's jail-bird'!"

"Who told you that?"

"It does not matter — I know it. I told you the truth, Miss Elsa; I came here from the hospital. But I may have to fight for my life. Against the Turner money and influence, I have only — this key. Shall I give it to you?"

I held it out to her on the palm of my hand. It was melodramatic, probably; but I was very young, and by that time wildly in love with her. I thought, for a moment, that she would take it; but she only drew a deep breath and pushed my hand away.

"Keep it," she said. "I am ashamed."

We were silent after that, she staring out over the rail at the deepening sky; and, looking at her as one looks at a star, I thought she had forgotten my presence, so long she sat silent. The voices of the men aft died away gradually, as, one by one, they rolled themselves in blankets on the deck, not to sleep, but to rest and watch. The lookout, in his lonely perch high above the deck, called down guardedly to ask for company, and one of the crew went up.

When she turned to me again, it was to find my eyes fixed on her.

"You say you have neither money nor influence. And yet, you are a gentleman."

"I hope so."

"You know what I mean"—impatiently. "You are not a common sailor."

"I did not claim to be one."

"You are quite determined we shall not know anything about you?"

"There is nothing to know. I have given you

137

my name, which is practically all I own in the world. I needed a chance to recover from an illness, and I was obliged to work. This offered the best opportunity to combine both."

"You are not getting much chance to rest," she said, with a sigh, and got up. I went with her to the companionway, and opened the door. She turned and looked at me.

"Good-night."

"Good-night, Miss Lee."

"I — I feel very safe with you on guard," she said, and held out her hand. I took it in mine, with my heart leaping. It was as cold as ice.

That night, at four bells, I mustered the crew as silently as possible around the jolly-boat, and we lowered it into the water. The possibility of a dead calm had convinced me that the sooner it was done the better. We arranged to tow the boat astern, and Charlie Jones suggested a white light in its bow, so we could be sure at night that it had not broken loose.

Accordingly, we attached to the bow of the jolly-boat a tailed block with an endless fall riven through it, so as to be able to haul in and refill the lantern. Five bells struck by the time we had arranged the towing-line.

We dropped the jolly-boat astern and made fast the rope. It gave me a curious feeling, that small boat rising and falling behind us, with its dead crew, and its rocking light, and, on its side above the water-line, the black cross — a curious feeling of pursuit, as if, across the water, they in the boat were following us. And, perhaps because the light varied, sometimes it seemed to drop behind, as if wearying of the chase, and again, in great leaps, to be overtaking us, to be almost upon us.

An open boat with a small white light and a black cross on the side.

CHAPTER XIV

FROM THE CROW'S NEST

THE night passed without incident, except for one thing that we were unable to verify. At six bells, during the darkest hour of the night that precedes the early dawn of summer, Adams, from the crow's-nest, called down, in a panic, that there was something crawling on all fours on the deck below him.

Burns, on watch at the companionway, ran forward with his revolver, and narrowly escaped being brained — Adams at that moment flinging down a marlinespike that he had carried aloft with him.

I heard the crash and joined Burns, and together we went over the deck and both houses. Everything was quiet: the crew in various attitudes of exhausted sleep, their chests and ditty-bags around them; Oleson at the wheel; and Singleton in his jail-room, breathing heavily.

Adams's nerve was completely gone, and, being now thoroughly awake, I joined him in the crow's-nest. Nothing could convince him that he had been the victim of a nervous hallucination. He stuck to his story firmly.

"It was on the forecastle-head first," he maintained. "I saw it gleaming."

"Gleaming?"

"Sort of shining," he explained. "It came up over the rail, and at first it stood up tall, like a white post."

"You did n't ay before that it was white."

"It was shining," he said slowly, trying to put his idea into words. "Maybe not exactly white, but light-colored. It stood still for so long, I thought I must be mistaken — that it was a light on the rigging. Then I got to thinking that there was n't no place for a light to come from just there."

That was true enough.

"First it was as tall as a man, or taller maybe," he went on. "Then it seemed about half that high and still in the same place. Then it got lower still, and it took to crawling along on its belly. It was then I yelled."

I looked down. The green starboard light threw a light over only a small part of the deck.

The red light did no better. The masthead was possibly thirty feet above the hull, and served no illuminating purpose whatever. From the bridge forward the deck was practically dark.

"You yelled, and then what happened?"

His reply was vague — troubled.

"I'm not sure," he said slowly. "It seemed to fade away. The white got smaller — went to nothing, like a cloud blown away in a gale. I flung the spike."

I accepted the story with outward belief and a mental reservation. But I did not relish the idea of the spike Adams had thrown lying below on deck. No more formidable weapon short of an axe, could be devised. I said as much.

"I'm going down for it," I said; "if you're nervous, you'd better keep it by you. But don't drop it on everything that moves below. You almost got Burns."

I went down cautiously, and struck a match where Adams had indicated the spike. It was not there. Nor had Burns picked it up. A splintered board showed where it had struck, and a smaller indentation where it had rebounded; but the marlinespike was gone, and Burns had not seen it. We got a lantern and searched systematically, without result. Burns turned to me a face ghastly in the oil light.

"Somebody has it," he said, "and there will be more murder! Oh, my God, Leslie!"

"When you went back after the alarm, did you count the men?"

"No; Oleson said no one had come forward. They could not have passed without his seeing them. He has the binnacle lantern and two other lights."

"And no one came from the after house?"

"No one."

Eight bells rang out sharply. The watch changed. I took the revolver and Burns's position at the companionway, while Burns went aft. He lined up the men by the binnacle light, and went over them carefully. The marlinespike was not found; but he took from the cook a long meat-knife, and brought both negro and knife forward to me. The man was almost collapsing with terror. He maintained that he had taken the knife for self-protection, and we let him go with a warning.

Dawn brought me an hour's sleep, the first since my awakening in the storeroom. When I roused, Jones at the wheel had thrown an extra blanket over me, for the morning was cool and a fine rain was falling.

The men were scattered around in attitudes of dejection, one or two of them leaning over the rail, watching the jolly-boat, riding easily behind us.

Jones heard me moving, and turned.

"Your friend below must be pretty bad, sir," he said. "Your lady-love has been asking for you. I would n't let them wake you."

"My — what?"

He waxed apologetic at once.

"That's just my foolishness, Leslie," he said. "No disrespect to the lady, I 'm sure. If it ain't so, it ain't, and no harm done. If it is so, why, you need n't be ashamed, boy. 'The way of a man with a maid,' says the Book."

"You should have called me, Jones," I said sharply. "And no nonsense of that sort with the men."

He looked hurt, but made no reply beyond touching his cap. And, while I am mentioning that, I may speak of the changed attitude of the men toward me from the time they put me in charge. Whether the deference was to the office rather than the man, or whether in placing me in authority they had merely expressed a general feeling that I was with them rather than of them, I do not know. I am inclined to think the former. The result, in any case, was the same. They deferred to me whenever possible, brought large and small issues alike to me, served me my food alone, against my protestations, and, while navigating the ship on their own responsibility, took care to come to me for authority for everything.

Before I went below that morning, I suggested that some of the spare canvas be used to erect a shelter on the after deck, and this was done. The rain by that time was driving steadily — a summer rain without wind. The men seemed glad to have occupation, and, from that time on, the tent which they erected over the hatchway aft of the wheel was their living and eating quarters. It added something to their comfort: I was not so certain that it added to their security.

Turner was violent that day. I found all four women awake and dressed, and Mrs. Turner, whose hour it was on duty, in a chair outside the door. The stewardess, her arm in a sling, was making tea over a spirit-lamp, and Elsa was helping her. Mrs. Johns was stretched on a divan, and on the table lay a small revolver.

Clearly, Elsa had told the incident of the key. I felt at once the atmosphere of antagonism. Mrs. Johns watched me coolly from under lowered eyelids. The stewardess openly scowled. And Mrs. Turner rose hastily, and glanced at Mrs. Johns, as if in doubt. Elsa had her back to me, and was busy with the cups.

"I'm afraid you've had a bad night," I said.

"A very bad night," Mrs. Turner replied stiffly.

"Delirium?"

"Very marked. He has talked of a white figure — we cannot quite make it out. It seems to be Wilmer — Mr. Vail."

She had not opened the door, but stood, nervously twisting her fingers, before it.

"The bromides had no effect?"

She glanced helplessly at the others. "None," she said, after a moment.

Elsa Lee wheeled suddenly and glanced scornfully at her sister.

"Why don't you tell him?" she demanded. "Why don't you say you did n't give the bromides?"

"Why not?"

Mrs. Johns raised herself on her elbow and looked at me.

"Why should we?" she asked. "How do we know what you are giving him? You are not friendly to him or to us. We know what you are trying to do — you are trying to save yourself, at any cost. You put a guard at the companionway. You rail off the deck for our safety. You drop the storeroom key in Mr. Turner's cabin, where Elsa will find it, and will be obliged to acknowledge she found it, and then take it from her by force, so you can show it later on and save yourself!"

Elsa turned on her quickly.

"I told you how he got it, Adèle. I tried to throw it —"

"Oh, if you intend to protect him!"

"I am rather bewildered," I said slowly; "but, under the circumstances, I suppose you do not wish me to look after Mr. Turner?"

"We think not" — from Mrs. Turner.

"How will you manage alone?"

Mrs. Johns got up and lounged to the table. She wore a long satin negligée of some sort, draped with lace. It lay around her on the floor in gleaming lines of soft beauty. Her reddish hair was low on her neck, and she held a cigarette, negligently, in her teeth. All the women smoked, Mrs. Johns incessantly.

She laid one hand lightly on the revolver, and flicked the ash from her cigarette with the other.

"We have decided," she said insolently, "that, if the crew may establish a dead-line, so may we. Our dead-line is the foot of the companionway. One of us will be on watch always. I am an excellent shot."

"I do not doubt it." I faced her. "I am afraid you will suffer for air; otherwise, the arrangement is good. You relieve me of part of the responsibility for your safety. Tom will

bring your food to the steps and leave it
there."

"Thank you."

"With good luck, two weeks will see us in
port, and then —"

"In port! You are taking us back?"

"Why not?"

She picked up the revolver and examined it
absently. Then she glanced at me, and shrugged
her shoulders. "How can we know? Perhaps
this is a mutiny, and you are on your way to
some God-forsaken island. That's the usual
thing among pirates, is n't it?"

"I have no answer to that, Mrs. Johns,"
I said quietly, and turned to where Elsa
sat.

"I shall not come back unless you send for
me," I said. "But I want you to know that
my one object in life from now on is to get you
back safely to land; that your safety comes
first, and that the vigilance on deck in your
interest will not be relaxed."

"Fine words!" the stewardess muttered.

The low mumbling from Turner's room had
persisted steadily. Now it rose again in the

sharp frenzy that had characterized it through the long night.

"Don't look at me like that, man!" he cried, and then — "He's lost a hand! A hand!"

Mrs. Turner went quickly into the cabin, and the sounds ceased. I looked at Elsa, but she avoided my eyes. I turned heavily and went up the companionway.

CHAPTER XV

A KNOCKING IN THE HOLD

IT rained heavily all that day. Late in the afternoon we got some wind, and all hands turned out to trim sail. Action was a relief, and the weather suited our disheartened state better than had the pitiless August sun, the glaring white of deck and canvas, and the heat.

The heavy drops splashed and broke on top of the jolly-boat, and, as the wind came up, it rode behind us like a live thing.

Our distress signal hung sodden, too wet to give more than a dejected response to the wind that tugged at it. Late in the afternoon we sighted a large steamer, and when, as darkness came on, she showed no indication of changing her course, Burns and I sent up a rocket and blew the fog-norn steadily. She altered her course then and came towards us, and we ran up our code flags for immediate assistance; but she veered off shortly after, and went on her way. We made no further effort to attract her attention. Burns thought her a passenger steamer for the Bermudas, and, as her way was not ours, she could not have been of much assistance.

One or two of the men were already showing signs of strain. Oleson, the Swede, developed a chill, followed by fever and a mild delirium, and Adams complained of sore throat and nausea. Oleson's illness was genuine enough. Adams I suspected of malingering. He had told the men he would not go up to the crow's-nest again without a revolver, and this I would not permit.

Our original crew had numbered nine — with the cook and Williams, eleven. But the two negroes were not seamen, and were frightened into a state bordering on collapse. Of the men actually useful, there were left only five: Clarke, McNamara, Charlie Jones, Burns, and myself; and I was a negligible quantity as regarded the working of the ship.

With Burns and myself on guard duty, the burden fell on Clarke, McNamara, and Jones. A suggestion of mine that we release Singleton was instantly vetoed by the men. It was arranged, finally, that Clarke and McNamara take alternate watches at the wheel, and Jones be given the lookout for the night, to be relieved by either Burns or myself.

I watched the weather anxiously. We were too short-handed to manage any sort of a gale; and yet, the urgency of our return made it unwise to shorten canvas too much. It was as well, perhaps, that I had so much to distract my mind from the situation in the after house.

The second of the series of curious incidents that complicated our return voyage occurred that night. I was on watch from eight bells midnight until four in the morning. Jones was in the crow's-nest, McNamara at the wheel. I was at the starboard forward corner of the after house, looking over the rail. I thought that I had seen the lights of a steamer.

The rain had ceased, but the night was still very dark. I heard a sort of rapping from the forward house, and took a step toward it, listening. Jones heard it, too, and called down to me, nervously, to see what was wrong.

I called up to him, cautiously, to come down

and take my place while I investigated. I thought it was Singleton. When Jones had taken up his position at the companionway, I went forward. The knocking continued, and I traced it to Singleton's cabin. His window was open, being too small for danger, but barred across with strips of wood outside, like those in the after house. But he was at the door, hammering frantically. I called to him through the open window, but the only answer was renewed and louder pounding.

I ran around to his door, and felt for the key, which I carried.

"What is the matter?" I called.

"Who is it?"

"Leslie."

"For God's sake, open the door!"

I unlocked it and threw it open. He retreated before me, with his hands out, and huddled against the wall beside the window. I struck a match. His face was drawn and distorted, and he held his arm up as if to ward off a blow.

I lighted the lamp, for there were no electric lights in the forward house, and stared at him, amazed. Satisfied that I was really Leslie, he had stooped, and was fumbling under the window. When he straightened, he held something out to me in the palm of his shaking hand. I saw, with surprise, that it was a tobacco-pouch.

"Well?" I demanded.

"It was on the ledge," he said hoarsely. "I put it there myself. All the time I was pounding, I kept saying that, if it was still there, it was n't true — I'd just fancied it. If the pouch was on the floor, I'd know."

"Know what?"

"It was there," he said, looking over his shoulder. "It's been there three times, looking in — all in white, and grinning at me."

"A man?"

"It — it has n't got any face."

"How could it grin at you if it has n't any face?" I demanded impatiently. "Pull yourself together and tell me what you saw."

It was some time before he could tell a connected story, and, when he did, I was inclined to suspect that he had heard us talking the night before, had heard Adams's description of the intruder on the forecastle-head, and that, what with drink and terror, he had fancied the rest. And yet, I was not so sure.

"I was asleep, the first time," he said. "I don't know how long ago it was. I woke up cold, with the feeling that something was looking at me. I raised up in bed, and there was a thing at the window. It was looking in."

"What sort of a thing?"

"What I told you — white."

"A white head?"

"It was n't a head. For God's sake, Leslie! I can't tell you any more than that. I saw it. That's enough. I saw it three times."

"It is n't enough for me," I said doggedly. "It had n't any head or face, but it looked in! It's dark out there. How could you see?"

For reply, he leaned over and, turning down the lamp, blew it out. We sat in the smoking darkness, and slowly, out of the thick night, the window outlined itself. I could see it distinctly. But how, white and faceless, had *it* stared in at the window, or reached through the bars, as Singleton declared it had done, and waved a fingerless hand at us?

He was in a state of mental and physical

collapse, and begged so pitifully not to be left, that at last I told him I would take him with me, on his promise to remain in a chair until dawn, and to go back without demur. He sat near me, amidships, huddled down among the cushions of one of the wicker chairs, not sleeping, but staring straight out, motionless.

With the first light of dawn Burns relieved me, and I went forward with Singleton. He dropped into his bunk, and was asleep almost immediately. Then, inch by inch, I went over the deck for footprints, for any clue to what, under happier circumstances, I should have considered a ghastly hoax. But the deck was slippery and sodden, the rail dripping, and between the davits where the jolly-boat had swung was stretched a line with a shirt of Burns's hung on it, absurdly enough, to dry. Poor Burns, promoted to the dignity of first mate, and trying to dress the part!

Oleson and Adams made no attempt to work that day; indeed, Oleson was not able. As I had promised, the breakfast for the after house was placed on the companion steps by Tom, the cook, whence it was removed by Mrs. Sloane. I saw nothing of either Elsa Lee or Mrs. Johns. Burns was inclined to resent the dead-line the women had drawn below, and suggested that, since they were so anxious to take care of themselves, we give up guarding the after house and let them do it. We were short-handed enough, he urged, and, if they were going to take that attitude, let them manage. I did not argue, but my eyes traveled over the rail to where the jolly-boat rose to meet the fresh sea of the morning, and he colored. After that he made no comment.

Singleton awakened before noon, and ate his first meal since the murders. He looked better, and we had a long talk, I outside the window and he within. He held to his story of the night before, but was still vague as to just how the thing looked. Of what it was he seemed to have no doubt. It was the specter of either the captain or Vail; he excluded the woman, because she was shorter. As I stood outside, he measured on me the approximate height of the apparition — somewhere about five feet eight. He could see Burns's shirt, he admitted, but the *thing* had been close to the window.

I found myself convinced against my will, and that afternoon, alone, I made a second and more thorough examination of the forecastle and the hold. In the former I found nothing. Having been closed for over twenty-four hours, it was stifling and full of odors. The crew, abandoning it in haste, had left it in disorder. I made a systematic search, beginning forward and working back. I prodded in and under bunks, and moved the clothing that hung on every hook and swung, to the undoing of my nerves, with every swell. Much curious salvage I found under mattresses and beneath bunks: a rosary and a dozen filthy pictures under the same pillow; more than one bottle of whiskey; and even, where it had been dropped in the haste of flight, a bottle of cocaine. The bottle set me to thinking: had we a "coke" fiend on board, and, if we had, who was it?

The examination of the hold led to one curious and not easily explained discovery. The Ella was in gravel ballast, and my search there was difficult and nerve-racking. The creaking of the girders and floor-plates, the groaning overhead of the trestle-trees, and once an unexpected list that sent me careening, head first, against a ballast-tank, made my position distinctly disagreeable. And above all the incidental noises of a ship's hold was one that I could not place — a regular knocking, which kept time with the list of the boat.

I located it at last, approximately, at one of the ballast ports, but there was nothing to be seen. The port had been carefully barred and calked over. The sound was not loud. Down there among the other noises, I seemed to feel as well as hear it. I sent Burns down, and he came up, puzzled.

"It's outside," he said. "Something cracking against her ribs."

"You did n't notice it yesterday, did you?"

"No; but yesterday we were not listening for noises."

The knocking was on the port side. We went forward together, and, leaning well out, looked over the rail.

The missing marlinespike was swinging there,

banging against the hull with every roll of the ship. It was fastened by a rope lanyard to a large bolt below the rail, and fastened with what Burns called a Blackwall hitch — a sailor's knot.

CHAPTER XVI

I FIND, from my journal, that the next seven days passed without marked incident. Several times during that period we sighted vessels, all outward bound, and once we were within communicating distance of a steam cargo boat on her way to Venezuela. She lay to and sent her first mate over to see what could be done.

He was a slim little man with dark eyes and a small mustache above a cheerful mouth. He listened in silence to my story, and shuddered when I showed him the jolly-boat. But we were only a few days out by that time, and, after all, what could they do? He offered to spare us a hand, if it could be arranged; but, Adams having recovered by that time, we decided to get along as we were. A strange sight we must have presented to the tidy little officer in his uniform and black tie: a haggard, unshaven lot of men, none too clean, all suffering from strain and lack of sleep, with nerves

ready to snap; a white yacht, motionless, her
sails drooping, — for not a breath of air
moved, — with unpolished brasses and dirty
decks; in charge of all, a tall youth, unshaven
like the rest, and gaunt from sickness, who
hardly knew a nautical phrase, who shook the
little officer's hand with a ferocity of welcome
that made him change color, and whose uniform consisted of a pair of dirty khaki trousers
and a khaki shirt, open at the neck; and behind us, wallowing in the trough of the sea as
the Ella lay to, the jolly-boat, so miscalled,
with its sinister cargo.

The Buenos Aires went on, leaving us a bit
cheered, perhaps, but none the better off, except that she verified our bearings. The after
house had taken no notice of the incident.
None of the women had appeared, nor did they
make any inquiry of the cook when he carried
down their dinner that night. As entirely as
possible, during the week that had passed, they
had kept to themselves. Turner was better,
I imagined; but, the few times when Elsa Lee
appeared at the companion for a breath of air,
I was off duty and missed her. I thought it

was by design, and I was desperate for a sight of her.

Mrs. Johns came on deck once or twice while I was there, but she chose to ignore me. The stewardess, however, was not so partisan, and, the day before we met the Buenos Aires, she spent a little time on deck, leaning against the rail and watching me with alert black eyes.

"What are you going to do when you get to land, Mr. Captain Leslie?" she asked. "Are you going to put us all in prison?"

"That's as may be," I evaded. She was a pretty little woman, plump and dark, and she slid her hand along the rail until it touched mine. Whereon, I did the thing she was expecting, and put my fingers over hers. She flushed a little, and dimpled.

"You *are* human, are n't you?" she asked archly. "I am not afraid of you."

"No one is, I am sure."

"Silly! Why, they are all afraid of you, down there." She jerked her head toward the after house. "They want to offer you something, but none of them will do it."

"Offer me something?"

She came a little closer, so that her round shoulder touched mine.

"Why not? You need money, I take it. And that's the one thing they have — money."

I began to understand her.

"I see," I said slowly. "They want to bribe me."

She shrugged her shoulders.

"That is a nasty word. They might wish to buy — a key or two that you carry."

"The storeroom key, of course. But what other?"

She looked around — we were alone. A light breeze filled the sails and flicked the end of a scarf she wore against my face.

"The key to the captain's cabin," she said, very low.

That was what they wished to buy: the incriminating key to the storeroom, found on Turner's floor, and access to the axe, with its telltale prints on the handle.

The stewardess saw my face harden, and put her hand on my arm.

"Now I *am* afraid of you!" she cried. "When you look like that!"

"Mrs. Sloane," I said, "I do not know that you were asked to do this — I think not. But if you were, say for me what I am willing to say for myself: I shall tell what I know, and there is not money enough in the world to prevent my telling it straight. The right man is going to be punished, and the key to the storeroom will be given to the police, and to no one else."

"But — the other key?"

"That is not in my keeping."

"I do not believe you!"

"I am sorry," I said shortly. "As a matter of fact, Burns has that."

By the look of triumph in her eyes I knew I had told her what she wanted to know. She went below soon after, and I warned Burns that he would probably be approached in the same way.

"Not that I am afraid," I added. "But — keep the little Sloane woman at a distance. She's quite capable of mesmerizing you with her eyes and robbing you with her hands at the same time."

"I'd rather you'd carry it," he said, "although I'm not afraid of the lady. It's not likely, after —"

He did not finish, but he glanced aft toward the jolly-boat. Poor Burns! I believe he had really cared for the Danish girl. Perhaps I was foolish, but I refused to take the key from him; I felt sure he could be trusted.

The murders had been committed on the early morning of Wednesday, the 12th. It was on the following Tuesday that Mrs. Sloane and I had our little conversation on deck, and on Wednesday we came up with the Buenos Aires.

It was on Friday, therefore, two days after the cargo steamer had slid over the edge of the ocean, and left us, motionless, a painted ship upon a painted sea, that the incident happened that completed the demoralization of the crew.

For almost a week the lookouts had reported "All's well" in response to the striking of the ship's bell. The hysteria, as Burns and I dubbed it, of the white figure had died away as the men's nerves grew less irritated. Although we had found no absolute explanation of the marlinespike, an obvious one suggested itself. The men, although giving up their weapons without protest, had grumbled somewhat over being left without means of defense. It was entirely possible, we agreed, that the marlinespike had been so disposed, as some seaman's resort in time of need.

The cook, taking down the dinner on Friday evening, reported Mr. Turner up and about and partly dressed. The heat was frightful. All day we had had a following breeze, and it had been necessary to lengthen the towing-rope, dropping the jolly-boat well behind us. The men, saying little or nothing, dozed under their canvas; the helmsman drooped at the wheel. Under our feet the boards sent up simmering heat waves, and the brasses were too hot to touch.

At four o'clock Elsa Lee came on deck, and spoke to me for the first time in several days. She started when she saw me, and no wonder. In the frenzied caution of the day after the crimes, I had flung every razor overboard, and the result was as villainous a set of men as I have ever seen.

"Have you been ill again?" she asked.

I put my hand to my chin. "Not ill," I said; "merely unshaven."

"But you are pale, and your eyes are sunk in your head."

"We are very short-handed and — no one has slept much."

"Or eaten at all, I imagine," she said. "When do we get in?"

"I can hardly say. With this wind, perhaps Tuesday."

"Where?"

"Philadelphia."

"You intend to turn the yacht over to the police?"

"Yes, Miss Lee."

"Every one on it?"

"That is up to the police. They will probably not hold the women. You will be released, I imagine, on your own recognizance."

"And — Mr. Turner?"

"He will have to take his luck with the rest of us."

She asked me no further questions, but switched at once to what had brought her on deck.

"The cabin is unbearable," she said. "We are willing to take the risk of opening the after companion door."

But I could not allow this, and I tried to explain my reasons. The crew were quartered there, for one; for the other, whether they were willing to take the risk or not, I would not open it without placing a guard there, and we had no one to spare for the duty. I suggested that they use the part of the deck reserved for them, where it was fairly cool under the awning; and, after a dispute below, they agreed to this. Turner, very weak, came up the few steps slowly, but refused my proffered help. A little later, he called me from the rail and offered me a cigar. The change in him was startling.

We took advantage of their being on deck to open the windows and air the after house. But all were securely locked and barred before they went below again. It was the first time they had all been on deck together since the night of the 11th. It was a different crowd of people that sat there, looking over the rail and speaking in monosyllables: no bridge, no glasses clinking with ice, no elaborate toilets and carefully dressed hair, no flash of jewels, no light laughter following one of poor Vail's sallies.

At ten o'clock they went below, but not until I had quietly located every member of the crew. I had the watch from eight to twelve that night, and at half after ten Mrs. Johns came on deck again. She did not speak to me, but dropped into a steamer-chair and yawned, stretching out her arms. By the light of the companion lantern, I saw that she had put on one of the loose negligées she affected for undress, and her arms were bare except for a fall of lace.

At eight bells (midnight) Burns took my place. Charlie Jones was at the wheel, and McNamara in the crow's-nest. Mrs. Johns was dozing in her chair. The yacht was making perhaps four knots, and, far behind, the small white light of the jolly-boat showed where she rode.

I slept heavily, and at eight bells I rolled off my blanket and prepared to relieve Burns. I was stiff, weary, unrefreshed. The air was very still and we were hardly moving. I took a pail of water that stood near the rail, and, leaning far out, poured it over my head and

171

shoulders. As I turned, dripping, Jones, relieved of the wheel, touched me on the arm.

"Go back to sleep, boy," he said kindly.
"We need you, and we're goin' to need you
more when we get ashore. You've been talkin'
in your sleep till you plumb scared me."

But I was wide awake by that time, and he
had had as little sleep as I had. I refused, and
we went forward together, Jones to get coffee,
which stood all night on the galley stove.

It was still dark. The dawn, even in the less
than four weeks we had been out, came perceptibly later. At the port forward corner of
the after house, Jones stumbled over something,
and gave a sharp exclamation. The next moment he was on his knees, lighting a match.

Burns lay there on his face, unconscious, and
bleeding profusely from a cut on the back of his
head — but not dead.

CHAPTER XVII

THE AXE IS GONE

MY first thought was of the after house. Jones, who had been fond of Burns, was working over him, muttering to himself. I felt his heart, which was beating slowly but regularly, and, convinced that he was not dying, ran down into the after house. The cabin was empty: evidently the guard around the pearl-handled revolver had been given up on the false promise of peace. All the lights were going, however, and the heat was suffocating.

I ran to Miss Lee's door, and tried it. It was locked, but almost instantly she spoke from inside: —

"What is it?"

"Nothing much. Can you come out?"

She came a moment later, and I asked her to call into each cabin to see if every one was safe. The result was reassuring — no one had been disturbed; and I was put to it to account to Miss Lee for my anxiety without telling her what had happened. I made some sort of excuse, which I have forgotten, except that she evidently did not believe it.

On deck, the men were gathered around Burns. There were ominous faces among them, and mutterings of hatred and revenge; for Burns had been popular — the best-liked man among them all. Jones, wrought to the highest pitch, had even shed a few shamefaced tears, and was obliterating the humiliating memory by an extra brusqueness of manner.

We carried the injured man aft, and with such implements as I had I cleaned and dressed the wound. It needed sewing, and it seemed best to do it before he regained consciousness. Jones and Adams went below to the forecastle, therefore, and brought up my amputating set, which contained, besides its knives, some curved needles and surgical silk, still in good condition.

I opened the case, and before the knives, the long surgeon's knives which were in use before the scalpel superseded them, they fell back, muttering and amazed.

I did not know that Elsa Lee also was watching until, having requested Jones, who had been a sailmaker, to thread the needles, his trembling hands refused their duty. I looked up, searching the group for a competent assistant, and saw the girl. She had dressed, and the light from the lantern beside me on the deck threw into relief her white figure among the dark ones. She came forward as my eyes fell on her.

"Let me try," she said; and, kneeling by the lantern, in a moment she held out the threaded needle. Her hand was quite steady. She made an able assistant, wiping clean the oozing edges of the wound so that I could see to clip the bleeding vessels, and working deftly with the silk and needles to keep me supplied. My old case yielded also a roll or so of bandage. By the time Burns was attempting an incoordinate movement or two, the operation was over and the instruments put out of sight.

His condition was good. The men carried him to the tent, where Jones sat beside him, and the other men stood outside, uneasy and watchful, looking in.

The operating-case, with its knives, came in

175

for its share of scrutiny, and I felt that an explanation was due the men. To tell the truth, I had forgotten all about the case. Perhaps I swaggered just a bit as I went over to wash my hands. It was my first opportunity, and I was young, and the Girl was there.

"I see you looking at my case, boys," I said. "Perhaps I'm a little late explaining, but I guess after what you've seen you'll understand. The case belonged to my grandfather, who was a surgeon. He was in the war. That case was at Gettysburg."

"And because of your grandfather you brought it on shipboard!" Clarke said nastily.

"No. I'm a cub doctor myself. I'd been sick, and I needed the sea and a rest."

They were not so impressed as I had expected — or perhaps they had known all along. Sailors are a secretive lot.

"I'm thinking we'll all be getting a rest soon," a voice said. "What are you going to do with them knives?"

I had an inspiration. "I'm going to leave that to you men," I said. "You may throw them overboard, if you wish — but, if you do, take out the needles and the silk; we may need them."

There followed a savage but restrained argument among the men. Jones, from the tent, called out irritably: —

"Don't be fools, you fellows. This happened while Leslie was asleep. I'll swear he never moved after he lay down."

The crew reached a decision shortly after that, and came to me in a body.

"We think," Oleson said, "that we'll lock them in the captain's cabin, with the axe."

"Very well," I said. "Burns has the key around his neck."

Clarke, I think it was, went into the tent, and came out again directly.

"There's no key around his neck," he said gruffly.

"It may have slipped around under his back."

"It isn't there at all."

I ran into the tent, where Jones, having exhausted the resources of the injured man's clothing, was searching among the blankets on which he lay. There was no key. I went out to the men again, bewildered. The dawn had come, a pink and rosy dawn that promised another stifling day. It revealed the disarray of the deck — the basins, the old mahogany amputating-case with its lock-plate of bone, the stained and reddened towels; and it showed the brooding and overcast faces of the men.

"Is n't it there?" I asked. "Our agreement was for me to carry the key to Singleton's cabin and Burns the captain's."

Miss Lee, by the rail, came forward slowly, and looked up at me.

"Is n't it possible," she said, "that, knowing where the key was, some one wished to get it, and so —" She indicated the tent and Burns.

I knew then. How dull I had been, and stupid! The men caught her meaning, too, and we tramped heavily forward, the girl and I leading.

The door into the captain's room was open, and the axe was gone from the bunk. The key, with the cord that Burns had worn around his neck, was in the door, the string torn and pulled as if it had been jerked away from the unconscious man. Later on we verified this by finding

178

on the back of Burns's neck an abraded line two inches or so in length.

It was a strong cord — the kind a sailor pins his faith to, and uses indiscriminately to hold his trousers or his knife.

I ordered a rigid search of the deck, but the axe was gone. Nor was it ever found. It had taken its bloody story many fathoms deep into the old Atlantic, and hidden it, where many crimes have been hidden, in the ooze and slime of the sea-bottom.

That day was memorable for more than the attack on Burns. It marked a complete revolution in my idea of the earlier crimes, and of the criminal.

Two things influenced my change of mental attitude. The attack on Burns was one. I did not believe that Turner had strength enough to fell so vigorous a man, even with the capstan bar which we found lying near by. Nor could he have jerked and broken the amberline. Mrs. Johns I eliminated for the same reason, of course. I could imagine her getting the key by subtlety, wheedling the impressionable young sailor into compliance. But force!

The second reason was the stronger.

Singleton, the mate, had become a tractable and almost amiable prisoner. Like Turner, he was ugly only when he was drinking, and there was not even enough liquor on the Ella to revive poor Burns. He spent his days devising, with bits of wire, a ring puzzle that he intended should make his fortune. And I believe he contrived, finally, a clever enough bit of foolery. He was anxious to talk, and complained bitterly of loneliness, using every excuse to hold Tom, the cook, when he carried him his meals. He had asked for a Bible, too, and read it now and then.

The morning of Burns's injury, I visited Singleton.

The new outrage, coming at a time when they were slowly recovering confidence, had turned the men surly. The loss of the axe, the handle of which I had told them would, under skillful eyes, reveal the murderer as accurately as a photograph, was a serious blow. Again arose the specter of the innocent suffering for the guilty. They went doggedly about their work, and wherever they gathered there was muttered talk of the white figure. There was grumbling, too, over their lack of weapons for defense.

The cook was a ringleader of the malcontents. Certain utensils were allowed him; but he was compelled at night to lock them in the galley, after either Burns's inspection or mine, and to turn over the key to one of us.

On the morning after the attack, therefore, Tom, carrying Singleton's breakfast to him, told him at length what had occurred in the night, and dilated on his lack of self-defense should an attack be directed toward him.

Singleton promptly offered to make him, out of wire, a key to the galley door, so that he could get what he wanted from it. The cook was to take an impression of the lock. In exchange, Tom was to fetch him, from a hiding-place which Singleton designated in the forward house, a bottle of whiskey.

The cook was a shrewd mulatto, and he let Singleton make the key. It was after ten that morning when he brought it to me. I was trying to get the details of his injury from Burns, at the time, in the tent.

"I didn't see or hear anything, Leslie,"

Burns said feebly. "I don't even remember
being hit. I felt there was some one behind me.
That was all."

"There had been nothing suspicious earlier
in the night?"

He lay thinking. He was still somewhat
confused.

"No — I think not. Or — yes, I thought
once I saw some one standing by the mainmast
— behind it. It was n't."

"How long was Mrs. Johns on deck?"

"Not long."

"Did she ask you to do something for her?"

Pale as he was, he colored; but he eyed me
honestly.

"Yes. Don't ask me any more, Leslie. It
had nothing to do with this."

"What did she ask you to do?" I persisted
remorselessly.

"I don't want to talk; my head aches."

"Very well. Then I'll tell you what happened
after I went off watch. No, I was n't spying.
I know the woman, that's all. She said you
looked tired, and would n't it be all right if you
sat down for a moment and talked to her."

"No; she said she was nervous."

"The same thing — only better. Then she persisted in talking of the crime, and finally she said she would like to see the axe. It would n't do any harm. She would n't touch it."

He watched me uneasily.

"She did n't either," he said. "I 'll swear to that, Leslie. She did n't go near the bunk. She covered her face with her hands, and leaned against the door. I thought she was going to faint."

"Against the door, of course! And got an impression of the key. The door opens in. She could take out the key, press it against a cake of wax or even a cake of soap in her hand, and slip it back into the lock again while you — What were you doing while she was doing all that?"

"She dropped her salts. I picked them up."

"Exactly! Well, the axe is gone."

He started up on his elbow.

"Gone!"

"Thrown overboard, probably. It is not in the cabin."

It was brutal, perhaps; but the situation was

all of that. As Burns fell back, colorless, Tom, the cook, brought into the tent the wire key that Singleton had made.

That morning I took from inside of Singleton's mattress a bunch of keys, a long steel file, and the leg of one of his chairs, carefully unscrewed and wrapped at the end with wire — a formidable club. One of the keys opened Singleton's door.

That was on Saturday. Early Monday morning we sighted land.

CHAPTER XVIII

A BAD COMBINATION

WE picked up a pilot outside the Lewes breakwater — a man of few words. I told him only the outlines of our story, and I believe he half discredited me at first. God knows, I was not a creditable object. When I took him aft and showed him the jolly-boat, he realized, at last, that he was face to face with a great tragedy, and paid it the tribute of throwing away his cigar.

He suggested our raising the yellow plague flag; and this we did, with a ready response from the quarantine officer. The quarantine officer came out in a power-boat, and mounted the ladder; and from that moment my command of the Ella ceased. Turner, immaculately dressed, pale, distinguished, member of the yacht club and partner in the Turner line, met him at the rail, and conducted him, with a sort of chastened affability, to the cabin.

Exhausted from lack of sleep, terrified with

what had gone by and what was yet to come, unshaven and unkempt, the men gathered on the forecastle-head and waited.

The conference below lasted perhaps an hour. At the end of that time the quarantine officer came up and shouted a direction from below, as a result of which the jolly-boat was cut loose, and, towed by the tug, taken to the quarantine station. There was an argument, I believe, between Turner and the officer, as to allowing us to proceed up the river without waiting for the police. Turner prevailed, however, and, from the time we hoisted the yellow flag, we were on our way to the city, a tug panting beside us, urging the broad and comfortable lines of the old cargo boat to a semblance of speed.

The quarantine officer, a dapper little man, remained on the boat, and busied himself officiously, getting the names of the men, peering at Singleton through his barred window, and expressing disappointment at my lack of foresight in having the bloodstains cleared away.

"Every stain is a clue, my man, to the trained eye," he chirruped. "With an axe, too! What a brutal method! Brutal! Where is the axe?"

186

"Gone," I said patiently. "It was stolen out of the captain's cabin."

He eyed me over his glasses.

"That's very strange," he commented. "No stains, no axe! You fellows have been mighty careful to destroy the evidence, have n't you?"

All that long day we made our deliberate progress up the river. The luggage from the after house was carried up on deck by Adams and Clarke, and stood waiting for the custom-house.

Turner, his hands behind him, paced the deck hour by hour, his heavy face colorless. His wife, dark, repressed, with a look of being always on guard, watched him furtively. Mrs. Johns, dressed in black, talked to the doctor; and, from the notes he made, I knew she was telling the story of the tragedy. And here, there, and everywhere, efficient, normal, and so lovely that it hurt me to look at her, was Elsa.

Williams, the butler, had emerged from his chrysalis of fright, and was ostentatiously looking after the family's comfort. No clearer indication could have been given of the new status of affairs than his changed attitude coward me. He came up to me, early in the afternoon, and demanded that I wash down the deck before the women came up.

I smiled down at him cheerfully.

"Williams," I said, "you are a coward — a mean, white-livered coward. You have skulked in the after house, behind women, when there was man's work to do. If I wash that deck, it will be with you as a mop."

He blustered something about speaking to Mr. Turner and seeing that I did the work I was brought on board to do, and, seeing Turner's eye on us, finished his speech with an ugly epithet. My nerves were strained to the utmost: lack of sleep and food had done their work. I was no longer in command of the Ella; I was a common sailor, ready to vent my spleen through my fists.

I knocked him down with my open hand.

It was a barbarous and a reckless thing to do. He picked himself up and limped away, muttering. Turner had watched the scene with his cold blue eyes, and the little doctor with his near-sighted ones.

"A dangerous man, that!" said the doctor.

"Dangerous and intelligent," replied Turner.
"A bad combination!"

It was late that night when the Ella anchored
in the river at Philadelphia. We were not
allowed to land. The police took charge of ship,
crew, and passengers. The men slept heavily on
deck, except Burns, who developed a slight fever
from his injury, and moved about restlessly.

It seemed to me that the vigilance of the
officers was exerted largely to prevent an escape
from the vessel, and not sufficiently for the safety
of those on board. I spoke of this, and a guard
was placed at the companionway again. Thus I
saw Elsa Lee for the last time until the trial.

She was dressed, as she had been in the afternoon, in a dark cloth suit of some sort, and I
did not see her until I had spoken to the officer
in charge. She turned, at my voice, and called
me to join her where she stood.

"We are back again, Leslie."

"Yes, Miss Lee."

"Back to — what? To live the whole thing
over again in a courtroom! If only we could
go away, anywhere, and try to forget!"

She had not expected any answer, and I had none ready. I was thinking — Heaven help me — that there were things I would not forget if I could: the lift of her lashes as she looked up at me; the few words we had had together, the day she had told me the deck was not clean; the night I had touched her hand with my lips.

"We are to be released, I believe," she said, "on our own — some legal term; I forget it."

"Recognizance, probably."

"Yes. You do not know law as well as medicine?"

"I am sorry — no; and I know very little medicine."

"But you sewed up a wound!"

"As a matter of fact," I admitted, "that was my initial performance, and it is badly done. It — it puckers."

She turned on me a trifle impatiently.

"Why do you make such a secret of your identity?" she demanded. "Is it a pose? Or — have you a reason for concealing it?"

"It is not a pose; and I have nothing to be ashamed of, unless poverty —"

"Of course not. What do you mean by poverty?"

"The common garden variety sort. I have hardly a dollar in the world. As to my identity, — if it interests you at all, — I graduated in medicine last June. I spent the last of the money that was to educate me in purchasing a dress suit to graduate in, and a supper by way of celebration. The dress suit helped me to my diploma. The supper gave me typhoid."

"So *that* was it!"

"Not jail, you see."

"And what are you going to do now?"

I glanced around to where a police officer stood behind us watchfully.

"Now? Why, now I go to jail in earnest."

"You have been very good to us," she said wistfully. "We have all been strained and nervous. Maybe you have not thought I noticed or — or appreciated what you were doing; but I have, always. You have given all of yourself for us. You have not slept or eaten. And now you are going to be imprisoned. It is n't just!"

I tried to speak lightly, to reassure her.

"Don't be unhappy about *that*," I said. "A nice, safe jail, where one may sleep and eat, and eat and sleep — oh, I shall be very comfortable! And if you wish to make me exceedingly happy, you will see that they let me have a razor."

But, to my surprise, she buried her face in her arms. I could not believe at first that she was crying. The policeman had wandered across to the other rail, and stood looking out at the city lights, his back to us. I put my hand out to touch her soft hair, then drew it back. I could not take advantage of her sympathy, of the hysterical excitement of that last night on the Ella. I put my hands in my pockets, and held them there, clenched, lest, in spite of my will, I reach out to take her in my arms.

CHAPTER XIX

I TAKE THE STAND

A ND now I come, with some hesitation, to the trial. Hesitation, because I relied on McWhirter to keep a record. And McWhirter, from his notes, appears to have been carried away at times by excitement, and either jotted down rows of unintelligible words, or waited until evening and made up his notes, like a woman's expense account, from a memory never noticeable for accuracy.

At dawn, the morning after we anchored, Charlie Jones roused me, grinning.

"Friend of yours over the rail, Leslie," he said. "Wants to take you ashore!"

I knew no one in Philadelphia except the chap who had taken me yachting once, and I felt pretty certain that he would not associate Leslie the football player with Leslie the sailor on the Ella. I went reluctantly to the rail, and looked down. Below me, just visible in the river mist of the early morning, was a small boat from which two men were looking up. One was McWhirter!

"Hello, old top," he cried. "Or *is* it you behind that beard?"

"It's I, all right, Mac," I said, somewhat huskily. What with seeing him again, his kindly face behind its glasses, the cheerful faith in me which was his contribution to our friendship, — even the way he shook his own hand in default of mine, — my throat tightened. Here, after all, was home and a friend.

He looked up at the rail, and motioned to a rope that hung there.

"Get your stuff and come with us for breakfast," he said. "You look as if you had n't eaten since you left."

"I'm afraid I can't, Mac."

"They're not going to hold you, are they?"

"For a day or so, yes."

Mac's reply to this was a violent résumé of the ancestry and present lost condition of the Philadelphia police, ending with a request that I jump over, and let them go to the place he had just designated as their abiding-place in eternity. On an officer lounging to the rail and looking down, however, he subsided into a low muttering.

The story of how McWhirter happened to be floating on the bosom of the Delaware River before five o'clock in the morning was a long one — it was months before I got it in full. Briefly, going home from the theater in New York the night before, he had bought an "extra" which had contained a brief account of the Ella's return. He seems to have gone into a frenzy of excitement at once. He borrowed a small car, — one scornfully designated as a "road louse," — and assembled in it, in wild confusion, one suit of clothes for me, his own and much too small, one hypodermic case, an armful of newspapers with red scare-heads, a bottle of brandy, a bottle of digitalis, one police card, and one excited young lawyer, of the same vintage in law that Mac and I were in medicine. At the last moment, fearful that the police might not know who I was, he had flung in a scrapbook in which he had pasted — with a glue that was to make his fortune — records of my exploits on the football field!

A dozen miles from Philadelphia the little

machine had turned over on a curve, knocking all the law and most of the enthusiasm out of Walters, the legal gentleman, and smashing the brandy-bottle. McWhirter had picked himself up, kicked viciously at the car, and, gathering up his impedimenta, had made the rest of the journey by foot and street-car.

His wrath at finding me a prisoner was unbounded; his scorn at Walters, the attorney, for not confounding the police with law enough to free me, was furious and contemptuous. He picked up the oars in sullen silence, and, leaning on them, called a loud and defiant farewell for the benefit of the officer.

"All right," he said. "An hour or so won't make much difference. But you'll be free to-day, all right, all right. And don't let them bluff you, boy. If the police get funny, tackle them and throw 'em overboard, one by one. You can do it."

He made an insulting gesture at the police, picked up his oars, and rowed away into the mist.

But I was not free that day, nor for many days. As I had expected, Turner, his family,

I TAKE THE STAND

Mrs. Johns, and the stewardess were released, after examination. The rest of us were taken to jail — Singleton as a suspect, the others to make sure of their presence at the trial.

The murders took place on the morning of August 12. The Grand Jury met late in September, and found an indictment against Singleton. The trial began on the 16th of November.

The confinement was terrible. Accustomed to regular exercise as I was, I suffered mentally and physically. I heard nothing from Elsa Lee, and I missed McWhirter, who had got his hospital appointment, and who wrote me cheering letters on pages torn from order-books or on prescription-blanks. He was in Boston.

He got leave of absence for the trial, and, as I explained, the following notes are his, not mine. The case was tried in the United States Court, before Circuit Judge Willard and District Judge McDowell. The United States was represented by a district attorney and two assistant attorneys. Singleton had retained a lawyer named Goldstein, a clever young Jew.

I was called first, as having found the bodies.

"Your name?"

"Ralph Leslie."

"Your age?"

"Twenty-four."

"When and where were you born?"

"November 18, 1887, in Columbus, Ohio."

"When did you ship on the yacht Ella?"

"On July 27."

"When did she sail?"

"July 28."

"Are you a sailor by occupation?"

"No; I am a graduate of a medical college."

"What were your duties on the ship?"

"They were not well defined. I had been ill and was not strong. I was a sort of deck-steward, I suppose. I also served a few meals in the cabin of the after house, when the butler was incapacitated."

"Where were you quartered?"

"In the forecastle, with the crew, until a day or so before the murders. Then I moved into the after house, and slept in a storeroom there."

"Why did you make the change?"

"Mrs. Johns, a guest, asked me to do so. She said she was nervous."

I TAKE THE STAND

"Who slept in the after house?"

"Mr. and Mrs. Turner, Miss Lee, Mrs. Johns, and Mr. Vail. The stewardess, Mrs. Sloane, and Karen Hansen, a maid; also slept there; but their room opened from the chart-room."

A diagram of the after house was here submitted to the jury. For the benefit of the reader, I reproduce it roughly. I have made no

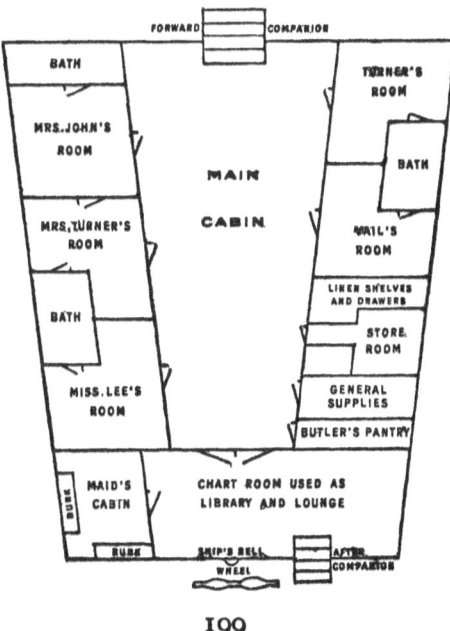

attempt to do more than to indicate the relative positions of rooms and companionways.

"State what happened on the night of August 11 and early morning of August 12."

"I slept in the storeroom in the after house. As it was very hot, I always left the door open. The storeroom itself was a small room, lined with shelves, and reached by a passageway. The door was at the end of the passage. I wakened because of the heat, and found the door locked on the outside. I lit a match, and found I could unscrew the lock with my knife. I thought I had been locked in as a joke by the crew. While I was kneeling, some one passed outside the door."

"How did you know that?"

"I felt a board rise under my knee as if the other end had been trod on. Shortly after, a woman screamed, and I burst open the door."

"How long after you felt the board rise?"

"Perhaps a minute, possibly two."

"Go on."

"Just after, the ship's bell struck six — three o'clock. The main cabin was dark. There was a light in the chart-room, from the binnacle light. I felt my way to Mr. Vail's room. I heard him breathing. His door was open. I struck a match and looked at him. He had stopped breathing."

"What was the state of his bunk?"

"Disordered — horrible. He was almost hacked to pieces."

"Go on."

"I ran back and got my revolver. I thought there had been a mutiny —"

"Confine yourself to what you saw and did. The court is not interested in what you thought."

"I am only trying to explain what I did. I ran back to the storeroom and got my revolver, and ran back through the chart-room to the after companion, which had a hood. I thought that if any one was lying in ambush, the hood would protect me until I could get to the deck. I told the helmsman what had happened, and ran forward. Mr. Singleton was on the fore-castle-head. We went below together, and found the captain lying at the foot of the forward companion, also dead."

"At this time, had you called the owner of the ship?"

"No. I called him then. But I could not rouse him."

"Explain what you mean by that."

"He had been drinking."

There followed a furious wrangle over this point; but the prosecuting attorney succeeded in having question and answer stand.

"What did you do next?"

"The mate had called the crew. I wakened Mrs. Turner, Miss Lee, and Mrs. Johns, and then went to the chart-room to call the women there. The door was open an inch or so. I received no answer to my knock, and pulled it open. Karen Hansen, the maid, was dead on the floor, and the stewardess was in her bunk, in a state of collapse."

"State where you found the axe with which the crimes were committed."

"It was found in the stewardess's bunk."

"Where is this axe now?"

"It was stolen from the captain's cabin, where it was locked for safe keeping, and presumably thrown overboard. At least, we did not find it."

"I see you are consulting a book to refresh your memory. What is this book?"

"The ship's log."

"How does it happen to be in your possession?"

"The crew appointed me captain. As such, I kept the log-book. It contains a full account of the discovery of the bodies, witnessed by all the men."

"Is it in your writing?"

"Yes; it is in my writing."

"You read it to the men, and they signed it?"

"No; they read it themselves before they signed it."

After a wrangle as to my having authority to make a record in the log-book, the prosecuting attorney succeeded in having the book admitted as evidence, and read to the jury the entry of August 13.

Having thus proved the crimes, I was excused, to be recalled later. The defense reserving its cross-examination, the doctor from the quarantine station was called next, and testified to the manner of death. His testimony was revolting, and bears in no way on the story, save in one particular — a curious uniformity in the mutilation of the bodies of Vail and Captain Richardson — a sinister similarity that was infinitely shocking. In each case the forehead, the two arms, and the abdomen had received a frightful blow. In the case of the Danish girl there was only one wound — the injury on the head.

CHAPTER XX

HENRIETTA SLOANE was called next.
"Your name?"

"Henrietta Sloane."

"Are you married?"

"A widow."

"When and where were you born?"

"Isle of Man, December 11, 1872."

"How long have you lived in the United States?"

"Since I was two."

"Your position on the yacht Ella?"

"Stewardess."

"Before that?"

"On the Baltic, between Liverpool and New York. That was how I met Mrs. Turner."

"Where was your room on the yacht Ella?"

"Off the chart-room."

"Will you indicate it on this diagram?"

"It was there." (Pointing.)

The diagram was shown to the jury.

"There are two bunks in this room. Which was yours?"

"The one at the side — the one opposite the door was Karen's."

"Tell what happened on the night of August 11 and morning of the 12th."

"I went to bed early. Karen Hansen had not come down by midnight. When I opened the door, I saw why. Mr. Turner and Mr. Singleton were there, drinking."

The defense objected to this but was overruled by the court.

"Mr. Vail was trying to persuade the mate to go on deck, before the captain came down."

"Did they go?"

"No."

"What comment did Mr. Singleton make?"

"He said he hoped the captain would come. He wanted a chance to get at him."

"What happened after that?"

"The captain came down and ordered the mate on deck. Mr. Vail and the captain got Mr. Turner to his room."

"How do you know that?"

"I opened my door."

"What then?"

"Karen came down at 12.30. We went to bed. At ten minutes to three the bell rang for Karen. She got up and put on a wrapper and slippers. She was grumbling and I told her to put out the light and let me sleep. As she opened the door she screamed and fell back on the floor. Something struck me on the shoulder, and I fainted. I learned later it was the axe."

"Did you hear any sound outside, before you opened the door?"

"A curious chopping sound. I spoke of it to her. It came from the chart-room."

"When the girl fell back into the room, did you see any one beyond her?"

"I saw something — I could n't say just what."

"Was what you saw a figure?"

"I — I am not certain. It was light — almost white."

"Can you not describe it?"

"I am afraid not — except that it seemed white."

"How tall was it?"

"I could n't say."

"As tall as the girl?"

"Just about, perhaps."

"Think of something that it resembled. This is important, Mrs. Sloane. You must make an effort."

"I think it looked most like a fountain."

Even the jury laughed at this, and yet, after all, Mrs. Sloane was right — or nearly so!

"That is curious. How did it resemble a fountain?"

"Perhaps I should have said a fountain in moonlight — white, and misty, and — and flowing."

"And yet, this curious-shaped object threw the axe at you, did n't it?"

There was an objection to the form of this question, but the court overruled it.

"I did not say *it* threw the axe. I did not see it thrown. I felt it."

"Did you know the first mate, Singleton, before you met on the Ella?"

"Yes, sir."

"Where?"

"We were on the same vessel two years ago, the American, for Bermuda."

"Were you friends?"

"Yes" — very low.

"Were you engaged to marry him at one time?"

"Yes."

"Why did you break it off?"

"We differed about a good many things."

After a long battle, the prosecuting attorney was allowed to show that, following the breaking off of her relations with Singleton, she had been a witness against him in an assault-and-battery case, and had testified to his violence of temper. The dispute took so long that there was only time for her cross-examination. The effect of the evidence, so far, was distinctly bad for Singleton.

His attorney, a young and intelligent Jew, cross-examined Mrs. Sloane.

Attorney for the defense: "Did you ever write a letter to the defendant, Mrs. Sloane, threatening him if he did not marry you?"

"I do not recall such a letter."

"Is this letter in your writing?"

"I think so. Yes."

"Mrs. Sloane, you testify that you 'opened

your door and saw' Mr. Vail and the captain taking Mr. Turner to his room. Is this correct?"

"Yes."

"Why did they take him? I mean, was he not able, apparently, to walk alone?"

"He was able to walk. They walked beside him."

"In your testimony, taken at the time and entered in the ship's log, you say you 'judged by the sounds.' Here you say you 'opened the door and saw them.' Which is correct?"

"I saw them."

"You say that Mr. Singleton said he wished to 'get at' the captain. Are those his exact words?"

"I do not recall his exact words."

"Perhaps I can refresh your mind. With the permission of the court, I shall read from the ship's log this woman's statement, recorded by the man who was in charge of the vessel, and therefore competent to make such record, and signed by the witness as having been read and approved by her: —

"'Mr. Singleton said that he hoped the captain would come, as he *and Mr. Turner* only wanted a chance to get at him. . . . There was a sound outside, and Karen thought it was Mr. Turner falling over something, and said that she hoped she would not meet him. Once or twice, when he had been drinking, he had made overtures to her, and she detested him. . . . She opened the door and came back into the room, touching me on the arm. " That beast is out there," she said, "sitting on the companion steps. If he tries to stop me, I 'll call you." ' "

The reading made a profound impression. The prosecution, having succeeded in having the log admitted as evidence, had put a trump card in the hands of the defense.

"What were the relations between Mr. Turner and the captain?"

"I don't know what you mean."

"Were they friendly?"

"No — not very."

"Did you overhear, on the night of August 9, a conversation between Mr. Turner and Mr. Vail?"

"Yes."

"What was its nature?"

"They were quarreling."

"What did Williams, the butler, give you to hide, that night?"

"Mr. Turner's revolver."

"What did he say when he gave it to you?"

"He said to throw it overboard or there would be trouble."

"Mrs. Sloane, do you recognize these two garments?"

He held up a man's dinner shirt and a white waistcoat. The stewardess, who had been calm enough, started and paled.

"I cannot tell without examining them." (They were given to her, and she looked at them.) "Yes, I have seen them."

"What are they?"

"A shirt and waistcoat of Mr. Turner's."

"When did you see them last?"

"I packed them in my trunk when we left the boat. They had been forgotten when the other trunks were packed."

"Had you washed them?"

"No."

"Were they washed on shipboard?"

"They look like it.. They have not been ironed."

"Who gave them to you to pack in your trunk?"

"Mrs. Johns."

"What did you do with them on reaching New York?"

"I left them in my trunk."

"Why did you not return them to Mr. Turner?"

"I was ill, and forgot. I'd like to know what right you have going through a person's things — and taking what you want!"

The stewardess was excused, the defense having scored perceptibly. It was clear what line the young Jew intended to follow.

Oleson, the Swede, was called next, and after the usual formalities: —

"Where were you between midnight and 4 A.M. on the morning of August 12?"

"In the crow's-nest of the Ella."

"State what you saw between midnight and one o'clock."

"I saw Mate Singleton walking on the forecastle-head. Every now and then he went to the rail. He seemed to be vomiting. It was too dark to see much. Then he went aft along the port side of the house, and came forward again on the starboard side. He went to where the axe was kept."

"Where was that?"

"Near the starboard corner of the forward house. All the Turner boats have an emergency box, with an axe and other tools, in easy reach. The officer on watch carried the key."

"Could you see what he was doing?"

"No; but he was fumbling at the box. I heard him."

"Where did he go after that?"

"He went aft."

"You could not see him?"

"I did n't look. I thought I saw something white moving below me, and I was watching it."

"This white thing — what did it look like?"

"Like a dog, I should say. It moved about, and then disappeared."

"How?"

"I don't understand."

"Over the rail?"

"Oh — no, sir. It faded away."

"Had you ever heard talk among the men of the Ella being a haunted ship?"

"Yes — but not until after I'd signed on her!"

"Was there some talk of this 'white thing'?"

"Yes."

"Before the murders?"

"No, sir; not till after. I guess I saw it first."

"What did the men say about it?"

"They thought it scared Mr. Schwartz overboard. The Ella's been unlucky as to crews. They call her a 'devil ship.'"

"Did you see Mr. Singleton on deck between two and three o'clock?"

"No, sir."

The cross-examination was very short: —

"What sort of night was it?"

"Very dark."

"Would the first mate, as officer on watch, be supposed to see that the emergency case you speak of was in order?"

"Yes, sir."

"Did the officer on watch remain on the forecastle-head?"

"Mr. Schwartz did not; Mr. Singleton did,

mostly except when he went back to strike the bells."

"Could Mr. Singleton have been on deck without you seeing him?"

"Yes, if he did not move around or smoke. I could see his pipe lighted."

"Did you see his pipe that night?"

"No, sir."

"If you were sick, would you be likely to smoke?"

This question, I believe, was ruled out.

"In case the wheel of the vessel were lashed for a short time, what would happen?"

"Depends on the weather. She'd be likely to come to or fall off considerable."

"Would the lookout know it?"

"Yes, sir."

"How?"

"The sails would show it, sir."

That closed the proceedings for the day. The crowd seemed reluctant to disperse. Turner's lawyers were in troubled consultation with him. Singleton was markedly more cheerful, and I thought the prosecution looked perturbed and uneasy. I went back to jail that night, and dreamed of Elsa — not as I had seen her that day, bending forward, watching every point of the evidence, but as I had seen her so often on the yacht, facing into the salt breeze as if she loved it, her hands in the pockets of her short white jacket, her hair blowing back from her forehead in damp, close-curling rings.

CHAPTER XXI

"A BAD WOMAN"

CHARLIE JONES was called first, on the second day of the trial. He gave his place of birth as Pennsylvania, and his present shore address as a Sailors' Christian Home in New York. He offered, without solicitation, the information that he had been twenty-eight years in the Turner service, and could have been "up at the top," but preferred the forecastle, so that he could be an influence to the men.

His rolling gait, twinkling blue eyes, and huge mustache, as well as the plug of tobacco which he sliced with a huge knife, put the crowd in good humor, and relieved somewhat the somberness of the proceedings.

"Where were you between midnight and 4 A.M. on the morning of August 12?"

"At the wheel."

"You did not leave the wheel during that time?"

"Yes, sir."

"When was that?"

"After they found the captain's body. I went to the forward companion and looked down."

"Is a helmsman permitted to leave his post?"

"With the captain lying dead down in a pool of blood, I should think —"

"Never mind thinking. Is he?"

"No."

"What did you do with the wheel when you left it?"

"Lashed it. There are two rope-ends, with loops, to lash it with. When I was on the Sarah Winters —"

"Stick to the question. Did you see the mate, Mr. Singleton, during your watch?"

"Every half-hour from 12.30 to 1.30. He struck the bells. After that he said he was sick. He thought he'd been poisoned. He said he was going forward to lie down, and for me to strike them."

"Who struck the bell at three o'clock?"

"I did, sir."

"When did you hear a woman scream?"

"Just before that."

"What did you do?"

"Nothing. It was the Hansen woman. I did n't like her. She was a bad woman. When I told her what she was, she laughed."

"Were you ever below in the after house?"

"No, sir; not since the boat was fixed up."

"What could you see through the window beside the wheel?"

"It looked into the chart-room. If the light was on, I could see all but the floor."

"Between the hours of 1 A.M. and 3 A.M., did any one leave or enter the after house by the after companion?"

"Yes, sir. Mr. Singleton went down into the chart-room, and came back again in five or ten minutes."

"At what time?"

"At four bells — two o'clock."

"No one else?"

"No, sir; but I saw Mr. Turner —"

"Confine yourself to the question. What was Mr. Singleton's manner at the time you mention?"

"He was excited. He brought up a bottle of

whiskey from the chart-room table, and drank what was left in it. Then he muttered something, and threw the empty bottle over the rail. He said he was still sick."

The cross-examination confined itself to one detail of Charlie Jones's testimony.

"Did you, between midnight and 3 A.M., see any one in the chart-room besides the mate?"

"Yes — Mr. Turner."

"You say you cannot see into the chart-room from the wheel at night. How did you see him?"

"He turned on the light. He seemed to be looking for something."

"Was he dressed?"

"Yes, sir."

"Can you describe what he wore?"

"Yes, sir. His coat was off. He had a white shirt and a white vest."

"Were the shirt and vest similar to these I show you?"

"Most of them things look alike to me. Yes, sir."

The defense had scored again. But it suffered at the hands of Burns, the next witness. I believe the prosecution had intended to call Turner at this time; but, after a whispered conference with Turner's attorneys, they made a change. Turner, indeed, was in no condition to go on the stand. He was pallid and twitching, and his face was covered with sweat.

Burns corroborated the testimony against Singleton — his surly temper, his outbursts of rage, his threats against the captain. And he brought out a new point: that Jones, the helmsman, had been afraid of Singleton that night, and had asked not to be left alone at the wheel.

During this examination the prosecution for the first time made clear their position: that the captain was murdered first; that Vail interfered, and, pursued by Singleton, took refuge in his bunk, where he was slaughtered; that the murderer, bending to inspect his horrid work, had unwittingly touched the bell that roused Karen Hansen, and, crouching in the chartroom with the axe, had struck her as she opened the door.

The prosecution questioned Burns about the axe and its disappearance.

"Who suggested that the axe be kept in the captain's cabin?"

"Leslie, acting as captain."

"Who had the key?"

"I carried it on a strong line around my neck."

"Whose arrangement was that?"

"Leslie's. He had the key to Mr. Singleton's cabin, and I carried this one. We divided the responsibility."

"Did you ever give the key to any one?"

"No, sir."

"Did it ever leave you?"

"Not until it was taken away."

"When was that?"

"On Saturday morning, August 22, shortly before dawn."

"Tell what happened."

"I was knocked down from behind, while I was standing at the port forward corner of the after house. The key was taken from me while I was unconscious."

"Did you ever see the white object that has been spoken of by the crew?"

"No, sir. I searched the deck one night

when Adams, the lookout, raised an alarm. We found nothing except —"

"Go on."

"He threw down a marlinespike at something moving in the bow. The spike disappeared. We could n't find it, although we could see where it had struck the deck. Afterwards we found a marlinespike hanging over the ship's side by a lanyard. It might have been the one we looked for."

"Explain 'lanyard.'"

"A cord — a sort of rope."

"It could not have fallen over the side and hung there?"

"It was fastened with a Blackwell hitch."

"Show us what you mean."

On cross-examination by Singleton's attorney, Burns was forced to relate the incident of the night before his injury — that Mrs. Johns had asked to see the axe, and he had shown it to her. He maintained stoutly that she had not been near the bunk, and that the axe was there when he locked the door.

Adams, called, testified to seeing a curious,

misty-white object on the forecastle-head. It had seemed to come over the bow. The marlinespike he threw had had no lanyard.

Mrs. Turner and Miss Lee escaped with a light examination. Their evidence amounted to little, and was practically the same. They had retired early, and did not rouse until I called them. They remained in their rooms most of the time after that, and were busy caring for Mr. Turner, who had been ill. Mrs. Turner was good enough to say that I had made them as safe and as comfortable as possible.

The number of witnesses to be examined, and the searching grilling to which most of them were subjected, would have dragged the case to interminable length, had it not been for the attitude of the judges, who discouraged quibbling and showed a desire to reach the truth with the least possible delay. One of the judges showed the wide and unbiased attitude of the court by a little speech after an especially venomous contest.

"Gentlemen," he said, "we are attempting to get to a solution of this thing. We are trying one man, it is true, but, in a certain

sense, we are trying every member of the crew,
every person who was on board the ship the
night of the crime. We have a curious situation. The murderer is before us, either in the
prisoner's dock or among the witnesses. Let
us get at the truth without bickering."

Mrs. Johns was called, following Miss Lee.
I watched her carefully on the stand. I had
never fathomed Mrs. Johns, or her attitude
toward the rest of the party. I had thought, at
the beginning of the cruise, that Vail and she
were incipient lovers. But she had taken his
death with a calmness that was close to indifference. There was something strange and
inexplicable in her tigerish championship of
Turner — and it remains inexplicable even
now. I have wondered since — was she in love
with Turner, or was she only a fiery partisan?
I wonder!

She testified with an insolent coolness that
clearly irritated the prosecution — thinking
over her replies, refusing to recall certain things,
and eyeing the jury with long, slanting glances
that set them, according to their type, either
wriggling or ogling.

The first questions were the usual ones.
Then: —

"Do you recall the night of the 31st ot
July?"

"Can you be more specific?"

"I refer to the night when Captain Richardson found the prisoner in the chart-room and
ordered him on deck."

"I recall that, yes."

"Where were you during the quarrel?"

"I was behind Mr. Vail."

"Tell us about it, please."

"It was an ordinary brawl. The captain
knocked the mate down."

"Did you hear the mate threaten the captain?"

"No. He went on deck, muttering; I did
not hear what was said."

"After the crimes, what did you do?"

"We established a dead-line at the foot of
the forward companion. The other was locked."

"Was there a guard at the top of the companion?"

"Yes; but we trusted no one."

"Where was Mr. Turner?"

"Ill, in his cabin."

"How ill?"

"Very. He was delirious."

"Did you allow any one down?"

"At first, Leslie, a sort of cabin-boy and deck-steward, who seemed to know something of medicine. Afterward we would not allow him, either."

"Why?"

"We did not trust him."

"This Leslie — why had you asked him to sleep in the storeroom?"

"I — was afraid."

"Will you explain why you were afraid?"

"Fear is difficult to explain, is n't it? If one knows why one is afraid, one — er — generally is n't."

"That's a bit subtle, I'm afraid. You were afraid, then, without knowing why?"

"Yes."

"Had you a revolver on board?"

"Yes."

"Whose revolver was kept on the cabin table?"

"Mine. I always carry one."

"Always?"

"Yes."

"Then — have you one with you now?"

"Yes."

"When you asked the sailor Burns to let you see the axe, what did you give as a reason?"

"The truth — curiosity."

"Then, having seen the axe, where did you go?"

"Below."

"Please explain the incident of the two articles Mr. Goldstein showed to the jury yesterday, the shirt and waistcoat."

"That was very simple. Mr. Turner had been very ill. We took turns in caring for him. I spilled a bowl of broth over the garments that were shown, and rubbed them out in the bathroom. They were hung in the cabin used by Mr. Vail to dry, and I forgot them when we were packing."

The attorney for the defense cross-examined her: —

"What color were the stains you speak of?"

"Darkish — red-brown."

"What sort of broth did you spill?"

"That's childish, is n't it? I don't recall."

"You recall its color."

"It was beef broth."

"Mrs. Johns, on the night you visited the forward house and viewed the axe, did you visit it again?"

"The axe, or the forward house?"

"The house."

She made one of her long pauses. Finally: —

"Yes."

"When?"

"Between three and four o'clock."

"Who went with you?"

"I went alone."

"Why did you go beyond the line that was railed off for your safety?"

(Sharply.) "Because I wished to. I was able to take care of myself."

"Why did you visit the forward house?"

"I was nervous and could not sleep. I thought no one safe while the axe was on the ship."

"Did you see the body of Burns, the sailor, lying on the deck at that time?"

"He might have been there; I did not see him."

"Are you saying that you went to the forward house to throw the axe overboard?"

"Yes — if I could get in."

"Did you know why the axe was being kept?"

"Because the murders had been committed with it."

"Had you heard of any finger-prints on the handle?"

"No."

"Did it occur to you that you were interfering with justice in disposing of the axe?"

"Do you mean justice or law? They are not the same."

"Tell us about your visit to the forward house."

"It was between two and three. I met no one. I had a bunch of keys from the trunks and from four doors in the after house. Miss Lee knew I intended to try to get rid of the axe. I did not need my keys. The door was open — wide open. I — I went in, and —"

Here, for the first time, Mrs. Johns's composure forsook her. She turned white, and her maid passed up to her a silver smelling-salts bottle.

"What happened when you went in?"

"It was dark. I stood just inside. Then — something rushed past me and out of the door, a something — I don't know what — a woman, I thought at first, in white."

"If the room was dark, how could you tell it was white?"

"There was a faint light — enough to see that. There was no noise — just a sort of swishing sound."

"What did you do then?"

"I waited a moment, and hurried back to the after house."

"Was the axe gone then?"

"I do not know."

"Did you see the axe at that time?"

"No."

"Did you touch it?"

"I have never touched it, at that time or before."

She could not be shaken in her testimony and was excused. She had borne her grilling exceedingly well, and, in spite of her flippancy, there was a ring of sincerity about the testimony that gave it weight.

Following her evidence, the testimony of Tom, the cook, made things look bad for Singleton, by connecting him with Mrs. Johns's intruder in the captain's room. He told of Singleton's offer to make him a key to the galley with wire. It was clear that Singleton had been a prisoner in name only, and this damaging statement was given weight when, on my recall later, I identified the bunch of keys, the file, and the club that I had taken from Singleton's mattress. It was plain enough that, with Singleton able to free himself as he wished, the attack on Burns and the disappearance of the axe were easily enough accounted for. It would have been possible, also, to account for the white figure that had so alarmed the men, on the same hypothesis.

Cross-examination of Tom by Mr. Goldstein, Singleton's attorney, brought out one curious fact. He had made no dark soup or broth for the after house. Turner had taken nothing during his illness but clam bouillon, made with milk, and the meals served to the four women had been very light. "They lived on toast and tea, mostly," he said.

That completed the taking of evidence for the day. In spite of the struggles of the clever young Jew, the weight of testimony was against Singleton. But there were curious discrepancies.

Turner went on the stand the next morning.

CHAPTER XXII

TURNER'S STORY

YOUR name?"

"Marshall Benedict Turner."

"Your residence?"

"——West 106th Street, New York City."

"Your occupation?"

"Member of the firm of L. Turner's Sons, shipowners. In the coast trade."

"Do you own the yacht Ella?"

"Yes."

"Do you recognize this chart?"

"Yes. It is the chart of the after house of the Ella."

"Will you show where your room is on the drawing?"

"Here."

"And Mr. Vail's?"

"Next, connecting through a bath-room."

"Where was Mr. Vail's bed on the chart?"

"Here, against the storeroom wall."

"With your knowledge of the ship and its

partitions, do you think that a crime could be committed, a crime of the violent nature of this one, without making a great deal of noise and being heard in the storeroom?"

Violent opposition developing to this question, it was changed in form and broken up. Eventually, Turner answered that the partitions were heavy and he thought it possible.

"Were the connecting doors between your room and Mr. Vail's generally locked at night?"

"Yes. Not always."

"Were they locked on this particular night?"

"I don't remember."

"When did you see Mr. Vail last?"

"At midnight, or about that. I — I was not well. He went with me to my room."

"What were your relations with Mr. Vail?"

"We were old friends."

"Did you hear any sound in Mr. Vail's cabin that night?"

"None. But, as I say, I was — ill. I might not have noticed."

"Did you leave your cabin that night of August 11 or early morning of the 12th?"

"Not that I remember."

"The steersman has testified to seeing you, without your coat, in the chart-room, at two o'clock. Were you there?"

"I may have been — I think not."

"Why do you say you 'may have been — I think not'?"

"I was ill. The next day I was delirious. I remember almost nothing of that time."

"Did you know the woman Karen Hansen?"

"Only as a maid in my wife's employ."

"Did you hear the crash when Leslie broke down the door of the storeroom?"

"No. I was in a sort of stupor."

"Did you know the prisoner before you employed him on the Ella?"

"Yes; he had been in our employ several times."

"What was his reputation — I mean, as a ship's officer?"

"Good."

"Do you recall the night of the 31st of July?"

"Quite well."

"Please tell what you know about it."

"I had asked Mr. Singleton below to have a drink with me. Captain Richardson came below and ordered him on deck. They had words, and he knocked Singleton down."

"Did you hear the mate threaten to 'get' the captain, then or later?"

"He may have made some such threat."

"Is there a bell in your cabin connecting with the maids' cabin off the chart-room?"

"No. My bell rang in the room back of the galley, where Williams slept. The boat was small, and I left my man at home. Williams looked after me."

"Where did the bell from Mr. Vail's room ring?"

"In the maids' room. Mr. Vail's room was designed for Mrs. Turner. When we asked Mrs. Johns to go with us, Mrs. Turner gave Vail her room. It was a question of baths."

"Did you ring any bell during the night?"

"No."

"Knowing the relation of the bell above Mr. Vail's berth to the bed itself, do you think he could have reached it after his injury?"

(Slowly.) "After what the doctor has said, no; he would have had to raise himself and reach up."

The cross-examination was brief but to the point: —

"What do you mean by 'ill'?"

"That night I had been somewhat ill; the next day I was in bad shape."

"Did you know the woman Karen Hansen before your wife employed her?"

"No."

"A previous witness has said that the Hansen woman, starting out of her room, saw you outside and retreated. Were you outside the door at any time during that night?"

"Only before midnight."

"You said you 'might have been' in the chart-room at two o'clock."

"I have said I was ill. I *might* have done almost anything."

"That is exactly what we are getting at, Mr. Turner. Going back to the 30th of July, when you were *not* ill, did you have any words with the captain?"

"We had a few. He was exceeding his authority."

"Do you recall what you said?"

"I was indignant."

"Think again, Mr. Turner. If you cannot recall, some one else will."

"I threatened to dismiss him and put the first mate in his place. I was angry, naturally."

"And what did the captain reply?"

"He made an absurd threat to put me in irons."

"What were your relations after that?"

"They were strained. We simply avoided each other."

"Just a few more questions, Mr. Turner, and I shall not detain you. Do you carry a key to the emergency case in the forward house, the case that contained the axe?"

Like many of the questions, this was disputed hotly. It was finally allowed, and Turner admitted the key. Similar cases were carried on all the Turner boats, and he had such a key on his ring.

"Did you ever see the white object that terrified the crew?"

"Never. Sailors are particularly liable to such — hysteria."

"During your delirium, did you ever see such a figure?"

"I do not recall any details of that part of my illness."

"Were you in favor of bringing the bodies back to port?"

"I — yes, certainly."

"Do you recall going on deck the morning after the murders were discovered?"

"Vaguely."

"What were the men doing at that time?"

"I believe — really, I do not like to repeat so often that I was ill that day."

"Have you any recollection of what you said to the men at that time?"

"None."

"Let me refresh your memory from the ship's log: —

(Reading.) "'Mr. Turner insisted that the bodies be buried at sea, and, on the crew opposing this, retired to his cabin, announcing that he considered the attitude of the men a mutiny.'"

"I recall being angry at the men — not much else. My position was rational enough, however. It was midsummer, and we had a long voyage before us."

"I wish to read something else to you. The witness Leslie testified to sleeping in the store-room, at the request of Mrs. Johns" (reading), "'giving as her reason a fear of something going wrong, as there was trouble between Mr. Turner and the captain.'"

Whatever question Mr. Goldstein had been framing, he was not permitted to use this part of the record. The log was admissible only as a record on the spot, made by a competent person and witnessed by all concerned, of the actual occurrences on the Ella. My record of Mrs. Johns's remark was ruled out; Turner was not on trial.

Turner, pale and shaking, left the stand at two o'clock that day, and I was recalled. My earlier testimony had merely established the finding of the bodies. I was now to have a bad two hours. I was an important witness, probably the most important. I had heard the scream that had revealed the tragedy, and had been in the main cabin of the after house only a moment or so after the murderer. I had found the bodies, Vail still living, and had been with the accused mate when he saw the

captain prostrate at the foot of the forward
companion.

All of this, aided by skillful questions, I told
as exactly as possible. I told of the mate's
strange manner on finding the bodies; I related,
to a breathless quiet, the placing of the bodies
in the jolly-boat, and the reading of the burial
service over them; I told of the little boat that
followed us, like some avenging spirit, carrying
by day a small American flag, union down, and
at night a white light. I told of having to increase the length of the towing-line as the heat
grew greater, and of a fear I had that the rope
would separate, or that the mysterious hand
that was the author of the misfortunes would
cut the line.

I told of the long nights without sleep, while,
with our few available men, we tried to work
the Ella back to land; of guarding the after
house; of a hundred false alarms that set our
nerves quivering and our hearts leaping. And
I made them feel, I think, the horror of a situation where each man suspected his neighbor,
feared and loathed him, and yet stayed close by

him because a known danger is better than an unknown horror.

The record of my examination is particularly faulty, McWhirter having allowed personal feeling to interfere with accuracy. Here and there in the margins of his notebook I find un-flattering allusions to the prosecuting attorney; and after one question, an impeachment of my motives, to which Mac took violent exception, no answer at all is recorded, and in a furious scrawl is written: "The —— little whipper-snapper! Leslie could smash him between his thumb and finger!"

I found another curious record — a leaf, torn out of the book, and evidently designed to be sent to me, but failing its destination, was as follows: "For Heaven's sake, don't look at the girl so much! The newspaper men are on."

But, to resume my examination. The first questions were not of particular interest. Then: —

"Did the prisoner know you had moved to the after house?"

"I do not know. The forecastle hands knew."

"Tell what you know of the quarrel on July 31 between Captain Richardson and the prisoner."

"I saw it from a deck window." I described it in detail.

"Why did you move to the after house?"

"At the request of Mrs. Johns. She said she was nervous."

"What reason did she give?"

"That Mr. Turner was in a dangerous mood; he had quarreled with the captain and was quarreling with Mr. Vail."

"Did you know the arrangement of rooms in the after house? How the people slept?"

"In a general way."

"What do you mean by that?"

"I knew Mr. Vail's room and Miss Lee's."

"Did you know where the maids slept?"

"Yes."

"You have testified that you were locked in. Was the key kept in the lock?"

"Yes."

"Would whoever locked you in have had only to move the key from one side of the door to the other?"

245

"Yes."

"Was the key left in the lock when you were fastened in?"

"No."

"Now, Dr. Leslie, we want you to tell us what the prisoner did that night when you told him what had happened."

"I called to him to come below, for God's sake. He seemed dazed and at a loss to know what to do. I told him to get his revolver and call the captain. He went into the forward house and got his revolver, but he did not call the captain. We went below and stumbled over the captain's body."

"What was the mate's condition?"

"When we found the body?"

"His general condition."

"He was intoxicated. He collapsed on the steps when we found the captain. We both almost collapsed."

"What was his mental condition?"

"If you mean, was he frightened, we both were."

"Was he pale?"

"I did not notice then. He was pale and

246

looked ill later, when the crew had gathered."

"About this key: was it ever found? The
key to the storeroom?"

"Yes."

"When?"

"That same morning."

"Where? And by whom?"

"Miss Lee found it on the floor in Mr.
Turner's room."

The prosecution was totally unprepared for
this reply, and proceedings were delayed for a
moment while the attorneys consulted. On
the resumption of my examination, they made
a desperate attempt to impeach my character
as a witness, trying to show that I had sailed
under false pretenses; that I was so feared in
the after house that the women refused to allow
me below, or to administer to Mr. Turner the
remedies I prepared; and, finally, that I had
surrendered myself to the crew as a suspect, of
my own accord.

Against this the cross-examination threw all
its weight. The prosecuting attorneys having
dropped the question of the key, the shrewd

young lawyer for the defense followed it up: —

"This key, Dr. Leslie, do you know where it is now?"

"Yes; I have it."

"Will you tell how it came into your possession?"

"Certainly. I picked it up on the deck, a night or so after the murders. Miss Lee had — dropped it." I caught Elsa Lee's eye, and she gave me a warm glance of gratitude.

"Have you the key with you?"

"Yes." I produced it.

"Are you a football player, Doctor?"

"I was."

"I thought I recalled you. I have seen you play several times. In spite of our friend the attorney for the commonwealth, I do not believe we will need to call character witnesses for you. Did you see Miss Lee pick up the key to the storeroom in Mr. Turner's room?"

"Yes."

"Did it occur to you at the time that the key had any significance?"

"I wondered how it got there."

"You say you listened inside the locked door, and heard no sound, but felt a board rise up under your knee. A moment or two later, when you called the prisoner, he was intoxicated, and reeled. Do you mean to tell us that a drunken man could have made his way in the darkness, through a cabin filled with chairs tables, and a piano, in absolute silence?"

The prosecuting attorney was on his feet in an instant, and the objection was sustained. I was next shown the keys, club, and file taken from Singleton's mattress. "You have identified these objects as having been found concealed in the prisoner's mattress. Do any of these keys fit the captain's cabin?"

"No."

"Who saw the prisoner during the days he was locked in his cabin?"

"I saw him occasionally. The cook saw him when he carried him his meals."

"Did you ever tell the prisoner where the axe was kept?"

"No."

"Did the members of the crew know?"

"I believe so. Yes."

249

"Was the fact that Burns carried the key to the captain's cabin a matter of general knowledge?"

"No. The crew knew that Burns and I carried the keys; they did not know which one each carried, unless —"

"Go on, please."

"If any one had seen Burns take Mrs. Johns forward and show her the axe, he would have known."

"Who were on deck at that time?"

"All the crew were on deck, the forecastle being closed. In the crow's-nest was McNamara; Jones was at the wheel."

"From the crow's-nest could the lookout have seen Burns and Mrs. Johns going forward?"

"No. The two houses were connected by an awning."

"What could the helmsman see?"

"Nothing forward of the after house."

The prosecution closed its case with me. The defense, having virtually conducted its case by cross-examination of the witnesses already called, contented itself with producing a few character witnesses, and "rested." Goldstein made an eloquent plea of "no case," and asked the judge so to instruct the jury.

This was refused, and the case went to the jury on the seventh day — a surprisingly short trial, considering the magnitude of the crimes.

The jury disagreed. But, while they wrangled, McWhirter and I were already on the right track. At the very hour that the jurymen were being discharged and steps taken for a retrial, we had the murderer locked in my room in a cheap lodging-house off Chestnut Street.

CHAPTER XXIII

FREE AGAIN

WITH the submission of the case to the jury, the witnesses were given their freedom. McWhirter had taken a room for me for a day or two to give me time to look about; and, his own leave of absence from his hospital being for ten days, we had some time together.

My situation was better than it had been in the summer. I had my strength again, although the long confinement had told on me. But my position was precarious enough. I had my pay from the Ella, and nothing else. And McWhirter, with a monthly stipend from his hospital of twenty-five dollars, was not much better off.

My first evening of freedom we spent at the theater. We bought the best seats in the house, and we dressed for the occasion — being in the position of having nothing to wear between shabby everyday wear and evening clothes.

"It is by way of celebration," Mac said, as he put a dab of shoe-blacking over a hole in his sock; "you having been restored to life, liberty, and the pursuit of happiness. That's the game, Leslie — the pursuit of happiness."

I was busy with a dress tie that I had washed and dried by pasting it on a mirror, an old trick of mine when funds ran low. I was trying to enter into Mac's festive humor, but I had not reacted yet from the horrors of the past few months.

"Happiness!" I said scornfully. "Do you call this happiness?"

He put up the blacking, and, coming to me, stood eyeing me in the mirror as I arranged my necktie.

"Don't be bitter," he said. "Happiness was my word. The Good Man was good to you when he made you. That ought to be a source of satisfaction. And as for the girl —"

"What girl?"

"If she could only see you now. Why in thunder didn't you take those clothes on board? I wanted you to. Could n't a captain wear a dress suit on special occasions?"

"Mac," I said gravely, "if you will think a moment, you will remember that the only special occasions on the Ella, after I took charge, were funerals. Have you sat through seven days of horrors without realizing that?"

Mac had once gone to Europe on a liner, and, having exhausted his funds, returned on a cattle-boat.

"All the captains I ever knew," he said largely, "were a fussy lot — dressed to kill, and navigating the boat from the head of a dinner-table. But I suppose you know. I was only regretting that she had n't seen you the way you're looking now. That's all. I suppose I may regret, without hurting your feelings!"

He dropped all mention of Elsa after that, for a long time. But I saw him looking at me, at intervals, during the evening, and sighing. He was still regretting!

We enjoyed the theater, after all, with the pent-up enthusiasm of long months of work and strain. We laughed at the puerile fun, encored

the prettiest of the girls, and swaggered in the
lobby between acts, with cigarettes. There
we ran across the one man I knew in Philadelphia, and had supper after the play with
three or four fellows who, on hearing my story,
persisted in believing that I had sailed on the
Ella as a lark or to follow a girl. My simple
statement that I had done it out of necessity
met with roars of laughter and finally I let
it go at that.

It was after one when we got back to the
lodging-house, being escorted there in a racing
car by a riotous crowd that stood outside the
door, as I fumbled for my key, and screeched in
unison: "Leslie! Leslie! Leslie! Sic 'em!"
before they drove away.

The light in the dingy lodging-house parlor
was burning full, but the hall was dark. I
stopped inside and lighted a cigarette.

"Life, liberty, and the pursuit of happiness,
Mac!" I said. "I've got the first two, and the
other can be had — for the pursuit."

Mac did not reply: he was staring into the
parlor. Elsa Lee was standing by a table,
looking at me.

255

She was very nervous, and tried to explain her presence in a breath — with the result that she broke down utterly and had to stop. Mac, his jovial face rather startled, was making for the stairs; but I sternly brought him back and presented him. Whereon, being utterly confounded, he made the tactful remark that he would have to go and put out the milk-bottles: it was almost morning!

She had been waiting since ten o'clock, she said. A taxicab, with her maid, was at the door. They were going back to New York in the morning, and things were terribly wrong.

"Wrong? You need not mind Mr. McWhirter. He is as anxious as I am to be helpful."

"There are detectives watching Marshall; we saw one to-day at the hotel. If the jury disagrees — and the lawyers think they will — they will arrest him."

I thought it probable. There was nothing I could say. McWhirter made an effort to re-assure her.

"It would n't be a hanging matter, anyhow," he said. "There's a lot against him, but hardly a jury in the country would hang a man for something he did, if he could prove he was delirious the next day." She paled at this dubious comfort, but it struck her sense of humor, too, for she threw me a fleeting smile.

"I was to ask you to do something," she said. "None of us can, for we are being watched. I was probably followed here. The Ella is still in the river, with only a watchman on board. We want you to go there to-night, if you can."

"To the Ella?"

She was feeling in her pocketbook, and now she held out to me an envelope addressed in a sprawling hand to Mr. Turner at his hotel.

"Am I to open it?"

"Please."

I unfolded a sheet of ruled note-paper of the most ordinary variety. It had been opened and laid flat, and on it, in black ink, was a crude drawing of the deck of the Ella, as one would look down on it from aloft. Here and there were small crosses in red ink, and, overlying it all from bow to stern, a red axe. Around the border, not written, but printed in childish

letters, were the words: "Not yet. Ha, ha."
In a corner was a drawing of a gallows, or what
passes in the everyday mind for a gallows, and
in the opposite corner an open book.

"You see," she said, "it was mailed downtown late this afternoon. The hotel got it at
seven o'clock. Marshall wanted to get a detective, but I thought of you. I knew — you knew
the boat, and then — you had said —"

"Anything in all the world that I can do to
help you, I will do," I said, looking at her. And
the thing that I could not keep out of my eyes
made her drop hers.

"Sweet little document!" said McWhirter,
looking over my shoulder. "Sent by some one
with a nice disposition. What do the crosses
mark?"

"The location of the bodies when found," I
explained — "these three. This looks like the
place where Burns lay unconscious. That one
near the rail I don't know about, nor this by
the mainmast."

"We thought they might mark places, clues,
perhaps, that had been overlooked. The whole
— the whole document is a taunt, is n't it? The

scaffold, and the axe, and 'not yet'; a piece of bravado!"

"Right you are," said McWhirter admiringly. "A little escape of glee from somebody who's laughing too soon. One-thirty — it will soon be the proper hour for something to happen on the Ella, won't it? If that was sent by some member of the crew — and it looks like it; they are loose to-day — the quicker we follow it up, the better, if there's anything to follow."

"We thought if you would go early in the morning, before any of them make an excuse to go back on board —"

"We will go right away; but, please — don't build too much on this. It's a good possibility, that's all. Will the watchman let us on board?"

"We thought of that. Here is a note to him from Marshall, and — will you do us one more kindness?"

"I will."

"Then — if you should find anything, bring it to us; to the police, later, if you must, but to us first."

"When?"

"In the morning. We will not leave until we hear from you."

She held out her hand, first to McWhirter, then to me. I kept it a little longer than I should have, perhaps, and she did not take it away.

"It is such a comfort," she said, "to have you with us and not against us! For Marshall did n't do it, Leslie — I mean — it is hard for me to think of you as Dr. Leslie! He did n't do it. At first, we thought he might have, and he was delirious and could not reassure us. He swears he did not. I think, just at first, he was afraid he had done it; but he did not. I believe that, and you must."

I believed her — I believed anything she said. I think that if she had chosen to say that I had wielded the murderer's axe on the Ella, I should have gone to the gallows rather than gainsay her. From that night, I was the devil's advocate, if you like. I was determined to save Marshall Turner.

She wished us to take her taxicab, dropping her at her hotel; and, reckless now of everything but being with her, I would have done so. But

FREE AGAIN

McWhirter's discreet cough reminded me of the street-car level of our finances, and I made the excuse of putting on more suitable clothing.

I stood in the street, bareheaded, watching her taxicab as it rattled down the street. McWhirter touched me on the arm.

"Wake up!" he said. "We have work to do, my friend."

We went upstairs together, cautiously, not to rouse the house. At the top, Mac turned and patted me on the elbow, my shoulder being a foot or so above him.

"Good boy!" he said. "And if that shirt-front and tie did n't knock into eternal oblivion the deck-washing on the Ella, I'll eat them!"

CHAPTER XXIV

THE THING

I DESERVE no credit for the solution of the Ella's mystery. I have a certain quality of force, perhaps, and I am not lacking in physical courage; but I have no finesse of intellect. McWhirter, a foot shorter than I, round of face, jovial and stocky, has as much subtlety in his little finger as I have in my six feet and a fraction of body.

All the way to the river, therefore, he was poring over the drawing. He named the paper at once.

"Ought to know it," he said, in reply to my surprise. "Sold enough paper at the drugstore to qualify as a stationery engineer." He writhed as was his habit over his jokes, and then fell to work at the drawing again. "A book," he said, "and an axe, and a gibbet or gallows. B-a-g — that makes 'bag.' Does n't go far, does it? Humorous duck, is n't he? Any one who can write 'ha! ha!' under a gallows has real humor. G-a-b, b-a-g!"

THE THING

The Ella still lay in the Delaware, half a mile or so from her original moorings. She carried the usual riding-lights — a white one in the bow, another at the stern, and the two vertical red lights which showed her not under command. In reply to repeated signals, we were unable to rouse the watchman. I had brought an electric flash with me, and by its aid we found a rope ladder over the side, with a small boat at its foot.

Although the boat indicated the presence of the watchman on board, we made our way to the deck without challenge. Here McWhirter suggested that the situation might be disagreeable, were the man to waken and get at us with a gun.

We stood by the top of the ladder, therefore, and made another effort to rouse him. "Hey, watchman!" I called. And McWhirter, in a deep bass, sang lustily: "Watchman, what of the night?" Neither of us made any perceptible impression on the silence and gloom of the Ella.

McWhirter grew less gay. The deserted decks of the ship, her tragic history, her isola-

263

tion, the darkness, which my small flash seemed only to intensify, all had their effect on him.

"It's got my goat," he admitted. "It smells like a tomb."

"Don't be an ass."

"Turn the light over the side, and see if we fastened that boat. We don't want to be left here indefinitely."

"That's folly, Mac," I said, but I obeyed him. "The watchman's boat is there, so we —"

But he caught me suddenly by the arm and shook me.

"My God!" he said. "What is that over there?"

It was a moment before my eyes, after the flashlight, could discern anything in the darkness. Mac was pointing forward. When I could see, Mac was ready to laugh at himself.

"I told you the place had my goat!" he said sheepishly. "I thought I saw something duck around the corner of that building; but I think it was a ray from a searchlight on one of those boats."

"The watchman, probably," I said quietly. But my heart beat a little faster. "The

watchman taking a look at us and gone **for**
his gun."

I thought rapidly. If Mac had seen anything,
I did not believe it was the watchman. But
there should be a watchman on board — in the
forward house, probably. I gave Mac my revolver and put the light in my pocket. I might
want both hands that night. I saw better
without the flash, and, guided partly by the bow
light, partly by my knowledge of the yacht, I
led the way across the deck. The forward house
was closed and locked, and no knocking produced any indication of life. The after house
we found not only locked, but barred across
with strips of wood nailed into place. The
forecastle was likewise closed. It was a dead
ship.

No figure reappearing to alarm him, Mac
took the drawing out of his pocket and focused
the flashlight on it.

"This cross by the mainmast," he said —
"that would be where?"

"Right behind you, there."

He walked to the mast, and examined carefully around its base. There was nothing there,

and even now I do not know to what that cross alluded, unless poor Schwartz —!

"Then this other one — forward, you call it, don't you? Suppose we locate that."

All expectation of the watchman having now died, we went forward on the port side to the approximate location of the cross. This being in the neighborhood where Mac had thought he saw something move, we approached with extreme caution. But nothing more ominous was discovered than the port lifeboat, nothing more ghostly heard than the occasional creak with which it rocked in its davits.

The lifeboat seemed to be indicated by the cross. It swung almost shoulder-high on McWhirter. We looked under and around it, with a growing feeling that we had misread the significance of the crosses, or that the sinister record extended to a time before the "she devil" of the Turner line was dressed in white and turned into a lady.

I was feeling underneath the boat, with a sense of absurdity that McWhirter put into words. "I only hope," he said, "that the watchman does not wake up now and see us. He'd

be justified in filling us with lead, or putting us
in strait-jackets."

But I had discovered something.

"Mac," I said, "some one has been at this
boat within the last few minutes."

"Why?"

"Take your revolver and watch the deck.
One of the *barécas* —"

"What's that?"

"One of the water-barrels has been upset,
and the plug is out. It is leaking into the boat.
It is leaking fast, and there's only a gallon or so
in the bottom! Give me the light."

The contents of the boat revealed the truth
of what I had said. The boat was in confusion.
Its cover had been thrown back, and tins of
biscuit, bailers, boat-hooks and extra rowlocks
were jumbled together in confusion. The
barécas lay on its side, and its plug had been
either knocked or drawn out.

McWhirter was for turning to inspect the
boat; but I ordered him sternly to watch the
deck. He was inclined to laugh at my caution,
which he claimed was a quality in me he had
not suspected. He lounged against the rail

near me, and, in spite of his chaff, kept a keen enough lookout.

The *barécas* of water were lashed amidships. In the bow and stern were small air-tight compartments, and in the stern was also a small locker from which the biscuit tins had been taken. I was about to abandon my search, when I saw something gleaming in the locker, and reached in and drew it out. It appeared to be an ordinary white sheet, but its presence there was curious. I turned the light on it. It was covered with dark-brown stains.

Even now the memory of that sheet turns me ill. I shook it out, and Mac, at my exclamation, came to me. It was not a sheet at all, that is, not a whole one. It was a circular piece of white cloth, on which, in black, were curious marks — a six-pointed star predominating. There were others — a crescent, a crude attempt to draw what might be either a dog or a lamb, and a cross. From edge to edge it was smeared with blood.

Of what followed just after, both McWhirter and I are vague. There seemed to be, simul-

taneously, a yell of fury from the rigging overhead, and the crash of a falling body on the
deck near us. Then we were closing with a
kicking, biting, screaming thing, that bore me
to the ground, extinguishing the little electric
flash, and that, rising suddenly from under me,
had McWhirter in the air, and almost overboard before I caught him. So dazed were we
by the onslaught that the thing — whatever it
was — could have escaped, and left us none the
wiser. But, although it eluded us in the darkness, it did not leave. It was there, whimpering
to itself, searching for something — the sheet.
As I steadied Mac, it passed me. I caught at it.
Immediately the struggle began all over again.
But this time we had the advantage, and kept
it. After a battle that seemed to last all night,
and that was actually fought all over that part
of the deck, we held the creature subdued,
and Mac, getting a hand free, struck a match.

It was Charlie Jones.

That, after all, is the story. Jones was a madman, a homicidal maniac of the worst type.
Always a madman, the homicidal element of his
disease was recurrent and of a curious nature.

He thought himself a priest of heaven, appointed
to make ghastly sacrifices at certain signals
from on high. The signals I am not sure of;
he turned taciturn after his capture and would
not talk. I am inclined to think that a shooting
star, perhaps in a particular quarter of the
heavens, was his signal. This is distinctly
possible, and is made probable by the stars
which he had painted with tar on his sacrificial
robe.

The story of the early morning of August 12
will never be fully known; but much of it,
in view of our knowledge, we were able to reconstruct. Thus — Jones ate his supper that
night, a mild and well-disposed individual.
During the afternoon before, he had read prayers for the soul of Schwartz, in whose departure he may or may not have had a part —
I am inclined to think not, Jones construing
his mission as being one to remove the wicked
and the oppressor, and Schwartz hardly coming
under either classification.

He was at the wheel from midnight until four
in the morning on the night of the murders. At

certain hours we believe that he went forward
to the forecastle-head, and performed, clad in
his priestly robe, such devotions as his disordered mind dictated. It is my idea that he looked,
at these times, for a heavenly signal, either a
meteor or some strange appearance of the heavens. It was known that he was a poor sleeper,
and spent much time at night wandering
around.

On the night of the crimes it is probable that
he performed his devotions early, and then got
the signal. This is evidenced by Singleton's
finding the axe against the captain's door before midnight. He had evidently been disturbed. We believe that he intended to kill
the captain and Mr. Turner, but made a mistake in the rooms. He clearly intended to kill
the Danish girl. Several passages in his Bible,
marked with a red cross, showed his inflamed
hatred of loose women; and he believed Karen
Hansen to be of that type.

He locked me in, slipping down from the
wheel to do so, and pocketing the key. The
night was fairly quiet. He could lash the wheel
safely, and he had in his favor the fact that

271

Oleson, the lookout, was a slow-thinking Swede who notoriously slept on his watch. He found the axe, not where he had left it, but back in the case. But the case was only closed, not locked — Singleton's error.

Armed with the axe, Jones slipped back to the wheel and waited. He had plenty of time. He had taken his robe from its hiding-place in the boat, and had it concealed near him with the axe. He was ready, but he was waiting for another signal. He got it at half-past two. He admitted the signal and the time, but concealed its nature — I think it was a shooting star. He killed Vail first, believing it to be Turner, and making with his axe, the four signs of the cross. Then he went to the Hansen girl's door. He did not know about the bell, and probably rang it by accident as he leaned over to listen if Vail still breathed.

The captain, in the mean time, had been watching Singleton. He had forbidden his entering the after house; if he caught him disobeying he meant to put him in irons. He was without shoes or coat, and he sat waiting on the after companion steps for developments.

THE THING

It was the captain, probably, whom Karen Hansen mistook for Turner. Later he went back to the forward companionway, either on his way back to his cabin, or still with an eye to Singleton's movements.

To the captain there must have appeared this grisly figure in flowing white, smeared with blood and armed with an axe. The sheet was worn over Jones's head — a long, narrow slit serving him to see through, and two other slits freeing his arms. The captain was a brave man, but the apparition, gleaming in the almost complete darkness, had been on him before he could do more than throw up his hands.

Jones had not finished. He went back to the chart-room and possibly even went on deck and took a look at the wheel. Then he went down again and killed the Hansen woman.

He was exceedingly cunning. He flung the axe into the room, and was up and at the wheel again, all within a few seconds. To tear off and fold up the sheet, to hide it under near-by cordage, to strike the ship's bell and light his pipe — all this was a matter of two or three minutes. I had only time to look at Vail.

When I got up to the wheel, Jones was smoking quietly.

I believe he tried to get Singleton later, and failed. But he continued his devotions on the forward deck, visible when clad in his robe, invisible when he took it off. It was Jones, of course, who attacked Burns and secured the key to the captain's cabin; Jones who threw the axe overboard after hearing the crew tell that on its handle were finger-prints to identify the murderer; Jones who, while on guard in the after house below, had pushed the key to the storeroom under Turner's door; Jones who hung the marlinespike over the side, waiting perhaps for another chance at Singleton; Jones, in his devotional attire, who had frightened the crew into hysteria, and who, discovered by Mrs. Johns in the captain's cabin, had rushed by her, and out, with the axe. It is noticeable that he made no attempt to attack her. He killed only in obedience to his signal, and he had had no signal.

Perhaps the most curious thing, after the murderer was known, was the story of the people in the after house. It was months before I got that in full. The belief among the women was that Turner, maddened by drink and unreasoning jealousy, had killed Vail, and then, running amuck or discovered by the other victims, had killed them. This was borne out by Turner's condition. His hands and parts of his clothing were blood-stained.

Their condition was pitiable. Unable to speak for himself, he lay raving in his room, talking to Vail and complaining of a white figure that bothered him. The key that Elsa Lee picked up was another clue, and in their attempt to get rid of it I had foiled them. Mrs. Johns, an old friend and, as I have said, an ardent partisan, undertook to get rid of the axe, with the result that we know. Even Turner's recovery brought little courage. He could only recall that he had gone into Vail's room and tried to wake him, without result; that he did not know of the blood until the next day, or that Vail was dead; and that he had a vague recollection of something white and ghostly that night — he was not sure where he had . seen it.

The failure of their attempt to get rid of the storeroom key was matched by their failure to smuggle Turner's linen off the ship. Singleton suspected Turner, and, with the skillful and not overscrupulous aid of his lawyer, had succeeded in finding in Mrs. Sloane's trunk the incriminating pieces.

As to the meaning of the keys, file, and club in Singleton's mattress, I believe the explanation is simple enough. He saw against him a strong case. He had little money and no influence, while Turner had both. I have every reason to believe that he hoped to make his escape before the ship anchored, and was frustrated by my discovery of the keys and by an extra bolt I put on his door and window.

The murders on the schooner-yacht Ella were solved.

McWhirter went back to his hospital, the day after our struggle, wearing a strip of plaster over the bridge of his nose and a new air of importance. The Turners went to New York soon after, and I was alone. I tried to put Elsa Lee out of my thoughts, as she had gone out of my life, and, receiving the hoped-for hospital appointment at that time, I tried to make up by hard work for a happiness that I had not lost because it had never been mine.

A curious thing has happened to me. I had thought this record finished, but perhaps —

Turner's health is bad. He and his wife and Miss Lee are going to Europe. He has asked me to go with him in my professional capacity!

It is more than a year since I have seen her.

The year has brought some changes. Singleton is again a member of the Turner forces, having signed a contract and a temperance pledge at the same sitting. Jones is in a hospital for the insane, where in the daytime he is a cheery old tar with twinkling eyes and a huge mustache, and where now and then, on Christmas and holidays, I send him a supply of tobacco. At night he sleeps in a room with opaque glass windows through which no heavenly signals can penetrate. He will not talk of his crimes, — not that he so regards them, —

but now and then in the night he wraps the drapery of his couch about him and performs strange orisons in the little room that is his. And at such times an attendant watches outside his door.

CHAPTER XXV

ONCE more the swish of spray against the side of a ship, the tang of salt, the lift and fall of the rail against the sea-line on the horizon. And once more a girl, in white from neck to heel, facing into the wind as if she loved it, her crisp skirts flying, her hair blown back from her forehead in damp curls.

And I am not washing down the deck. With all the poise of white flannels and a good cigar, I am lounging in a deck-chair, watching her. Then —

"Come here!" I say.

"I am busy."

"You are not busy. You are disgracefully idle."

"Why do you want me?"

She comes closer, and looks down at me. She likes me to sit, so she may look superior and scornful, this being impossible when one looks up. When she has approached —

"Just to show that I can order you about."

"I shall go back!" — with raised chin. How I remember that raised chin, and how (whisper it) I used to fear it!

"You cannot. I am holding the edge of your skirt."

"Ralph! And all the other passengers looking!"

"Then sit down — and, before you do, tuck that rug under my feet, will you?"

"Certainly not."

"Under my feet!"

She does it, under protest, whereon I release her skirts. She is sulky, quite distinctly sulky. I slide my hand under the rug into her lap. She ignores it.

"Now," I say calmly, "we are even. And you might as well hold my hand. Every one thinks you are."

She brings her hands hastily from under her rug and puts them over her head. "I don't know what has got into you," she says coldly. "And why are we even?"

"For the day you told me the deck was **not** clean."

THE SEA AGAIN

"It was n't clean."

"I think I am going to kiss you."

"Ralph!"

"It is coming on. About the time that the bishop gets here, I shall lean over and —"

She eyes me, and sees determination in my face. She changes color.

"You would n't!"

"Would n't I!"

She rises hastily, and stands looking down at me. I am quite sure at that moment that she detests me, and I rather like it. There are always times when we detest the people we love.

"If you are going to be arbitrary just because you can —"

"Yes?"

"Marsh and the rest are in the smoking-room. Their sitting-room is empty."

Quite calmly, as if we are going below for a clean handkerchief or a veil or a cigarette, we stroll down the great staircase of the liner to the Turners' sitting-room, and close the door.

And — I kiss her.

THE END

THE BUCKLED BAG

THE BUCKLED BAG

I HAVE broken down in health lately—nothing serious; but a nurse lasts only so long, and during the last five years I have been under a double strain. Caring for the sick has been only a part of it. The other?

Well, put it like this: The world's pretty crowded after all. We are always touching elbows, and there is never a deviation from the usual, the normal, that is not felt all the way down the line. Stand a row of dominoes on edge and knock down the end one. Do you see? And generally somebody goes down for fair. We do not know much about it among the poor; they have to manage the best way they can, and maybe they are blunted—some of them. They have not the time for mental agony. And the thing works both ways. Their lapses are generally obvious—cause and result; motive and crime.

In the lower walks of life people are more elemental. But get up higher. Crime exists there; but, instead of a passion, it is a craft. In its detection it is brain against brain, not intellect against brute force or instinct. If anything gives, it is the body.

Illness follows crime—it does not always follow the criminal; but somebody goes down for fair. There is a breach in the wall. The doctor and the clergyman come in then. One way and another they get the story. There

1

is nothing hidden from them. They get it, but they do not want it. They cannot use it. The clergyman's vows and the medical man's legal status forbid their using their knowledge; but, where a few years ago there were only two, now each crisis, mental or physical, finds three—the trained nurse.

Do you see what I mean? The thing is thrust at her. She does not want the story either. Her business is bodies, doctors' orders, nourishments; but unless she's a fool she ends by holding the family secret in the hollow of her hand. It worries her. She needs her hands. She gets rid of it as soon as she can and forgets it. She is safe; the secret is safe. Without the clergyman's vows or the doctor's legal status, she is as silent as either.

That is the ethical side. That is what the nurse does. There is another side, which is mine. The criminal uses every means against society. Why not society against the criminal? And this is my defense. Every trained nurse plays a game, a sort of sporting proposition—her wits against wretchedness. I play a double game—the fight against misery and the fight against crime—like a man running two chessboards at once.

I hated it in the beginning. It has me by the throat now. It is the criminal I find absorbing. And I have learned some things—not new, of course—that to be honest because one is untempted is to be strong with the strength of a child; that the great virtues often link arms with the great vices; that the big criminal thinks big thoughts.

I have had my chance to learn and I know. A nurse gets under the very skin of the soul. She finds a mind surrendered, all the crooked little motives that have fired

the guns of life revealed in their pitifulness.   Even now,
sometimes, it hurts me to look back.

It is five years since George L. Patton was shot in the
leg during a raid on the Hengst Place, in Cherry Run.
He is at the head of one of the big private agencies now,
but he was a county detective then; and Hengst shot him
from a cupboard.   Well, that does not matter particularly, except that Mr. Patton was brought to the hospital
that night and I was given the case.

He took it very calmly—said he guessed he would rest
a while, now he had the chance, and slept eighteen hours
without moving.   I made caps, I remember, and tried to
plan what I would do when I left the house.   My time
was about up and I dreaded private duty.   I had been
accustomed to the excitement of a hospital, and there was
something horrible to me in the idea of spending the rest
of my life in darkened rooms, with the doctor's daily visit
for excitement and a walk round the block for recreation.

I gave Mr. Patton his dinner that night and we had
our first clash.   He looked at the soup and toast, and
demanded steak and onions.

"I'm sorry," I said.   "You're to have light diet for a
day or two.   We don't want any fever from that leg."

"Leg!   What has my leg to do with my stomach?   I
want a medium steak.   I'll do without the onions if I
have to."

"Doctor's orders," I said firmly.   "You may have an
egg custard if you want it, or some cornstarch."

We had a downright argument and he took the soup.
When he had finished he looked up at me and smiled.

"I don't like you," he said, "but darned if I don't

respect you, young woman. Absolute obedience to orders is about the hardest thing in the world to get. And now send for that fool interne and we'll have a steak for breakfast."

Well, he did; and pretty soon he was getting about everything the hospital could give him. He was a politician, of course, and we depended on our state appropriation for support; but he got nothing from me without an order. He always said he did not like me, but I think he did after a while. I could beat him at chess, for one thing.

"You have a good head, Miss Adams," he said to me one day when he was almost well. "Are you going to spend the rest of your life changing pillowslips and shaking down a thermometer?"

"I've thought of institutional work; I dare say I'd be changing nurses and shaking down internes," I said with some bitterness.

"How old are you?—not, of course, for publication."

"Twenty-nine."

"Any family?"

"The nearest relatives I have are two old aunts, in the country."

He was silent for a minute or two. Then: "I've been thinking of something; I may take it up with you later. There's only one objection—you're rather too good-looking."

"I'm not really good-looking at all," I admitted frankly. "I have too high a forehead. It's the cap."

"Like 'em high!" said Mr. Patton.

I made an eggnog and brought it in to him. He was sitting propped in a chair, and when I gave him the glass he smiled up at me. He had never attempted any sentimentalities with me, which is more than can be said of the usual convalescent male over forty.

"It isn't all the cap," he said.

That afternoon he tried to learn from me something about the other patients on the floor; but of course I would tell him nothing. He seemed rather irritated and tried to bully me, but I was firm.

"Don't be childish, Mr. Patton!" I said at last. "We don't tell about other patients. If you want to find out get one of your men in here." To my surprise he laughed.

"Good girl!" he said. "You've stood a cracking test and come through A 1. You've got silence and obedience to orders, and you have a brain. I've mentioned the forehead. Now I'm going to make my proposition. Has it ever occurred to you that every crisis, practically, among the better classes, finds a trained nurse on hand?"

"Cause or result?"

"Result, of course. Upset the ordinary routine of a family, have a robbery, an elopement or a murder, and somebody goes to bed, with a trained nurse in attendance. Fact, isn't it?" I admitted it. "It's a fault of the tension people live under," he went on. "Any extra strain and something snaps. And who is it who is in the very bosom of the family? You know and I know. The nurse gets it all—the intimate details that the police miss; the family disputes, the inner motives; the—you go to your room and think it over. And when you decide I have a case for you."

I tried to object, but he cut me short; so I put the thermometer in his mouth and managed to tell him how I felt.

"It just doesn't seem honest," I finished. "I'm in a position of confidence and I violate it. That's the truth. A nurse is supposed to work for good; if she has any place it's an uplift place—if you can see what I mean. And to go into a house and pry out its secrets——"

He jerked the thermometer out wrathfully.

"Uplift!" he said. "Isn't it uplifting to place a criminal where he won't injure society? If you can't see it that way, we don't want you. Now go away and think about it."

I went up to my room and stood in front of the mirror, which is where I do most of my thinking. I talk things over with myself, I suppose. And I saw the lines behind my ears that said: "Twenty-nine, almost thirty!"—and the row of caps ready for private duty, with only the doctor's visits for excitement and a walk round the block for recreation. And I thought of institutional work, with its daily round of small worries, its monotonous years, with my soul gradually shrinking and shaping itself to fit a set of rules. And over against it all I put Mr. Patton's offer.

I recall it all—the color that came to my face at the chance to use my head instead of only a trained obedience to orders; the prospect of adventure; the chance to pit my wits against other wits and perhaps win out. I put on one of the new caps and went down to Mr. Patton's room.

"I'll do it!" I said calmly.

My time was up two days later. Mr. Patton was practically well and gave me my instructions while I helped him pack his bag.

"Do the things the other nurses do," he advised. "Go

to the Nurses' Home, but don't register for cases right away. Make an excuse that you're tired and need a few days' rest. When I telephone you I shall call myself Doctor Patton—not that I pretend to do any medical work, but for extra caution."

"You said you had a case for me."

"I had, but it isn't big enough. I want you for something worth while, and it will be along soon. It's about due."

"And—just one thing, Mr. Patton: I will take my first case on trial. If I find that I am doing harm and not good by revealing the secrets of a family, I shall give it up. A doctor would be answerable to the law for doing the things I am about to do."

"You have no legal status."

"I have a moral status," I replied grimly, and he found no answer to that.

Before he left, however, he said something that rather cheered me.

"You will never be required to tell anything you learn, except what is directly pertinent to the matter in hand," he said. "I would not give such latitude to any other woman I know—but you have brains and you will know what we want."

"I cannot work in the dark—I must know what you are after."

"We will lay all our cards on your table face up. I wouldn't insult you by asking you to play blindfolded. And remember this, Miss Adams—it's as high a duty to explore and heal the moral sores of a community as it is to probe and dress, for instance, the wound of a man who has been shot in the leg."

Two days later I left the hospital and took a room at the Nurses' Home he had recommended. He would arrange with the secretary, he said, that I should be called for any case on which he wished me placed.

I put in a bad week. One of the staff of the hospital located me and called me to a case. I got out of it by saying I needed a few days' rest, and he rang off irritably. Then, on the third day, I had my handbag cut off my arm in a department store, and went home depressed and ill-humored.

"You're a fine detective!" I said to myself in the mirror. "You're not so clever as Mr. Patton thinks, and if you're honest you'll go and tell him so."

I think I should have done so—I was so abashed; but our arrangement was that I should not try to see him under any circumstances. There was to be no suspicion of me in any way. He would see me when necessary. I still had the strap of my bag, which had been left hanging to my arm; and, as a constant reminder, I fastened it to the frame of my mirror. Even now, when the department gives me its best cases, and when I have been successful enough to justify a little pride, I look at that bit of leather and become meek and normal again.

II

In spite of Mr. Patton's promise I went on my first case for him without any preparation. Miss Shinn, the secretary, asked me if I would take a case that evening.

"For whom?"

She was turning over the pages of her ledger in the parlor-office of the Home and she did not look up.

"A Doctor Patton telephoned," she said. "I believe he had spoken to you of the case."

My throat tightened, but, after all, this was what I had been waiting for.

"Do you know what sort of case it is?" I asked. "I'm not doing obstetrics, you know."

"It is not an obstetric case. You are to take a taxicab at eight o'clock tonight."

Miss Shinn was a heavy, rather bilious brunette, who rarely smiled; but I caught an amused twinkle as she glanced up. Quite suddenly I liked her. Clearly she knew what I was about to do and she did not disapprove; and yet she was a very ethical person. I gathered that she would be very hard on a nurse who wore frivolous uniforms, or gossiped about her patients, or went to the theater with a doctor, or cut rates. And yet she was indulgent to me—she was more than indulgent. I was certain, somehow, from the very quiver of her wide back as she marked me "Engaged" on her register, that she was wildly interested and curious. It gave me confidence.

At eight o'clock that evening I went downstairs with my suitcase and ordered a taxicab. No word had come from Mr. Patton and I had nothing but a name and address to go by. The name—we will call it G. W. March. It was not, of course. You would know the name at once if I told it. The address was a street fronting one of the parks—a good neighborhood, I knew—old families, substantial properties, traditions, all that sort of thing. Certainly not a place to look for crime.

As I waited for the cab I searched the newspapers for something to throw light on my new enterprise. There was nothing at all except a notice that Mr. and Mrs.

George W. March had returned from their summer home
on the Maine coast a few days before and had opened
their city home.

It looked like a robbery. I was vaguely disappointed.
I had it all worked out in five minutes—Mrs. March in
bed, collapsed; missing pictures or jewels; house full of
trusted servants; and myself trying to solve the mystery
between an alcohol rub and a dose of bromide. I hated
to go on with it, but I was ashamed not to. I said to
myself savagely that I was not a quitter, and got into the
taxicab.

The March case was not a robbery, however. It was
not a criminal case, strictly speaking, at all. It was the
disappearance of a girl and in some ways it was a remark-
able mystery—particularly baffling because for so long it
seemed to be a result without a cause. How we found
the cause at last; how we located the family in Brickyard
Road and solved the puzzle of the buckled bag; how we
learned the identity of the little old woman with the jet
bonnet, and her connection with the garden door—-all
this makes up the record of my first case.

The buckled bag is lying on my desk now. It is a
shabby, quaint old bag, about eight inches long, round-
bellied, brown with wear. It still contains what was
in it when Mr. Patton found it—a cotton handkerchief,
marked with a J; two keys—one a house-door key, the
other a flat one; a scrawled note in a soiled lavender
envelope; a newspaper clipping of a sale of blankets.

It is one of my most painful memories that for a month
I examined that newspaper cutting frequently and that I
failed entirely to grasp the significance of the reverse side.
We all have a mental blind spot. That was mine.

Clare March was missing. That was my case; to find her, or to help to find her, was my task at first. Later it grew more complicated. I had not thought Mr. Patton would violate our agreement about working in the dark and my confidence was justified. At the first corner he hailed the machine and got in.

"Fine work!" he said. "You're a dependable person, Miss Adams."

"I'm rather a scared person."

"Nonsense! And don't take yourself or this affair too seriously. Do your durnedest—'Angels could do no more.' "

"Is it something stolen?"

"A small matter of a daughter. It's a queer thing, Miss Adams. I'll tell you about it." He leaned out and asked the driver to go slowly. "Time us to get there at eight-thirty," he said. "Now, Miss Adams, here are the facts: You are going to the home of George March, the banker—you know the name probably—Mrs. March is your patient. She's not ill; she's hysterical and frightened—that's all. It's not a hard case."

"It's the hardest sort of a case."

"Well, you like work," he replied cheerfully. "The family has been away for four months. Until a month ago Clare, the daughter, was with them. One month ago, on the third of September, Clare, who is an only child, twenty years old, left the country place in Maine for home. She traveled alone, leaving her maid in the country. The city house had not been closed; a housekeeper and two maids were there through the summer. She was expected at the house for breakfast on the morning of the fourth. She did not arrive—or, rather, she did not

go home. She reached the city safely. We have traced
her into the railroad station and out again—and that has
been about all. She's not been seen since."

"Perhaps she has eloped."

"Possibly; but the man she is engaged to is in the city,
almost frantic. Besides, there is more than I have told
you. We know that she took a taxicab at the station;
that before she got in she met and accepted a small parcel
from a blond young man, rather shabbily dressed; and
that they seemed to be having an argument, though a
quiet one. We have found the taxicab she took, and a
shop where she bought a couple of books—a Browning
and a recent novel. From the bookshop she went to a
department store. There she dismissed the taxicab. We
have traced her in the store to a department where she
bought a pair of blankets. They made a large parcel, but
she took it with her. From that time we have lost her
absolutely."

"The third of September, and this is the fifth of October—almost five weeks!"

"Exactly," he said dryly. "That's why I've sent for
you. We have tried all the usual things; we've combed
the city fine—and we are just where we started. If we
could make a noise about it we should have some chance.
Set the general public looking—that's the way to get
information. You get a million clues worth nothing, and
out of the lot one that helps. But you know these people.
They won't listen to any publicity. They have only one
argument—if she is dead publicity won't help her, and
if she is alive it will hurt her."

I was conscious of a vague disappointment. In the last
half-hour I had keyed myself to the highest pitch. I was

seeing red, really—nothing but the bloodiest sort of crime would have come up to my expectation. Certainly nothing less than a murder had been in my thoughts.

"I don't see how I can help," I said, a bit resentfully. "You've had five weeks and got nowhere," I continued: "and if you are going to ask me to put myself in her place, and try to imagine what could have happened, and to follow her mental processes, I can't do it. I can't imagine myself idle and rich and twenty. I can't imagine taking a taxicab when a street car would do, or having a lady's maid——"

Mr. Patton laid a hand on my arm.

"Did you ever hear Lincoln's story of the little Mississippi steamboat with a whistle so large that every time they blew it the boat stopped? No? Well, no matter. I don't want you to put yourself in her place; I want a little inside help—that's all. There's a curious story behind this case, Miss Adams. We've only scratched the top. Get in there and get their confidence. They won't talk to me—too much family pride. Get the mother to talk. That's part of her trouble—family pride and bottling up her emotions. I can't get close to any of them. After five weeks Mrs. March still calls me Mr. Peyton." He smiled ruefully.

"She bought blankets! That's curious, isn't it?"

"It's almost ridiculous under the circumstances. You may not be able to imagine yourself twenty, and so on, but you can certainly get your wits to work on those blankets. If she had bought a revolver now—but blankets!"

"She was engaged, you say? Were there any other men who—who liked her?"

"Half a dozen, I believe—all accounted for."

"Any neurasthenic tendency?"

"In the half-dozen? I dare say yes, when she announced her engagement; in the girl—I think not. She was temperamental rather. The picture I get of her is of an attractive and indulged young woman, engaged to a man she seems to have cared about. And yet, with all the gods smiling, she disappears."

I sat thoughtful. The cab was moving along beside the park now. We were almost there.

"She may be dead," I said at last.

"She may indeed."

He rapped on the window, and when the driver stopped he got out, with a quick handshake.

"Now go to it!" he said. "Go out for a breath of air between seven and eight each evening, and—keep your eyes open. I have a hunch that you'll get this thing— beginner's luck."

The March house was an old-fashioned, rather stately residence. Instead of going upstairs to the drawing room there was a reception room opening into the lower hall. Behind that was a music room and, still farther back, a library.

At the very rear of the lower floor was a dining room, quite the largest in the house, extending as it did the entire width of the building. In this room was a large bay window extending out into a city garden, and in the bay, shut off by tall plants, was a small table, where the family breakfasted and even, when alone, sometimes dined.

A long flight of stairs, uncarpeted, led to the second

floor. On that first evening I got merely the vaguest outlines of the house, of course. It was silent, immaculate, rather heavy. I had a glimpse of two men in the library talking—one middle-aged, rather stout; the other much younger. Over everything hung the hush of suspense—that hush which accompanies birth and death and great trouble.

A parlor maid admitted me and led me upstairs to my room.

"Mr. March would like to see you in the library when you have taken off your things," she said.

I changed quickly into my uniform—all white, of course, with rubber-soled white shoes. With the familiar garb I was myself again; I could face anything, do anything. Clothes are queer things.

Mr. March turned when he heard me at the door and rose.

"I am Miss Adams, the nurse," I said. "Do you wish to see me?"

"Will you come in, Miss Adams? This is Mr. Plummer. Have you seen Mrs. March?"

"No; I thought it best to see you first."

"I am glad of that. Perhaps I ought to tell you—we are in great trouble, Miss Adams. Our—our only daughter has gone away, disappeared. It is over a month since—" He stopped.

"That is very terrible," I said. I liked his face.

"We wish absolute secrecy—of course I need hardly say that; but you understand Mrs. March is highly nervous. I—I hope you can quiet her. What we want you to do is to be as cheerful and optimistic as possible. You know what I mean. She will talk to you about Clare

—about Miss March. Reassure her if you can. Be certain that Miss March will be found soon."

"I will do what I can. Has the doctor left any orders?"

"Very few. She is to be soothed. There's a bromide, I believe. Her maid has the instructions."

There was nothing for me in that glimpse of the two men most nearly concerned—two gentlemen unaffectedly distressed and under great strain in a quiet, well-ordered house. It looked like poor material, from Mr. Patton's point of view. Mr. March followed me into the hall. "If you need anything let me know, Miss Adams. Or will you speak to the servants?"

"I can tell better later on. If I am going to be up tonight—and I think I would better, this first night anyhow—I should like a lunch; something cold on a tray."

"Do you wish it upstairs?" I hesitated. There was a picture in a silver frame on the library table—I thought it probably one of the missing girl. I wanted to see it.

"It will be a change to come down."

"Very well," he said. "There will be a supper left in the dining room. There is a small table there in the bay window. It will be more comfortable—not quite so lonely."

"Thank you," I replied and went upstairs. Opposite the library door I glanced in. I had been right about the picture. Mr. Plummer had picked it up and was looking at it. I felt certain that he was the fiancé—a manly looking fellow; not very tall, but solid and dependable looking, with a good head and earnest eyes.

My patient was in bed—a pretty little woman in a boudoir cap, with a pink light beside her. She held out a nervous hand.

"How big and strong and competent you look!" she said, and quite unexpectedly fell to crying. I had a difficult evening. She was entirely unstrung—must have me sit down by the bed at once and listen to the trouble, as she called it—and as it was indeed.

"She wouldn't go away and leave me like this!" she said more than once. "If you only knew her, Miss Adams—so full of character; so determined; so gifted! And beautiful—haven't you seen her picture in the newspapers?"

I evaded that—I never read society news.

"And happy too?" I said. "She must have been very happy."

I saw a change in Mrs. March's rather childish face.

"We thought she was, of course; but lately—I've remembered so many things while I've been lying here. She was very strange all summer—moody sometimes, and again so gay that she frightened me."

"Perhaps she was gay when Mr. Plummer was there and moody when he was away."

"But he wasn't there at all. That's another thing, Miss Adams. She would not let me ask Walter up. She —she really kept him away all summer. I don't believe Mr. March told the detective that—he forgot so many things."

She wanted me to telephone this piece of information to the police at once, but I persuaded her to wait. I gave her an alcohol rub and a cup of hot milk; and, finding them without effect, I took a massage vibrator I found on her dressing table and ran it up and down her spine. She relaxed with the treatment finally and even asked me to use it on her face.

"I'm an old woman with all the worry," she said apologetically. "It will tone up the facial muscles, won't it? And would you mind putting some cold cream on first?"

I did not mind; and after a time she fell asleep. I was glad of a respite. In my two hours over the bed I had accumulated many ill-assorted bits of information. I wanted time to catalogue them in my mind. I have the notes I made that night on one of my records:

"C. has been missing since September third; today is October fifth—a total of thirty-two days.

"Was moody all summer—would not see Mr. Plummer, but wrote him daily.

"She had been engaged once before, to a Wilson Page, but broke engagement. Cause of trouble not known. C. suffered much at the time. Note—Have Mr. P. look up Wilson Page.

"C. usually undemonstrative, but rather affected when she said goodbye to her mother. Was she planning something, unknown to them?

"But if she was planning an elopement why did she make careful appointments with her dressmakers and milliners? Is she more crafty than they think or was her decision made unexpectedly?

"She forgot her jewel case, which she always carried with her. An inventory reveals only a part of her jewelry. She wore, when she left, only the sapphire ring Mr. Plummer gave her. She had less than a hundred dollars in money.

"Wilson Page is dark. The man who met her in the station was thin and fair.

"Her picture is on her mother's dressing table—an attractive face; dark-eyed, full of character, but rather wistful. A thoughtful face. Is she living or dead? Did she go voluntarily or was she lured away? If she went voluntarily—why?"

I looked round the handsome room where my patient slept calmly, her petulant features relaxed and peaceful. I glanced across the hall to Miss Clare's room, where a light burned every evening; where an ivory dressing set, with carved monogram, was spread on the toilet table; where every luxury a young woman could demand had been gathered together for her use. And I recalled the look in the face of the man downstairs as he gazed at her picture—the tragedy in the eyes of her father. How had she gone and why? How and why?

III

My first night at the March house was marked by a disagreeable and rather mystifying occurrence. I had got my patient quiet and asleep and had had a telephone talk with the doctor by eleven.

"There is very little to do," the doctor said. "I'll come in in the morning. Just keep her comfortable and cheerful. She needs someone to talk to. Let her talk all she wants."

I darkened the room where she lay and placed a screen in the hall outside the door, with a comfortable chair beside it and a shaded lamp. I had made up my mind to sit up for that one night at least. I had had nervous cases before; and I knew that sometime between then and morning she would waken, and that the sight of someone alert and watchful would be a comfort.

At midnight I took off my cap, eased my hair and

removed my stiff collar. With the neck of my dress turned in I was fairly comfortable. Also I was hungry. I had eaten almost no dinner. It was too early to eat. I got a book from the library and read.

At two o'clock Mrs. March was still sleeping quietly and I decided to get my night supper. I slipped as noiselessly as possible down the stairs. An English hall lamp was turned on in the lower hall near the music-room door, and far back in the dining room a candle light in a wall bracket showed me where to go.

My progress in my rubber-soled shoes was practically noiseless. I made my way along the hall back to the dining room. The room was very large, as I have said before, paneled in oak, with a heavy fireplace and a tapestry in an overmantel above. At one corner, beside the deep bay window, were French doors, hung with casement cloths, leading out evidently into the garden.

I was deliberate in all my movements, I remember. I went to the fireplace and stood looking up at the overmantel; I found the switch that would throw the light over my small table and thus give me a more cheerful place to eat. The bay, walled off by palms and flowering oleanders in tubs, was dark and rather uninviting at that hour. I made no particular attempt to be silent, but I dare say it is a result of my training that I make no unnecessary noise.

One of the older nurses said to me once:

"When you go out on private duty you'll have to fuss about your night supper generally. An orange and a glass of milk is about what most cooks set out. Keep them up to the mark. Insist on cold meat or sandwiches; and if there's an alcohol coffee pot have them leave it ready. Coffee is your best friend at three in the morning, and your next best is a shawl to lay over your knees."

I was thinking of that and rather smiling when I entered the recess and sat down at the small table. I was absolutely calm and beginning to be mightily interested in my case. The tray was ready; and there was a small alcohol coffee pot ready, with a box of matches beside it.

I lit the lamp and inspected the tray. The cook seemed to have been trained by some predecessor. There was chicken, a bit of salad, brown bread and fruit. I ate slowly while my coffee cooked—ate with an ear toward the staircase for a sound from my patient above, and with an occasional eye toward the garden below. A late moon showed a brick terrace under the windows, and three steps lower was a formal design of flower-bed and path, with a small cement circle, evidently a pool in summer. Somehow the garden looked uncanny—bushes became figures, moving about, waving arms in the breeze. I was a distinct object from outside as I sat in my nook; and, having now eaten and waiting only for the coffee, I reached up and extinguished the light over my head.

It was then, still standing, that I saw the hand. It was coming down the staircase rail, moving slowly and grasping tight. It was near the music room when I saw it first and therefore going away from me, but descending. There was something terribly stealthy about it. It must have been that quality in it which made me shrink back behind an oleander. Surely there was nothing unusual in people being about in a house where there was both illness and trouble, and yet——

At the foot of the stairs the hand, still on the rail, hesitated, disappeared. A moment later there rounded the newel post a little old woman dressed in black. She limped slightly, but for all that she came swiftly. Every detail is stamped on my mind. I can see her now, bent forward, something that was probably jet on her old-fashioned bonnet catching the faint light as she came. She had a quaint loose black wrap on—a dolman, I think they used to call them—and hanging to her arm a shabby leather handbag.

Stealthy as her movements were, they were extremely natural. Just inside the door she stopped, took off her spectacles and put them in a case, which she put in her bag, and then extracted from it another pair, which she put on. The bag was a quaint one, fastened with two straps and steel buckles. The buckles were troublesome and she was in a hurry. More than once she turned and looked back.

I waited for her to see me. It was an old servant, of course, come to tell me I was wanted upstairs. I was so sure of it that I bent down and put out my alcohol lamp. When I straightened up she had passed the bay and was at the French door leading to the garden. She opened the door, went out, closed it noiselessly behind her, and was gone. I tried to see her in the garden, but if she went that way she was lost in the shadows.

Even then I was rather amused than puzzled. I went over to the door and tried it. There was a lock on it. Unless she had a key she had locked herself out.

I drank my coffee and went upstairs. My patient was still asleep. From Mr. March's room came heavy, deep breathing, telling that he was forgetting his anxieties, for a time at least. But my book—the book I had left on my chair in the hall—was gone!

It seemed rather absurd. I thought I might have taken it with me; and I searched the dining room, without result. It was not to be found. I thought of the little old housekeeper, or whatever she was—but that was ridiculous. Besides, she had carried no book. She had a black leather handbag over her arm. She might, of course, have put the book—what idiocy was I thinking! The book was about. Every one has laid things down and seen them disappear. Sometimes they turn up and sometimes they do not—the fourth dimension perhaps.

I met Mr. Patton the next evening as he had arranged. He fell into step beside me.

"How's it going?" he asked.

"I'm learning to be a first-rate lady's maid," I said, rather peevishly I am afraid. "I massage, manicure and give scalp treatments, and I've got a smirk from trying to look cheerful. The experiment is a failure, Mr. Patton. I'm not nursing, for there's no real illness; and I'm not helping you any. And the dreadful decorum of the house gets me. If I were twenty I'd run away too. Nothing ever gets dusty or out of place. No door ever slams. When I raise a window for air I put in a gauze-filled frame to keep the dirt out!"

"Has the mother talked at all?"

"All the time—about herself. I've learned a little, of course. The girl has been moody—would not let Mr. Plummer, her fiancé, visit her this summer. Seemed to be in trouble; but confided in no one. The family relationships seem to have been all right. They adore her."

"Have you seen many of the people who come and go about the house—intimate friends and relatives?"

"Nearly all, I think."

"Any one who could answer the description of the man she met at the station—the light-haired chap?"

I considered.

"None, I am sure."

"She and her mother got along well?"

"I think so. They were always together."

"Is there any trace of another love affair?"

"Yes, she was engaged once before. To a Mr. Wilson Page. She broke the engagement herself."

That interested him. He said he would look up Mr. Page.

"And don't be impatient," he advised me. We had made our circuit of the block and were in sight of the house again. "These are long cases sometimes—but the longer the time the more sure I am that the girl is alive. Murder will out; it's self-limiting, like a case of measles. But take a girl who wants to stay hidden, and if she's intelligent there's hardly any way to locate her. How many servants in the house?"

"Seven, I believe."

"Keep an eye on them. If one of them is garrulous let her talk. They know more of the family than any member of it."

This brought to my mind the curious episode of the old woman, and I told him about it. He listened without interruption.

"When you say old, how old?"

"Seventy, I should say. She was stooped—and rather lame, but very active."

"You are sure you saw her? You could not possibly have been dozing?"

"I was making coffee; I don't customarily do that in

my sleep. I think it must have been the cook. She is the
only servant I have not seen. And, as to dozing, does
anybody dream a handbag with straps and buckles?"

He put a hand on my arm impressively.

"It may interest you to know," he said, "that the cook
is a young woman; I interviewed her myself. There is
no person such as you describe in the house!"

"But why—at three in the morning——"

"Exactly," he said dryly. "Why? That's for us to
find out."

He got a careful description of the old woman from
me, and an account of her exit by the French door from
the dining room into the garden. He was excited, for
him, and rather triumphant.

"Now was it a mistake to put you there?" he demanded. "Of course not! And the next thing is to find
the old lady. You can help there. Tell your story to the
family. Set them to wondering and guessing. They may
place her for us at once. In this business try direct
methods whenever you can. They save time."

He left me at the corner and I went on alone. Just
before I reached the house a man ran down the steps and
went away rapidly. The parlor maid was just closing
the door.

"Did that gentleman inquire for me, Mimi?" I asked.
"I am expecting my brother." I was learning!

"No, miss. He asked for Miss March." Her eyes
were wide and excited. "When I said she was not here
he ran down the steps in a hurry."

"My brother," I persisted, "is short and dark. Perhaps
you——"

"He asked for Miss March," she repeated. "And,

anyhow, he was thin and lightish." She turned to see whether any of the family might overhear. "He's been here before, miss," she confided, lowering her voice—"twice, in the last week. He—he isn't one of Miss March's friends—I know that. And tonight he left this."

She showed me her tray on the hall table. There was a note on it addressed: "Miss Clare March. Important."

"I'll take this up to Mrs. March, Mimi," I said. "And if he comes again ask him in and call me."

"Call you, miss?"

"Call me," I said quietly. "When he asks for Miss March merely ask him to come in. Then call me. Mrs. March has requested me to see him."

I took the letter and went upstairs, but I did not give it to Mrs. March at once. That night, while I made my coffee, I steamed open the envelope and read the contents. It was on pale lavender paper and was as follows:

"I implore you to see me as soon as posible. Come to the old place. I am up against it for sure. Don't let this go any longer! It's life or death with me!"

I made a careful copy of the note, even to the misspelled word, and sealed it again. Mr. March was out that night—a girl had been found in a hospital. He was always following some such forlorn hope, returning each time a little sadder, a little grayer.

Mrs. March was unusually exacting that morning. She wakened at dawn with a cry and I went to her. I was sleeping on the couch at the foot of the bed. She was sitting up, terrified, in the gray dawn. She wailed that Clare needed her, was calling for her. She had heard her distinctly.

"Surely you do not believe in dreams!" I said sternly.

"Not in dreams perhaps," she replied. She was still pallid. "But don't you think, Miss Adams, that people hear things in sleep that waking ears do not catch? You know what I mean. It's subconscious, or something."

"It's subnormal," I commented, and brought her back to earth with a cup of hot tea.

That morning I gave Mr. March the note. We were at breakfast and Mr. Plummer had dropped in, as he usually did, on his way to his downtown office. Mr. March read it without comment and passed it to the other man. He was younger, less poised. I saw him change color.

"Who brought this?" he demanded.

"Mimi got it. It was left by a thin, fair-haired young man."

They called Mimi, but she knew no more than I had told them, except for one fact: She said the man had tried to push by her into the house and that he had insisted that Miss March was at home. They sent the girl out. They seemed to have no scruple about talking before me.

"It is mystifying enough," Mr. Plummer said. "Patton ought to see it. But it doesn't help much. Whoever wrote that did not know that Clare was—not at home."

"Thin and fair-haired!" repeated ·Mr. March. "That's what Patton said, Walter—about the man at the railroad station, isn't it?"

"Patton is a fool!"

I gathered that the idea of the fair-haired man was extremely distasteful to him. He was almost surly.

We were sitting at the small breakfast table in the bay. I thought it a good time to speak about the little old

woman. Any lingering doubt I may have had as to her
right to be where I had seen her was dispelled by their
manner. They were abstracted at first, then interested,
then astounded.

"But, my dear young woman," Mr. March exclaimed,
"why did you not rouse the house? And why did you
wait for thirty hours before telling us?"

"It would be necessary for you to have seen her in
order to understand. It never occurred to me that she
was not a member of the household—she was so respectable. Only now, when I have seen all the servants, I
begin to realize—she went out through that door."

"Is anything missing?" Mr. Plummer asked. "Mrs.
March's jewels?"

"Still in the safe-deposit vault. We have had no heart
to think of them."

Nevertheless a search of the house was made that day.
Nothing was missing. Under Mrs. March's flushed directions, as she sat up in bed, I went round with great
bunches of keys, verifying lists, looking up laces, locating
furs. Such jewelry as she had about was safe.

As for the old lady with the jet on her bonnet, with the
dolman and the buckled handbag—none of the family
had ever known such a person. She answered no description, fitted into no place. Family and servants alike
disclaimed her.

Life has a curious way of picking up threads and dropping them. The romantic young man with the blond hair,
the little old lady with the limp, came and went; and for
two weeks there was nothing more. Clare March remained missing. Mrs. March spoke of her in the past
tense. Mr. Plummer grew thinner and took to coming

into Mrs. March's room and sitting for long stretches without speech, his hands hanging listlessly between his knees.

I had my first real talk with Mr. Plummer late one afternoon while the invalid dozed in her chair. He was a good-looking man, something over thirty and already growing gray. He had sat for some time apparently busy with his own thoughts—in reality watching me as I put away Mrs. March's various pretty trifles—she was always littered—ribbon bows, a nail file, a magazine, letters.

"Do you never make an unnecessary movement?" he asked at last.

"Frequently, I'm afraid."

"Must you put all those things away? Or will you sit down and talk for five minutes?"

I sat down near him. Mrs. March was sound asleep.

"Do you want me to sit down and talk, or to sit down and listen?"

"To listen, and to answer some questions. Just a minute." He went quietly to the dressing table, returning with the photograph of Clare that stood there.

"You nurses know a lot about people," he said. "That's your business. You're a psychologist even if you don't realize it. I've watched you with Mrs. March. Now what do you read in that picture?"

"It is a lovely face," I replied, doing my best, but feeling utterly inadequate. Womanlike, I dare say I was anxious to say the thing he wanted to hear. "A—a pleasant face, I should say, but with character and temperament."

"What about the eyes?"

"They are well apart—that's a good sign, though cows are that way, aren't they! They are very direct and honest too. Really, Mr. Plummer——"

"Here is a later picture, taken this summer. Now, what do you see?"

I was puzzled and uncomfortable.

"She looks older, more serious."

"Look at the eyes."

Well, there was a difference. I could not say where it lay. The effect was curious. In the early picture she was looking at the camera, and the eyes were limpid and clear. In the picture he took from his pocketbook she gazed into the camera also; but there was a sort of elusiveness about the eyes. It gave me a strange feeling of indirectness, evasion—I hardly know what. They might have been the eyes of a woman who had lived hard and suffered. And yet this girl of twenty had hardly lived as yet. It was almost a tragic face. I have seen the same drooping lines in eye cases, where vision is faulty and seeing an effort. What was this, then—astigmatism or evasion?

"You see it, don't you? Miss Adams, she has had some real trouble to make a change of that sort. I—I thought she was happy in our engagement; but as I look back there are things——"

Mrs. March stirred and opened her eyes.

"I hate to waken," she said querulously. "It is only when I am asleep that I can forget, and even then I dream. Go out now, please, Walter; Miss Adams is going to use the vibrator."

That afternoon at five o'clock Mr. Patton called me over the telephone for the first time.

"I think we have something," he said. "When you go out for your walk tonight dress for the street. There will be a taxicab at the corner and I shall be inside."

"At what time?"

"Seven-thirty."

"Will an hour be enough?"

"Ask for two hours."

Mrs. March was rather peevish about my going out.

"I dare say you need air," she said, "but you could get it by opening a window. And what about my hot milk?"

"I'll ask Hortense to sit with you and she will heat the milk. I do not need air, of course. But I do need some exercise."

She let me go grudgingly. Mr. Patton would not tell me where we were going, but insisted on talking of indifferent things. As it turned out we were headed for a police station; and at last he voiced his errand.

"We are going to show you a lot of handbags," he said. "A woman pickpocket was brought in here yesterday with four in a pocket under a skirt. I was looking over them today and it occurred to me that you might recognize one of them."

"Mine! I hope you send her up for a year!"

"Not yours. And do not jump to conclusions; it is fatal in this business."

I knew the bag at once when I saw it. Surely no other bag in the city of that size had two straps fastened with steel buckles. The handles of two of the other bags had been cut off, but the heavy leather handle of this one was entire.

"This is the one you mean, of course. Yes, it looks

like the one the old lady carried; but there may be others. It is foreign, isn't it?"

"What was she doing that night when you noticed the bag?"

"She opened it and put in a pair of spectacles in a case."

He unfastened the bag and emptied on to a table a tin spectacle case, as quaint as the bag; two keys, one for a patent lock, the other an ordinary house key. Last of all he drew from a pocket inside the bag a soiled and creased lavender envelope, stamped and ready for mailing. It was addressed with pencil to Mrs. March and had been opened. Mr. Patton drew out the communication inside and watched me as I read it. It was hardly decipherable and was written on a piece of wrapping paper:

"Am all right. Clare."

I stared at it.

"Interesting, isn't it?" commented Mr. Patton. "Did she write it or didn't she? If she's all right why isn`t she home? Why do all our little communications arrive in lavender envelopes? Who's the old lady? What was she doing in the house that night? What's the answer?"

"That's the key to the garden door," I said dully.

IV

The doctor made a late call that night and dismissed Mrs. March as a patient.

"I'll drop in now and then to learn what the news is," he said as he prepared to leave. "You don't need me professionally. Just keep cheerful. It will all come out right."

I followed him into the hall. It seemed to me that, if any one knew the inside history I had failed to secure, it was he. And up to that time I had failed with him.

"I hope you will stay on, Miss Adams. I am leaving her in your hands—remember, no drugs so long as she is normal; at any symptoms of nervousness again, start them early."

"It's a trying case," I said slowly. "It takes it out of me, doctor. She asks me for theories, and—of course I didn't know the girl or her life—I cannot give her what she wants."

He hesitated. We were in the lower hall by that time.

"Just what does she want?"

"Encouragement."

"That Clare is living, of course. Well, tell her this the next time she is down. It is true enough. Tell her Clare was unhappy in her engagement and that I believe there is another man; that she has eloped with him; and that her message to the family has miscarried."

"Wilson Page?"

He eyed me. For the first time it occurred to me that he suspected my business in the house and that he was giving me information that ethically he would have refused.

"No; a blond fellow, rather thin. I have seen her meeting him in the park, and once I believe she met him in my reception room."

He seemed to regret this information the moment I had it and left immediately.

That night, after I had rubbed Mrs. March with cocoanut oil, used the vibrator, given her hot milk and read her finally to sleep, I slipped into my room and sat down by the window. The autumn garden lay beneath, with no moon to bring out its geometrical desolation. And there, elbows on the sill, the chill air blowing about me, I tried to piece together the scraps I held—the little old lady; the blond man and his frantic note; the letter in the buckled bag. And again I recalled the conversation Mr. Patton and I had in the taxicab on our way back that evening.

"She's alive," he had said; "and she is in the city—if that note is hers, and I think it is. I'll show it to the father and the other chap in the morning. Then she is in hiding. Why?"

I lay down on a couch at the foot of Mrs. March's bed, but did not get to sleep, for some reason. The slightest movement of my patient found me wide-eyed and alert. Small sounds were exaggerated. A regular footstep that seemed to ascend the stairs for hours turned out to be a drip from a bathroom tap. The slow chiming of the hall clock set me crazy.

At two o'clock I got up and went downstairs. In the waitress' pantry, off the dining room, there were beef cubes. It seemed to me that if I drank a cup of bouillon I might sleep. As usual the light was burning in the lower hall. The dining room was dark—I no longer required a night supper—and the little table in the bay window was bare. A street light beyond the garden showed the window and the longer rectangle of the garden door. I was not nervous.

I made my way through the unlighted dining room to the pantry, a small room, painted white, with a butler's slide to the basement kitchen, and a small white glass-and-silver refrigerator built in the wall, where the waitress kept the dining-room butter and cream. The electric light was out of order there; I pressed the switch, but there was no answering flood of light. I had matches with me for the alcohol lamp, however, and found my capsules easily. Thus I was still in darkness when I opened the swinging door into the dining room.

Some one was trying the lock of the garden door! I do not mind saying I was terrified. The door was glass. To cross the room to the lighted hall would throw my whole figure into relief. I shrank back, breathing with difficulty, into my corner. Beyond the thin casement cloth of the door I could see a moving shadow.

The lock did not give. It seemed to me, all at once, that I knew the silhouette—that here again was the little old lady, but now without her key. My heart ceased pounding! I was able to think, to calculate. I wondered whether she would break the glass. I planned to let her get in if she could and then to cut off her retreat by advancing on her from behind. I was very calm by that time—rather exalted, I dare say, at my own bravery. I put the packet of beef cubes into my pocket in order to have both hands free.

I do not know just when I realized that it was not the little old lady—I believe it was after one of the panes had been broken and had fallen with a soft crash on to the rug inside. The figure straightened; it was much taller than I had expected. I recall my heart almost stopping and then racing on at a mad pace; I saw what I knew was a hand put through the opening; I heard the lock turn and the cautious opening of the door. The intruder was in the room with me.

Panic possessed me then. I turned wildly and threw

myself headlong against the swinging pantry door. It was madness, of course. There was no exit from the little room, no way to fasten the door. I was in a cul-de-sac and in the black dark. I believe I opened a drawer and got a cake knife; at least, eons after, I found myself clutching one. I do not remember how I got it.

The swinging door remained undisturbed. When I could hear—above the pounding in my ears—there was no sound anywhere except the hall clock's slow chiming.

Many things I have never recalled clearly about that hideous night. I do not know, for instance, how long I stood at bay in the pantry; or how my courage rose from my knees, which ceased trembling, to my spinal cord, to my pulse, which went down from about a hundred and eighty, thin and stringy, to what I judged was almost normal, still irregular, but stronger. When my courage reached my brain, which was in perhaps fifteen minutes, though I would have sworn it was daylight by that time and I had stood there most of the night, I put my ear against the door and listened. There was no sound.

The instinct of my training asserted itself. Whatever was happening, my patient must not be alone. I must get up to the sick-room. In a few moments it was an obsession. I must get back. My sense of duty was stronger than my terror.

I made the break at last, opening the door an inch or so. The room was quiet. With infinite caution I pushed the door farther open. I could see the room, solidly handsome, rather heavy, empty! I made my first few steps of progress with deliberate slowness. I knew that if I ran panic would follow at my heels. I dared not look over my shoulder. Even the lighted hall brought small comfort, with the dark rooms opening off from it, sheltering I knew not what; but I reached the foot of the stairs in safety. There I stopped.

A woman, dressed in rags, lay huddled at the foot of the steps in a faint. She lay face down. Even when I had turned her over and had recognized the features of the photographs in the house, I was still incredulous. Nevertheless it was true. Bruised and torn, clad in rags, gaunt to the point of emaciation, Clare March had come home again.

It was the end of one mystery—the beginning of another.

V

My first feeling was one of horror. Her condition was frankly terrible. I even feared at first that she was dead. I found a pulse, however. I am big and strong; I got her down off the staircase and laid her flat on the floor. All the time I was praying that none of the family or the servants had been roused. I did not want anyone to see her yet.

I brought down some aromatic ammonia and gave it to her in water. Mrs. March was sleeping calmly; across the hall Mr. March also slept, audibly. I had a little time; I wanted an hour—maybe two.

She came to very gradually, throwing an arm over her head, moving a little, and finally opening her eyes. Always I talked soothingly to her.

"Now don't be alarmed," I said over and over. "You are at home and everything is all right. I am a nurse. Everything is all right."

"I want—Julie," she said at last feebly.

I had never heard the name.

"Julie is coming. Can you sit up if I hold you?"

She made an effort and by degrees I got her into the music room. She collapsed again there; and, there being no couch, I put her down on the floor with a cushion under her head. Terrible thoughts had been running through my head. The papers had been full of abduction stories, and I confess at once I thought nothing else could explain her condition, her rags.

"I am hungry," she said when I got her settled. "I am—I am starving! I don't know when I have had anything to eat."

She looked it too. I had the beef capsules in my pocket and I left her there while I made some broth. I brought it back, with crackers. She was into a chair by that time; and she drank the stuff greedily, blistering hot as it was.

I had my first chance to take an inventory of her appearance. It was startling. Her hands were abraded and blistered. She held one out to me pathetically, but without comment. Over one eye was a deep bluish bruise. Her face was almost colorless, and her forearm where the sleeve had been torn away was thin to emaciation. Every trace of beauty was eclipsed for the time. She was shocking—that is all.

Her clothing was thin and inadequate—a torn white waist, much soiled; a short, ragged black skirt; and satin bedroom slippers, frayed and cut. She had nothing on her head and no wrap, though the night was cold. She looked up at me when she held out the empty cup.

"How is mother?"

"She has not been well. She is all right."

"Was it worry?"

"Yes. Do you think you can get up the stairs?"

"Is that all I am to have to eat?"

"I'll get more soon. You mustn't take too much at once."

She rose and I put my arm around her. She had taken me for granted, childishly, but at the foot of the stairs she halted our further progress to ask me:

"Who are you? You are not a servant."

"I am a trained nurse. I've been caring for your mother during her illness."

We went up the stairs and into her room.

Mrs. March wakened about the time I had got the girl to her own room.

"Don't tell mother yet," she begged. "Give me a little time. I—I'd frighten her now."

I promised. When I went back, half an hour later, Clare had undressed herself and put on a negligee from the closet. She was sitting in front of the fire I had lighted, brushing out her hair. For the first time she was reminiscent of the girl of the photographs. She was not like them yet—she was too gaunt.

I tried to coax her to bed, but she would not go. I was puzzled. Her nervous excitement was extreme; more than once she stopped, with brush poised, as if she was on the point of asking me some question; but she never asked it—her courage evidently failed her. It was a horrible night. I sat inside the door of my patient's room, in darkness, and watched the door across. I could hear the girl pacing back and forth; I was almost crazy.

I offered her a bromide, which she refused to take; but about half-past three I heard her lie down on the bed, and some of the tension relaxed. I had a chance to think, to work out a course of action. Mr. Patton should be notified at once; and as soon as the girl was really composed I would rouse Mr. March. I knew I would be criticized in the family for not rousing them all at once, but I am always willing to take the responsibility for what I do—the doctor's orders first and my own judgment next is my motto. And there have been times when the doctor's orders—but never mind about that.

I looked at my watch. It was almost four o'clock and still black dark. I went down to the library, where the telephone stood on a stand behind a teakwood screen, and called up Mr. Patton's apartment; but I could not get him.

I hung up the receiver and sat there in the darkness, meaning to try again in a moment or so. It was while I was still there that I heard Clare on the stairs.

She came slowly and painfully—a step; a pause for rest; another step. Once down in the lower hall, she made better progress. She came directly into the library, through the music room, and turned on the lights.

I was curious. It was easy to watch her through the carved margin of the screen. It was only curiosity. I had no idea there would be further mystery to solve. In the morning she would tell her story, the law would take hold, and that would be all. But I recall distinctly every movement she made.

First she went to the long table littered with magazines, with the bronze reading lamp in the center. She glanced over the magazines as they lay, picked up the framed picture of herself and looked at it for a long moment, her hands visibly trembling. Then she took a survey of the room.

There was an English fender about the fireplace, with a tufted leather top. Mr. Plummer habitually sat there, with his back to the fire. And just inside, thrown carelessly, lay a newspaper. It was the newspaper she wanted. It was not easy for her to reach it in her weakened condition. She stooped, staggered, bent again, and got it.

The wood fire had burnt itself out, but the warm bricks and ashes still threw out a comforting heat. She curled up on the floor by the fender and proceeded to go over the pages, running a shaking finger through paragraph after paragraph. I was most uncomfortable, half-ashamed, and cramped from my position.

When I felt that I could stand no more she found what she was looking for. I heard her gasp and then saw her throw herself forward, her face in her arms, crying silently but fiercely, her shoulders shaking. She paid no attention when I bent over her, except to draw herself away from my hand. When I tried to take the newspaper, however, she snatched it from my hand and sat up.

"Go away!" she said hysterically. "You're always round watching me. Can't I even cry alone?"

I was rather offended. I was raw and new, and it hurt. I drew back, like a fool, and lost a clew that we did not find until weeks later.

"I'm sorry you feel that way," I said coldly and went out and up the stairs.

She burned the paper before she made a laborious and faltering ascent of the staircase half an hour later—at least, when I went down there was no sign of it or of any of the newspapers that had littered the room. And, though Mr. Patton secured them all later and we went over them patiently, we could find nothing that seemed to have the remotest bearing on what we were trying to learn.

She was much better by morning—had slept a little; was calmer; had a bit of color in her ears, which had been wax-white; but the bruise on her forehead was blacker.

I broke the news of her return very gently to Mr. March at dawn and left it to him to tell his wife. I went in afterward and found her hysterically impatient to see her daughter. I induced her to wait, however, until she had had an egg and a piece of toast. I do not believe in excitement on an entirely empty stomach. We covered the bruise with a loop of Clare's heavy hair; and then her father and mother went in and I closed the door.

Somebody had telephoned for Mr. Plummer; but she sent her father out to say she would not see him just yet. It was like a blow in the face. He almost reeled.

"That's the message, boy," Mr. March said. "I don't understand it any more than you do. She's in frightful condition; we've sent for the doctor. Tomorrow I am sure——"

"But what does she say?" Mr. Plummer broke in. "Where has she been? I'll wait until she wants to see me, of course, but for God's sake tell me where she has been!"

"She has told us very little," Mr. March had to confess. "She is hardly coherent yet. She says she will talk to the police sometime today. She has been imprisoned—that is all we know."

Mrs. March's sitting room was open and Mr. Plum-

mer went in and sat down heavily. Some time later, as
I passed the door, he called me in.

"You let her in, didn't you?" he asked. "Will you sit
down and tell me all you know about it?"

I was glad to talk—I had been bottled up for so long.
I told him everything—except my reason for being down
in the library behind the screen.

"Did she ask for me at all?" he asked when I had
finished.

"I—I think so. Naturally she would."

He smiled at me wryly.

"You know she did not ask for me," he said and got up.

I was very sorry for him. He was so earnest, so bewildered. He waited round all morning, hoping for a
message, and about noon she said she would see him.
Her own maid dressed her and together we put a little
rouge on her face and touched up her colorless lips. Except for the hollows in her cheeks, she looked lovely. I
told her message to him.

"Tell him I want to see him," she said to me; "but he
is not to ask a lot of questions, and he is to stay only a
minute or two—I am so very tired."

He was uncertain of his welcome, I think. I took him
to the door. She was on a couch, propped up with pillows, and the bruise was covered. And when I saw the
look in his eyes and the assuring flame in hers I knew
that, whatever else was wrong, it was nothing that lay
between them. The vision of the blond man as Clare's
lover died at that moment and never came to life again.

The story of the almost two months of Clare March's
disappearance she told to Mr. Patton that afternoon. She
would not allow her father and mother to be present, and

only Mr. Patton's insistence that the nurse should be there to see that she did not overtax her strength secured my admission. The story was short and was told haltingly. It gave me the impression of truth, but of being only a part of the truth. Her descriptions of the people and of the surroundings, for instance, were undoubtedly drawn from painful memory. They were photographic—raw with truth. The same was true of her story of the escape.

"It was on the third of September that you started home," Mr. Patton said. "We know that, and that you arrived on the morning of the fourth. We lost you from the time you got into a taxicab at the station. Did you order the man to drive you home?"

"Not directly. I went to—" She named the department store to which she had been traced. "I had made my purchase when a young man came up to me and introduced himself. He said I did not know him, but that he was living in the same house with an old German teacher of mine, Fräulein Julie Schlenker. She had taught me at boarding school and I was very fond of her. He said she was—dying."

Tears came into her eyes. Mr. Patton caught my eye for the fraction of a second.

"Was this before you bought the blankets or after?"

She looked startled, but he was smiling pleasantly. If she had to reassemble her story she did it well and quickly.

"Before. I was terribly worried about Julie," she said. "I agreed to go there at once, and I asked him what I could take her to make her comfortable. He said she couldn't eat, but perhaps blankets—or something like that. I bought blankets and had them put in the taxicab.'

"What address did this blond young man give you?"

"I did not say he was a blond young man," she objected. "I do not remember what he looked like. I should not know him again."

Mr. Patton nodded gravely.

"My mistake," he said. "Was this the same taxicab?"

"No; I had dismissed the other. I got into the taxicab and the man gave an address to the driver. I paid no attention to it. I was upset about Julie. I hardly looked out. We went very fast. All the time I was seeing Julie lying dead, with her poor old face—" She shuddered. Clearly that part of the story was true enough and painful. "We drove for a long time. I was worried about the bill. When the register said four dollars I was anxious. I had checks, but very little money."

She stopped herself suddenly and gave Mr. Patton a startled glance, but he was blandness itself.

"Four dollars!" he said. "Did you know the neighborhood?"

"Not at all. I was angry and accused the driver of taking a roundabout way. He said he had gone directly and offered to ask a corner man."

"You were still in the city then?"

"Yes; but it was far out. When the driver drew up I had just enough money to pay him. It was almost five dollars."

"Can you remember exactly?"

"Four dollars and eighty cents. I gave that man five dollars. I had only a dollar left."

"The young man was still with you?"

"No, indeed. I was quite alone. I wish you would not interrupt me."

Mr. Patton sat back good-humoredly and folded his hands. I knew why he had continually broken in on the story. I thought he had caught something, by his look.

"I got out. I had the blankets and they were bulky. The man carried them to the doorstep and drove away. I thought it was a queer neighborhood. It was a mean little house, off by itself, with only an unoccupied house near.

"I felt very strange, but Julie was always queer.

"I asked for Julie. A hideous old woman answered the door. The whole place was filthy. I felt terribly for Julie—she was always so neat. I went in and up the stairs. The stairs were narrow and steep, and shut off below with a door. All I could think of was Julie in that horrible place. There were cobwebs along the stairs. I held my skirt away from them. We turned toward the back of the house and stopped before a door. The old woman did not rap. She opened it and said: 'In here, miss.' I went in. The room was empty. I said: 'Why, where is Julie?' But the old woman had gone. I heard her outside locking the door."

That was a strange story we listened to that afternoon —a story of futile calls for help; of bread and water passed through a panel in the door; of a drugged sleep, from which she wakened to find her clothing gone and rags substituted; of drunken revels below; and of the constant, maddening surveillance through the panel by a man with a squint. She described the room with absolute accuracy and even drew it roughly for Mr. Patton—a low attic room with two small windows; a sloping roof; discolored plaster from a leak above; a washstand without bowl or pitcher; for light a glass lamp with a smoked chimney; and for furniture a cot under the lowest part of the ceiling, and a chair.

Once a day, she said, the old woman brought her a tin basin for washing, and a towel, rough-dried. The basin had a red string to hang it up by, she said. The towels were checked—pink and white.

"Like glass towels," she said. "There was a grate for coal and a wooden shelf above it, with an old steel engraving tacked up on the wall. One corner was loose, and if I left the window open it flapped all the time. I had a fire only once; but I did not suffer from cold—the kitchen was beneath, and the flue was always warm."

"This steel engraving—do you remember what it was?"

"The Landing of the Pilgrims," she said promptly. "Some one had colored a part of it with crayons—a child probably."

Mr. Patton looked puzzled. She might have invented the panel in the door or the man with the squint; but parts of her story bore the absolute imprint of truth—the chimney flue being warm; the flapping picture; the rough-dried towels; the basin with a red string through its rim.

"In a moment I want you to tell us how you got away," Mr. Patton said; "but first—I want a reason for all this. Was it—did they try to force you to anything?"

"Nothing at all."

"They were not white-slavers then?"

She colored.

"No."

"They never threatened you?"

She hesitated, considered.

"Only when I cried out—and that would have done no good. There was only an empty house near."

"Miss March, this is an almost incredible story. A crime must have a motive. You are saying that you were imprisoned in an isolated house for two months, were unharmed and unthreatened, but under constant surveillance, and finally made your escape. And you can imagine no reason for it!"

"I haven't said that at all—I imagined plenty of reasons. Couldn't they have wanted a ransom?"

"They made no attempt to secure one."

She told of her escape rather briefly. If I can give in so many words my impression of her story it was that here and there she was on sure ground, and that the escape was drawn absolutely from memory and was accurate in every detail.

"Every now and then they all got drunk," she said. "I—I always thought they would set the house on fire. The two younger women would sing—and it was horrible."

"You did not say there were younger women."

She was confused.

"There were two. One was married to the man. They called the old woman ma. And there was a man with a wooden leg who visited the house. He came over the field; I saw him often. For the last two days they'd been drinking, and the old woman fell down and hurt herself. I could hear her groaning. And I was hungry—I was terribly hungry." She looked at me. "You know how hungry I was. I had not even water."

"She was starving," I said.

"Nobody came. I was frightened. I kept thinking that something had happened." She checked herself, started again. "All evening I lay in darkness. I could hear them yelling and singing and now and then the old woman groaning. And I was so thirsty I hoped it would rain and the roof would leak. That's how thirsty I was. I slept a little—not very much. Mostly I walked about and worried. The house was so quiet that it drove me crazy."

"Quiet! Were they asleep?"

She looked at him quickly.

"They went away—all of them. There was only the old woman, and she was hurt. When I called nobody answered."

"How was your door fastened?"

"On the outside."

"Couldn't you have put your arm through the broken panel and unlocked it?"

"The key was not in the lock. It never was. It was always on a nail at the top of the staircase. I could see it."

No one could have doubted her. The key was kept at the top of the stairs on a nail. It takes a perceptible second to invent such a detail. She had not invented it.

"All the next day no one came near me. One of the windowpanes was broken. I called through it for help. Sometimes there were people in the fields beyond the house. There was nobody that day except some little boys. They paid no attention; perhaps they did not hear me. I was getting weaker all the time. I thought that pretty soon I would be too weak to try to escape. The fire was out below and my room was cold. My hands were so stiff I could hardly move them. I worked a long time at the window. They had driven nails in all round it. I worked them loose."

She held out her hands. They were cut and blistered.

"I got them out at last, but I broke a pane of glass. I hardly cared whether it was heard or not. I had never been able before to see what lay below the window. There was a sort of shed there.

"I had to wait until night. The room was freezing, with the window out. They were still away, except the old woman. She lay and groaned down below. I lay on the mattress the rest of the day and shivered. As soon as it was dark I crawled up on the windowsill. I was frightened—it looked so far down. I lowered myself by my hands and then dropped; but I slipped. I thought I had broken my ankle. The loose boards on the shed made a frightful noise."

"How did you find your way home?"

"I walked for hours. I do not know anything about the streets. I just walked toward the glow of the city lights against the sky. When I got into the city proper I knew where I was."

"Where were you when you first recognized your surroundings?"

"I saw the North Market."

"Do you remember from which direction you approached it?"

"The west side, I believe." Her tone was reluctant.

Mr. Patton drew a soiled lavender envelope from his pocket and took out its inclosure.

"'Am all right. Clare,'" he read. "Now, Miss March, just when and where did you write this little note?"

Her only answer was to break into hysterical crying. "Julie! Julie!" she cried. She absolutely refused to explain the note. It was an *impasse*. She could neither explain it nor ignore it. She took refuge in tears and silence.

That was the end of Clare March's story. It sounded like madness; but there was proof of a sort—her general condition; her hands; her brief but photographic descriptions. It was true—at least in part. It was not the whole truth. She had not spoken of the blond man or of the little old lady in black; and yet I was convinced she knew about them both. Mr. Patton thought as I did; for when she was quieter he asked for a description of the old woman of her story.

"She was very stout," she said slowly, "and very dirty. She always wore the same things—a blue calico dress and an apron. She seemed to be washing all the time; the apron was always wet and soapy. And she had thin gray hair drawn into a hard knot."

"Could you tell her nationality by her voice—her accent?"

"I'm afraid not."

"Did you ever see her dressed for the street?"

"Never."

"Then you never saw her in a black bonnet trimmed with jet, and an old-fashioned dolman, and carrying a pocketbook fastened with two buckles?"

She leaned over suddenly and caught Mr. Patton by the wrist.

"I can't stand it any longer!" she cried. "What do you know? Was the paper wrong?"

When she saw by his face that he did not understand and could not help her, she sank back among her pillows. She would not answer any more questions and lapsed into a watchful silence.

VI

Naturally I have never taken any credit for the solution of the Clare March mystery. Even now, when I am writing under an assumed name, I am uneasy. To be suspected would be my professional ruin. So far I have been able to keep my double calling a profound secret. I may have been in your house. Think over it, those of you who have something to conceal—are you certain that the soft-walking, starched, white young woman to whom in your weakness you talked so freely—are you sure it was not myself? Under the skin, I said in the beginning —aye, and under the flesh and its weaknesses. Do you recall that day when you and a visitor talked at the bedside and I wrote letters in a corner by a window? How do you know but that your entire conversation, word by word, was at the Central Office in two hours? Did it ever occur to you before?

I wrote many letters that week. Mrs. March was up and about, bustling and busy; Clare was my patient. I no longer met Mr. Patton in the evenings. He was combing the outskirts of the city, I believe, and interviewing taxicab drivers. I sent a daily report by mail to him:

MONDAY—I notice one curious thing: She will not let me do much for her. Hortense, her maid, does some things—not much. She gets rid of us both whenever she can. I feel worse than useless. I have offered to give her massage, but she refuses. Mr. Plummer only comes to the door—she does not wish him to come in.

TUESDAY—Still weak and inert. A box of flowers every day from Mr. Plummer. I had thought possibly she did not care for him; but today I saw her eyes when she looked at the roses—I believe she is crazy about him. She would like to get rid of me, but her parents insist she needs me. Her hands are healing. There is one curious thing—her wrists are abraded. Did she say her hands were tied?

WEDNESDAY—The blond man has been here. I saw him from the stairs and went down. He is not what we thought at all. He is untidy and shabby. He was waiting inside the door, turning his hat round in his hands. I told him Miss March was ill, but he refused to leave. He said: "Tell her it is Samuels, and this is the last call. She'll know what I mean." I said: "I think she has had a letter from you." He turned livid. "Then she got it!" he stormed. "And she paid no attention to it! You tell her, for me, that she'll fix things with me now—today— or I'll tell the whole story!" He felt in his watch pocket and seemed to remember that his watch was gone. That added to his rage. "You tell her that. Tell her she'll have it at the old place by three this afternoon or I'll go to her precious sweetheart and tell him some things he ought to know." I tried to follow him when he left, but by the time I'd got my hat and ulster he was out of sight. If Samuels is his real name you can probably find him. He is blond and smooth-shaved, and has a gold tooth— right side, upper jaw; wears a tan overcoat and a soft green felt hat.

WEDNESDAY, four P. M.—I have just come back from an errand for Clare. I have been to the "old place" with a parcel for Samuels. It was money. He was so greedy that he tore it open while I waited. It seemed to be con- siderable—well over a hundred dollars. When he had

counted it he put it in his pocket. He looked better than
in the morning and was calmer. He looked at me after
he had counted it. "Don't look so damned virtuous!" he
said. "This isn't backmail. It's for value received."

The "old place" is at the corner of Tenth Street and
the Embankment. We stood in the doorway of a vacant
building and talked. Samuels looks decayed—as if he
has seen better days. I tried to get you by telephone to
follow me. You were out.

THURSDAY—A very curious thing happened today:
Clare asked for some chicken cooked in cream. The cook
had never done it and I volunteered. It took some time;
I was in the basement more than an hour. When I came
up with the chicken she had disappeared. We were all
terribly frightened. I called the office twice, but you were
out as usual—you will have to arrange some way for me
to get you in emergencies. She had taken her wraps and
gone out by the garden door. The parlor maid had not
seen her. It was two hours later when she came back,
exhausted. She locked herself in her room and it was
almost the dinner hour before she would admit me.

Her father had a talk with her tonight. He said:

"You must not do such unwise things. You will drive
your mother frantic."

"Poor mother!" she replied. "I'll tell you before long
where I was. Don't ask me."

I thought she had been crying. I believe she has
pawned or sold her sapphire ring; I do not see it.

That letter, sent special delivery, and unsigned as all
of them were, brought a telephone message from the
detective and an appointment for that evening.

"Ask for an evening off," he said. "I think I've got it
And I want to talk to you."

He had a taxi at the corner that night. It was when it
was well under way that he began to talk.

"We've got the house," he said. "The man with the
squint did it—but that's a long story. In her anxiety to
tell as much as she dared of the truth she went a little too
far. Given a four-dollar-and-eighty-cent taxicab radius,
an isolated house with two young women, an old hag and
a man with a squint—put a shed on the back of the house
and a bad reputation all over it—and you have perhaps
two dozen possibilities. Add such graphic touches as a
built-in stairway and a tin basin hung up by a red string
as identification marks, and an empty house and a man
with a wooden leg for neighbors, and out of the two
dozen there will be one house that fits. We've found it."

"Is that where we are going?"

"To that neighborhood. I really wanted a chance to
go over the whole thing with you. Now, then, what do
you think? You've been close to the case—closer than I
have. How much of that story of hers is true?"

"About half of it."

"Which half?"

"Well, I think she was not a prisoner. I believe she
was a voluntary guest in the house she described and that
she was hiding from something."

"I see. And not expecting us to find the house, she
gave a circumstantial description. But what was she
hiding from? So far as we can learn, her past has been
an open book—she was away at school for four years,
and spent a year abroad with a party of girls and a
chaperon. She came out two years ago—I remember

reading about the coming-out ball, something very elaborate. That first winter she went about with young Page, became engaged and broke it off. Page has been away ever since. It can't have anything to do with Page. Last spring she took on this Plummer—has been with her family all summer—has never, except during the year abroad, been away from her mother for any length of time. That doesn't look like anything to hide from. What do you think of the Julie story?"

"I don't believe it. But there is a Julie."

"Does the family know the name?"

"No. The girl is paying blackmail, Mr. Patton."

"The blond chap?"

"Yes."

"That was rotten luck, my being out of touch that day. If we had him—or if we had your friend the little old lady!"

He stopped the taxicab shortly after and we got out. We were well out of the center of town, in a scattering suburb. I had never seen it. And before us stretched one of those empty spaces that are left here and there, without apparent cause, during the growth of the city. House-builders are gregarious—they build in clusters. Perhaps it's a matter of sewers or of gas and water. To right and left of us stretched a sort of field, almost bare of grass, with straggling paths across it. Long before, a street had been cut through; its edges were still intact—a pitfall for the unwary.

I did not see all this that night. It was late October and very dark. Mr. Patton had a pocket flash, and with that and his hand I managed fairly. Our destination was before us—a little house faintly lighted.

"I'm afraid this isn't very pleasant, Miss Adams," he apologized; "and I haven't a good reason for bringing you. But I'm up against it in a way. I want you to see this place and perhaps your instinct will tell you what I fail to make out. I've been here once today and it stumps me. They swear they've never had a girl there; that the man with the wooden leg sleeps in the garret sometimes. He's a watchman at the railroad over there. By the way, did she speak of a railroad?"

"I think not."

"It's a bad place. The police protection doesn't amount to much, but over there in the town they say it's a speakeasy. The cellar's full of beer. They say other things too—that the old woman is a white slaver, for one thing. That bears out the story partly. And another thing does also—the hag hurt herself lately. She's going about with a cane. On the other hand—well, if they were lying today they did a good piece of work."

There was a wagon near the house as we approached. At first we thought they were moving out. Then Mr. Patton laughed.

"Getting rid of the beer and the empties," he said. "Got them scared! Now don't be nervous. You needn't speak to them. I want you to keep your eyes open—that's all."

I was nervous. There was something sinister about the very location. I have even now rather a hazy recollection of Mr. Patton's rap at the door, the imperious summons of the law, and of a hideous old woman who peered out into the darkness.

"Well, mother," Mr. Patton said cheerfully, "here I am again. I want to look round a little."

The hag made to close the door, but a woman spoke from behind.

"Let him in, ma," she said. "We ain't got nothing to hide. Come in, mister."

A man came up from a cellarway with a box of bottles. I can still see his face over the bottles—his sickening pallor, his squint. He thought it was a raid, clearly. Then he saw me and his color came back.

"I guess a man's 'ouse is 'is own," he snarled. "We drink a little beer ourselves. That ain't again' the law, I reckon."

"Not at all," Mr. Patton said good-humoredly. "I'll have a lamp, please."

It appeared to be a four-roomed house. We stood in the front room, an untidy place with a bed in a corner and heavy with stale odors. Behind there was a kitchen with a table littered with the remains of the evening meal. Between the two rooms was a narrow, steep staircase shut off with a door below and ending above in a small landing. From this landing two doorways opened—one into a front room, the other into a half room, or attic, over the kitchen. It was into this room that Mr. Patton, carrying a smoky lamp, led the way.

"This is the room," he said. "That is the window with the shed below. Here is where the flue comes up from the kitchen."

I looked round. It was a sordid, filthy place. The plaster had broken away here and there. Where it was intact it was discolored from a leaking roof. For furniture there was a mattress on the floor, with soiled bedding, a chair with a broken seat, and a washstand. Clare had said the washstand was unfurnished, but had men-

tioned a tin basin. Here was a tin basin with a red string.
Mr. Patton was watching me grimly.

"Well, what do you make of it?" he said.

"It looks queer," I admitted. "Only there are some
things—the panel in the door, for instance. There is no
door."

"I asked about that. They say it came off the hinges
a month or so ago and they chopped it up for firewood."

I was still looking about. He had stooped and was
examining the door-hinges.

"She said she broke the glass. One window is broken,
but this one over the shed is not."

He came over and ran his hand over the window frame.

"Sash is nailed in, which I believe was also mentioned!"
he said. Our eyes met in the dim light—a friendly clash;
he was so sure of the place and I was so doubtful.

As I stood there peering into the squalid corners of the
attic I remembered the daintiness of the girl's room at
home—its bright chintz and shining silver; its soft lamps;
its cushions; its white bath beyond. I remembered the
exquisite service of the March household and tried to
picture the hag below climbing that ladder of a staircase
with a platter of greasy food. I tried to forget Clare, in
her lovely negligee, and to recall the haggard creature
who had dropped in her rags at the foot of the staircase.
And I tried to place the wretched girl of that night in this
wretched place. I could not do it. There was something
wrong.

Mr. Patton turned to me, gravely smiling.

"Now, then, your instinct against my training," he
said. "Is this the place?"

"I do not believe she was ever here," I said. "Don't

ask me why—I just don't believe it." But a moment later I felt that my instinct had received a justification. "Do you remember," I said, "a graphic description of a steel engraving that flapped in the wind?"

"By George!"

"There is not only no engraving—there are no nail holes in the plaster. There has never been such an engraving here," I said in triumph.

VII

I have often wondered what would have happened had we taken Clare March the next day to that untidy house in Brickyard Road. Brickyard Road was the local name of the street that had been cut through and forgotten.

Would she have told the real story or not? If not, how would she have explained the discrepancy, for instance, of the missing engraving? Would she have taken refuge in silence? Had she hoped by the very detail of her description to throw us off the track? Did she wonder, those dreadful days, how the bag with the buckles had come into the hands of the police and yet had not led us farther? Did she suspect me at any time?

Sometimes I thought she did. She would not let me do much for her. I gave her the medicines that were ordered, saw to her nourishment, read to her occasionally. Her own maid looked after her personally. It rather irritated me. More than once I found her watching me. I would glance up from my book and find her eyes on me with a question in them; but she never asked it.

Mr. Patton was waiting eagerly to take her out to

Brickyard Road; but she was still very weak and she showed a distaste for the excursion that was understandable enough under the circumstances. Other things puzzled me, however—her unwillingness to see Mr. Plummer was one. Yet she sat for hours looking at his picture. I suspected, too, that her maid was closely in her confidence. More than once I caught a glance of understanding between them. Sometimes I wondered if she was quite normal—not insane, of course, but with some queer mental bias.

Outwardly everything was calm. She lay or sat in her fairylike room, with flowers all about her. Her color was coming back. In her soft negligees she looked flowerlike herself. The picture was quite complete—a lovely convalescent; a starched and capped nurse; a maid in black and white; flowers; order; decorum; with a lover hovering in the background. But the nurse was making notes that were not of symptoms on her record, the maid was not clever enough to mask her air of mystery, and the lover paced back and forth downstairs waiting for a word that never came.

On the day following my excursion with Mr. Patton, going into my own room unexpectedly, I found Hortense, the maid, in my clothes closet. She made profuse apologies and backed out. She had been looking, she said, for a frock that had been mislaid. I did not believe her.

After she had gone I made a careful examination of the closet. A row of my white linen dresses hung there, my street clothes, my mackintosh. In a far end, where I had placed them the night she arrived, were the ragged garments in which Clare had come home. I locked my door and, taking them out, went over them carefully.

There was a worn black skirt, rather short; a ragged and filthy waist of poor material and carelessly made, put together by hand with large stitches and coarse thread. The undergarments were similarly sewed. They might have come from just such a place as the house in Brick-yard Road. The skirt was different. Though ragged, it was well made, and it had been shortened. It had been altered at the top, too, I decided—the belt taken off and put on again inside out.

I found something just then. On the inside of the belt was woven the name of one of the leading tailors in the city. I thought over that a while. The skirt could hardly belong to Brickyard Road. It seemed to me that this was a valuable clew. Also it seemed to me that Hortense knew this also, and that there was no time to be lost.

The situation was put up to me that day in an unexpected fashion. Mr. Patton slipped on the first ice of the season and injured the leg that had been hurt before. He was almost wild with vexation.

"Just keep wide awake," he wrote me by special delivery, "and send me the usual daily bulletins. If anything very important happens come round and see me. The people we saw are being watched. If you meet the blond chap follow him until you get a chance to telephone. I'll send some one to relieve you. We haven't got it all yet by any means."

It rather knocked my plans, especially as I could tell by the shaky writing that he was suffering when he wrote the letter. It seemed to me that for a day or so I should have to get along alone.

At least I could do something—I could perhaps trace the skirt.

I had been in the March house now for eight weeks and had had practically no time off. When I asked for two hours Mrs. March offered me the remainder of the day.

I took it; I was glad to get it.

I took the skirt along, carrying it out quite calmly under Hortense's not too friendly eyes. I thought it probable she would miss it, but I could see no other way. I wanted to identify the skirt. If it had been made for Clare her story of having had all her clothing taken away from her fell to shreds. If it had not I meant to trace it. And trace it I did that autumn afternoon while the dead leaves in the park made crackling eddies under the trees; while the wind held me back at every corner; while fashionable women donned the first furs of the season and sallied forth to the tailors for their winter garments. I, too, went to a tailor.

I dare say I was not fashionable enough to be worth while. It was a long time before I received attention and my few hours were flying. When at last the manager turned to me I indicated my bundle.

"I want to trace a skirt that was made here," I began. "Your name is on the belt. It is very important."

"But, madam," he said, "we cannot give any information that concerns our customers."

"This is vitally important."

"It would be impossible. We turn out a great many costumes. We keep no record of the styles."

"There is a number on the belt."

I believe he suspected me of divorce proclivities. He held out both hands, palm up.

"Madam surely understands—it is impossible!"

I turned over the lapel of my coat and he saw a badge that Mr. Patton had given me. He had said:

"Don't use it unless you need to; but when the time comes flash it!"

I flashed it. I got my information within ten minutes, but it did not help at first. He gave me the name of the woman for whom it had been made. I had never heard of her—a Mrs. Kershaw.

"You are quite positive?"

"Positive, madam. The number is distinct. Also one of the skirtmakers recalls—it was part of a trousseau a year or so ago."

A sort of lust of investigation seized me. I had started the thing and I would see it out. With a new deference the tailor handed me my rewrapped bundle and saw me to the door.

"No trouble with the Kershaws, I hope?" he said.

"None whatever," I answered at random. "She gave the skirt away and I am tracing it."

That was it, of course. I said it first and believed it afterward. She had given the skirt away.

It took an hour and a half of my shortening afternoon to locate and interview Mrs. Kershaw. She was quite affable. I did not show my badge—it was not necessary. I made up a story about some stolen goods, with this skirt among them. She was anxious to help, she said, but——

"I hardly remember," she said. "I gave away a lot of my wedding clothes—the styles changed so quickly. Why, I remember exactly what I did with that! I gave it to the Fräulein—Fräulein Schlenker. But stolen goods! She's the honestest old soul in the world."

"She is old then?"

"Oh, yes—quite. Such a quaint little figure. She taught me at boarding school, but she grew too old. Poor Fräulein Julie!"

My lips were dry. Julie!

"Would you mind describing the Fräulein, Mrs. Kershaw?"

"You do not suspect her of anything?"

"No, indeed; but I should like to find her."

"Well, she is a little thing, stooped and lame. She hurt her ankle after I knew her first. She is very saving —we all thought she was rich; but I believe not. There's a brother, or some one, that she helps. She wears a rusty black bonnet with jet on it, and a queer old wrap; and— oh, yes—she always carries the same bag—a foreign one, with buckles. I really think the bag was the reason we thought she was wealthy. It seemed such a secure affair."

Julie, then, was my little old lady of the dining room and the garden door! And there was more than that—the school was the school from which Clare had graduated.

"Have you seen the Fräulein lately?"

"We have been away all summer. She may have called. I'll ask."

The little old lady had not called, however. I got her address. It seemed to me that things were closing up.

It was quite dark when I left the Kershaw house. It was very cold and I was hungry; but excitement would not let me eat. I was getting my first zest for this new game I was playing, and I was losing my shrinking horror of spying into affairs that were not my own. It seemed to me that my cause was just; for if Clare March had not been incarcerated in the Brickyard Road house she might still, out of terror of the truth, insist that she had been. Hysterical young women had done such things before. I held no brief for the family in Brickyard Road; but if they were innocent they were not to suffer. I was after the truth, and I felt that I should get it. I had no course of action mapped out. I wanted to confront the little old lady—I got no farther.

It was seven o'clock when I reached the house. I had crossed the city again. I was empty and shivering with cold, and I still carried the parcel under my arm. For the first time that day I was nervous. The fear of failure assailed me. I used to have the same feeling when I had charge of the operating room and a strange surgeon was about to operate. Would he want silk or catgut? What solutions did he use? Would the assistant get there in time to lay out the instruments? So now with the Fräulein—would she deny the skirt? If she did, should I accuse her of the night visit to the March house? Or of the letter in the buckled bag?

The house was a small one on a by-street, a comfortable two-story brick, with a wooden stoop and a cheerful glow through the curtains of a vestibule door. The woman who answered my ring was clearly the mistress. She wore a white apron and there was an agreeable odor of cooking food in the air.

"Fräulein Schlenker?" she said. "Yes; she made her home here. She is not here now."

"Can't you tell me where I may find her?"

She hesitated.

"I don't know exactly. We've been anxious about her lately. She went away for a vacation about two months ago. Did you want to see her about renting the house in Brickyard Road?"

For just a minute I distinctly saw two white aprons and two vestibule doors!

"Yes," I said as coolly as I could. "When—when will it be empty?"

"It is empty," she replied. "I hardly know what to do. She's been anxious to rent it; but now that she's away and no word from her— Would you like the key?"

The empty house in Brickyard Road!

"If I might have it."

"You'll return it soon, won't you?" She went into the hall and got a key from the drawer of a table. "She'll do anything that's reasonable—paper the lower floor and fix the roof. It's a nice little house." I took the key, still rather dazed. "It's a growing neighborhood out that way," she went on, evidently eager to do her roomer a good turn. "Some of these days that street will be paved." She had an air of doubt; she was clearly divided between eagerness and trepidation. "You'll be sure to return the key?"

"I'll have it back here tomorrow."

She watched me down the street, still vaguely uneasy. I tried to make my back honest, to step as one who walks the straight and narrow path. I had a feeling that she might suddenly change her mind and pursue me, commanding the return of the key. I hardly breathed until I had turned the corner.

I got something to eat at the first restaurant I saw. I needed food and time to think. I meant at first to telephone Mr. Patton. As I grew warmer and less fatigued I decided to go on alone. It was my first case; I wanted to make good—frankly I desired Mr. Patton's approval, and something he had said to me once came back.

"In this business," he said, "there are times when two's a crowd." I remembered that.

I ate deliberately. I never hurry with my food—I've seen too many stomachs treated like coal-cellars on the first cold day of fall. And as I ate, the key lay before me on the cloth. It had a yellow tag tied to it, indorsed in a small, neat script, very German.

"Key to the house in Brickyard Road," it said. "Kitchen door."

I had, at the best, about two hours and a half when I left the restaurant. That meant a taxicab. I counted my money. I had thirteen dollars. It would surely be enough.

Brickyard Road lay a square or two away from where I alighted. I retained the cab—out there in that potter's field of dead-and-gone real-estate hopes it was a tie with the living world. Its lamps made a comfortable glow. The chauffeur was broad-shouldered. I turned back and borrowed a box of matches from him. I have often wondered since what he thought.

The house Mr. Patton and I had examined was dimly lighted, as before. I passed it at a safe distance. The empty house, that was the only other building in Brickyard Road, was my destination. The two houses were alike—clearly built by the same builder. Only the courage of an idea took me on. In the lighted house the crone was singing—a maudlin voice. Some one was walking along the rickety boardwalk round the place—a step and a tap, a step and a tap—the one-legged man, of course.

There is something horrible about an empty house at night. A house is an intimate place; its every emanation

is human. Life has begun and ended in it. Thoughts
are things, I have always believed—things that leave their
mark.

I had such a feeling about the little house in Brickyard
Road. I was very nervous. The other house was near
enough to be dangerous—too far away to be company.
I felt terribly alone. There was not even starlight. I
stumbled and fumbled along, feeling my way by the side
of the house to the rear. There was a dispute going on
next door. The crone had ceased singing. Some one
broke a bottle with a crash.

I found the kitchen door at last. To reach it I had to
go through a wooden shed. In the safety of the shed I
struck a match and found the keyhole. The key turned
easily. As I opened the door a breath of musty air
greeted me and blew out my match. The thick darkness
closed down on me like a veil; I was frightened.

It was a moment or two before I could light a fresh
match, and it took more than that for me to survey the
kitchen. It had been in use not very long before. There
was a kettle on the stove and a few odds and ends of
dishes in orderly stacks on an upturned box. And there
was a loaf of bread, covered with gray-green mold.
There was no table, no chair—only, in a corner, there was
a cot bed, neatly made up. I remember distinctly the
comfort of discovering that orderly bed, with a log-cabin
quilt spread over it.

My match went out, but the box was almost full. I
was not uneasy now. The peace of the log-cabin quilt
was on my soul. I found a smoky lamp with a very little
oil in it, and lighted it. My nerves are pretty good. I've
laid out more than one body in the mortuary at night and

alone. I was not going to be daunted by an empty house. Nevertheless the glow of the lamp was comforting. I put down my bundle and went into the front room.

I had a real fright there. Something shadowy stood in the center of the room, moving very slightly. I almost dropped the lamp. I had a patient once who used to say her heart "dropped a stitch." Mine did. Then I saw that it was a woman's black dress hanging to a gas fixture and moving in the air from the open kitchen door.

I began to feel uneasy. What if the house were inhabited? Certainly it had been occupied recently. I dare say I move softly by habit, but I doubled my ordinary caution. I wanted to get away, but I wanted more than that. I wanted desperately to see whether there was a steel engraving of the Landing of the Pilgrims in the attic room over the kitchen. If I was right—if in this house Clare March had been imprisoned—if her detail of the house next door was merely what she had gained from a window—what was the meaning of it all? Where was Julie? If I knew anything this old black silk swaying in the air belonged to her.

Not, of course, that I reasoned this all out. I felt it partly; for the next moment I heard a door open at the top of the stairs. I blew out the lamp instantly, but a sort of paralysis of fright kept me from flight. I could have made it. The stairs, like the house next door, were closed off with a door—a dash past this door and I should have been in the kitchen; but I hesitated, and it was too late. The steps were at the lower door.

Now and then since that evening I have a nightmare, and it is always the same. I am standing in a dark room and there are stealthy steps drawing nearer and nearer.

At last the thing comes toward me; I can hear it; but there is nothing to see. And then it touches me with ice-cold hands—and I waken with a scream. I frightened a nervous patient almost into convulsions once with that dream of mine.

The darkness was terrible. Behind me the dress swayed, touched me. I almost fainted. The staircase door did not open immediately. I wondered frantically what was standing and waiting there. It showed my abnormal mental condition when it occurred to me that perhaps the old woman, Julie—perhaps she was dead, and that this on the staircase was she again, come back. I almost dropped the lamp.

I braced myself against I knew not what when I heard the door opening. Whoever it was, was listening, I felt sure. Through the open kitchen door came the sound of singing from next door and of some one hammering on a table in time. It covered my gasping breaths, I dare say. The stair door opened wider and some one stepped down into the tiny passage. We were perhaps eight feet apart.

I lived a century, waiting to hear which way the footsteps turned. They went toward the kitchen, still stealthily, with a caution that was more terrible than curses. I had a moment's respite then, and I felt my way toward the front door. If the key was there I might yet escape. I found the door. The key was gone. Even in that moment of frenzy I knew where the key was—in the buckled bag at the police station. I was trapped!

There were various sounds now from the kitchen—a match struck, and a wavering search, probably for the lamp I held; then a dim but steady light, as though from a candle followed by the cautious lifting of stovelids and much rustling of paper. The paper reminded me of something—my bundle lay on the cot!

I knew the exact moment when it was discovered. I heard it torn open and I shivered in the silence that followed. Then the candle went out and there was complete silence again; but this time it was the quiet of strained ears and quickened senses. I dream of that, too, sometimes—of a silence that is a horror.

I dared not move a muscle. I felt that if I relaxed I should stagger. I breathed with only the upper part of my lungs. Then, very slowly, there was movement in the next room—a step and then another. It was coming. While the light was burning I had been terrified by something desperate, but at least quick with life. Now, in the darkness, it became disembodied horror again! It came slowly but inevitably, and directly toward me. I tried to move, but I could not. The black dress moved in the air; a chill breath blew on me. Then, out of the black void all round, a cold hand touched my cheek. I must have collapsed without a sound.

VIII

When I came to I was lying on the floor of the empty room, with the black dress swaying above me. There was a faint light in the room. By turning my head I saw that it came from the kitchen. Some one was moving quickly there; there was a rattle of china. A moment later a figure appeared in the doorway and peered in.

"Are you awake, Miss Adams?"

It was Clare! I struggled to a sitting position and stared at her.

"Was it—you—before?" I asked.

"Yes. Don't talk about it just now. I have a fire going and soon we can have some tea. I think you are almost frozen—and I know I am."

It was curious to see how our positions had been reversed. And there was a change in Clare—she was almost cheerful. She helped me out into the kitchen and on to the cot, and then busied herself about the room.

"I am sure there is tea somewhere," she said. "Julie was always making tea."

She was dressed for the street—suit and hat and furs. She tried to make talk as she moved about the room, but the really vital things of the evening she avoided. She fussed with the fire, filled the kettle afresh from a hydrant outside, rinsed out two cups, found tea, searched for sugar. And still her eyes had not met mine.

She found me staring at an engraving that lay on the floor, however, and she dropped her artificial manner.

"The Landing of the Pilgrims!" she said gravely. "I was going to burn it."

The sounds in the next house died away. The kettle on the stove began to boil cheerfully. The little room grew bright with firelight. Clare drew the box before the cot and poured two steaming cups of tea.

"We will drink our tea," she said, "and then I shall tell you, Miss Adams. I am very happy tonight—I have only one grief."

What that was she did not say. She had found a box of biscuits and opened it. She took very little herself. She was plainly intent on making up to me for my fright. She seemed to bear me no malice for being there. It was not until I had drained my cup that she put hers down.

"Now we'll begin," she said, and took off her jacket. Next she drew up the sleeve of the soft blouse she wore beneath and held out her arm for me to see. I gave a shocked exclamation.

"Cocaine!" she said briefly. "The other arm is also scarred. I got it first at school for toothache." I could not say anything; I only stared. "But that's all over now," she went on briskly. "Today I have—but I'll tell you about that later. I knew there was only one way out, Miss Adams—to do it myself. Father and mother would have helped me, of course; but it would have been their will, not mine. I had to educate my own will to be strong enough. Oh, I'd thought it all out. And then— I did not want them to know. Even now, when I know it's over, I'm afraid to have them know. I've lied to keep it from them; but the detective knew it wasn't true."

She told me the whole story eagerly, frankly. It was clearly a relief. She had made her plans that summer and made them thoroughly. She had tried before and failed. This time there was the great incentive—she wished to marry.

"I wanted to bring children into the world, Miss Adams," she said. "I should not have dared—the way things were. All summer I tried and broke over. I was almost crazy. Then I got a letter from Julie—she had been my German teacher at school and I was fond of her. She had been taking care of an insane brother, who had died. She wanted to work again. Poor Julie!

"I thought she could help me. I knew it would be hard, though I didn't know—well, I wrote her the whole story and told her my plan. I had been here to see the brother with her; I knew the house. I asked her to send out after night for just enough to keep us going for a time. I did not want the house opened. I thought there would be a hue and cry and they might trace me to Julie."

"Your father and mother said they knew of no one named Julie."

"They would have known of her as Fräulein Schlenker. They had never seen her. I came to the city, bought some blankets and a book or two, and came out here. She was here and partly settled. She was against the plan even then; but I showed her my arms and she knew it was desperate. I had a supply of cocaine—I had got it in town. I was to have it—I should have died without—but she was to reduce the quantity. I locked myself in and gave her the key."

"You had been getting the cocaine from the man with the blond hair?"

"Yes. He was in a pharmacy at first—where I got the prescription filled. He suspected me after a time. When he lost his position he still got it for me. I met him wherever I could—on the street, in the park, anywhere; but generally we met by the Embankment. He robbed me, I think. I owed him a great deal finally. He took to bothering me about it. It used up all my allowance and more.

"I gave Julie the cocaine; and she was to reduce it—a little at a time. I suffered the tortures of the lost, Miss Adams—but perhaps you know. There were many days when I wanted to kill myself; and once Julie tied my hands behind my back. She was wonderful—wonderful! I owe it all to her. I was lost, Miss Adams—I would lie, steal, almost murder, to get the cocaine. I lived for it."

"All this was here in this house?"

"Upstairs—in the back room one window looked out over a field and could be kept unshuttered. I chose it. Besides, the fire from below heated it. We had only a little coal left in the cellar, and we could get none. Julie went out after night and did our buying. It—it all took longer than I had thought. I planned for a month. It was more than that. We were running out of money. At the end of five weeks we were desperate—and I sent Julie to the house."

I remembered that well enough! But I did not interrupt.

"Father always gave me the fees from directors' meetings; and, as they were in gold, I dropped them under the cushion of a silver box on my dressing table. Sometimes there would be several; most of them went eventually to—to the man I spoke of. Before we went away in the summer I had put some there; I could not remember how many—my mind was hazy—but I was sure there was perhaps fifty dollars. I had my own house keys with me and I gave Julie the key to the garden door. She was terribly frightened, but we were desperate. She got in without any trouble and got it. There was forty dollars."

I remembered something.

"Forty dollars and a book," I said, smiling.

"Forty dollars and a book—was it yours? The day came when she told me I had had no cocaine for a week. I was faint and dizzy, but I wrote a line to father and mother. I shouldn't have written it. It could never be reconciled with anything but the truth, and I was morbid about that. They were never to know. I did not want Mr. Plummer to know—I thought he would never trust me again. But I wrote it and Julie took it out. She never came back—and I was locked in, upstairs!"

"She never came back!"

"She was killed—struck by an automobile. I thought —didn't the detective know that? He had her bag."

So my little old lady was dead after all! I was sorry. What a spirit she had!

"I was locked in," Clare was saying. "I waited—and she did not come. I had not eaten for a day or so before, and there were two days and a night without even water. I was so desperate that I tried to call the other house; but the old woman had hurt herself, and there was no one about outside. I tried to break down the door. There was a panel in it—for the brother who was crazy. I could almost reach the key on the nail outside. The last day I think I was delirious. The key made faces at me through the panel. I told you, didn't I, about getting out of the window?"

"Yes. When did you learn about Julie?"

"The night I went home. I went down to the library and searched the newspapers. I felt that she had been hurt. As soon as I was strong enough I slipped away from the house; and—they were going to give her a pauper burial. I pawned a ring and, at least, she did not have that."

She broke down, after keeping up bravely for so long. I gathered from broken sentences her terrible fear of having the facts known; her despair over the tissue of falsehood and truth that she had told Mr. Patton; her fear of seeing her lover again until she was sure of herself; her grief for Julie's death and her self-accusation of it; her terror that day when Hortense had been able to discover in my closet only a part of the clothing she had worn. But after a time she looked up, smiling through her tears.

"I am really only crying over Julie," she said. "The rest is—all gone, Miss Adams. I am cured—really cured! Today I sat for an hour with a bottle of cocaine beside me, and—I did not touch it!"

That was my first case for Mr. Patton; and, though I really discovered nothing that Clare would not have told eventually herself, he was kind enough to say some very pleasant things.

"Though," he said, wincing as he tried to move his foot, "courage carried to the nth power is often foolishness! What possessed you to go to that house alone?"

"I wanted to locate the Landing of the Pilgrims."

He leaned back and looked up at me, smiling.

"Curiosity!" he said. "That was the only quality I was afraid you lacked." He took an envelope from the stand at his elbow and held it out.

"Your check, as per agreement."

"I don't want money, Mr. Patton. I—don't think I am silly; but I had my reward—if I deserved one, which, of course, I don't—when I saw Mr. Plummer's eyes last night. She went straight into his arms."

"You won't take the check?"

"No, thank you."

"Then I'll bank it for you. We are going to have some interesting cases together, Miss Adams, but I wish you were back here to look after me. There's a spineless creature here who lets me bully her. Do you know—

you're a queer woman! Taking as remuneration the sight of a young girl going into her lover's arms!"

"I've taken most of my pleasures and all of my sentiment vicariously for a number of years," I retorted. "And, even if it's the other person's, sentiment one has to have!"

"Yes," said Mr. Patton, looking at me curiously. "Sentiment one has to have!"

The bag is before me as I write. There are two keys—one to the house in Brickyard Road; the other to the garden door at the March home. The lavender envelope is there and its note from the blond youth—simply explained, as are all confusing things when one has a key. The envelope had contained the vial of cocaine that Clare took with her on her flight, and had come, of course, from the pharmacy clerk. I never examined the clipping carefully until today. It is curious to locate one's mental blind spot. I had read it many times.

The reverse is an advertisement for the cure of the drug habit.

LOCKED DOORS

LOCKED DOORS

"YOU promised," I reminded Mr. Patton, "to play with cards on the table."

"My dear young lady," he replied, "I have no cards! I suspect a game, that's all."

"Then—do you need me?"

The detective bent forward, his arms on his desk, and looked me over carefully.

"What sort of shape are you in? Tired?"

"No."

"Nervous?"

"Not enough to hurt."

"I want you to take another case, following a nurse who has gone to pieces," he said, selecting his words carefully. "I don't want to tell you a lot—I want you to go in with a fresh mind. It promises to be an extraordinary case."

"How long was the other nurse there?"

"Four days."

"She went to pieces in four days!"

"Well, she's pretty much unstrung. The worst is, she hasn't any real reason. A family chooses to live in an unusual manner, because they like it, or perhaps they're afraid of something. The girl was, that's sure. I had never seen her until this morning, a big, healthy-looking

1

young woman; but she came in looking back over her shoulder as if she expected a knife in her back. She said she was a nurse from St. Luke's and that she'd been on a case for four days. She'd left that morning after about three hours' sleep in that time, being locked in a room most of the time, and having little but crackers and milk for food. She thought it was a case for the police."

"Who is ill in the house? Who was her patient?"

"There is no illness, I believe. The French governess had gone, and they wished the children competently cared for until they replaced her. That was the reason given her when she went. Afterward she—well, she was puzzled."

"How are you going to get me there?"

He gathered acquiescence from my question and smiled approval.

"Good girl!" he said. "Never mind how I'll get you there. You are the most dependable woman I know."

"The most curious, perhaps?" I retorted. "Four days on the case, three hours' sleep, locked in and yelling 'Police'! Is it out of town?"

"No, in the heart of the city, on Beauregard Square. Can you get some St. Luke's uniforms? They want another St. Luke's nurse."

I said I could get the uniforms, and he wrote the address on a card.

"Better arrive about five," he said.

"But—if they are not expecting me?"

"They will be expecting you," he replied enigmatically.

"The doctor, if he's a St. Luke's man——"

"There is no doctor."

It was six months since I had solved, or helped to solve, the mystery of the buckled bag for Mr. Patton. I had had other cases for him in the interval, cases where the police could not get close enough. As I said when I began this record of my crusade against crime and the criminal, a trained nurse gets under the very skin of the soul. She finds a mind surrendered, all the crooked little motives that have fired the guns of life revealed in their pitifulness.

Gradually I had come to see that Mr. Patton's point of view was right; that if the criminal uses every means against society, why not society against the criminal? At first I had used this as a flag of truce to my nurse's ethical training; now I flaunted it, a mental and moral banner. The criminal against society, and I against the criminal! And, more than that, against misery, healing pain by augmenting it sometimes, but working like a surgeon, for good.

I had had six cases in six months. Only in one had I failed to land my criminal, and that without any suspicion of my white uniform and rubber-soled shoes. Although I played a double game no patient of mine had suffered. I was a nurse first and a police agent second. If it was a question between turpentine compresses—stupes, professionally—and seeing what letters came in or went out of the house, the compress went on first, and cracking hot too. I am not boasting. That is my method, the only way I can work, and it speaks well for it that, as I say, only one man escaped arrest—an arson case where the factory owner hanged himself in the bathroom needle shower in the house he had bought with the insurance money, while I was fixing his breakfast tray. And even he might have been saved for justice had the cook not burned the toast and been obliged to make it fresh.

I was no longer staying at a nurses' home. I had taken a bachelor suite of three rooms and bath, comfortably downtown. I cooked my own breakfasts when I was off duty and I dined at a restaurant near. Luncheon I did not bother much about. Now and then Mr. Patton telephoned me and we lunched together in remote places where we would not be known. He would tell me of his cases and sometimes he asked my advice.

I bought my uniforms that day and took them home in a taxicab. The dresses were blue, and over them for the street the St. Luke's girls wear long cloaks, English fashion, of navy blue serge, and a blue bonnet with a white ruching and white lawn ties. I felt curious in it, but it was becoming and convenient. Certainly I looked professional.

At three o'clock that afternoon a messenger brought a small box, registered. It contained a St. Luke's badge of gold and blue enamel.

At four o'clock my telephone rang. I was packing my suitcase according to the list I keep pasted in the lid. Under the list, which was of uniforms, aprons, thermometer, instruments, a nurse's simple set of probe, forceps and bandage scissors, was the word "box." This always went in first—a wooden box with a lock, the key of which was round my neck. It contained skeleton keys, a small black revolver of which I was in deadly fear, a pair of handcuffs, a pocket flashlight, and my badge from the chief of police. I was examining the revolver nervously when the telephone rang, and I came within an ace of sending a bullet into the flat below.

Did you ever notice how much you get out of a telephone voice? We can dissemble with our faces, but under stress the vocal cords seem to draw up tight and the voice comes thin and colorless. There's a little woman in the flat beneath—the one I nearly bombarded—who sings like a bird at her piano half the day, scaling vocal heights that make me dizzy. Now and then she has a visitor, a nice young man, and she disgraces herself, flats F, fogs E even, finally takes cowardly refuge in a wretched mezzo-soprano and cries herself to sleep, doubtless, later on.

The man who called me had the thin-drawn voice of extreme strain—a youngish voice.

"Miss Adams," he said, "this is Francis Reed speaking. I have called St. Luke's and they referred me to you. Are you free to take a case this afternoon?"

I fenced. I was trying to read the voice.

"This afternoon?"

"Well, before night anyhow; as—as early this evening as possible."

The voice was strained and tired, desperately tired. It was not peevish. It was even rather pleasant.

"What is the case, Mr. Reed?"

He hesitated. "It is not illness. It is merely—the governess has gone and there are two small children. We want some one to give her undivided attention to the children."

"I see."

"Are you a heavy sleeper, Miss Adams?"

"A very light one." I fancied he breathed freer.

"I hope you are not tired from a previous case?" I was beginning to like the voice.

"I'm quite fresh," I replied almost gayly. "Even if I were not, I like children, especially well ones. I shan't find looking after them very wearying, I'm sure."

Again the odd little pause. Then he gave me the address on Beauregard Square, and asked me to be sure not to be late.

"I must warn you," he added; "we are living in a sort of casual way. Our servants left us without warning. Mrs. Reed has been getting along as best she could. Most of our meals are being sent in."

I was thinking fast. No servants! A good many people think a trained nurse is a sort of upper servant. I've been in houses where they were amazed to discover that I was a college woman and, finding the two things irreconcilable, have openly accused me of having been driven to such a desperate course as a hospital training by an unfortunate love affair.

"Of course you understand that I will look after the children to the best of my ability, but that I will not replace the servants."

I fancied he smiled grimly.

"That of course. Will you ring twice when you come?"

"Ring twice?"

"The doorbell," he replied impatiently.

I said I would ring the doorbell twice.

The young woman below was caroling gayly, ignorant of the six-barreled menace over her head. I knelt again by my suitcase, but packed little and thought a great deal. I was to arrive before dusk at a house where there were no servants and to ring the doorbell twice. I was to be a light sleeper, although I was to look after two healthy children. It was not much in itself, but, taken in connection with the previous nurse's appeal to the police, it took on new possibilities.

At six I started out to dinner. It was early spring and cold, but quite light. At the first corner I saw Mr. Patton waiting for a street car, and at his quick nod I saw I was to get in also. He did not pay my fare or speak to me. It was a part of the game that we were never seen together except at the remote restaurant I mentioned before. The car thinned out and I could watch him easily. Far downtown he alighted and so did I. The restaurant was near. I went in alone and sat down at a table in a recess, and very soon he joined me. We were in the main dining room but not of it, a sop at once to the conventions and to the necessity, where he was so well known, for caution.

"I got a little information—on—the affair we were talking of," he said as he sat down. "I'm not so sure I want you to take the case after all."

"Certainly I shall take it," I retorted with some sharpness. "I've promised to go."

"Tut! I'm not going to send you into danger unnecessarily."

"I am not afraid."

"Exactly. A lot of generals were lost in the Civil War because they were not afraid and wanted to lead their troops instead of saving themselves and their expensive West Point training by sitting back in a safe spot and directing the fight. Any fool can run into danger. It takes intellect to keep out."

I felt my color rising indignantly.

"Then you brought me here to tell me I am not to go?"

"Will you let me read you two reports?"

"You could have told me that at the corner!"

"Will you let me read you two reports?"

"If you don't mind I'll first order something to eat. I'm to be there before dark."

"Will you let me——"

"I'm going, and you know I'm going. If you don't want me to represent you I'll go on my own. They want a nurse, and they're in trouble."

I think he was really angry. I know I was. If there is anything that takes the very soul out of a woman, it is to be kept from doing a thing she has set her heart on, because some man thinks it dangerous. If she has any spirit, that rouses it.

Mr. Patton quietly replaced the reports in his wallet and his wallet in the inside pocket of his coat, and fell to a judicial survey of the menu. But although he did not even glance at me he must have felt the determination in my face, for he ordered things that were quickly prepared and told the waiter to hurry.

"I have wondered lately," he said slowly, "whether the mildness of your manner at the hospital was acting, or the chastening effect of three years under an order book."

"A man always likes a woman to be a sheep."

"Not at all. But it is rather disconcerting to have a pet lamb turn round and take a bite out of one."

"Will you read the reports now?"

"I think," he said quietly, "they would better wait until we have eaten. We will probably both feel calmer. Suppose we arrange that nothing said before the oysters counts?"

I agreed, rather sulkily, and the meal went off well enough. I was anxious enough to hurry but he ate deliberately, drank his demi-tasse, paid the waiter, and at last met my impatient eyes and smiled.

"After all," he said, "since you are determined to go anyhow, what's the use of reading the reports? Inside of an hour you'll know all you need to know." But he saw that I did not take his teasing well, and drew out his pocketbook.

They were two typewritten papers clamped together.

They are on my desk before me now. The first one is indorsed:

Statement by Laura J. Bosworth, nurse, of St. Luke's Home for Graduate Nurses.

Miss Bosworth says:

I do not know just why I came here. But I know I'm frightened. That's the fact. I think there is something terribly wrong in the house of Francis M. Reed, 71 Beauregard Square. I think a crime of some sort has been committed. There are four people in the family, Mr. and Mrs. Reed and two children. I was to look after the children.

I was there four days and the children were never allowed out of the room. At night we were locked in. I kept wondering what I would do if there was a fire. The telephone wires are cut so no one can call the house, and I believe the doorbell is disconnected too. But that's fixed now. Mrs. Reed went round all the time with a face like chalk and her eyes staring. At all hours of the night she'd unlock the bedroom door and come in and look at the children.

Almost all the doors through the house were locked. If I wanted to get to the kitchen to boil eggs for the children's breakfast—for there were no servants, and Mrs. Reed was young and didn't know anything about cooking—Mr. Reed had to unlock about four doors for me.

If Mrs. Reed looked bad, he was dreadful—sunken eyed and white and wouldn't eat. I think he has killed somebody and is making away with the body.

Last night I said I had to have air, and they let me go out. I called up a friend from a pay-station, another nurse. This morning she sent me a special-delivery letter that l was needed on another case, and I got away. That's all; it sounds foolish, but try it and see if it doesn't get on you r nerves.

Mr. Patton looked up at me as he finished reading.

"Now you see what I mean," he said. "That woman was there four days, and she is as temperamental as a cow, but in those four days her nervous system went to smash."

"Doors locked!" I reflected. "Servants gone; state of fear—it looks like a siege!"

"But why a trained nurse? Why not a policeman, if there is danger? Why any one at all, if there is something that the police are not to know?"

"That is what I intend to find out," I replied. He shrugged his shoulders and read the other paper:

Report of Detective Bennett on Francis M. Reed, April 5, 1913:

Francis M. Reed is thirty-six years of age, married, a chemist at the Olympic Paint Works. He has two children, both boys. Has a small independent income and owns the house on Beauregard Square, which was built by his grandfather, General F. R. Reed. Is supposed to be living beyond his means. House is usually full of servants, and grocer in the neighborhood has had to wait for money several times.

On March twenty-ninth he dismissed all servants without warning. No reason given, but a week's wages instead of notice.

On March thirtieth he applied to the owners of the paint factory for two weeks' vacation. Gave as his reason nervousness and insomnia. He said he was "going to lay off and get some sleep." Has not been back at the works since. House under surveillance this afternoon. No visitors.

Mr. Reed telephoned for a nurse at four o'clock from a store on Eleventh Street. Explained that his telephone was out of order.

Mr. Patton folded up the papers and thrust them back into his pocket. Evidently he saw I was determined, for he only said:

"Have you got your revolver?"

"Yes."

"Do you know anything about telephones? Could you repair that one in an emergency?"

"In an emergency," I retorted, "there is no time to repair a telephone. But I've got a voice and there are

windows. If I really put my mind to it you will hear
me yell at headquarters."

He smiled grimly.

II

The Reed house is on Beauregard Square. It is a
small, exclusive community, the Beauregard neighborhood; a dozen or more solid citizens built their homes
there in the early 70's, occupying large lots, the houses
flush with the streets and with gardens behind. Six on
one street, six on another, back to back with the gardens
in the center, they occupied the whole block. And the
gardens were not fenced off, but made a sort of small
park unsuspected from the streets. Here and there bits
of flowering shrubbery sketchily outlined a property, but
the general impression was of lawn and trees, free of
access to all the owners. Thus with the square in front
and the gardens in the rear, the Reed house faced in two
directions on the early spring green.

In the gardens the old tar walks were still there, and
a fountain which no longer played, but on whose stone
coping I believe the young Beauregard Squarites made
their first climbing ventures.

The gardens were always alive with birds, and later
on from my windows I learned the reason. It seems to
have been a custom sanctified by years, that the crumbs
from the twelve tables should be thrown into the dry
basin of the fountain for the birds. It was a common
sight to see stately butlers and *chic* little waitresses in
black and white coming out after luncheon or dinner with
silver trays of crumbs. Many a scrap of gossip, as well

as scrap of food, has been passed along at the old stone fountain, I believe. I know that it was there that I heard of the "basement ghost" of Beauregard Square—a whisper at first, a panic later.

I arrived at eight o'clock and rang the doorbell twice. The door was opened at once by Mr. Reed, a tall, blond young man carefully dressed. He threw away his cigarette when he saw me and shook hands. The hall was brightly lighted and most cheerful; in fact the whole house was ablaze with light. Certainly nothing could be less mysterious than the house, or than the debonair young man who motioned me into the library.

"I told Mrs. Reed I would talk to you before you go upstairs," he said. "Will you sit down?"

I sat down. The library was even brighter than the hall, and now I saw that although he smiled as cheerfully as ever his face was almost colorless, and his eyes, which looked frankly enough into mine for a moment, went wandering off round the room. I had the impression somehow that Mr. Patton had had of the nurse at headquarters that morning—that he looked as if he expected a knife in his back. It seemed to me that he wanted to look over his shoulder and by sheer will-power did not.

"You know the rule, Miss Adams," he said: "When there's an emergency get a trained nurse. I told you our emergency—no servants and two small children."

"This should be a good time to secure servants," I said briskly. "City houses are being deserted for country places, and a percentage of servants won't leave town."

He hesitated.

"We've been doing very nicely, although of course it's

hardly more than just living. Our meals are sent in from a hotel, and—well, we thought, since we are going away so soon, that perhaps we could manage."

The impulse was too strong for him at that moment. He wheeled and looked behind him, not a hasty glance, but a deliberate inspection that took in every part of that end of the room. It was so unexpected that it left me gasping.

The next moment he was himself again.

"When I say that there is no illness," he said, "I am hardly exact. There is no illness, but there has been an epidemic of children's diseases among the Beauregard Square children and we are keeping the youngsters indoors."

"Don't you think they could be safeguarded without being shut up in the house?"

He responded eagerly

"If I only thought——" he checked himself. "No," he said decidedly; "for a time at least I believe it is not wise."

I did not argue with him. There was nothing to be gained by antagonizing him. And as Mrs. Reed came in just then, the subject was dropped. She was hardly more than a girl, almost as blond as her husband, very pretty, and with the weariest eyes I have ever seen, unless perhaps the eyes of a man who has waited a long time for deathly tuberculosis.

I liked her at once. She did not attempt to smile. She rather clung to my hand when I held it out.

"I am glad St. Luke's still trusts us," she said. "I was afraid the other nurse—— Frank, will you take Miss Adams' suitcase upstairs?"

She held out a key. He took it, but he turned at the door:

"I wish you wouldn't wear those things, Anne. You gave me your promise yesterday, you remember."

"I can't work round the children in anything else," she protested.

"Those things" were charming. She wore a rose silk negligee trimmed with soft bands of lace and blue satin flowers, a petticoat to match that garment, and a lace cap.

He hesitated in the doorway and looked at her—a curious glance, I thought, full of tenderness, reproof—apprehension perhaps.

"I'll take it off, dear," she replied to the glance. "I wanted Miss Adams to know that, even if we haven't a servant in the house, we are at least civilized. I—I haven't taken cold." This last was clearly an afterthought.

He went out then and left us together. She came over to me swiftly.

"What did the other nurse say?" she demanded.

"I do not know her at all. I have not seen her."

"Didn't she report at the hospital that we were—queer?"

I smiled.

"That's hardly likely, is it?"

Unexpectedly she went to the door opening into the hall and closed it, coming back swiftly.

"Mr. Reed thinks it is not necessary, but—there are some things that will puzzle you. Perhaps I should have spoken to the other nurse. If—if anything strikes you as unusual, Miss Adams, just please don't see it! It is all right, everything is all right. But something has occurred—not very much, but disturbing—and we are all of us doing the very best we can."

She was quivering with nervousness.

I was not the police agent then, I'm afraid.

"Nurses are accustomed to disturbing things. Perhaps I can help."

"You can, by watching the children. That's the only thing that matters to me—the children. I don't want them left alone. If you have to leave them call me."

"Don't you think I will be able to watch them more intelligently if I know just what the danger is?"

I think she very nearly told me. She was so tired, evidently so anxious to shift her burden to fresh shoulders.

"Mr. Reed said," I prompted her, "that there was an epidemic of children's diseases. But from what you say——"

But I was not to learn, after all, for her husband opened the hall door.

"Yes, children's diseases," she said vaguely. "So many children are down. Shall we go up, Frank?"

The extraordinary bareness of the house had been dawning on me for some time. It was well lighted and well furnished. But the floors were innocent of rugs, the handsome furniture was without arrangement and, in the library at least, stood huddled in the center of the room. The hall and stairs were also uncarpeted, but there were marks where carpets had recently lain and had been jerked up.

The progress up the staircase was not calculated to soothe my nerves. The thought of my little revolver, locked in my suitcase, was poor comfort. For with every four steps or so Mr. Reed, who led the way, turned automatically and peered into the hallway below; he was listening, too, his head bent slightly forward. And each time that he turned, his wife behind me turned also. Cold terror suddenly got me by the spine, and yet the hall was bright with light.

(Note: Surely fear is a contagion. Could one isolate the germ of it and find an antitoxin? Or is it merely a form of nervous activity run amuck, like a runaway locomotive, colliding with other nervous activities and causing catastrophe? Take this up with Mr. Patton. But would he know? He, I am almost sure, has never been really afraid.)

I had a vision of my oxlike predecessor making this head-over-shoulder journey up the staircase, and in spite of my nervousness I smiled. But at that moment Mrs. Reed behind me put a hand on my arm, and I screamed. I remember yet the way she dropped back against the wall and turned white.

Mr. Reed whirled on me instantly.

"What did you see?" he demanded.

"Nothing at all." I was horribly ashamed. "Your wife touched my arm unexpectedly. I dare say I am nervous."

"It's all right, Anne," he reassured her. And to me, almost irritably:

"I thought you nurses had no nerves."

"Under ordinary circumstances I have none."

It was all ridiculous. We were still on the staircase.

"Just what do you mean by that?"

"If you will stop looking down into that hall I'll be calm enough. You make me jumpy."

He muttered something about being sorry and went on quickly. But at the top he went through an inward struggle, evidently succumbed, and took a final furtive survey of the hallway below. I was so wrought up that had a door slammed anywhere just then I think I should have dropped where I stood.

The absolute silence of the house added to the strangeness of the situation. Beauregard Square is not close to a trolley line, and quiet is the neighborhood tradition. The first rubber-tired vehicles in the city drew up before Beauregard Square houses. Beauregard Square children speak in low voices and never bang their spoons on their plates. Beauregard Square servants wear felt-soled shoes. And such outside noises as venture to intrude themselves must filter through double brick walls and doors built when lumber was selling by the thousand acres instead of the square foot.

Through this silence our feet echoed along the bare floor of the upper hall, as well lighted as belowstairs and as dismantled, to the door of the day nursery. The door was locked—double locked, in fact. For the key had been turned in the old-fashioned lock, and in addition an ordinary bolt had been newly fastened on the outside of the door. On the outside! Was that to keep me in? It was certainly not to keep any one or anything out. The feeblest touch moved the bolt.

We were all three outside the door. We seemed to keep our compactness by common consent. No one of us left the group willingly; or, leaving it, we slid back again quickly. That was my impression, at least. But the bolt rather alarmed me.

"This is your room," Mrs. Reed said. "It is generally

the day nursery, but we have put a bed and some other things in it. I hope you will be comfortable."

I touched the bolt with my finger and smiled into Mr. Reed's eyes.

"I hope I am not to be fastened in!" I said.

He looked back squarely enough, but somehow I knew he lied.

"Certainly not," he replied, and opened the door.

If there had been mystery outside, and bareness, the nursery was charming—a corner room with many windows, hung with the simplest of nursery papers and full of glass-doored closets filled with orderly rows of toys. In one corner a small single bed had been added without spoiling the room. The window-sills were full of flowering plants. There was a bowl of goldfish on a stand, and a tiny dwarf parrot in a cage was covered against the night air by a bright afghan. A white-tiled bathroom connected with this room and also with the night nursery beyond.

Mr. Reed did not come in, I had an uneasy feeling, however, that he was just beyond the door. The children were not asleep. Mrs. Reed left me to let me put on my uniform. When she came back her face was troubled.

"They are not sleeping well," she complained. "I suppose it comes from having no exercise. They are always excited."

"I'll take their temperatures," I said. "Sometimes a tepid bath and a cup of hot milk will make them sleep."

The two little boys were wide awake. They sat up to look at me and both spoke at once.

"Can you tell fairy tales out of your head?"

"Did you see Chang?"

They were small, sleek-headed, fair-skinned youngsters, adorably clean and rumpled.

"Chang is their dog, a Pekingese," explained the mother. "He has been lost for several days."

"But he isn't lost, mother. I can hear him crying every now and then. You'll look again, mother, won't you?"

"We heard him through the furnace pipe," shrilled the smaller of the two. "You said you would look."

"I did look, darlings. He isn't there. And you promised not to cry about him, Freddie."

Freddie, thus put on his honor, protested he was not crying for the dog.

"I want to go out and take a walk, that's why I'm crying," he wailed. "And I want Mademoiselle, and my buttons are all off. And my ear aches when I lie on it."

The room was close. I threw up the windows, and turned to find Mrs. Reed at my elbows. She was glancing out apprehensively.

"I suppose the air is necessary," she said, "and these windows are all right. But—I have a reason for asking it—please do not open the others."

She went very soon, and I listened as she went out. I had promised to lock the door behind her, and I did so. The bolt outside was not shot.

After I had quieted the children with my mildest fairy story I made a quiet inventory of my new quarters. The rough diagram of the second floor is the one I gave Mr. Patton later. That night, of course, I investigated only the two nurseries. But, so strangely had the fear that hung over the house infected me, I confess that I made

my little tour of bathroom and clothes-closet with my
revolver in my hand!

I found nothing, of course. The disorder of the house
had not extended itself here. The bathroom was spotless
with white tile, the large clothes-closet which opened off
the passage between the two rooms was full of neatly
folded clothing for the children. The closet was to play
its part later, a darkish little room faintly lighted by a
ground glass transom opening into the center hall, but
dependent mostly on electric light.

Outside the windows Mrs. Reed had asked me not to
open was a porte-cochère roof almost level with the sills.
Then was it an outside intruder she feared? And in
that case, why the bolts on the outside of the two nursery
doors? For the night nursery, I found, must have one
also. I turned the key, but the door would not open.

I decided not to try to sleep that night, but to keep
on watch. So powerfully had the mother's anxiety about
her children and their mysterious danger impressed me
that I made frequent excursions into the back room. Up
to midnight there was nothing whatever to alarm me. I
darkened both rooms and sat, waiting for I know not
what; for some sound to show that the house stirred,
perhaps. At a few minutes after twelve faint noises penetrated to my room from the hall, Mr. Reed's nervous
voice and a piece of furniture scraping over the floor.
Then silence again for half an hour or so.

Then—I was quite certain that the bolt on my door
had been shot. I did not hear it, I think. Perhaps I
felt it. Perhaps I only feared it. I unlocked the door;
it was fastened outside.

There is a hideous feeling of helplessness about being

locked in. I pretended to myself at first that I was only interested and curious. But I was frightened; I know that now. I sat there in the dark and wondered what I would do if the house took fire, or if some hideous tragedy enacted itself outside that locked door and I were helpless.

By two o'clock I had worked myself into a panic. The house was no longer silent. Some one was moving about downstairs, and not stealthily. The sounds came up through the heavy joists and flooring of the old house.

I determined to make at least a struggle to free myself. There was no way to get at the bolts, of course. The porte-cochère roof remained and the transom in the clothes-closet. True, I might have raised an alarm and been freed at once, but naturally I rejected this method. The roof of the porte-cochère proved impracticable. The tin bent and cracked under my first step. The transom then.

I carried a chair into the closet and found the transom easy to lower. But it threatened to creak. I put liquid soap on the hinges—it was all I had, and it worked very well—and lowered the transom inch by inch. Even then I could not see over it. I had worked so far without a sound, but in climbing to a shelf my foot slipped and I thought I heard a sharp movement outside. It was five minutes before I stirred. I hung there, every muscle cramped, listening and waiting. Then I lifted myself by sheer force of muscle and looked out. The upper landing of the staircase, brilliantly lighted, was to my right. Across the head of the stairs had been pushed a cotbed, made up for the night, but it was unoccupied.

Mrs. Reed, in a long, dark ulster, was standing beside it, staring with fixed and glassy eyes at something in the lower hall.

III

Some time after four o'clock my door was unlocked from without; the bolt slipped as noiselessly as it had been shot. I got a little sleep until seven, when the boys trotted into my room in their bathrobes and slippers and perched on my bed.

"It's a nice day," observed Harry, the elder. "Is that bump your feet?"

I wriggled my toes and assured him he had surmised correctly.

"You're pretty long, aren't you? Do you think we can play in the fountain to-day?"

"We'll make a try for it, son. It will do us all good to get out into the sunshine."

"We always took Chang for a walk every day, Mademoiselle and Chang and Freddie and I."

Freddie had found my cap on the dressing table and had put it on his yellow head. But now, on hearing the beloved name of his pet, he burst into loud grief-stricken howls.

"Want Mam'selle," he cried. "Want Chang too. Poor Freddie!"

The children were adorable. I bathed and dressed them and, mindful of my predecessor's story of crackers and milk, prepared for an excursion kitchenward. The nights might be full of mystery, murder might romp from room to room, but I intended to see that the youngsters breakfasted. But before I was ready to go down breakfast arrived.

Perhaps the other nurse had told the Reeds a few plain truths before she left; perhaps, and this I think was the case, the cloud had lifted just a little. Whatever it may have been, two rather flushed and blistered young people tapped at the door that morning and were admitted, Mr. Reed first, with a tray, Mrs. Reed following with a coffee-pot and cream.

The little nursery table was small for five, but we made room somehow. What if the eggs were underdone and the toast dry? The children munched blissfully. What if Mr. Reed's face was still drawn and haggard and his wife a limp little huddle on the floor? She sat with her head against his knee and her eyes on the little boys, and drank her pale coffee slowly. She was very tired, poor thing. She dropped asleep sitting there, and he sat for a long time, not liking to disturb her.

It made me feel homesick for the home I didn't have. I've had the same feeling before, of being a rank outsider, a sort of defrauded feeling. I've had it when I've seen the look in a man's eyes when his wife comes-to after an operation. And I've had it, for that matter, when I've put a new baby in its mother's arms for the first time. I had it for sure that morning, while she slept there and he stroked her pretty hair.

I put in my plea for the children then.

"It's bright and sunny," I argued. "And if you are nervous I'll keep them away from other children. But if you want to keep them well you must give them exercise."

It was the argument about keeping them well that

influenced him, I think. He sat silent for a long time. His wife was still asleep, her lips parted.

"Very well," he said finally, "from two to three, Miss Adams. But not in the garden back of the house. Take them on the street."

I agreed to that.

"I shall want a short walk every evening myself," I added. "That is a rule of mine. I am a more useful person and a more agreeable one if I have it."

I think he would have demurred if he dared. But one does not easily deny so sane a request. He yielded grudgingly.

That first day was calm and quiet enough. Had it not been for the strange condition of the house and the necessity for keeping the children locked in I would have smiled at my terror of the night. Luncheon was sent in; so was dinner. The children and I lunched and supped alone. As far as I could see, Mrs. Reed made no attempt at housework; but the cot at the head of the stairs disappeared in the early morning and the dog did not howl again.

I took the boys out for an hour in the early afternoon. Two incidents occurred, both of them significant. I bought myself a screw driver—that was one. The other was our meeting with a slender young woman in black who knew the boys and stopped them. She proved to be one of the dismissed servants—the waitress, she said.

"Why, Freddie!" she cried. "And Harry too! Aren't you going to speak to Nora?"

After a moment or two she turned to me, and I felt she wanted to say something, but hardly dared.

"How is Mrs. Reed?" she asked. "Not sick, I hope?"

She glanced at my St. Luke's cloak and bonnet.

"No, she is quite well."

"And Mr. Reed?"

"Quite well also."

"Is Mademoiselle still there?"

"No, there is no one there but the family. There are no maids in the house."

She stared at me curiously

"Mademoiselle has gone? Are you cer—— Excuse me, Miss. But I thought she would never go. The children were like her own."

"She is not there, Nora."

She stood for a moment debating, I thought. Then she burst out:

"Mr. Reed made a mistake, miss. You can't take a houseful of first-class servants and dismiss them the way he did, without half an hour to get out bag and baggage, without making talk. And there's talk enough all through the neighborhood."

"What sort of talk?"

"Different people say different things. They say Mademoiselle is still there, locked in her room on the third floor. There's a light there sometimes, but nobody sees her. And other folks say Mr. Reed is crazy. And there is worse being said than that."

But she refused to tell me any more—evidently concluded she had said too much and got away as quickly as she could, looking rather worried.

I was a trifle over my hour getting back, but nothing was said. To leave the clean and tidy street for the disordered house was not pleasant. But once in the children's suite, with the goldfish in the aquarium darting like tongues of flame in the sunlight, with the tulips and hyacinths of the window-boxes glowing and the orderly toys on their white shelves, I felt comforted. After all, disorder and dust did not imply crime.

But one thing I did that afternoon—did it with firmness and no attempt at secrecy, and after asking permission of no one. I took the new screw driver and unfastened the bolt from the outside of my door.

I was prepared, if necessary, to make a stand on that issue. But although it was noticed, I knew, no mention of it was made to me.

Mrs. Reed pleaded a headache that evening, and I believe her husband ate alone in the dismantled dining room. For every room on the lower floor, I had discovered, was in the same curious disorder.

At seven Mr. Reed relieved me to go out. The children were in bed. He did not go into the day nursery, but placed a straight chair outside the door of the back room and sat there, bent over, elbows on knees, chin cupped in his palm, staring at the staircase. He roused enough to ask me to bring an evening paper when I returned.

When I am on a department case I always take my off-duty in the evening by arrangement and walk round the block. Some time in my walk I am sure to see Mr. Patton himself if the case is big enough, or one of his agents if he cannot come. If I have nothing to communicate it resolves itself into a bow and nothing more.

I was nervous on this particular jaunt. For one thing my St. Luke's cloak and bonnet marked me at once, made me conspicuous; for another, I was afraid Mr. Patton would think the Reed house no place for a woman and order me home.

It was a quarter to eight and quite dark before he fell into step beside me.

"Well," I replied rather shakily; "I'm still alive, as you see."

"Then it is pretty bad?"

"It's exceedingly queer," I admitted, and told my story. I had meant to conceal the bolt on the outside of my door, and one or two other things, but I blurted them all out right then and there, and felt a lot better at once.

He listened intently.

"It's fear of the deadliest sort," I finished.

"Fear of the police?"

"I—I think not. It is fear of something in the house. They are always listening and watching at the top of the front stairs. They have lifted all the carpets, so that every footstep echoes through the whole house. Mrs. Reed goes down to the first door, but never alone. To-day I found that the back staircase is locked off at top and bottom. There are doors."

I gave him my rough diagram of the house. It was too dark to see it.

"It is only tentative," I explained. "So much of the house is locked up, and every movement of mine is under surveillance. Without baths there are about twelve large rooms, counting the third floor. I've not been able to get there, but I thought that to-night I'd try to look about."

"You had no sleep last night?"

"Three hours—from four to seven this morning."

We had crossed into the public square and were walking slowly under the trees. Now he stopped and faced me.

"I don't like the look of it, Miss Adams," he said. "Ordinary panic goes and hides. But here's a fear that knows what it's afraid of and takes methodical steps for protection. I didn't want you to take the case, you know that; but now I'm not going to insult you by asking you to give it up. But I'm going to see that you are protected. There will be some one across the street every night as long as you are in the house."

"Have you any theory?" I asked him. He is not strong for theories generally. He is very practical. "That is, do you think the other nurse was right and there is some sort of crime being concealed?"

"Well, think about it," he prompted me. "If a murder has been committed, what are they afraid of? The police? Then why a trained nurse and all this caution about the children? A ghost? Would they lift the carpets so that they could hear the specter tramping about?"

"If there is no crime, but something—a lunatic perhaps?" I asked.

"Possibly. But then why this secrecy and keeping out the police? It is, of course, possible that your respected employers have both gone off mentally, and the whole thing is a nightmare delusion. On my word it sounds like it. But it's too much for credulity to believe they've both gone crazy with the same form of delusion."

"Perhaps I'm the lunatic," I said despairingly. "When you reduce it like that to an absurdity I wonder if I didn't imagine it all, the lights burning everywhere and the carpets up, and Mrs. Reed staring down the staircase, and

I locked in a room and hanging on by my nails to peer out through a closet transom."

"Perhaps.   But how about the deadly sane young woman who preceded you?   She had no imagination. Now about Reed and his wife—how do they strike you?   They get along all right and that sort of thing, I suppose?"

"They are nice people," I said emphatically.   "He's a gentleman and they're devoted.   He just looks like a big boy who's got into an awful mess and doesn't know how to get out.   And she's backing him up.   She's a dear."

"Humph!" said Mr. Patton.   "Don't suppress any evidence because she's a dear and he's a handsome big boy!"

"I didn't say he was handsome," I snapped.

"Did you ever see a ghost or think you saw one?" he inquired suddenly.

"No, but one of my aunts has.   Hers always carry their heads.   She asked one a question once and the head nodded."

"Then you believe in things of that sort?"

"Not a particle—but I'm afraid of them."

He smiled, and shortly after that I went back to the house.   I think he was sorry about the ghost question, for he explained that he had been trying me out, and that I looked well in my cloak and bonnet.

"I'm afraid of your chin generally," he said; "but the white lawn ties have a softening effect.   In view of the ties I have almost the courage——"

"Yes?"

"I think not, after all," he decided.   "The chin is there,

ties or no ties. Good-night, and—for heaven's sake don't run any unnecessary risks."

The change from his facetious tone to earnestness was so unexpected that I was still standing there on the pavement when he plunged into the darkness of the square and disappeared.

IV

At ten minutes after eight I was back in the house. Mr. Reed admitted me, going through the tedious process of unlocking outer and inner vestibule doors and fastening them again behind me. He inquired politely if I had had a pleasant walk, and without waiting for my reply fell to reading the evening paper. He seemed to have forgotten me absolutely. First he scanned the headlines; then he turned feverishly to something farther on and ran his fingers down along a column. His lips were twitching, but evidently he did not find what he expected—or feared—for he threw the paper away and did not glance at it again. I watched him from the angle of the stairs.

Even for that short interval Mrs. Reed had taken his place at the children's door.

She wore a black dress, long sleeved and high at the throat, instead of the silk negligee of the previous evening, and she held a book. But she was not reading. She smiled rather wistfully when she saw me.

"How fresh you always look!" she said. "And so self-reliant. I wish I had your courage."

"I am perfectly well. I dare say that explains a lot. Kiddies asleep?"

"Freddie isn't. He has been crying for Chang. I hate

night, Miss Adams.   I'm like Freddie.   All my troubles
come up about this time.   I'm horribly depressed."

Her blue eyes filled with tears.

"I haven't been sleeping well," she confessed.

I should think not!

Without taking off my things I went down to Mr.
Reed in the lower hall.

"I'm going to insist on something," I said.   "Mrs.
Reed is highly nervous.   She says she has not been sleeping.   I think if I give her an opiate and she gets an
entire night's sleep it may save her a breakdown."

I looked straight in his eyes, and for once he did
evade me.

"I'm afraid I've been very selfish," he said.   "Of
course she must have sleep.   I'll give you a powder, unless
you have something you prefer to use."

I remembered then that he was a chemist, and said I
would gladly use whatever he gave me.

"There is another thing I wanted to speak about, Mr.
Reed," I said.   "The children are mourning their dog.
Don't you think he may have been accidentally shut up
somewhere in the house in one of the upper floors?"

"Why do you say that?" he demanded sharply.

"They say they have heard him howling."

He hesitated for barely a moment.   Then:

"Possibly," he said.   "But they will not hear him
again.   The little chap has been sick, and he—died to-day.
Of course the boys are not to know."

No one watched the staircase that night.   I gave Mrs.
Reed the opiate and saw her comfortably into bed.   When
I went back fifteen minutes later she was resting, but not

asleep. Opiates sometimes make people garrulous for a little while—sheer comfort, perhaps, and relaxed tension. I've had stockbrokers and bankers in the hospital give me tips, after a hypodermic of morphia, that would have made me wealthy had I not been limited to my training allowance of twelve dollars a month.

"I was just wondering," she said as I tucked her up, "where a woman owes the most allegiance—to her husband or to her children?"

"Why not split it up," I said cheerfully, "and try doing what seems best for both?"

"But that's only a compromise!" she complained, and was asleep almost immediately. I lowered the light and closed the door, and shortly after I heard Mr. Reed locking it from the outside.

With the bolt off my door and Mrs. Reed asleep my plan for the night was easily carried out. I went to bed for a couple of hours and slept calmly. I awakened once with the feeling that some one was looking at me from the passage into the night nursery, but there was no one there. However, so strong had been the feeling that I got up and went into the back room. The children were asleep, and all doors opening into the hall were locked. But the window on to the porte-cochère roof was open and the curtain blowing. There was no one on the roof.

It was not twelve o'clock and I still had an hour. I went back to bed.

At one I prepared to make a thorough search of the house. Looking from one of my windows I thought I saw the shadowy figure of a man across the street, and I was comforted. Help was always close, I felt. And yet, as I stood inside my door in my rubber-soled shoes, with my ulster over my uniform and a revolver and my skeleton keys in my pockets, my heart was going very fast. The stupid story of the ghost came back and made me shudder, and the next instant I was remembering Mrs. Reed the night before, staring down into the lower hall with fixed glassy eyes.

My plan was to begin at the top of the house and work down. The thing was the more hazardous, of course, because Mr. Reed was most certainly somewhere about. I had no excuse for being on the third floor. Down below I could say I wanted tea, or hot water—anything. But I did not expect to find Mr. Reed up above. The terror, whatever it was, seemed to lie below.

Access to the third floor was not easy. The main staircase did not go up. To get there I was obliged to unlock the door at the rear of the hall with my own keys. I was working in bright light, trying my keys one after another, and watching over my shoulder as I did so. When the door finally gave it was a relief to slip into the darkness beyond, ghosts or no ghosts.

I am always a silent worker. Caution about closing doors and squeaking hinges is second nature to me. One learns to be cautious when one's only chance of sleep is not to rouse a peevish patient and have to give a body-massage, as like as not, or listen to domestic troubles— "I said" and "he said"—until one is almost crazy.

So I made no noise. I closed the door behind me and stood blinking in the darkness. I listened. There was no sound above or below. Now houses at night have no terror for me. Every nurse is obliged to do more or less going about in the dark. But I was not easy. Suppose Mr. Reed should call me? True, I had locked my door and had the key in my pocket. But a dozen emergencies flew through my mind as I felt for the stair rail.

There was a curious odor through all the back staircase, a pungent, aromatic scent that, with all my familiarity with drugs, was strange to me. As I slowly climbed the stairs it grew more powerful. The air was heavy with it, as though no windows had been opened in that part of the house. There was no door at the top of this staircase, as there was on the second floor. It opened into an upper hall, and across from the head of the stairs was a door leading into a room. This door was closed. On this staircase, as on all the others, the carpet had been newly lifted. My electric flash showed the white boards and painted borders, the carpet tacks, many of them still in place. One, lying loose, penetrated my rubber sole and went into my foot.

I sat down in the dark and took off the shoe. As I did so my flash, on the step beside me, rolled over and down with a crash. I caught it on the next step, but the noise had been like a pistol shot.

Almost immediately a voice spoke above me sharply. At first I thought it was out in the upper hall. Then I realized that the closed door was between it and me.

"Ees that you, Meester Reed?"

Mademoiselle!

"Meester Reed!" plaintively. "Eet comes up again, Meester Reed! I die! To-morrow I die!"

She listened. On no reply coming she began to groan rhythmically, to a curious accompaniment of creaking. When I had gathered up my nerves again I realized that she must be sitting in a rocking chair. The groans were really little plaintive grunts.

By the time I had got my shoe on she was up again, and I could hear her pacing the room, the heavy step of a woman well fleshed and not young. Now and then she stopped inside the door and listened; once she shook the knob and mumbled querulously to herself.

I recovered the flash, and with infinite caution worked my way to the top of the stairs. Mademoiselle was locked in, doubly bolted in. Two strong bolts, above and below, supplemented the door lock.

Her ears must have been very quick, or else she felt my softly padding feet on the boards outside, for suddenly she flung herself against the door and begged for a priest, begged piteously, in jumbled French and English. She wanted food; she was dying of hunger. She wanted a priest.

And all the while I stood outside the door and wondered what I should do. Should I release the woman? Should I go down to the lower floor and get the detective across the street to come in and force the door? Was this the terror that held the house in thrall—this babbling old Frenchwoman calling for food and a priest in one breath?

Surely not. This was a part of the mystery, not all. The real terror lay below. It was not Mademoiselle, locked in her room on the upper floor, that the Reeds waited for at the top of the stairs. But why was Mademoiselle locked in her room? Why were the children locked in? What was this thing that had turned a home into a jail, a barracks, that had sent away the servants, imprisoned and probably killed the dog, sapped the joy of life from two young people? What was it that Mademoiselle cried "comes up again"?

I looked toward the staircase. Was it coming up the staircase?

I am not afraid of the thing I can see, but it seemed to me, all at once, that if anything was going to come up the staircase I might as well get down first. A staircase is no place to meet anything, especially if one doesn't know what it is.

I listened again. Mademoiselle was quiet. I flashed my light down the narrow stairs. They were quite empty. I shut off the flash and went down. I tried to go slowly, to retreat with dignity, and by the time I had reached the landing below I was heartily ashamed of myself. Was this shivering girl the young woman Mr. Patton called his right hand?

I dare say I should have stopped there, for that night at least. My nerves were frayed. But I forced myself on. The mystery lay below. Well, then, I was going down. It could not be so terrible. At least it was nothing supernatural. There must be a natural explanation. And then that silly story about the headless things must pop into my head and start me down trembling.

The lower rear staircase was black dark, like the upper, but just at the foot a light came in through a barred window. I could see it plainly and the shadows of the iron grating on the bare floor. I stood there listening. There was not a sound.

It was not easy to tell exactly what followed. I stood there with my hand on the rail. I'd been very silent; my rubber shoes attended to that. And one moment the staircase was clear, with a patch of light at the bottom. The next, something was there, half way down—a head, it seemed to be, with a pointed hood like a monk's cowl.

There was no body. It seemed to lie at my feet. But it was living. It moved. I could tell the moment when the eyes lifted and saw my feet, the slow back-tilting of the head as they followed up my body. All the air was squeezed out of my lungs; a heavy hand seemed to press on my chest. I remember raising a shaking hand and flinging my flashlight at the head. The flash clattered on the stair tread harmless. Then the head was gone and something living slid over my foot.

I stumbled back to my room and locked the door. It was two hours before I had strength enough to get my aromatic ammonia bottle.

V

It seemed to me that I had hardly dropped asleep before the children were in the room, clamoring.

"The goldfish are dead!" Harry said, standing soberly by the bed. "They are all dead with their stummicks turned up."

I sat up. My head ached violently.

"They can't be dead, old chap." I was feeling about for my kimono, but I remembered that when I had found my way back to the nursery after my fright on the back stairs I had lain down in my uniform. I crawled out, hardly able to stand. "We gave them fresh water yesterday, and——"

I had got to the aquarium. Harry was right. The little darting flames of pink and gold were still. They floated about, rolling gently as Freddie prodded them with a forefinger, dull eyed, pale bellies upturned. In his cage above the little parrot watched out of a crooked eye.

I ran to the medicine closet in the bathroom. Freddie had a weakness for administering medicine. I had only just rescued the parrot from the result of his curiosity and a headache tablet the day before.

"What did you give them?" I demanded.

"Bread," said Freddie stoutly.

"Only bread?"

"Dirty bread," Harry put in. "I told him it was dirty."

"Where did you get it?"

"On the roof of the porte-cochère!"

Shade of Montessori! The rascals had been out on that sloping tin roof. It turned me rather sick to think of it.

Accused, they admitted it frankly.

"I unlocked the window," Harry said, "and Freddie got the bread. It was out in the gutter. He slipped once."

"Almost went over and made a squash on the pavement," added Freddie. "We gave the little fishes the bread for breakfast, and now they're gone to God."

The bread had contained poison, of course. Even the two little snails that crawled over the sand in the aquarium were motionless. I sniffed the water. It had a slightly foreign odor. I did not recognize it.

Panic seized me then. I wanted to get away and take the children with me. The situation was too hideous. But it was still early. I could only wait until the family roused. In the meantime, however, I made a nerve-racking excursion out on to the tin roof and down to the gutter. There was no more of the bread there. The porte-cochère was at the side of the house. As I stood balancing myself perilously on the edge, summoning my courage to climb back to the window above, I suddenly remembered the guard Mr. Patton had promised and glanced toward the square.

The guard was still there. More than that, he was running across the street toward me. It was Mr. Patton himself. He brought up between the two houses with absolute fury in his face.

"Go back!" he waved. "What are you doing out there anyhow? That roof's as slippery as the devil!"

I turned meekly and crawled back with as much dignity as I could. I did not say anything. There was nothing I could bawl from the roof. I could only close and lock the window and hope that the people in the next house still slept. Mr. Patton must have gone shortly after, for I did not see him again.

I wondered if he had relieved the night watch, or if he could possibly have been on guard himself all that chilly April night.

Mr. Reed did not breakfast with us. I made a point of being cheerful before the children, and their mother was rested and brighter than I had seen her. But more than once I found her staring at me in a puzzled way. She asked me if I had slept.

"I wakened only once," she said. "I thought I heard a crash of some sort. Did you hear it?"

"What sort of a crash?" I evaded.

The children had forgotten the goldfish for a time. Now they remembered and clamored their news to her.

"Dead?" she said, and looked at me.

"Poisoned," I explained. "I shall nail the windows

over the porte-cochère shut, Mrs. Reed. The boys got
out there early this morning and picked up something—
bread, I believe. They fed it to the fish and—they are
dead."

All the light went out of her face. She looked tired
and harassed as she got up.

"I wanted to nail the window," she said vaguely, "but
Mr. Reed—— Suppose they had eaten that bread, Miss
Adams, instead of giving it to the fish!"

The same thought had chilled me with horror. We
gazed at each other over the unconscious heads of the
children and my heart ached for her. I made a sudden
resolution.

"When I first came," I said to her, "I told you I
wanted to help. That's what I'm here for. But how
am I to help either you or the children when I do not
know what danger it is that threatens? It isn't fair to
you, or to them, or even to me."

She was much shaken by the poison incident. I thought
she wavered.

"Are you afraid the children will be stolen?"

"Oh, no."

"Or hurt in any way?" I was thinking of the bread
on the roof.

"No."

"But you are afraid of something?"

Harry looked up suddenly.

"Mother's never afraid," he said stoutly.

I sent them both in to see if the fish were still dead.

"There is something in the house downstairs that you
are afraid of?" I persisted.

She took a step forward and caught my arm.

"I had no idea it would be like this, Miss Adams. I'm dying of fear!"

I had a quick vision of the swathed head on the back staircase, and some of my night's terror came back to me. I believe we stared at each other with dilated pupils for a moment. Then I asked:

"Is it a real thing?—surely you can tell me this. Are you afraid of a reality, or—is it something supernatural?" I was ashamed of the question. It sounded so absurd in the broad light of that April morning.

"It is a real danger," she replied. Then I think she decided that she had gone as far as she dared, and I went through the ceremony of letting her out and of locking the door behind her.

The day was warm. I threw up some of the windows and the boys and I played ball, using a rolled handkerchief. My part, being to sit on the floor with a newspaper folded into a bat and to bang at the handkerchief as it flew past me, became automatic after a time.

As I look back I see a pair of disordered young rascals in Russian blouses and bare round knees doing a great deal of yelling and some very crooked throwing; a nurse sitting tailor fashion on the floor, alternately ducking to save her cap and making vigorous but ineffectual passes at the ball with her newspaper bat. And I see sunshine in the room and the dwarf parrot eating sugar out of his claw. And below, the fish in the aquarium floating belly-up with dull eyes.

Mr. Reed brought up our luncheon tray. He looked tired and depressed and avoided my eyes. I watched him while I spread the bread and butter for the children. He nailed shut the windows that opened on to the porte-cochère roof and when he thought I was not looking he examined the registers in the wall to see if the gratings were closed. The boys put the dead fish in a box and made him promise a decent interment in the garden. They called on me for an epitaph, and I scrawled on top of the box:

> *These fish are dead*
> *Because a boy called Fred*
> *Went out on a porch roof when he should*
> *Have been in bed.*

I was much pleased with it. It seemed to me that an epitaph, which can do no good to the departed, should at least convey a moral. But to my horror Freddie broke into loud wails and would not be comforted.

It was three o'clock, therefore, before they were both settled for their afternoon naps and I was free. I had determined to do one thing, and to do it in daylight—to examine the back staircase inch by inch. I knew I would be courting discovery, but the thing had to be done, and no power on earth would have made me essay such an investigation after dark.

It was all well enough for me to say to myself that there was a natural explanation; that this had been a human head, of a certainty; that something living and not spectral had slid over my foot in the darkness. I would not have gone back there again at night for youth, love or money. But I did not investigate the staircase that day, after all.

I made a curious discovery after the boys had settled down in their small white beds. A venturesome fly had sailed in through an open window, and I was immediately in pursuit of him with my paper bat. Driven from the cornice to the chandelier, harried here, swatted there, finally he took refuge inside the furnace register.

Perhaps it is my training—I used to know how many million germs a fly packed about with it, and the generous benevolence with which it distributed them; I've forgotten—but the sight of a single fly maddens me. I said that to Mr. Patton once, and he asked what the sight of a married one would do. So I sat down by the register and waited. It was then that I made the curious discovery that the furnace belowstairs was burning, and burning hard. A fierce heat assailed me as I opened the grating. I drove the fly out of cover, but I had no time for him. The furnace going full on a warm spring day! It was strange.

Perhaps I was stupid. Perhaps the whole thing should have been clear to me. But it was not. I sat there bewildered and tried to figure it out. I went over it point by point:

The carpets up all over the house, lights going full all night and doors locked.

The cot at the top of the stairs and Mrs. Reed staring down.

The bolt outside my door to lock me in.

The death of Chang.

Mademoiselle locked in her room upstairs and begging for a priest.

The poison on the porch roof.

The head without a body on the staircase and the thing that slid over my foot.

The furnace going, and the thing I recognized as I

sat there beside the register—the unmistakable odor of burning cloth.

Should I have known? I wonder. It looks so clear to me now.

I did not investigate the staircase, for the simple reason that my skeleton key, which unfastened the lock of the door at the rear of the second-floor hall, did not open the door. I did not understand at once and stood stupidly working with the lock. The door was bolted on the other side. I wandered as aimlessly as I could down the main staircase and tried the corresponding door on the lower floor. It, too, was locked. Here was an *impasse* for sure. As far as I could discover the only other entrance to the back staircase was through the window with the iron grating.

As I turned to go back I saw my electric flash, badly broken, lying on a table in the hall. I did not claim it.

The lower floor seemed entirely deserted. The drawing room and library were in their usual disorder, undusted and bare of floor. The air everywhere was close and heavy; there was not a window open. I sauntered through the various rooms, picked up a book in the library as an excuse and tried the door of the room behind. It was locked. I thought at first that something moved behind it, but if anything lived there it did not stir again. And yet I had a vivid impression that just on the other side of the door ears as keen as mine were listening. It was broad day, but I backed away from the door and out into the wide hall. My nerves were still raw, no doubt, from the night before.

I was to meet Mr. Patton at half after seven that night, and when Mrs. Reed relieved me at seven I had half an hour to myself. I spent it in Beauregard Gardens, with the dry fountain in the center. The place itself was charming, the trees still black but lightly fringed with new green, early spring flowers in the borders, neat paths and, bordering it all, the solid, dignified backs of the Beauregard houses. I sat down on the coping of the fountain and surveyed the Reed house. Those windows above were Mademoiselle's. The shades were drawn, but no light came through or round them. The prisoner— for prisoner she was by every rule of bolt and lock— must be sitting in the dark. Was she still begging for her priest? Had she had any food? Was she still listening inside her door for whatever it was that was "coming up"?

In all the other houses windows were open; curtains waved gently in the spring air; the cheerful signs of the dinner hour were evident near by—moving servants, a gleam of stately shirt bosom as a butler mixed a salad, a warm radiance of candle-light from dining room tables and the reflected glow of flowers. Only the Reed house stood gloomy, unlighted, almost sinister.

Beauregard Place dined early. It was one of the traditions, I believe. It liked to get to the theater or the opera early, and it believed in allowing the servants a little time in the evenings. So, although it was only something after seven, the evening rite of the table crumbs began to be observed. Came a colored butler, bowed to me with a word of apology, and dumped the contents of a silver tray into the basin; came a pretty mulatto, flung her crumbs gracefully and smiled with a flash of teeth at the butler.

Then for five minutes I was alone.

It was Nora, the girl we had met on the street, who came next. She saw me and came round to me with a little air of triumph.

"Well, I'm back in the square again, after all, miss," she said. "And a better place than the Reeds. I don't have the doilies to do."

"I'm very glad you are settled again, Nora."

She lowered her voice.

"I'm just trying it out," she observed. "The girl that left said I wouldn't stay. She was scared off. There have been some queer doings—not that I believe in ghosts or anything like that. But my mother in the old country had the second-sight, and if there's anything going on I'll be right sure to see it."

It took encouragement to get her story, and it was secondhand at that, of course. But it appeared that a state of panic had seized the Beauregard servants. The alarm was all belowstairs and had been started by a cook who, coming in late and going to the basement to prepare herself a cup of tea, had found her kitchen door locked and a light going beyond. Suspecting another maid of violating the tea canister she had gone soft-footed to the outside of the house and had distinctly seen a gray figure crouching in a corner of the room. She had called the butler, and they had made an examination of the entire basement without result. Nothing was missing from the house.

"And that figure has been seen again and again, miss," Nora finished. "McKenna's butler Joseph saw it in this very spot, walking without a sound and the street light beyond there shining straight through it. Over in the Smythe house the laundress, coming in late and going down to the basement to soak her clothes for the morning, met the thing on the basement staircase and fainted dead away."

I had listened intently.

"What do they think it is?" I asked.

She shrugged her shoulders and picked up her tray.

"I'm not trying to say and I guess nobody is. But if there's been a murder it's pretty well known that the ghost walks about until the burial service is read and it's properly buried."

She glanced at the Reed house.

"For instance," she demanded, "where is Mademoiselle?"

"She is alive," I said rather sharply. "And even if what you say were true, what in the world would make her wander about the basements? It seems so silly, Nora, a ghost haunting damp cellars and laundries with stationary tubs and all that."

"Well," she contended, "it seems silly for them to sit on cold tombstones—and yet that's where they generally sit, isn't it?"

Mr. Patton listened gravely to my story that night.

"I don't like it," he said when I had finished. "Of course the head on the staircase is nonsense. Your nerves were ragged and our eyes play tricks on all of us. But as for the Frenchwoman——"

"If you accept her you must accept the head," I snapped. "It was there—it was a head without a body and it looked up at me."

We were walking through a quiet street, and he bent over and caught my wrist.

"Pulse racing," he commented. "I'm going to take you away, that's certain. I can't afford to lose my best assistant. You're too close, Miss Adams; you've lost your perspective."

"I've lost my temper!" I retorted. "I shall not leave until I know what this thing is, unless you choose to ring the doorbell and tell them I'm a spy."

He gave in when he saw that I was firm, but not without a final protest.

".I'm directly responsible for you to your friends," he said. "There's probably a young man somewhere who will come gunning for me if anything happens to you. And I don't care to be gunned for. I get enough of that in my regular line."

"There is no young man," I said shortly.

"Have you been able to see the cellars?"

"No, everything is locked off."

"Do you think the rear staircase goes all the way down?"

"I haven't the slightest idea."

"You are in the house. Have you any suggestions as to the best method of getting into the house? Is Reed on guard all night?"

"I think he is."

"It may interest you to know," he said finally, "that I sent a reliable man to break in there last night quietly, and that he—couldn't do it. He got a leg through a cellar window, and came near not getting it out again. Reed was just inside in the dark." He laughed a little, but I guessed that the thing galled him.

"I do not believe that he would have found anything if he had succeeded in getting in. There has been no crime, Mr. Patton, I am sure of that. But there is a menace of some sort in the house."

"Then why does Mrs. Reed stay and keep the children if there is danger?"

"I believe she is afraid to leave him. There are times when I think that he is desperate."

"Does he ever leave the house?"

"I think not, unless——"

"Yes?"

"Unless he is the basement ghost of the other houses."

He stopped in his slow walk and considered it.

"It's possible. In that case I could have him waylaid tonight in the gardens and left there, tied. It would be a hold-up, you understand. The police have no excuse for coming in yet. Or, if we found him breaking into one of the other houses we could get him there. He'd be released, of course, but it would give us time. I want to clean the thing up. I'm not easy while you are in that house."

We agreed that I was to wait inside one of my windows that night, and that on a given signal I should go down and open the front door. The whole thing, of course, was contingent on Mr. Reed leaving the house some time that night. It was only a chance.

"The house is barred like a fortress," Mr. Patton said as he left me. "The window with the grating is hopeless. We tried it last night."

VI

I find that my notes of that last night in the house on Beauregard Square are rather confused, some written at the time, some just before. For instance, on the edge of a newspaper clipping I find this:

"Evidently this is the item. R—— went pale on reading it. Did not allow wife to see paper."

The clipping is an account of the sudden death of an elderly gentleman named Smythe, one of the Beauregard families.

The next clipping is less hasty and is on a yellow symptom record. It has been much folded—I believe I tucked it in my apron belt:

"If the rear staircase is bolted everywhere from the inside, how did the person who locked it, either Mr. or Mrs. Reed, get back into the body of the house again? Or did Mademoiselle do it? In that case she is no longer a prisoner and the bolts outside her room are not fastened.

"At eleven o'clock tonight Harry wakened with earache. I went to the kitchen to heat some mullein oil and laudanum. Mrs. Reed was with the boy and Mr. Reed was not in sight. I slipped into the library and used my skeleton keys on the locked door to the rear room. It was empty even of furniture, but there is a huge box there, with a lid that fastens down with steel hooks. The lid is full of small airholes. I had no time to examine further.

"It is one o'clock. Harry is asleep and his mother is dozing across the foot of his bed. I have found the way to get to the rear staircase. There are outside steps from the basement to the garden. The staircase goes down all the way to the cellar evidently. Then the lower door in the cellar must be only locked, not bolted from the inside. I shall try to get to the cellar."

The next is a scrawl:

"Cannot get to the outside basement steps. Mr. Reed is wandering round lower floor. I reported Harry's condition and came up again. I must get to the back staircase."

I wonder if I have been able to convey, even faintly, the situation in that highly respectable old house that night: The fear that hung over it, a fear so great that even I, an outsider and stout of nerve, felt it and grew cold; the unnatural brilliancy of light that bespoke dread of the dark; the hushed voices, the locked doors and staring, peering eyes; the babbling Frenchwoman on an upper floor, the dead fish, the dead dog. And, always in my mind, that vision of dread on the back staircase and the thing that slid over my foot.

At two o'clock I saw Mr. Patton, or whoever was on guard in the park across the street, walk quickly toward the house and disappear round the corner toward the gardens in the rear. There had been no signal, but I felt sure that Mr. Reed had left the house. His wife was still asleep across Harry's bed. As I went out I locked the door behind me, and I took also the key to the night nursery. I thought that something disagreeable, to say the least, was inevitable, and why let her in for it?

The lower hall was lighted as usual and empty. I listened, but there were no restless footsteps. I did not like the lower hall. Only a thin wooden door stood between me and the rear staircase, and any one who thinks about the matter will realize that a door is no barrier to a head that can move about without a body. I am afraid I looked over my shoulder while I unlocked the front door, and I know I breathed better when I was out in the air.

I wore my dark ulster over my uniform and I had my revolver and keys. My flash, of course, was useless. I missed it horribly. But to get to the staircase was an obsession by that time, in spite of my fear of it, to find what it guarded, to solve its mystery. I worked round the house, keeping close to the wall, until I reached the garden. The night was the city night, never absolutely dark. As I hesitated at the top of the basement steps it seemed to me that figures were moving about among the trees.

The basement door was unlocked and open. I was not prepared for that, and it made me, if anything, more uneasy. I had a box of matches with me, and I wanted light as a starving man wants food. But I dared not light them. I could only keep a tight grip on my courage and go on. A small passage first, with whitewashed stone walls, cold and scaly under my hand; then a large room, and still darkness. Worse than darkness, something crawling and scratching round the floor.

I struck my match, then, and it seemed to me that something white flashed into a corner and disappeared. My hands were shaking, but I managed to light a gas jet and to see that I was in the laundry. The staircase came down here, narrower than above, and closed off with a door.

The door was closed and there was a heavy bolt on it but no lock.

And now, with the staircase accessible and a gaslight to keep up my courage, I grew brave, almost reckless. I would tell Mr. Patton all about this cellar, which his best men had not been able to enter. I would make a sketch for him—coal-bins, laundry tubs, everything. Foolish, of course, but hold the gas jet responsible—the reckless bravery of light after hideous darkness.

So I went on, forward. The glow from the laundry followed me. I struck matches, found potatoes and cases of mineral water, bruised my knees on a discarded bicycle, stumbled over a box of soap. Twice out of the corner of my eye and never there when I looked I caught the white flash that had frightened me before. Then at last I brought up before a door and stopped. It was a curiously barricaded door, nailed against disturbance by a plank fastened across, and, as if to make intrusion without discovery impossible, pasted round every crack and over the keyhole with strips of strong yellow paper. It was an ominous door. I wanted to run away from it, and I wanted also desperately to stand and look at it and imagine what might lie beyond. Here again was the strange, spicy odor that I had noticed in the back staircase.

I think it is indicative of my state of mind that I backed away from the door. I did not turn and run. Nothing in the world would have made me turn my back to it.

Somehow or other I got back into the laundry and jerked myself together.

It was ten minutes after two. I had been just ten minutes in the basement!

The staircase daunted me in my shaken condition. I made excuses for delaying my venture, looked for another box of matches, listened at the end of the passage, finally slid the bolts and opened the door. The silence was impressive. In the laundry there were small, familiar sounds—the dripping of water from a faucet, the muffled measure of a gas meter, the ticking of a clock on the shelf. To leave it all, to climb into that silence——

Lying on the lower step was a curious instrument. It was a sort of tongs made of steel, about two feet long, and fastened together like a pair of scissors, the joint about five inches from the flattened ends. I carried it to the light and examined it. One end was smeared with blood and short, brownish hairs. It made me shudder, but—from that time on I think I knew. Not the whole story, of course, but somewhere in the back of my head, as I climbed in that hideous quiet, the explanation was developing itself. I did not think it out. It worked itself out as, step after step, match after match, I climbed the staircase.

Up to the first floor there was nothing. The landing was bare of carpet. I was on the first floor now. On each side, doors, carefully bolted, led into the house. I opened the one into the hall and listened. I had been gone from the children fifteen minutes and they were on my mind. But everything was quiet.

The sight of the lights and the familiar hall gave me courage. After all, if I was right, what could the head on the staircase have been but an optical delusion? And I was right. The evidence—the tongs—was in my hand. I closed and bolted the door and felt my way back to the stairs. I lighted no matches this time. I had only a few, and on this landing there was a little light from the grated window, although the staircase above was in black shadow.

I had one foot on the lowest stair, when suddenly overhead came the thudding of hands on a closed door. It broke the silence like an explosion. It sent chills up and down my spine. I could not move for a moment. It was the Frenchwoman!

I believe I thought of fire. The idea had obsessed me in that house of locked doors. I remember a strangling weight of fright on my chest and of trying to breathe. Then I started up the staircase, running as fast as I could lift my weighted feet, I remember that, and getting up perhaps a third of the way. Then there came a plunging forward into space, my hands out, a shriek frozen on my lips, and——quiet.

I do not think I fainted. I know I was always conscious of my arm doubled under me, a pain and darkness. I could hear myself moaning, but almost as if it were some one else. There were other sounds, but they did not concern me much. I was not even curious about my location. I seemed to be a very small consciousness surrounded by a great deal of pain.

Several centuries later a light came and leaned over me from somewhere above. Then the light said:

"Here she is!"

"Alive?" I knew that voice, but I could not think whose it was.

"I'm not—— Yes, she's moaning." '

They got me out somewhere and I believe I still clung to the tongs. I had fallen on them and had a cut on my chin. I could stand, I found, although I swayed. There was plenty of light now in the back hallway, and a man I had never seen was investigating the staircase.

"Four steps off," he said. "Risers and treads gone and the supports sawed away. It's a trap of some sort."

Mr. Patton was examining my broken arm and paid no attention. The man let himself down into the pit

under the staircase. When he straightened, only his head
rose above the steps. Although I was white with pain
to the very lips I laughed hysterically.

"The head!" I cried. Mr. Patton swore under his
breath.

They half led, half carried me into the library. Mr.
Reed was there, with a detective on guard over him. He
was sitting in his old position, bent forward, chin in
palms. In the blaze of light he was a pitiable figure,
smeared with dust, disheveled from what had evidently
been a struggle. Mr. Patton put me in a chair and dis-
patched one of the two men for the nearest doctor.

"This young lady," he said curtly to Mr. Reed, "fell
into that damnable trap you made in the rear staircase."

"I locked off the staircase—but I am sorry she is hurt.
My—my wife will be shocked. Only I wish you'd tell
me what all this is about. You can't arrest me for going
into a friend's house."

"If I send for some member of the Smythe family will
they acquit you?"

"Certainly they will," he said. "I—I've been raised
with the Smythes. You can send for any one you like."
But his tone lacked conviction.

Mr. Patton made me as comfortable as possible, and
then, sending the remaining detective out into the hall,
he turned to his prisoner.

"Now, Mr. Reed," he said. "I want you to be sensible.
For some days a figure has been seen in the basements of
the various Beauregard houses. Your friends, the
Smythes, reported it. Tonight we are on watch, and we
see you breaking into the basement of the Smythe house.

We already know some curious things about you, such as dismissing all the servants on half an hour's notice and the disappearance of the French governess."

"Mademoiselle! Why, she——" He checked himself.

"When we bring you here tonight, and you ask to be allowed to go upstairs and prepare your wife, she is locked in. The nurse is missing. We find her at last, also locked away and badly hurt, lying in a staircase trap, where some one, probably yourself, has removed the steps. I do not want to arrest you, but, now I've started, I'm going to get to the bottom of all this."

Mr. Reed was ghastly, but he straightened in his chair.

"The Smythes reported this thing, did they?" he asked. "Well, tell me one thing. What killed the old gentleman—old Smythe?"

"I don't know."

"Well, go a little further." His cunning was boyish, pitiful. "How did he die? Or don't you know that either?"

Up to this point I had been rather a detached part of the scene, but now my eyes fell on the tongs beside me.

"Mr. Reed," I said, "isn't this thing too big for you to handle by yourself?"

"What thing?"

"You know what I mean. You've protected yourself well enough, but even if the—the thing you know of did not kill old Mr. Smythe you cannot tell what will happen next."

"I've got almost all of them," he muttered sullenly. "Another night or two and I'd have had the lot."

"But even then the mischief may go on. It means a

crusade; it means rousing the city. Isn't it the square thing now to spread the alarm?"

Mr. Patton could stand the suspense no longer.

"Perhaps, Miss Adams," he said, "you will be good enough to let me know what you are talking about."

Mr. Reed looked up at him with heavy eyes.

"Rats," he said. "They got away, twenty of them, loaded with bubonic plague."

I went to the hospital the next morning. Mr. Patton thought it best. There was no one in my little flat to look after me, and although the pain in my arm subsided after the fracture was set I was still shaken.

He came the next afternoon to see me. I was propped up in bed, with my hair braided down in two pigtails and great hollows under my eyes.

"I'm comfortable enough," I said, in response to his inquiry; "but I'm feeling all of my years. This is my birthday. I am thirty today."

"I wonder," he said reflectively, "if I ever reach the mature age of one hundred, if I will carry in my head as many odds and ends of information as you have at thirty!"

"I?"

"You. How in the world did you know, for instance, about those tongs?"

"It was quite simple. I'd seen something like them in the laboratory here. Of course I didn't know what animals he'd used, but the grayish brown hair looked like rats. The laboratory must be the cellar room. I knew it had been fumigated—it was sealed with paper, even over the keyhole."

So, sitting there beside me, Mr. Patton told me the story as he had got it from Mr. Reed—a tale of the offer in an English scientific journal of a large reward from some plague-ridden country of the East for an anti-plague serum. Mr. Reed had been working along bacteriological lines in his basement laboratory, mostly with guinea pigs and tuberculosis. He was in debt; the offer loomed large.

"He seems to think he was on the right track," Mr. Patton said. "He had twenty of the creatures in deep zinc cans with perforated lids. He says the disease is spread by fleas that infest the rats. So he had muslin as well over the lids. One can had infected rats, six of them. Then one day the Frenchwoman tried to give the dog a bath in a laundry tub and the dog bolted. The laboratory door was open in some way and he ran between the cans, upsetting them. Every rat was out in an instant. The Frenchwoman was frantic. She shut the door and tried to drive the things back. One bit her on the foot. The dog was not bitten, but there was the question of fleas.

"Well, the rats got away, and Mademoiselle retired to her room to die of plague. She was a loyal old soul; she wouldn't let them call a doctor. It would mean exposure, and after all what could the doctors do? Reed used his serum and she's alive.

"Reed was frantic. His wife would not leave. There was the Frenchwoman to look after, and I think she was afraid he would do something desperate. They did the best they could, under the circumstances, for the children. They burned most of the carpets for fear of fleas, and put poison everywhere. Of course he had traps too.

"He had brass tags on the necks of the rats, and he got back a few—the uninfected ones. The other ones were probably dead. But he couldn't stop at that. He had to be sure that the trouble had not spread. And to add to their horror the sewer along the street was being relaid, and they had an influx of rats into the house. They found them everywhere in the lower floor. They even climbed the stairs. He says that the night you came he caught a big fellow on the front staircase. There was always the danger that the fleas that carry the trouble had deserted the dead creatures for new fields. They took up all the rest of the carpets and burned them. To add to the general misery the dog Chang developed unmistakable symptoms and had to be killed."

"But the broken staircase?" I asked. "And what was it that Mademoiselle said was coming up?"

"The steps were up for two reasons: The rats could not climb up, and beneath the steps Reed says he caught in a trap two of the tagged ones. As for Mademoiselle the thing that was coming up was her temperature—pure fright. The head you saw was poor Reed himself, wrapped in gauze against trouble and baiting his traps. He caught a lot in the neighbors' cellars and some in the garden."

"But why," I demanded, "why didn't he make it all known?"

Mr. Patton laughed while he shrugged his shoulders.

"A man hardly cares to announce that he has menaced the health of a city."

"But that night when I fell—was it only last night?—some one was pounding above. I thought there was a fire."

"The Frenchwoman had seen us waylay Reed from her window. She was crazy."

"And the trouble is over now?"

"Not at all," he replied cheerfully. "The trouble may be only beginning. We're keeping Reed's name out, but the Board of Health has issued a general warning. Personally I think his six pets died without passing anything along."

"But there was a big box with a lid——"

"Ferrets," he assured me. "Nice white ferrets with pink eyes and a taste for rats." He held out a thumb, carefully bandaged. "Reed had a couple under his coat when we took him in the garden. Probably one ran over your foot that night when you surprised him on the back staircase."

I went pale. "But if they are infected!" I cried; "and you are bitten——"

"The first thing a nurse should learn," he bent forward smiling, "is not to alarm her patient."

"But you don't understand the danger," I said despairingly. "Oh, if only men had a little bit of sense!"

"I must do something desperate then? Have the thumb cut off, perhaps?"

I did not answer. I lay back on my pillows with my eyes shut. I had given him the plague, had seen him die and be buried, before he spoke again.

"The chin," he said, "is not so firm as I had thought. The outlines are savage, but the dimple—— You poor little thing; are you really frightened?"

"I don't like you," I said furiously. "But I'd hate to see any one with—with that trouble."

"Then I'll confess. I was trying to take your mind

off your troubles. The bite is there, but harmless. Those were new ferrets; had never been out."

I did not speak to him again. I was seething with indignation. He stood for a time looking down at me; then, unexpectedly, he bent over and touched his lips to my bandaged arm.

"Poor arm!" he said. "Poor, brave little arm!" Then he tiptoed out of the room. His very back was sheepish.

THE RED LAMP

THE RED LAMP

Introduction to the Journal of William A. Porter,
A. B., M. A., Ph. D., Litt. D., etc.

June 30, 1924.

A FEW weeks ago, at a dinner, a discussion arose as to the unfinished dramas recorded in the daily press. The argument was, if I remember correctly, that they give us the beginning of many stories, and the endings of as many more. But that what followed those beginnings, or preceded those endings, was seldom or never told.

It was Pettingill, of all persons, who turned the attention of the table to me.

"Take that curious case of yours, Porter," he said. "Not yours, of course, but near your summer place two years ago. What ever happened there? Grace and I used to sit up all night to see who would get the morning paper first; then—it quit on us. That's all. Quit on us." He surveyed the table with an aggrieved air.

Helena Lear glanced across at me maliciously.

"Do tell us, Willie," she said. She is the only person in the world who calls me Willie. "And give us all the horrible details. You know, I have always had a sneaking belief that you did the things yourself!"

Under cover of the laugh that went up, I glanced at my wife. She was sitting erect and unsmiling, her face drained of all its color, staring across the flowers and candles into the semi-darkness above the buffet. As though she saw something.

I do not know, I never shall know, probably. I saw little Pettingill watching her unobtrusively, and following her eyes to the space over the buffet behind me, but I did not turn around. Possibly it was only the memories aroused by that frivolous conversation which made me feel, for a moment, that there was a cold wind eddying behind my back . . .

It occurred to me then that many people throughout the country had been intensely interested in our Oakville drama, and had been left with that same irritating sense of non-completion. But not only that. At least three of the women had heard me make that absurd statement of mine, relative to the circle enclosing a triangle. There were more than Helena Lear, undoubtedly, who had remembered it when, early in July, the newspapers had announced the finding of that diabolical symbol along with the bodies of the slain sheep.

It seemed to me that it might be a duty I owed to myself as well as to the University, to clarify the matter; to complete the incomplete; to present to them the entire story with its amazing climax, and in effect to say to them and to the world at large:

"This is what happened. As you see, the problem is solved, and here is your answer. But do not blame me if here and there is found an unknown factor in the equation; an X we do not know what to do with, but without which there would have been no solution. I can show you the X. I have used it. But I cannot explain it." . . .

As will be seen, I have taken that portion of my Journal extending from June 16th, 1922, to September 10th of the same year. Before that period, and after it,

it is merely the day by day record of an uneventful life.
Rather fully detailed, since like Pepys I have used it as
a reservoir into which to pour much of that residue
which remains in a man's mind over and above the little
he gives out each day. Rather more fully detailed, too,
since I keep it in shorthand, an accomplishment acquired
in my student days, and used not to insure the privacy
of the diary itself, although I think my dear wife so
believes, but to enable me, frankly, to exercise that taste
for writing which exists in all of us whose business is
English literature.

Show me any man who teaches literature, and I will
show you a man thwarted. For it is our universal,
hidden conviction that we too could write, were it not
for the necessity of earning our daily bread. We start
in as writers, only temporarily side-tracked. "Some
day——" we say to ourselves, and go to our daily task
of Milton or Dryden or Pope as those who, seeking the
beauties of the country, must travel through a business
thoroughfare to get there.

But time goes by, and still we do not write. We find,
as life goes on, that all the great thoughts have already
been recorded; that there is not much to say that has
not been already said. And, because we are always staring at the stars, we learn the shortness of our arms.

We find a vicarious consolation in turning out, now
and then, a man who is not daunted by tradition, and
who puts his old wine into new bottles. We read papers
before small and critical societies. And we sometimes
keep Journals.

And so—this Journal. Much the same as when, under
stress of violent excitement or in the peaceful interludes,
I went to it as one goes to a friend, secure against be-
trayal. Here and there I have detailed more fully conversations which have seemed to bear on the mystery;

now and again I have rounded a sentence. But in the main it remains as it was, the daily history of that strange series of events which culminated so dramatically on the night of September 10th in the panelled room of the main house at Twin Hollows. . . .

Of this house itself, since it figures so largely in the narrative, a few words should be said. The main portion of it, the hall which extended from the terrace toward the sea through to the rear and the drive, the panelled den and the large library in front of it are very old. To this portion, in the seventies, had been added across the hall by some long forgotten builder a dining room opposite the library and facing the sea, pantries, kitchen, laundry, and beyond the laundry a nondescript room originally built as a gun room and still containing the gun cases on the walls.

In later years the gun room, still so called, had fallen from its previous dignity and served divers purposes. In my Uncle Horace's time old Thomas, the gardener, used it on occasion as a potting room. And on wet days washing was hung up in it to dry. But it remained the "gun room," and so figures in this narrative.

In the re-building considerable judgment had been shown, and the broad white structure, with its colonial columns to the roof, makes a handsome appearance from the bay. It stands on a slight rise, facing the water, and its lawn extends to the edge of the salt marsh which divides it from the sea.

This is Twin Hollows. A place restful and beautiful to the eye; a gentleman's home, with its larkspurs and zinnias, its roses and its sun-dial, its broad terrace, its great sheltered porch and its old panelling. Some lovely woman should sweep down its wide polished staircase, or armed with basket and shears, should cut roses in the garden with its sun-dial—that sun-dial where I stood the night the bell clanged. But it stands idle. It will, so long as I live, always stand idle.

Of my Uncle Horace, who also figures largely in the Journal, a few words are necessary. He was born in 1848, and graduated from this University with the class of '70. He had died suddenly in June of the year before the Journal takes up the narrative, presumably of cardiac asthma, from which he had long suffered. A gentleman and a scholar, an essential solitary, there had been no real intimacy between us. Once in awhile I passed a week-end in the country with him, and until the summer of the narrative, my chief memory of him had been of a rather small and truculent elderly gentleman, with the dry sharp cough of the heart sufferer, pacing the terrace beneath my window at night in the endless search of the asthmatic for air, and smoking for relief some particu-larly obnoxious brand of herbal cigarette.

Until the summer of the narrative— . . .

Ever since I have been considering the making public of the Journal, I have been asking myself this question, as one which will undoubtedly be asked when the book is published: What effect have the events of that sum-mer had on my previous convictions?

Have I changed? Do I now believe that death is but a veil, and that through that veil we may now and then, as through a glass, see darkly?

I can only answer that as time has gone on I find they have exerted no permanent effect whatever. I am still profoundly agnostic. My wife and I have emerged from it, I imagine, as one emerges from a seance room where the phenomena have been particularly puzzling; that is, bewildered and half convinced for the moment, but without any change in our fundamental incredulity.

The truth is that if these things be, they are too great for our human comprehension; the revolution demanded in our ideas of the universe is too basic. And, as the Journal will show, too dangerous. . . .

"All houses in which men have lived and suffered and died are haunted houses," I have written somewhere in the Journal. And if thoughts are entities, which may impress themselves on their surroundings, perhaps this is true.

But dare I go further? Re-state my conviction at the time that the solution of our crimes had been facilitated by assistance from some unseen source? And that, having achieved its purpose, this force forthwith departed from us? I do not know.

The X remains unsolved.

But I admit that more than once, during the recent editing of this Journal for publication, I have wakened at night covered with a cold sweat, from a dream in which I am once more standing in the den of the house at Twin Hollows, the red lamp lighted behind me, and am looking out into the hall at a dim figure standing at the foot of the staircase.

A figure which could not possibly be there. But was there.

(Signed)
WILLIAM A. PORTER.

June 16th.

COMMENCEMENT Week is over at last, thank heaven, and with no more than the usual casualties. Defeated at the ball game, 9—6. Lear down with ptomaine, result of bad ice-cream somewhere or other. Usual reunions of old boys, with porters staggering under the suitcases, which seem to grow heavier each year.

Nevertheless, the very old 'uns always give me a lump in the throat, and I fancy there was a considerable amount of *globus hystericus* as the class of '70 marched onto the Field on Class Day. Only eight of them this year, Uncle Horace being missing. Poor old boy!

Which reminds me that Jane thought she saw him with the others as they marched in. Wonderful woman, Jane! No imagination ordinarily, meticulous mind and only a faint sense of humor. Yet she drags poor old Horace out of his year-old grave and marches him onto the Field, and then becomes slightly sulky with me when I laugh!

"I told you to bring your glasses, my dear," I said.

"How many men are in that group?" she demanded tensely.

"Eight. And for heaven's sake lower your voice."

"I see nine, William," she said quietly. And when she stood up to take her usual snap-shots of the Alumni procession she was trembling.

A curious woman, Jane. . . .

So another year is over, and what have I to show for it? A small addition to my account in the savings bank, a volume or two of this uneventful diary, some hundreds of men who perhaps know the Cavalier Poets and perhaps not, and some few who have now an inkling that English literature did not begin with Shakespeare.

What have I to look forward to? Three months of uneventful summering, perhaps at Twin Hollows—if Larkin ever gets the estate settled—and then the old round again. Milton and Dryden and Pope. Addison and Swift.

"Mr. Sims, have you any idea who wrote the Ancient Mariner? Or have you by chance ever heard of the Ancient Mariner?"

"Wordsworth, I believe, sir."

Yet I am not so much discontented as afraid of sinking into a lethargy of smug iconoclasm. It is bad for the soul to cease to expect grapes of a thistle, for the next stage is to be "old and a cynic; a carrion crow," like the old man in Prince Otto, with rotten eggs the burthen of my song.

Yet what is it that I want? My little rut is comfortable; so long have I lain in it that now my very body has conformed. I fit my easy chair beside my reading lamp; my thumbs are broadened with much holding of books. *I depend on my tea.*

Yesterday, calling on Lear, I must have voiced my uneasiness, for he at once suggested a hobby. His bed was littered with mutilated envelopes.

"Nothing like it," he said. "It's the safety valve of middle life, and the solace of age."

"I'm not quite sure I want a safety valve," I said, and I fancied he looked at me suspiciously.

A hobby! Shall I gather postage stamps, and inquire of a letter not from whom it comes, but from where? Or adopt Jane's camera, and take little pictures of unimportant folk doing uninteresting things? Or go, as Lear finally suggested, a-fishing? Is it to be my greatest adventure to pull a fish out of the water and watch it drown with wide-opened mouth, in the air? Ah me!

"Greatest rest in the world for the brain," Lear said, "Fishing."

"I'm not sure I want a rest for my brain," I protested. "I dare say what I need is a complete change."

"Well, try ptomaine," he said drily, and with that I went away.

But I dare say Lear is right. The prospect of my three months' vacation has gone to my head somewhat. And I dare say too that I am much like the solitary water-beetle Jock found on the kitchen floor last night. That is, willing enough to leave my snug spot behind the warm pipes of life until danger threatens, or discomfort, and then all for scurrying back, a-tremble, into unexciting security again.

June 17th.

A FTER all, security has its points.
I am the object of a certain amount of suspicion to-day on the part of my household! There is no place in the world, I imagine, for a philosopher with a sense of humor, a new leisure, and an inquiring turn of mind! In fact, I sometimes wonder whether any philosopher belongs in the present day and generation. These are times of action. Men think and then act; sometimes, indeed, they simply act.

But a philosopher, of course, should only think. . . .

And all this because last night I set Jane's clock forward one hour. Because, forsooth, I had determined to cease casting my eyes out on the world, and to study intensively that small domain of my own which lies behind the drain pipe!

During some nine months of the year I bring home to Jane from the lecture room the mere husk of a man; exhausted with the endeavor to implant one single thought into a brain where it will germinate, I sink into my easy chair and accept the life of my household. Tea. Dinner. A book. Bed. And this is my life. My existence, rather.

But with the close of the spring term I find a faint life stirring within me.

"Isn't this a new tea?" I will say.

"You have been drinking it all winter," Jane will reply, rather shortly.

Yesterday was my first free day, and last night I wandered about the house, looking over my possessions and re-discovering them.

"You've had the sofa done over, my dear."

"Before Christmas," Jane replied, and glanced at me. In return I glanced at Jane.

It dawns on a man now and then that he knows very little about his wife. He knows, of course, the surface attributes of her mind, her sense of order,—Jane is orderly—her thrift, and Jane is thrifty. She has had to be! But it came to me suddenly that I knew very little of Jane, after all.

She is making one of those endless bits of tapestry, which some day she will put on the seat of a chair, and thereafter I shall not be expected to sit in that chair. But it is not a work which requires profound attention. She was working at it at the moment, her head bent, her face impassive.

"What are you thinking about, Jane?" I asked her.

"I really wasn't thinking at all."

I dare say from that I fell to speculating on Jane's mind, and that does not imply a criticism. Rather on the contrary, for Jane has an excellent mental equipment. But I am sometimes aware that she possesses certain qualities I do not possess. For example, it would be impossible for me to imagine, as Jane did on Class Day, that I saw Uncle Horace. Although, like all men with defective vision, I have occasional optical illusions. But it is equally impossible for me to deny that she did see Uncle Horace, and there has been a certain subtle change in her since which convinces me of her sincerity.

What then, I considered, is the difference between Jane's mind and my own? She has some curious ability, which she hides like one of the seven deadly sins, and which makes her at times a difficult person with whom to live.

I have already recorded in this Journal that one occasion in my life when at the reunion of my class,

(1896), some wag proposed mixing all that was left of the various liquors in the punch bowl and drinking a stirrup cup out of it, and the fact that I was extremely dizzy on my way home.

But I did not record, I think, the fact that after I had quietly entered the house and got myself to bed, Jane came into my room.

"Oh! So you are back!" she said.

"Certainly I am back, my dear."

It seemed unnecessary to state that neither she nor the doorway in which she stood seemed entirely steady at the moment, nor did I so state. But perhaps it was not necessary, for after eyeing me coldly for a moment, she said:

"Were you supporting the chapel half an hour ago, William, or was it supporting you?"

"I don't know what you are talking about!"

"Don't you?" she observed, and retired quietly, after removing my shoes from the top of my book case.

But the humiliating fact remains that I *had* stopped for a moment's rest beside the chapel, and that somehow Jane knew it.

Or take again that incident already recorded in this Journal, under the date of June 28th of last year, when she wakened me at seven o'clock and said she had seen Uncle Horace lying dead on the floor of the library at Twin Hollows.

"Dreams," I said drowsily, "are simply wish fulfillments. Go on back to bed, my dear. The old boy's all right."

"I wasn't asleep," she said quietly. "And you will have a telephone message soon telling you I was not."

And so true was this that she had hardly ceased speaking before Annie Cochran called up to tell us she had found him, at seven o'clock, dead on the library floor.

(Note: In preparing these notes for publication one thing occurs to me very strongly, and that is this: it is curious that my wife's vision, or whatever it may be called, did not occur until some hours after the death. If there came some mental call to her, why not when he was *in extremis?* Not only would it have helped us greatly in the mystery which was so soon to develop, but it would have been more true to the usual type of such phenomena.

In this case, if we are to admit anything but coincidence, it is easier to accept the fact that we are dealing with mental telepathy. In other words, that the servant Annie Cochran, who actually found the body at seven in the morning, at once thought of Jane and so flashed the scene to her.

But I admit that this is merely explaining one mystery with another.)

So I was reflecting, as Jane pushed her needle through her tapestry, slow, infinitely plodding and absolutely composed. What portion of Jane, then, wandered out at night, and saw me with a death-grip on the chapel wall? Or, with a fine contempt of distance and a house she loathed, went to Twin Hollows and found Uncle Horace on the floor?

It was an interesting thought, and I played with it out of sheer joy in idleness. The Jane then, whom I could reach out and touch at night, might only be the shell of Jane, while the real Jane might be off on some spirit adventure of her own! I considered this. It has, one must admit, its possibilities. And just then she glanced up at me.

"What are you thinking about?" she asked.

"My dear," I said gravely, "I am worrying."

"What about?"

"About you."

"I'm all right," she said. "Although of course I'd like to get away somewhere."

"That's precisely what I'm worrying about!" I observed, and she looked puzzled but said nothing.

I went back to Jane's mind, with a volume of von Humboldt unnoticed on my knee. Had she true clairvoyance, whatever that may mean? Or was telepathy the answer? She is Scotch, and the Scots sometimes claim what is called "second sight." I know that in her heart she believes she has this curious gift. She was, they say, a queer child, seeing and hearing things unseen and unheard by others. And I know she fears and hates it; it is somehow irreligious to her.

But—has she?

No immediate answer being forthcoming, I went back to my book, and very soon I happened on the following paragraph: "A presumptuous scepticism which rejects facts without examining them to see if they are real, is more blameworthy than an irrational credulity."

It was, in a way, a challenge, but there were no facts to examine. I could believe that Jane is merely a fine recording instrument on which telepathic impressions are recorded, or I could accept that she is able to leave that still lovely but slightly matronly body of hers on occasion and travel on the wings of space. But, because my interest was aroused, I consulted the dictionary on clairvoyance, and found that it was the faculty of being able to perceive objects without the customary use of the senses.

It was "vision without eyes."

Even then—on so small a base does one's comfort behind the pipe sometimes depend—all would have been well had not Clara entered with the dish of fruit which is my method of telling the seasons; the winter orange and banana gradually giving way to the early berries which mark the spring, and so on. And with that Jane looked at the clock.

That glance was at once my downfall and my triumph. For it occurred to me then to make a simple experiment, and to "examine the facts."

"Jane," I argued, "rises by her bedroom clock every morning, and punctually to the minute. But Jane does not look at her clock. Then, if I set it forward one hour——?"

And set it forward one hour I did, after Jane was asleep. And at the moment its hands indicated seven-thirty, although it was but half past six, did Jane open her eyes, rise from her bed without so much as a glance toward the clock, and call her household.

So Jane saw her clock without eyes, Clara has been sulky all day, and I am in extreme disfavor.

"Really, William," Jane said with a sigh this after-noon, "you are very difficult in the holidays."

"Difficult?"

"You know perfectly well you turned my clock on."

"Why in the world should I turn your clock on?"

"It is your idea of being funny, I dare say."

"It isn't funny to be wakened an hour too soon, my dear."

But she is suspicious of me, and cold toward me. Thus I suffer the usual lot of the seeker after truth. And Jane, my dear Jane, can see without her eyes. But she cannot understand why I turned her clock on for all her curious ability. Nor, after eating the burned biscuits Clara served to-night, can I.

But if Jane can see without her eyes, if she can perceive objects not visible to those of us who depend on the usual senses, then is one to admit that she saw Uncle Horace, as she said she did, marching at the head of his class procession last Tuesday?

June 18th.

I FEEL to-night rather like the man who had caught a bull by the tail and daren't let go. And yet I am certain there is a perfectly natural explanation.

The difficulty is that I cannot very well go to Jane about it. If it is what it appears to be, and not a double exposure, it will frighten her. If it *is* a double exposure, she will wonder at my inquiry, and think I am watching her. She has not, even to-day, quite forgotten the clock.

But certain things are very curious; she thought she saw Uncle Horace marching onto the Field with his class. So much did this upset her that, when she stood up to take her picture, the camera shook in her hands. Then she takes the picture, and instead of the eight old men of the class of '70 there are nine.

And she knows it. Why else would she hide the print, and pretend that she had mislaid it? It was that fact which made me suspicious.

"I'll look them up for you later, William," she said. "You aren't in a hurry, are you?"

"In the bright lexicon of vacation there is no such word as hurry," I observed, brightly. And she who usually smiles at my feeblest effort turned abruptly away.

So Jane had lost her picture. Jane, whose closets are marvels of mathematical exactness, who keeps my clothing so exactly that I can find it in the dark, save for that one incident, duly noted in this Journal, when I unfolded a washcloth at the President's dinner, having taken it from my handkerchief box.

And shortly after Jane went out for a walk, Jane who never exercises save about her household. Poor Jane, I feel to-night, face to face with the inexplicable and hiding it like one of the seven deadly sins.

There are nine men in the picture; there is no getting

away from it. And there is no denying, either, a faint difference in the ninth figure, a sort of shadowiness, a lack of definition. Under Jane's reading glass it gains nothing. The features, owing to the distance, are indistinct, but if one could imagine the ghost of old Horace, in his brocaded dressing gown and slightly stooped to cough, in that blare of noise, shouting and sunshine, it is there.

Later: I have shown the picture to Lear, and he says it is undoubtedly a case of double exposure.

"What else could it be?" he said, with that peculiar irritation induced in some people by any suggestion of the supernatural.

"I don't think she ever took a picture of him in her life."

"Well, somebody has," he said, and handed the print back to me. "If you don't believe me, show it to Cameron. He's a shark on that sort of thing."

(Note: Cameron, Exchange Professor of Physics, at our University. A member of the Society for Psychical Research, and known, I understand, among the students as "Spooks" Cameron.)

But I have not shown it to Cameron, and I do not intend to. I hardly know the man, for one thing. And for another, Lear is right. The University looks with suspicion on the few among the faculty who have on occasion dabbled with such matters.

"Personally," he said, "I think it's a double exposure. But whether it is or not I'm damned certain of one thing, the less said about it the better."

June 19th.

CURIOUS, when one begins to think on a subject, how it sometimes comes up in the most unexpected places.

I dropped into the dining room for tea this afternoon after Jane's bridge party, to find Jane looking uncomfortable and an animated conversation on spiritualism going on, with Helena Lear leading it.

"Ah!" she said when she saw me, "here comes our cynic. I suppose you don't believe in automatic writing either?"

"I should," I replied gravely. "I have seen as many as fifty men taking notes while in a trance in my lecture room."

"Nor in spirits?"

"Certainly I do. And in the Smoke of Prophecy, and the Powder of Death."

She looked rather blank, and Jane flushed a trifle.

"What is more," I said, a trifle carried away by the tenseness of the room, perhaps, "I know that if I take a piece of chalk—have you any chalk, Jane?—and draw on the floor here the magic circle, and a triangle within it, no evil spirits can approach me. Get the chalk, dear; I promise I shall not be disturbed by so much as one demon."

In the laughter which followed the subject was dropped. But Helena Lear, when she gave me my tea, eyed me with amusement.

"You and your circle!" she said. "Don't you know that half these women more than half believe you?"

"And don't you?"

"You don't believe yourself."

"Still," I said, remembering von Humboldt, "I am not an out and out sceptic. I will admit that Jock there, who is acting as a vacuum cleaner under the table, can hear and see and smell things that I cannot. But I do not therefore believe he communicates with the spirit world."

"But he sees things you don't see. You admit that."

"Certainly. He may see further into the spectrum than I do."

"Then *what* does he see?" she said triumphantly.

A fortunate digression enabled me to escape with a whole skin, but I think there was something rather quizzical in her smiling farewell. After all, if Jock does see things I do not, what does he see? I'm blessed if I know.

June 20th.

JANE knows that I have seen the picture, and that I know it lies behind her refusal to go to Twin Hollows for the summer. When I came back from Larkin's office to-day, the final papers having been signed, I could see her almost physically bracing herself.

"So it's all set, my dear," I said. "And if we can get Annie Cochran to clean the place a bit——"

"Would you mind so very much," she asked, almost wistfully, "if we don't go there?"

"But it's all settled. Edith is coming back on purpose."

(Note: The "Edith" of the Journal is my niece, who makes her home with us. At this time she was absent on a round of house-parties. A very lovely and popular girl, of whom more hereafter.)

"It's too large for us," said Jane. "I need a rest in the summer, not a big house to care for."

And there was a certain definiteness in her statement which ended the conversation. As a result, and following our usual course when there is a difference between us, we have taken refuge in a polite silence all day, the familiar armed neutrality of marriage. An uncomfortable state of affairs, and aggravated by Edith's absence.

When she is here her bright talk fills in the gaps, and in the end she forces a *rapprochement*. . . .

Lear has told Cameron about the picture. I met Cameron while taking Jock for his evening walk to-night, and he re-introduced himself to me. After to-day's repression I fear I was a bit talkative, but he was a good listener.

Evidently he has a certain understanding of Jane's refusal to go to Twin Hollows, although he said very little.

"Houses are curious, sometimes," was his comment.

But on the matter of the picture he was frankly interested.

"There is," he said, "a certain weight in the evidence for psychic photography, Mr. Porter. Of course it is absurd to claim that all the curious photographs—and thousands of them come to me—are produced by discarnate intelligences. But there is something; I don't know just what."

Jane has gone to bed, still politely silent, and I am left alone to wrestle with my two problems; where to spend the summer, and why Jane finds the house at Twin Hollows what Cameron describes as curious.

A mild term, that, for Jane's feeling about the house. Actually, she hates it. Has always hated it. She has had no pride in our acquisition of it; she has even stead-fastly refused to bring away from it any of that early American furniture with which old Horace had filled it.

Yet she collects early American furniture. I write to-night at an utterly inadequate early American desk, because of this taste of hers: Jock has at this moment curled his long length on the hard seat of a Windsor chair, because of it! And yet she will have none of Uncle Horace's really fine collection.

Nor is she of the type to listen to Annie Cochran's

story that the old portion of the house is haunted by the man killed there.

(Note: An old story and not authenticated, of the shooting of a man many years ago as he hid to escape the Excise. As a matter of fact, none of our later experiences in the house bore out this particular tradition at all.)

If she has a distaste for it, it may possibly relate to the occupancy of the house by the Riggs woman before Uncle Horace bought it. But even here I am doubtful, for Mrs. Riggs was caught in most unblushing fraud and entirely discredited as a medium.

June 21st.

EDITH is back. She came in this morning, kissed Jock, Jane and myself, Jock first, demanded an enormous breakfast and all the hot water in the house, and descended gaily a half hour later to the table, in her usual aura of bath salts, bath powder and sunshine.

"Well," she said, attacking her melon, "and when do we go to the haunted house?"

"Ask your Aunt."

She glanced at me and then shrewdly at Jane.

"Good heavens!" she said. "Don't tell me there's any question about it?"

"It isn't decided yet," Jane said uneasily. "It's a big house, Edith, and——"

"All the more reason for taking it," said Edith, and having finished her melon flung out her pretty arms. "Grass," she said, *"and* flowers, *and* the sea. I shall swim," she went on. "And old Father William shall fish, and Jane shall sew a fine seam. And at night the ghosts shall walk. And everything will be lovely."

She turned to me.

"You do believe in ghosts, don't you, Father William?"

And somehow even Jane caught some of the infection of her gaiety. "Ask him about the triangle in a circle," she said.

"What's that?" Edith inquired.

"The triangle in a circle, drawn around you, will keep off demons," I explained gravely. "Surely you know that?"

"How—convenient!"

"And that the skins of four frogs, killed on a moon-less night, will make one invisible if worn as a cap? And that the spirits obey solomon's seal—not the plant, of course! And that if you eat a stew of the eyes of a vulture, and the ear-tufts of an owl, you will be wise beyond all dreams of wisdom?"

"Who wants to be wise?" said Edith. "But go on. I love to hear you."

"Very well," I agreed, with an eye on Jane, "now take the figure five. Five is the magic number, not seven. We have five fingers, five toes, five senses. There are five points to a star. Perhaps you noticed my wild excitement when my automobile license this year was 555."

Jane got up, and I saw that my nonsense had had its effect. She was smiling, for the first time in days.

"If you care to go out and look at the house to-morrow, William," she said, "I will go."

And perhaps Edith had sensed a situation she did not understand, for she kissed her, and as I left the room I heard her requesting Jane to bring back with her marketing some frog skins and the ear-tufts of an owl. . . .

So this afternoon things are looking brighter. And thus does man deceive himself! Only three days ago I was filled with vague yearnings and aspirations; I re-corded here that my little rut was comfortable, but that

I feared it. I wrote: "Was my greatest adventure to be to drag a fish out of the water, and watch it drown, open-mouthed, in the air?"

And yet, at the mere thought of not going to Twin Hollows, of being thrown on the mercies of some Mountain House, or set on a horse in the far west, I have been frightened almost into a panic.

The water-beetle indeed. . . .

The town is very quiet to-night. The annual student exodus is almost over, although still an occasional truck goes by, piled high with trunks. The Lears intend to stay. Sulzer and Mackintyre are off for the Scottish Lakes, and Cameron, I hear, is going soon to the Adirondacks, where he spends his summer in a boat, and minus ghosts, I dare say.

I have mailed him the picture to-day, and can only hope Jane does not miss it.

One wonders about men like Cameron. Slight, almost negligible, as is my acquaintance with him—I would not know him in a crowd, even now—there is something of Scottish dourness in him. He neither smokes nor drinks; he lives austerely and alone. He has a reputation as a relentless investigator; it was he who exposed the hauntings at the house on Sabbathday Lake, in Massachusetts.

But he is a believer. That is, he believes in conscious survival after death, and I suspect that he has his own small group here. Among them little Pettingill. It would be a humiliating thought, for me, to feel that after I passed over, as they say, little Pettingill might hale me to him, in the light of a red lamp, and request me to lift a table! . . .

Warren Halliday is on the verandah with Edith. I can hear her bubbling laughter, and his quiet, deep voice.

After all, I dare say we must make up our minds to lose her sometime, but it hurts.

And it will not be soon. He has not a penny to bless himself with, nor has she. I think, if I were very rich, I would provide an endowment fund for lovers.

But something is wrong with our university system. It takes too long to put a man on a wife-supporting basis. Halliday is twenty-six; he lost two years in the war, and he has another year of law. Truly, Edith will need the eyes of a vulture and the ear-tufts of an owl.

June 22nd.

A LL houses in which men have lived and suffered and died are haunted houses." But then, all houses are haunted. Why, then, did Jock refuse to enter the house at Twin Hollows to-day, but crawled under the automobile and remained there, a picture of craven terror, until our departure?

This old house where I am writing to-night, undoubtedly it has seen the passing of more than one human soul. Yet Jock moves through it unconcernedly, his stump of a tail proudly upraised, his head unbowed. His attitude to-night, too, is even slightly more flamboyant than usual, as though to testify that although he may have given the impression of terror during the day, we are laboring under a misapprehension. He but sought the shelter of the car for coolness.

"He may see further into the spectrum than I do," I said to Helena Lear the other day, and she countered: "Yes. But *what* does he see?"

Old Thomas met us in Oakville with the keys, and we drove out to the house. I sensed in Jane a reluctance to enter, but she fought it back bravely, and we examined it with a view to our own occupancy. It is in excellent condition and repair, although the white covers over the library furniture and in the den behind gave those rooms a rather ghostly appearance. Jane, I saw, gave only a cursory glance into those rooms, and soon after, pleading the chill inside, moved out into the sunlight.

Edith, however, was enchanted with it all, and said so. She danced through the house, shamelessly courting old Thomas, selecting bedrooms for us all, and peering into closets, and I caught up with her at last on the second floor, looking at the boat-house on the beach beyond the marsh.

"What's above it?" she asked. "Rooms?"

"When the old sloop was in commission, the captain slept there," I told her.

"How many rooms?"

"Two, I think, and a sort of kitchenette."

"Are they furnished?"

Old Thomas, being appealed to, said they were, and Edith's face assumed that air of mysterious calculation which I have learned to associate with what she calls "an idea." Whatever it was, however, she kept it to herself, and I left her selecting a bedroom for herself, and putting into it sufficient thought to have served a better purpose.

Her surroundings and belongings are very important to her; and yet I believe she is in love with young Halliday, who can, so far as I see, give her neither.

It is a curious thing, to go into a house left, as Twin Hollows has been, without change since old Horace died, and not to find him there; his big arm chair near the fireplace in the library, his very pens still on the flat-topped desk which is the only modern piece in the room, the books he was reading still in the desk rack. I had a curious feeling to-day that if I raised my voice, I would hear the little cough which was so often his preliminary to speech, from the den beyond.

The den too is unchanged. (Note: From an ugly room, the original kitchen of the old house, he had made it a sort of treasure house of early American old pewter, brought over perhaps in ships which had anchored in the very bay outside; of early framed charters and deeds of land, signed by English kings and hung on the walls above the old panelling, which he himself had found somewhere and installed; of quaint chairs, a settle and an old chest, hooked rugs on the floor, and old glass candlesticks.)

I threw back the covering which protected the desk top, and sat down at it. Just there, in all probability, he had been sitting when the fatal attack took place. He may have felt it coming on, but there was no one to call, poor old chap. We had not been overly close, but the thought of him, writing perhaps, or reading, the sudden consciousness that all was not well, an instant of comprehension, and then the end—it got me, rather.

I think he had been reading. Among the other books on the desk was the one with a scrap of paper thrust in it to mark the place, and a pencil line drawn on the margin of the page to mark a paragraph. But it gives me rather a new line on him. I had always thought that his purchase of a house locally reputed to be haunted, a reputation considerably enhanced by the Riggs woman's tenancy, was a rather magnificent gesture of pure Calvinism.

But to-night I am wondering. The marked paragraph is in a book entitled "Eugenia Riggs and the Oakville Phenomena," and I have brought it home with me. It is a creepy sort of thing, and I find myself looking back over my shoulder as I copy it into this record.

"It is to be borne in mind that the room was always subjected to the most careful preliminary examination. Its walls were plastered, and no doors or windows (see photograph) were near the cabinet. As an additional precaution strings of small bells were placed across all possible entrances and exits, which were also closed and locked.

"It is also to be remembered that the medium herself was always willing to be searched, and this was frequently done by Madame B——. This had been done on the night when the hand was distinctly seen by all present, reaching out and touching those nearest on the shoulder, and later making the impression in the pan of soft putty left in the cabinet.

"It is to be borne in mind too that, except when the controls rapped for no light, there was always sufficient illumination for us to see the medium clearly. A small red lamp was found to offer least disturbance and was customarily used.

"There was occasional fraud, but *there were also genuine phenomena.*"

The last few words are italicized.

So to-night I am wondering. Does one find, as life goes on, that the lonely human spirit revolts at the thought of eternal peace, and craves a relief in action in the life beyond? Would I not myself, for instance, prefer even coming back and lifting little Pettingill's table to the unadulterated society of the saints?

June 23rd.

THERE is a division in my family. Edith has come out with her plan, which is to "spread out," as she puts it, in the main house at Twin Hollows, and to let Warren Halliday spend his vacation at the boathouse!

"*Renting* it to him, I suppose?" I inquired over my breakfast bacon.

"Renting it?" she said indignantly. "You wouldn't

have the nerve to ask money for that tumble-down place, would you? And anyhow, you can't get blood out of a stone."

There is a terrible frankness about Edith at times.

But Jane is as equally determined not to occupy the house at any cost. It was written all over her yesterday, and there is still an ominous set look about her mouth. Between them I am more or less trimming skiff.

If Jane would be more open it would be easier; if she would only come to me and say that she is afraid of the house I think I could reassure her. It may be that that silly photograph is still in her mind. But why would she not even stay in the house yesterday? She went out into the garden and picked some of its neglected flowers instead.

"It's a pity not to use them," she said, and then looked at me with such a white and pitiful face that I put my arm around her.

"I must have been a very bad husband," I said, "if you think I am going to force you to live here. Who am I," I added, "against you and Jock?"

But she did not smile.

"If you want to come here," she said, making what I felt was a painful concession, "why couldn't we live at the Lodge? It is really quite sweet. And we could rent this."

"Would that be quite moral, under the circumstances? I'm not asking the circumstances," I added hastily. "I'm simply putting the question."

"We could ask a lower rent."

There is, I sometimes think, a fundamental difference in the ethical views of men and women. To Jane it is quite proper to let a house with what she believes is a most undesirable quality, if she lowers the price. She does not suggest advertising: "One house, furnished, reputed to be haunted." On the contrary, she proposes to entice tenants with a lower rent, and once having got them there, to be able to say, in effect: "What would you? The house is cheap. True, it has certain disadvantages; I am sorry you have been bothered. But you have saved money."

Aside from this viewpoint, however, the idea is sound enough. We can be comfortable at the Lodge. And—let me always be frank in this Journal—I may have my occasional yearnings for adventure, but they have their limitations, and the talk Edith has reported as taking place between old Thomas and herself yesterday after I left them has revealed them to myself.

Edith, on the contrary, finds the situation "really thrilling."

"It's a good house, yes'm," said Thomas. For them as likes it. I wouldn't be caught dead in it at night myself."

"I hope you never will be," said Edith.

"It ain't nothing you can put your finger on," said Thomas. "It's just knocks and raps, and doors opening and closing. But I say that's enough."

"It sounds like plenty," said Edith. "Of course it may be rats."

"It's a right husky rat that'll open a closed door, and I ain't yet seen a rat that could move a chair. Besides, I ain't ever heard that rats are partial to a red light."

"Now see here, Thomas," Edith reports herself as saying, "either you've said too much or you've said too little. What about a red light? Nothing scandalous, I hope!"

Stripped of further trimming, it appears that some two years ago a small red lamp was installed in the den at Twin Hollows, and is now still there, Thomas having declined to destroy it for fear of some dire and mysterious vengeance.

"Not for light, as far as I could see, miss," he said. "I never seen him read by it. But put in it was, and the night it first came Annie Cochran said something came into her room and pulled the covers off her bed."

"How—shameless!" said Edith.

"More than that," he went on stolidly, "the furniture was moving through the house all night, and the next morning she found the tea-kettle sitting in the pantry, and tea had been made in the tea-pot."

"But surely she did not begrudge the poor things their tea, Thomas? It must be thirsty work, moving furniture and chasing about rapping on things."

"She'd left the kettle on the stove, and there it was," he said, doggedly.

Like the lady of color who said to the judge that she had "just sort of lost her taste" for her husband, I begin to lose my taste for this lamp. But one wonders whether its evil reputation is not a survival from the days of Mrs. Riggs, when "a small red lamp was found to offer least disturbance, and was customarily used."

June 24th.

EDITH has lost and Jane has won. We shall spend the summer at the Lodge.

But I feel that Jane's victory brings her no particular pleasure, that even to go to the Lodge is a concession she is making against some hidden apprehension. Yet to show just how baseless are most of these things, this morning Clara has been in a low mood, and I heard Jane inquire the reason.

"I dreamed last night that I'd lost a tooth," said Clara. "That's a sign of death, sure, Mrs. Porter."

Edith, however, has won in one way. Warren Halliday is to have the boat-house.

We motored out together to-day, I to look over the Lodge more carefully, and Halliday to inspect his prospective quarters. He is thoroughly likeable, a nice clean-cut young fellow, not too handsome but manly and with a good war record, and badly cut up at his failure to find a job for the summer.

"I'd do anything," he said. "Sell neckties if necessary! But I can't even land that. Although—" he forced a grin "—I have a nice taste in neckties!"

On the way out I told him something of the history of the house, and a little—very little—of Jane's nervousness concerning it.

"Of course," he said, "it's all nonsense. But a surprising number of people are going bugs on it."

"Darned uncomfortable nonsense, too."

"It's not only that, sir. It's dangerous. Imagine what a general conviction of this sort would do. Think of the fellows who find things getting a bit thick for them here, and how quickly they'd hop out of it! Think of the crimes it would cause. And take wars. Nobody would care whether he lived or not. Talk about civilization going! Why, the whole darned populace would go!"

In view of that conversation, it was interesting later that day, at the Lodge, to have old Thomas intimate that Uncle Horace had not died a natural death, but had "seen something" which had caused it.

As a matter of fact, he brought out certain rather curious facts, which appear to have been somehow overlooked, or at least considered unimportant, at the inquest.

For instance, he had been writing at his desk when the attack came on. His pen was found on the floor. But there was no sign of what he had been writing, save for a mark on the fresh blotter, as if he had blotted something there. The most curious thing, however, according to old Thomas, was the matter of lights.

When Annie Cochran found him the following morning, on the floor beside his desk, all the lights were out, including his desk lamp.

"But the red lamp was going in the den," said old Thomas. "It didn't make much light, so nobody noticed it until the doctor came. He saw it right off. I leave it to you, what shut off that desk lamp?"

I rather gather from Thomas that the ill-repute of the red lamp has spread over the country-side. The house had a bad reputation to start with, which Mrs. Riggs' tenancy did nothing to redeem, and now comes Annie Cochran and her red lamp, and a fairly poor outlook so far as renting the property is concerned.

There has been, according to Thomas, considerable interest as to whether we will inhabit the house or not, and if ever I saw relief in a man's face it was in his when I announced the decision. As Halliday observes, it would be interesting to know if either Annie Cochran or Thomas has ever heard that red is the best light for so-called psychic phenomena.

The Lodge proves to be weatherproof and in good condition, and the boat-house quite liveable, with the addition of a few things from the main house.

It will need thorough screening, however, on account of the mosquitos.

(Note: It is necessary, for the sake of the narrative, to describe the boat-house. It is built up on piles which raise it above tide level, and the dory and canoe belonging to the house are stored in the lower portion of it in winter. The old sloop, however, not in commission for several years, was at this time anchored to a buoy about a hundred yards out in the bay, and showed the buffetings of wind and tide.

Across the salt marsh, from the foot of the lawn, extended a raised wooden run-way which led to the boat-house and the beach. This walk also prolongs itself into a sort of ramshackle pier, from which a run-way extends to a wooden float. At the time of our visit examination showed the float badly in need of repair, a number of the barrels which supported it having more or less gone to pieces.

It was, as will be seen, during Halliday's repair of this float that he made that discovery which was later to see the commencement of my troubles.)

All in all, Jane's scheme is practical, although Edith is frankly disappointed.

"I would have looked so sweet on that terrace!" she says, and makes a dreadful face at me.

I have asked her to say nothing to Jane about old Thomas's ravings, as she calls them. She has agreed, but accuses me of extreme terror, and maintains that I am merely putting the responsibility on Jane.

"You know perfectly well," she says, "that you believe in ghosts. And if you rent that house old Horace *ought* to come back and haunt you."

But she is secretly pleased. She sees herself in the cottage, in a bungalow apron, presenting a picture of lovely but humble domesticity to young Halliday, and thus forcing his hand. For if I know anything of Edith, she is going to marry him. And if I know anything of Halliday, he is going to marry nobody he cannot support.

It may be an interesting summer. . . .

Curious about that lamp on the desk, the night the poor old chap passed out. Of course, he might have turned it out and risen to go upstairs when he felt the attack coming on. But wouldn't he have laid the pen down first? One would do that automatically.

It's a pity the blotting pad has been destroyed.

June 25th.

THE last, or almost the last, word Uncle Horace wrote the night of his death was "danger."

But how much significance am I to attach to that? We speak of the danger of taking cold, of levity in the lecture room, of combining lobster and ice-cream. To poor old Horace there would have been danger in over-exertion; in that sense of the word he was always in danger. But it was not a word he was apt to use lightly.

Yet what conceivable danger could have threatened him? . . .

This morning, clearing my desk preparatory to our exodus, I resorted to an old trick of mine. I turned over my large desk blotter and presented a fresh and unblemished side to the world. It came to me then that thus probably since the invention of blotters had neatness been established with a minimum of effort, and that it might have been resorted to by Annie Cochran.

After luncheon I started to Twin Hollows with the back of the car piled high with a varied assortment of breakable toilet articles, a lamp or two, and a certain number of dishes. The Lodge was open, and Annie Cochran vigorously cleaning it, and having deposited my fragile load there, I wandered up to the house.

Thomas was cutting the lawn, with a mare borrowed for the purpose pulling the old horse mower, and the Oakville constable, Starr, who is also the local carpenter, was replacing old boards with new on the raised walk to the beach. What with the sunlight, the put-put of a two-cycle engine in a passing motor boat, a flock of knock-abouts and sloops poised on the water like great butterflies, and the human activities about, the absurdity of abandoning the old house to some unappreciative tenant grew on me.

"Hear you're going to live in the Lodge," said Starr, spitting over the rail.

"Mrs. Porter feels the main house is too large for us."

He eyed me sharply.

"Yes," he said. "Pretty big house. Well, I'm in a dollar on it."

"A dollar?"

"I bet you'd never live in it," he said, and there was a furtive gleam of amusement in his eye as he marked a board preparatory to sawing it.

"It's my opinion, Starr," I said, "that you people around here have talked this place into disrepute."

"Maybe we have," he said, non-committally.

"Mr. Horace Porter lived there for twenty years."

"And *died* there," he reminded me.

"Of chronic heart trouble."

"So the doctor says."

"But you don't think so?"

"I know he had got a right forcible knock on the head, too."

"I thought that came from his fall."

"Well, it may have," he said, and signified the end of the conversation by falling to work with his saw. I waited, but he evidently felt he had said enough, and his further speech was guarded in the extreme. He didn't know whether Mr. Porter had been writing or not when it happened. No, he'd been the first to get there, and he had seen no paper.

Asked if he had had any reason, any experience of his own, to make him wager we would not live in the house, he only shook his head. But as I started back he called after me.

"I don't know as there's any truth in it," he said. "But

they do say, on still nights, that he's been heard coughing around the place. I ain't ever heard it myself."

So Thomas thinks that Uncle Horace was frightened to death, and Starr intimates that he was murdered, and all this was seething in the minds of these country people a year ago, without it reaching me at all. There had been no inquest; simply, as I recall, Doctor Hayward notifying the Coroner by telephone, and giving organic heart disease as the cause.

I was, I admit, startled this morning as I turned back to the main house. But I knew the tendency of small inbred communities to feed on themselves, for lack of outside nutriment, and by the time I had reached the terrace I was putting Starr's statement about a blow in the same class with the cough heard at night. I stood looking out over the sweep of lawn, and the words occurred to me of that other ancient Horace, confirmed city-dweller that he was.

"There was ever among the number of my wishes, a portion of ground, not over large, in which was a garden and a fountain, with a continual stream close to my house, and a little woodland besides. The gods have done more abundantly, and better for me, than this."

So I felt that the gods had done even better for me than I had thought. My little woodland, to my left as I faced the sea, covered thirty acres, extending beyond Robinson's Point; true, I had no fountain, but I had a garden of sorts. And I had a ship, which apparently the old Roman had never dreamed of. The old sloop bobbed and swung in the wash of a passing tug.

I turned and went into the house to find that Annie Cochran had turned the blotter and that the last word the poor old boy had written had been "danger."

June 26th.

WOMEN are curious creatures. Throughout the winter it is of vital importance to Jane that her tea cups are old Chelsea, and that the mirror over the hall table is pure early colonial, even if it does raise my right eye an inch or so. The Queen Anne chairs in her bedroom, the Adam sideboard in the dining room, apparently divide her affection with me, and she has been known to make considerably more fuss over a scratch on the Sheraton cabinet than over a similar injury to myself.

We are settled to-night in the Lodge, and whatever Edith may say as to its romantic outside appearance, within it is frankly hideous. It is all a cottage should not be. From the old parlor organ downstairs to beds that dip in the center above, it is atrocious. Yet to-night Jane is a happy woman.

Can it be that women require rest from their possessions, as for instance I do from my dinner clothes? That it gives them the same sense of freedom to don, speaking figuratively, a parlor organ and the cheapest of other furnishings, as it does me to put on my ancient fishing garments?

Or is Jane simply relieved?

I confess that to-night with Larkin's advertisement for the other house before me, I feel not only in the position of a man attempting to sell a gold brick, but that I have a secret hankering for the gold brick myself.

"For rent for the season, large handsomely furnished house on bay three miles from Oakville. Beautiful location. Thirty-two acres, landscaped. Flower and kitchen gardens. Low rental."

Yet I dare say we shall do well enough. After all, there comes a time when ambition ceases to burn, or

romance to stir, and the highest cry of the human heart
is for peace. Here, I feel, is peace.

I have brought with me those books which all the
year I have promised myself to read, so that my small
room overflows with them; a spare note-book or two
for this Journal, to be filled probably with the weights
of fish and the readings of the barometer; Jane for solid
affection, Edith for the joy of life, and Jock for com-
panionship.

But the latter I am questioning to-night. Jock has
deserted me. He will not occupy the window seat of my
room, although his comforter is neatly spread upon it.
When I showed it to him he leaped up obediently, then
glanced out the window toward the main house, emitted
a long and melancholy howl, and with an air of firmness
not to be gainsaid, retired under the bed in Jane's room,
which faces toward the highroad. Nor could I later coax
him past the main house for a moonlight stroll upon the
beach.

He joined me there later, having reached it by some
devious route of his own through the marsh, but without enthusiasm.

Later: There has been wild excitement here, and
only now have we quieted down. It is clear that already
Clara has heard some of the local talk.

At eleven o'clock we heard wild screams from Clara's
attic bedroom, and all three of us arrived there in varying stages of undress. Clara was outside her door, which
was closed, and was hysterically shrieking that there was
a blue light under her bed.

I opened the door, entered the room, which was dark,
and stooped down. There *was* a blue light there,
luminous and spectral, and my very scalp prickled. I
think, had it not been for the women outside, I would
have howled like a dog. And the worst of it was that

it had an eye, a large staring eye that gazed at me with all the concentrated malevolence in the world.

It was a moment before I could say in an unshaken voice:

"Turn on the lights, somebody."

There was a delay until the switch was found, and for that moment the blue light stared at me and I at it. I heard Edith flop down on the floor beside me and give a little yelp, and Clara snivelling outside and saying she would never go into that room again. Never.

Then Jane turned on the lights, and I saw under the bed the large phosphorescent head of a dead fish, brought by Jock from the beach and carefully *cached* there!

June 27th.

I HAVE found Uncle Horace's letter, and in a manner so curious that there can be, it seems to me, but two interpretations of it. One is that, somehow, I have had all along a subconscious knowledge of its presence behind the drawer. But I hesitate to accept that. I am orderly by instinct, and when I went over the desk after his death, the merest indication of a paper caught behind the drawer would have sent me after it.

The other explanation is that I received a telepathic message. It came, as I fancy such messages must come, not from outside but from within. I heard nothing; it welled up, above the incoherent and vague wanderings of a mind not definitely in action, in a clear cut and definite form. "Take out the bottom drawer on the right."

But if I am to accept telepathy, I am to believe that I am not alone in my knowledge of this letter. Yet considering the tone of it, the awful possibility it indicates, who could have such a knowledge and yet keep it to himself? , . .

How did it get behind the drawer? If the brownish smudge on the corner turns out to be blood, and I think it is, then it was placed in the drawer after he died. Annie Cochran and Thomas both deny having seen any paper about. The doctor, perhaps? But would he not have read it first?

It had been crumpled into a ball and thrown into the drawer, and the subsequent opening of the drawer had pushed it back, out of sight. So much is clear.

But—after he fell!

Suppose—and in the privacy of this Journal I may surely let my imagination wander—suppose then, that some other hand picked up this paper, ignorant of its contents, and in a hurried attempt to put the room in order, flung it into the drawer? Or toward the waste basket beside it, and it fell short? Suppose, in a word, that he was not alone when he died? Suppose that some other hand, again, turned out the desk light and the others, and somehow overlooked the dim red lamp in the next room, or left it to see the way to escape?

I must not let my nerves run away with me. Murder is an ugly word, and after all we have Hayward's verdict of death by heart failure. But a sufficient shock, or a blow, might have brought that on. Fright, even, for the poor old chap was frightened when he wrote that letter. Trembling but uncompromising. That was like him.

"I realize fully the unpleasantness of my own situation; even, if you are consistent, its danger. But——"

But what? But in spite of this I shall do as I have threatened, probably.

I am profoundly moved to-night. We did not love one another, but he was old and alone, and menaced by some monstrous wickedness. Just what that wickedness was

no one can say, but I fully believe to-night that he died
of it. . . .

This morning I went with Edith to the main house,
she to select some odds and ends for the boat-house,
against Halliday's coming, and I to clear out the library
desk, to have it moved to the Lodge.

Edith was in high spirits as I unlocked the front door,
and was gravely telling Thomas, who accompanied us,
that we had seen a blue light under Clara's bed the night
before. But he expressed no surprise.

"Plenty of them, folks tell me," he said. "First time
I've heard of them in the Lodge, though."

"Oh!" said Edith slightly daunted. "So there are
lights, too."

"Yes'm," he replied. "Annie Cochran, she had one
here, used to hang around the shower-bath off the
gun room. And there used to be plenty outside. Fellows
setting trawl out in the bay used to see them over the
swamp."

"Marsh gas," I suggested.

"Maybe," he said, with his take-it or leave-it attitude,
and we went into the house.

There Edith and Thomas left me, and I opened the
shutters of the library and sat down at the desk. I
could hear Edith insisting on seeing the shower-bath off
the gun room. Then their voices died away, and I
began to go through the desk once more. All important
papers had been taken away after the death, and the
drawers contained the usual riff-raff of such depositories,
old keys, ancient check books, their stubs filled in Uncle
Horace's neat hand.

Naturally, I was thinking of him. More or less, I
was concentrated on him, if this is any comfort to my
spiritualistic friends. He had, indeed, fallen out of the
very chair in which I sat when he was stricken, and had

apparently cut his head badly on the corner of the desk. All this was in my mind, as I closed the last drawer and surveyed the heap of rubbish on the desk.

I suppose I was subconsciously reconstructing the night of his death, when he had penned that word "danger" which now lay, clearly outlined in reverse, on the blotter. And that when I wandered into the den, looking for a place to store what Lear calls the detritus piled up on the desk, I was still thinking of it. But I cannot feel that my entrance into the room, or my idly switching on the red lamp which stood there, had the slightest connection with the message I seemed at that moment to receive: "Take out the bottom drawer on the right."

I have heard people who believe in this sort of thing emphasize the peculiar insistence of the messages, and this was true in this case. I do not recall that there was any question in my mind, either, as to which bottom drawer on the right I was to remove. But I must record here a rather curious incident which my spiritualistic friends would add to the picture as proof positive of its other-earth origin.

Edith came back. I could hear her in the library.

"I've found Annie Cochran's blue light," she called. "A piece of phosphorescent wood. No wonder this neighborhood's haunted!" Then she came into the doorway, with Thomas behind her, and suddenly stopped.

"Why!" she said, "what funny shadows!"

"Shadows?"

Then she laughed and ran her fingers across her eyes.

"My error," she said. "When I came in I seemed to see a sort of cloud under the ceiling. It's gone now."

Old Thomas stood by, quietly.

"Lots of folks have seen them shadows," he said. "Some say they're red and some brown. I ain't ever seen them myself, so I can't say." He turned to go. "Maybe it's phosphorescence!" he said, and went away with a sort of hideous silent mirth shaking him.

Behind the drawer I found the letter.

(Note: I made no copy of the letter in the original Journal, so I give it here.)

Unfinished letter of Mr. Horace Porter, addressed to some one unknown, and dated the day of his death, June 27th of the preceding year:

"I am writing this in great distress of mind, and in what I feel is a righteous anger. It is incredible to me that you cannot see the wickedness of the course you have proposed.

"In all earnestness I appeal to you to consider the enormity of the idea. Your failure to comprehend my own attitude to it, however, makes me believe that you may be tempted to go on with it. In that case I shall feel it my duty, not only to go to the police but to warn society in general.

"I realize fully the unpleasantness of my own situation; even, if you are consistent, its danger. But——"

The letter had not been finished.

June 28th.

I SLEPT very little last night, and this morning made an excuse to go up to town with the letter. Larkin had telephoned me that he had an inquiry on the house through Cameron, and this gave me a pretext. Jane at first wished to go with me, but Edith coaxed her into helping with the rooms over the boat-house, and I finally got away.

Larkin is impressed with the letter, but does not necessarily see its connection with Uncle Horace's death.

"After all," he said, "you've got your medical man's statement that he died of heart failure. Suppose he *was* scared to death? That isn't a crime in law. And you've got to remember the old gentleman was pretty much of a pepper pot. He attacked me almost as violently as that once for my politics!"

"He didn't threaten you with the police, did he?"

"No; he recommended a Sanitarium, I think. You haven't an idea who it's meant for, you say?"

"Not the slightest. He hadn't any friends, intimates, so far as I know. The Livingstones, very decent people with a big place about six miles from him, his doctor, and myself—that's about all."

" 'Enormity of the idea,' " he read again. "Of course that might be a new poison gas, or this thing the press is always scaring up, the death ray. Some fellow with a bee in his bonnet, you may be sure."

"That wouldn't imply danger to himself."

"Any fellow with a bee in his bonnet is dangerous," he said, and gave me back the letter.

"Of course," he went on, "you've made a nice point about the stain on the corner. If it's blood, it's hardly likely he got up again and put it where you found it. But I think you'll find the servant there, what's her name, picked it up in her excitement and threw it into the drawer. People don't always know what they do at such times. However, if you like, I'll have that stain tested and see what it is."

I tore off the corner, and left him putting it carefully into an envelope. He glanced up as I prepared to go.

"What's this I hear about your keeping off demons by drawing some sort of a cabalistic design around yourself?" he asked. "You'd better let me in on it; I need a refuge now and then."

Which proves that a man may shout the eternal virtues and be unheard forever, but if he babble nonsense in a wilderness it will travel around the world.

Nevertheless, I am the better for the talk with him. I have been too closely consorting with my womenkind, probably; the most virile man can become effeminized in time. And Larkin's attitude as to renting the house is an eminently sane one.

"Rent it without saying anything," he said, "and ten to one whoever takes it will have a peaceable summer. But do as you suggest, tell the tenant the place has the reputation of being haunted, and ghosts will be as thick as mosquitos from the start."

He has asked for some photographs of the property, and I have promised them for the day after to-morrow. . . .

We have settled down into our routine here very comfortably. Our eggs and milk are brought each morning by a buxom farmer's daughter, one Maggie Morrison, a sturdy red-cheeked girl who drives in a small truck, and backs and turns before the Lodge rather than circle around the main house.

"Surely," I said to her yesterday, "you aren't afraid of the place in daylight?"

"Not afraid," she said, "but it gives me the shivers." And weakened that somewhat by her statement that she never liked a place where there had been a death. Yet she handles callously the cold corpses of her chickens, pulling up their poor rigid wings to show the tenderness of the dead skin beneath, and bending their stilled breast-bones to prove that they have died young!

With the lawns cut and the shrubbery trimmed, the place grows increasingly lovely. At low tide the beach is covered with odds and ends from the mysterious life of the sea, red and white starfish, sea urchins, and disintegrated jelly fish. Sea-gulls pick up mussels, hover over a flat-topped rock, drop them onto its surface and then swoop down upon the broken shell, with a warning cry to other gulls to keep away.

So clear was the water this afternoon that, rowing to the old sloop, I could see the barnacles encrusting it, and the long strings of kelp which hang from it like green and matted hair. Edith, bare-armed and slim in the canoe, paddled around it appraisingly.

"Needs a shave and a hair cut," she decided.

The boat-house is ready for young Halliday. She has put in it a great deal of love and one or two of my most treasured personal possessions.

"That isn't by any chance my smoking stand?"

"But you aren't going to smoke much this summer, Father William," she says, and tucks a hand into my arm. "I heard you say so yourself."

It has a sitting room, bedroom and kitchenette, but no bath.

"He can use the sea," says Edith, easily. "And take a cake of soap in with him."

"And wash himself ashore," I suggest, and am frowned down, probably as too old for such ribaldry.

Jane is very serene. Now and then, as she sits on our small verandah with her tapestry, I see her raise her eyes and glance toward the other house, but she does not mention it, nor do I. I notice that, like Maggie Morrison, she does not go very near to it, but she appears to have adopted an attitude of *laissez faire.*

But she absolutely refused to take the pictures of the house Larkin asks for. Not that she put it like that.

"I haven't had any luck with the camera lately," she said. "You take them, or let Edith do it."

The result of the collaboration, which followed early

this afternoon is still in doubt. Jane intends to develop and print them this evening.

And so our life goes on. We retire early, I generally slightly scented from the cold cream of Edith's good night kiss. Clara, too, goes up early, probably looking under her bed before retiring into it. And Jane sits and sews while I make my nightly entry in this Journal; she is, I think, both jealous and faintly suspicious of it!

At ten o'clock or so we let Jock out, and he looks toward the main house and then turns out the gates and into the highroad, where for a half hour or so he chases rabbits and possibly looks for a bear. At ten-thirty he scratches at the door, and we admit him and go up to bed. Behind the drain pipe!

Later: I have just had a surprise amounting to shock. Jane finds she has forgotten the black japanned lantern with a red slide which she uses in the mysterious rites of developing pictures, and suggests that we go to the other house and use the red lamp there.

"But I can bring it here."

"I am through being silly about the other house, William," she says with an air of resolution. "Anyhow, the pantry there is better, and you can sit in the kitchen. Bring a book or something."

She has, poor Jane, very much the air of Helena Lear's kitten the day Jock cornered it and it came out resolutely and looked him in the eye. In effect, Jane is going out to meet her bugaboo and stare it down.

June 29th.

JANE is in bed to-day, and I am not all I might be, although I managed to get an indifferent print or two to Larkin this morning.

It is well enough for cold-blooded and nerveless individuals to speak of fear as a survival of that time when, in our savage state, we were surrounded by enemies, dangers, and a thousand portents in skies we could not comprehend, and to insist that when knowledge comes in at the door, fear and superstition fly out of the window.

It is only in his head that man is heroic; in the pit of his stomach he is always a coward.

Yet, stripped of its trimmings,—the empty, echoing house, its reputation, and my own private thoughts about its possible tragedy, the incident loses much of its terror; is capable, indeed, of a quite normal explanation.

That is, that Jane either saw someone outside the pantry window, or was the victim of a subjective image of her own producing. . . .

To put the affair in consecutive shape.

At eleven o'clock I had moved the red lamp from the den in the other house to the pantry and there connected it. I also lighted the kitchen, and established myself there with "The Life and Times of Cavour," a book which I considered safe and sufficiently unexciting under the circumstances.

Jane seemed to be going very well beyond the pantry door, and after a time I ceased the reassuring whistling with which I had been affirming my continued presence within call, and grew absorbed in my book.

It must have been 11:15 when she called out to me sharply to know where a cold wind was coming from, and although I felt no such air I closed the kitchen door. It was within a couple of minutes of that, or thereabouts, that I suddenly heard her give a low moan, and the next instant there was the crash of a falling body.

When I opened the pantry door I found her in a dead faint, underneath the window. When she revived, she maintained that she had seen Uncle Horace.

Her statement runs about as follows: She had not felt particularly uneasy on entering the house, "although I had expected to," she admits. Nor at the beginning of operations in the pantry. The cold air, however, had had a peculiar quality to it; it "froze" her, she says; she felt rigid with it.

And it continued after she heard me close the kitchen door.

This wind, she says, was not only so cold that she called to me, but she had an impression that it was coming from somewhere near at hand, and she seemed to see the curtains blowing out at the window. The lower sash was down, as she could tell by the reflection of the red lamp in it, but she went to the window to see if the upper sash had been lowered.

With the darkness outside, the glass had become a sort of mirror, and she said her own figure in it startled her for a moment. She stood staring at it, when she realized that she was not alone in the room. Clearly reflected, behind and over her right shoulder, was a face.

It disappeared almost immediately, and I have my own private doubts about her recognition of it as Uncle Horace, which I believe is *post facto*. But I am obliged to admit that Jane saw something, either outside the window and looking in, or the creation of her own excited fancy.

As soon as I could leave her I went outside, but I could find no one there, and this morning I find that my own foot prints under the window have entirely obliterated anything else that may have been there.

Jane herself believes it was Uncle Horace, but I cannot find that she received anything more than an indistinct impression of a face. She rather startled me this morning, however, by asking me if I had ever thought that Uncle Horace had not died a natural death. "Why in the world should I think such a thing?"

But pressed for an explanation she merely said she had heard that the spirits of those who have died violent deaths are more likely to appear than of others who have passed peaceably away; that the desire to acquaint the world with the circumstances of the tragedy is overwhelming!

What seems much more likely is that she has caught from me, with that queer gift of hers, some inkling of my own anxiety. . . .

Larkin's report from the laboratory shows that the stain on the corner of the letter is blood. One lives and learns. Not only does the report state that it is blood, but that it is human blood. Moreover, that it is about a year old, and that it is the imprint of a human finger, but is too badly blurred for identification, as it was made while the blood was fresh.

So does science come to the aid of the police to-day. Truly one lives and learns.

Larkin watched me while I read the report.

"You see?" I said. "It is human blood."

"What else did you expect it to be?"

"Still, it shows something."

"Certainly it does," he agreed easily. "It may even show a crime, for all I know. But where do you go from there? That finger-print is valueless. Say there was a crime,—where's your criminal? You can't go through the world rounding up all the individuals society ought to be warned against."

"No," I said, rather feebly. "No, I dare say not."

He went with me to the door of his office, and put his hand on my shoulder.

"Go on out to the country and forget about it," he advised. "You're looking rather shot, Porter. Draw your magic circle or whatever it is about your cottage, and retire inside it! Whatever happened there last year, it's too late to do anything about it now."

He is right. I shall get out my fishing gear to-morrow and perhaps Edith will spare me young Halliday now and then. He is, she said the other day in the inelegant vernacular of present day youth, "about as psychic as a door knob."

June 30th.

I HAVE been brought to-day, for the first time, into active contact with the feeling of the country people against my house, and especially against the red lamp. It is an amazing situation.

Thomas came to the doorway this morning while I was at breakfast, followed by Starr the constable, who remained somewhat uneasily behind him. It developed that half a dozen sheep, in a meadow beyond Robinson's Point, were found the night before last with their throats cut. The farmer who owned them heard them milling about and ran out, and he declares he saw a dark figure dart out of the field and run into my woods at the head of Robinson's Point.

It appears that the farmer, whose name is Nylie, abandoned the pursuit as soon as he saw where the fugitive was headed, and went back to his dead sheep. They were neatly laid out in a row.

"At what time was all this?" I asked.

"Eleven o'clock, or thereabouts."

"How about a dog?" I asked. "They kill sheep, don't they? Catch them by the throat or something?"

"They don't stab them with a knife. Not around here, anyhow," said Starr.

The ostensible object of the visit was to ask if we had been disturbed that night, and for some reason or other I did not at once connect the situation with Jane's curious experience.

"No," I said. "You'll probably find that Nylie has an enemy somewhere, some hand he has discharged, perhaps."

Starr took himself away very soon after that, but before he left he exchanged a glance with Thomas, and I had a feeling that something lay behind this morning visit. It was not long before Thomas brought it out. It appears that Nylie ran after the figure to the edge of the wood, and there stood hesitating. The woods, I gather, share in the ill-repute of the house. And as he stood there, although everyone knew the house was empty, he distinctly saw the evil glow of the red lamp from it!

I dare say Jane is right, and my sense of humor is perverted, but I could not resist the opportunity of baiting Thomas. In which I realize now I made a tactical error.

"Really?" I said. "Nylie was certain of that, was he?"

"Saw it as plain as I see you," said Thomas. "I know you don't believe me——"

"But I do believe you. What about the red lamp?"

"Well," he said, "it's pretty well known about these parts that that lamp ain't healthy. Some say one thing and some say another, but most folks is agreed on that."

"Still, I don't see how it could kill sheep, do you?"

And even now I do not distinctly see the connection. I imagine the local belief is that the lamp exerts some malign influence, possibly even that it liberates some sinister spirit. Not, I imagine, that this is ever put into words. The nearest they come to that is the statement that the lamp is not "healthy," and that "George" has come back.

At least that is all that I can make out of that strange mixture of hysteria, superstitious fears and local mishaps to which Thomas gave birth in the next ten minutes or so. It began with Annie Cochran in the house after the lamp came, and gradually extended into the country-side; cows had mysteriously and prematurely calved; a meteorite had dropped into a field nearby; a fisherman's boat had been found empty in the bay on a quiet day and its owner never seen again; blight, pestilence and death had visited the community, equalled only in its history by the last few months of Mrs. Riggs' occupancy of the house. And the tradition was that Mrs. Riggs had used a red lamp to call her particular spirit.

" 'George' was his name," said Thomas, "and by and large he gave us a lot of trouble."

"Let me get this, Thomas," I said. "You mean that you think this 'George' has come back?"

"I'm not saying that," he said with his usual caution. "But there's some talk of it."

"And killed those sheep?"

"I'm not saying that either. But there's not a man, woman or child around these parts would have gone into those woods night before last, heading for the big house."

I felt that I had gone far enough, and I proceeded to explain the lighting of the lamp that night. But, although I saw that he believed me readily enough, it did not for a moment alter his attitude toward the red lamp.

"And, as a matter of fact," I concluded, "I think Mrs. Porter actually saw the man Nylie chased, looking in through the pantry window."

"That'll have been 'George' all right," said Thomas, and creaked heavily out of the room. . . .

To leaven the gloom of the morning, Halliday arrived to-day, in boisterous high spirits, broken with a sort of husky emotion when he saw his quarters.

"It's so darned good of you all," he said, and although the words were to Jane the look was for Edith.

We all escorted him down, Thomas carrying his kit bag, I his overcoat, Jock the newspaper and Warren himself staggering under a box of groceries and the canned goods on which he apparently intends to subsist. He has definitely refused Jane's offer to take his meals at our table.

"I'm the world's best cook with a can opener," he said boastfully. "And when bacon and beans begin to pall on me, I'll come up for a hand-out."

We stood around, Edith with entire shamelessness, while he unpacked and settled them. She herself insisted on arranging the top of the chest of drawers, and I saw her there, handling his hairbrushes caressingly. Poor little Edith, so frankly in love, so ready to believe that love is enough, and that such things as she has always taken for granted, food and shelter, will automatically follow in its train.

Afterwards we had tea on the narrow verandah over the water, and Halliday examined the old sloop with a professional eye.

"Pretty well out of condition, I'm afraid."

"Any boat's a good boat, sir," he said with his quick smile. "You shall be the skipper, and I'll be the midshipmite, the bo'sun tight and the crew of the—what's its name, anyhow?"

There followed a prolonged dispute between Edith and the new crew as to a name for the sloop, which was compromised by their announcing that it was to be called "The Cheese."

"Why? It has no holes in it," I protested.

"Because it's to have a skipper in it," said Edith conclusively.

After the women left we sat on the small verandah which surrounds the boat-house on three sides, and smoked. He told me his circumstances; he has exactly enough money to finish his course which will take another year. At the end of that time he is to have a junior partnership in a law firm in Boston.

"But you know what that means, at first," he said. "A sort of sublimated clerical job. It will be a long time before I am independent."

Before he could marry, was what he meant. And again I thought of my endowment fund for lovers. There are so many funds for preserving human life, and so few to make it worth the preserving. But I must talk to Edith. It is no use making the boy more unhappy than he is, or breaking down the restraints he is clearly putting on himself.

"I lost two years in the war," he said. "That threw me back, you see."

"I dare say it was not lost."

"No," he agreed. "I suppose a man must gain something by a thing like that, if he survives."

From that to the stories about the main house, and to Thomas's recital this morning, was not a long step, nor from that to the history of the house itself and to Mrs. Riggs.

"Curious," he said, "how these people rise, prosper, and then are found fraudulent, without discrediting the next generation of their kind. Eventually they are all caught between bases, and it begins all over again."

But the red lamp interested him.

"Some night, sir," he suggested, "you and I might go up there and try rubbing the thing; see if we can evoke the *genii*. . . ."

About 8:30 to-night I took Jock and walked to Nylie's farm, where the sheep had been killed. I found the field, and wandered idly in. To my surprise, a man with a shot-gun rose from a fence corner and confronted me, and Jock's hair rose as he prepared to spring.

"What do you want here?" he demanded, suspiciously.

"Go easy with that gun," I said. "My name's Porter, and I'm out for a stroll. That's all."

He apologized gruffly, while I held Jock by the collar, and even condescended to point out where the dead sheep had been found, but there was certainly no cordiality in his manner, and even a trace of hostility.

July 1st.

MORE sheep were killed last night. The Livingstones have lost a dozen of their blooded stock, and several farmers have suffered.

In each case the method is the same; the sheep are neatly stabbed in the jugular vein and then as neatly laid out in a row.

We are buying no mutton from the local butcher!

I assured Thomas this morning that I had not lighted the red lamp again, but he did not smile. He is quite capable of believing, I dare say, that I have summoned a demon I cannot control.

But he tells me that a county detective from town, sent by the sheriff, is coming out to look into the matter. And there is a certain relief in this. It seems to me that we have to do with some form of religious mania, symbolistic in its manifestation. The sheep is the ancient sacrifice of many faiths.

This belief is strengthened by Thomas's statement that in each case save the first one there has been left on a nearby rock or, in one instance, on a fence, a small cabalistic design roughly drawn in chalk. . . .

8:00 P.M. I feel like a man who has dreamed of some horrible or grotesque figure, and wakes to find it perched on his bed-post.

The detective sent by Benchley, the Sheriff, has just been here, a man named Greenough, a heavy-set individual with a pleasant enough manner and a damnable smile, behind which he conceals a considerable amount of shrewdness.

He had, of course, gathered together the local superstitions, and he was inclined to be facetious concerning my ownership of the red lamp. But he was serious enough about the business that had brought him.

"It's probably psychopathic," he said, "and the psychopath is a poor individual to let loose in any community, especially when he's got a knife."

My own suggestion of religious mania seemed to interest him.

"It's possible," he said. "It's a queer time in the world, Mr. Porter. People seem ready to do anything, think anything, to escape reality. And from that to delusional insanity isn't very far."

I suppose I looked surprised at that, for he smiled.

"I read a good bit," he said, "and my kind of work is about nine-tenths psychology, anyhow. You've got to know what your criminal was thinking, and then try to think like him. The third degree is nothing but applied psychology." He smiled again. "But that's a long way from sheep-killing. Now I'll ask you something. Did you ever hear of a circle, with a triangle inside it?"

I suppose I started, and I had a quick impression that his eyes were on me, shrewdly speculative behind his glasses. But the next moment he had reached into his pocket and drawn out a pencil and an envelope. "Like this," he said, and drawing the infernal symbol slowly and painstakingly, held it out to me.

To save my life I could not keep my hand steady; the envelope visibly quivered, and I saw his eyes on it.

"What do you mean, hear of it?" I asked. And then it came to me suddenly that that ridiculous statement of mine had somehow got to the fellow's ears, and that he was quietly hoaxing me. "Good Lord!" I said, and groaned. "So you've happened on that too!"

"So you know something about it?" he said quietly, and leaned forward. "Now, do you mind telling me what you know?"

He had not been hoaxing me. There was a curious significance in his manner, in the way he was looking at me, and it persisted while I told my absurd story. Told it badly, I realize, and haltingly; that I had picked up a book on Black Magic somewhere or other, and had as promptly forgotten it, save for one or two catch phrases and that infernal symbol of a triangle in a circle; how I had foolishly repeated them to a group of women, and now seemed likely never to hear the last of it.

"As I gather, the Lear woman has spread it all over town," I said. "She dabbles in spiritualism, or something, and it seems to have appealed to her imagination."

"It has certainly appealed to somebody's imagination," he said. "That's the mark our friend the sheep-killer has been leaving."

He was very cordial as he picked up his hat and prepared to depart. He was sorry to have had to trouble me; nice little place I had there. He understood I was fighting shy of the other house. He would do the same thing; he didn't believe in ghosts, but he was afraid of them.

And so out onto the drive, leaving me with a full and firm conviction that he suspects me of killing some forty odd sheep in the last few nights, probably in the celebration of some Black Mass of my own psychopathic devising.

July 2nd.

L ARKIN thinks he has rented the house. I made a telephone message from him the excuse to go to town this morning. Mr. Bethel was not present, but his secretary was, a thin boy with a bad skin and with his hair pomaded until it looks as though it is painted on his head. He smoked one cigarette after another as we talked.

If to-morrow is fair, Mr. Bethel will motor out and look over the property. It appears that he is in feeble health. If it is not, Gordon, the secretary, will come alone. It develops that, although the boy is a local product, and not one to be particularly proud of, Mr. Bethel comes from the west; Cameron's note to Larkin merely introduced him, but assumed no responsibility. As, however, he offers the rent in advance, the matter of references becomes, as Larkin says, an unimportant detail.

I get the impression from the secretary that the old man is writing a book, and wishes to be undisturbed, and if his choice of a secretary fairly represents him, he will be.

From Larkin I learned that he had heard of the circle in a triangle from Helena Lear herself, at a dinner table, and that he has no idea that it is at all wide-spread. He regards the use of it by the sheep-killer as purely coincidence, which greatly cheers me.

Nevertheless, I went to the Lears and lunched there. Helena has agreed to spread the thing no further, and I came away with a great sense of relief. Into the bargain, Lear tells me that Cameron, after studying the photograph I sent him, is inclined to think it is the result of a double exposure.

"Double exposure or a thought image," Lear says. "He has had some success himself in getting curious forms on a sensitized plate. Got the number five once, after concentrating on it for an hour! I asked him about Doyle's fairies, but he only laughed."

All in all, I feel to-day that I was unduly apprehensive last night. The weather is magnificent; Edith, in knickerbockers and a sweater, has been holding nails for young Halliday to-day while he repairs the float. Jane has taken over from Thomas the care of the flower beds around the cottage, and has been busy there all afternoon with a weed-puller and a hoe, and I have found the sails for the sloop, mildewed but usable, in the attic of the Lodge.

No more sheep were killed last night. I understand Greenough has put guards on all the nearby flocks, and advised outlying farms to do the same thing. Maggie Morrison told us this morning that they were doing it, but in, I gathered, a half-hearted manner. Most of them believe that, by his very nature, the marauder is impervious to shot and shell.

"Joe Willing," she says, "saw something moving around his cow barn a night or so ago, and he fired right into it. But when he ran up there was nothing there."

One curious thing, however, has been brought in by Starr, who stopped on his way past to-day. In a meadow not far from the Livingstone place two large stones, which had lain there for years, have been moved together and stood on their edges, and a flat slab of rock laid across them. On top of this, when it was found, there lay a small heap of fine sand.

One can figure, of course, that here is an altar, erected by the same unbalanced mind which has been killing the sheep. But no offering has yet been laid on it.

Later: Halliday spent the evening here, and I walked back with him. He tells me that on his first night in the boat-house, he saw a light moving over the salt marsh, about three hundred feet away.

He was sitting on the small balcony of the boat-house, which surrounds it on three sides, and glancing toward the marsh, saw a light there. It seemed to float above the marsh at a distance of three or four feet, and was intermittent.

At first he thought it was someone on the way to the beach, with a flash light or a lantern, and he watched with some curiosity. Earlier in the evening he had himself walked along the edge of the swamp and decided it was not passable. But half way through the marsh the light stopped and then disappeared.

"I decided the chap, whoever it was, was in trouble," he said, "so I called to him. But there was no answer, and the light didn't appear again."

"Marsh gas, probably," I explained. "Methane, C.H., of course."

"Marsh gas burns with a thin blue flame, doesn't it? This was a small light, rather white. I waited an hour or so, but it didn't show again."

I have, since my return, looked up the book on the Oakville phenomena which I discovered on the desk of the main house. It is not significant, but it is interesting, to find that Mrs. Riggs produced fleeting lights, sometimes of a bluish-green, from the cabinet, again a sparkling point which generally localized itself near her head. But I cannot find any record of a light persisting for any length of time, or following a definite course.

July 3rd.

THE house is rented. As it rained this morning, the secretary came alone, and seemed very well satisfied.

But at the last moment my conscience began to worry me, and perhaps too, for none of our motives are unmixed, I was afraid he suspected something. He made some observation about the rent being low for a property of that size, and glanced at me as he said it, so I plunged.

"I think I'd better be honest with you, even if it costs me money," I said. "The house is cheap because it —well, it isn't an easy house to rent."

"Too lonely, eh?"

"Partly that, and partly because—a portion of the house is very old, and there have been some stories about it circulating in the neighborhood for years."

"Ghost stories?"

"You can call them that."

He seemed to be amused, rather than alarmed. He grinned broadly and took out a cigarette.

"Ghosts won't bother me any," he said rather boastfully. "What kind of a ghost?"

"I don't believe anyone claims to have seen anything. The reports are mostly of raps and various noises."

He seemed to take a peculiar, almost a furtive, enjoyment out of my statement, my confession, rather.

"Hot dog!" he said. "Well, raps won't bother me, and Mr. Bethel's got a deaf ear; he can turn that up at night if they worry him."

So the house is rented, unless something unexpected turns up, and I have done my part. But I confess to an extreme distaste for the secretary and Edith may find herself with a small problem on her hands. For just before we left he spied her on the float, and gave her a careful inspection.

"That looks pretty good to me," he said. And although his gesture embraced the water front his eyes were on her.

I have arranged with Annie Cochran, following Gordon's query about a servant, to resume her old position at the main house. She refuses to remain after dark, but I presume this will be satisfactory. She will also commence to-morrow to get the house in readiness.

With that strange swiftness with which news travels in the country, already the word has gone out that the place is rented, and I lay to that our sudden popularity this afternoon. The first to arrive was Doctor Hayward, as nervous and jerky as ever, fiddling with his collar, and when for a moment excluded from the talk, gnawing abstractedly at his finger ends. Nothing escapes the man; I sometimes feel that he goes about on his rounds, collecting gossip as assiduously as he disperses the medicines he puts up in his small dispensary, and that his mind is similarly stocked with it, put up neatly on shelves and in order, so that he can conveniently put his hand on it.

He addressed himself mostly to Jane—there is a certain type of medical man who wins his way into families by the favor of women, and is more at his ease with them than with its men-folk—and only beat a circuitous route to the subject uppermost in his mind, which clearly was that an elderly invalid had taken Twin Hollows and would probably require a physician.

In the course of this roundabout talk, however, I came finally to the conclusion that, like the detective, he was watching me. And, as had happened with Greenough, I became absurdly self-conscious. The very knowledge that, the moment I looked away, his eyes slid to me and

there remained, made me awkward. As a result I upset my tea-cup, and while Jane was hurrying for a cloth
to repair the damage, he said:

"Pretty nervous, aren't you?"

"Not particularly. But I happen to specialize in upsetting tea-cups."

"How are you sleeping?"

"Like a top," I assured him with a certain truculence,
I dare say. But he is fairly thick-skinned. He passed
it over by giving his collar a twitch.

"Dream any?" he inquired.

By heaven! The fellow was not only watching me; he
was analyzing me. And with that peculiar perverse
humor which, I feel to-night, may get me into trouble
yet, I answered. I who seldom dream, and then the be-
nign dreams of an uneventful life and an easy conscience,
I answered:

"Horribly!"

He leaned back and took to biting a finger, staring
at me over it. "What do you mean by 'horribly'?" he
inquired. But some gleam of reason came to me then,
and I laughed.

"Sorry, Hayward," I said, "I couldn't resist it. I
never dream, at least nothing I can remember. But you
were being so professional——"

Jane's return prevented the apology which was on his
lips, and he went back to the local gossip. Once I mentioned the matter of the sheep, but he rather dexterously
side-stepped it, and finally brought the talk around to
the renting of the house. But I am confident that
Greenough has been to him about me, and has asked him
to give him an opinion on my mental balance.

I was on guard after that; determined to exhibit myself in my most rational manner. But there is something upsetting in the mere thought that one's sanity is

being brought into question. One's usually automatic acts become self-conscious ones. And to-night I could laugh, if I were not somewhat disturbed by it, at the care with which I placed my cigarette on the saucer of my tea-cup and flung the silver spoon into the grate; at the sudden comprehension of what I had done, and my wild leap to recover the spoon; and at Hayward's intent expression as I turned from the fireplace with the spoon in my hand, and muttered something about being the original man who put his umbrella to bed and stood himself in the corner. He was too absorbed to smile.

He left finally, when the Livingstones arrived.

"You must take good care of this fine husband of yours, Mrs. Porter," he said, holding her hand in the paternal fashion of his type. "He's probably been overdoing it a bit." The result of which is that Jane herself has taken to watching me quietly, over her tapestry, and that she suggested this evening that I take a course of bromide for my nerves.

Irritated at Hayward as I was, and annoyed at myself, I saw him to his car, and asked him the question which has been in the back of my mind ever since I found the letter in the library desk.

"By the way," I said, "you knew my Uncle Horace pretty well. Better than I did, in recent years. Did he have many friends—I mean, locally?"

He straightened his tie with a jerk.

"He had no intimates at all, so far as I know. I knew him as well as anybody. He rather liked Mrs. Livingstone, but he had no use for Livingstone himself."

"Well, I'll change the question. Do you know of any quarrel he had had, shortly before he died?"

"That's easier. He quarreled with a good many people. I imagine you know that as well as I do."

"He never mentioned to you that he had had a definite difference of opinion with anyone?"

Looking back to-night over that conversation, I am inclined to think that he had an answer for that question, and that he almost gave it. But he changed his mind. The purpose of his visit must have come to him, Greenough's story about that idiotic circle and my own lame explanation of it, and all the outrageous mess in which I had involved myself.

"I'd like to know why you ask me that," he said instead.

"He had never talked to you about calling on the police, in some emergency?"

"Never. I see what you're driving at, Porter," he added. "I admit, I had some thought of that myself at the time. But the autopsy showed the cause of death all right. He wasn't murdered."

"The blow on the head had nothing to do with it, then?"

He glanced at me quickly.

"If it *was* a blow," he said, "it didn't help matters any, of course. But I prefer to think that the head injury was received as he fell." He hesitated. "Don't you?"

"Naturally," I agreed.

But there was a significance in that pause of his, followed by "don't you" which has stayed with me ever since. It was almost as though, in view of Greenough's visit to him and my own questions, I had been somehow responsible for the poor old boy's death, and was seeking reassurance. . . .

1:00 A.M. I am not able to sleep, and so, recipient of all my repressions, I come to you. I have repeated my little formula over and over, as some people count sheep. "Milton and Dryden and Pope." "Milton and

Dryden and Pope," but without result. Yet I have seen whole class-rooms succumb to the soporific effect of that or some similar phrase in the early hours of a bright morning.

I have even been out, in dressing gown and slippers, and wandered a way down the main road, where I was surprised by a countryman with a truck load of produce and probably recognized. If any more sheep are killed to-night!

What am I to think about this red lamp business?

Into every situation it insistently intrudes itself. It was burning when old Horace died; I had turned it on in the closed and shuttered den the day I received that curious message about the letter; Jane lights it to develop the pictures of the house for Larkin, and Nylie's sheep are killed. What is more, Jane sees a face, either outside the window or behind her in the pantry. From the moment of its entrance into the house, after eighteen years of quiet, the old stories of hauntings are revived, raps are heard, footsteps wander about, and furniture appears to move.

Is Greenough right, and am I ready for the psychopathic ward of some hospital? Is this accumulation of evidence actual, or have I imagined it? And yet I am sane enough, apparently. I listen, and I hear the familiar sounds of night-time here, Jock moving about uneasily in Jane's bedroom next to mine; the rhythmic creaking of the run-way to the float, as the wash of the tide swings it to and fro on its rollers. I hear no voices whispering. . . .

Yet Mrs. Livingstone was most explicit this afternoon. She clearly has no nerves, being complacent with the complacence of fat rapidly gained in middle age, and no imagination, or she would have taken lemon in her tea, and no sugar. But she sat there, ignoring little Livingstone's attempts to change the subject, and soberly warned me against renting the house.

Jane's face was a study. So far I had been able to keep from her much of the local gossip about the house, and all of the talk about the red lamp. But now she heard it all, garnished and embellished, and I caught her eyes fixed on me piteously.

"Is it too late, William?" she asked. "Must we rent it now?"

"It's all signed, sealed and delivered, my dear," I said. "But all is not lost. To-morrow morning I shall take my little hatchet and smash that lamp to kingdom come."

Mrs. Livingstone took a slice of cake.

"I'm sure you have my permission," she said, "and as I gave it to your Uncle Horace, I dare say I have a right to say so."

"Perhaps you would like to have it back?"

"God forbid!" she said quickly.

"Oh, for heaven's sake," Livingstone put in irritably, "let's talk about something else. Mrs. Porter, will you show me your garden?"

I had a feeling that his wife had wanted just this, perhaps had given him some secret signal, for she settled back the moment they had gone and, so to speak, opened fire.

"You're not a spiritist, Mr. Porter?"

" 'I am a cynic; I am a carrion crow,' " I quoted. But I saw the words had no meaning for her. She may have felt some underlying amusement in them, however, for she stiffened somewhat, and rather abruptly changed her point of attack.

"I have often wondered," she said slowly, "whether you have ever considered your uncle's death as—unusual."

"You mean that you do?"

"Personally," she said, looking directly at me, "I think he was frightened to death." She hesitated. She gave me the impression of venturing on ground which was unpleasant to her. "Either that or—" She abandoned that, and began again, hurriedly.

"My husband dislikes the subject," she said. "But I will tell you why I believe what I do, and you can see what you can make of it. You remember that Mrs. Porter was not well when you both came out, the day he was found dead, and toward evening you took her home? Well, Annie Cochran would not stay alone that night, and I stayed with her. It was very—curious."

"Just what do you mean by curious?"

"That there was somebody in the house that night, or something."

"And you don't believe it was somebody?"

"I don't know what I believe," she said, rather breathlessly. "I suppose, since you claim to be a cynic you will laugh, but I have to tell you just the same."

Stripping her narrative to the skeleton, she had been sceptical before, but that night the house had been strangely uncanny. They had sat in the kitchen with all the lights on, and at two o'clock in the morning she distinctly heard somebody walking in the hall overhead, on the second floor. Doors seemed to open and shut, and finally, on a crash from somewhere in the dining room, "like a doubled fist striking the table," Annie Cochran had bolted outside and stayed there. At dawn she came back, and said she had distinctly seen a ball of light floating in the room over the den, shortly after she went out.

"And was the red lamp lighted, while all this was going on?"

"That's one of the most curious things about it. It

was not, when I made a round of that floor early in the evening. But it was going at dawn."

There is, of course, one thing I can do. I can meet Mr. Bethel when he arrives and lay my cards on the table. It will take all my courage; I know how I should feel if I had taken a house, and at the moment of my arrival a wild-eyed owner came to turn me away, on the ground that his house is haunted. Or, we will say, subject to inexplicable nocturnal visits. . . .

Shall I take Halliday into my confidence? I need a fresh brain on the matter, certainly. Someone who will see that the local connection of the murdered sheep with the red lamp, and so with old Horace's death, is the absurdity it must be.

July 4th.

A QUIET Fourth, but in spite of all precautions, more sheep were killed last night, and in fear of my life I have been expecting a visit from Greenough this morning. But perhaps old Morrison—it looked like the Morrison truck—did not recognize me last night.

But to make things more unpleasant all around, the fellow this time did not leave his infernal chalk mark! One can imagine Greenough straightening from his investigation and deciding that his recent talk with me has put me on my guard. Heigh ho!

The neighborhood is in a wild state of alarm. The failure of the detective from town to stop the killings has probably added to the superstitious fears which seem mixed up in it. But the more intelligent farmers have got out their rifles and duck guns, and there will be short shrift for the fellow if he is seen at work.

Public opinion appears to be divided between a demon and a dangerous lunatic at large. . . .

Otherwise, I have recovered from last night's hysteria.

The cleaning of the house for Mr. Bethel begins to-day, and I have decided to let it go on. If on hearing my story he decides not to stay no harm will be done; if he remains, it is in order for him.

Jane said at breakfast: "Are you letting him come, William?"

"I shall tell him all I know, my dear. After that it is up to him."

"But is it? Suppose something happens to him?"

"What on earth could happen?" I inquired irritably. "He doesn't need to light that silly lamp. Anyhow, I'm going to destroy it. And as for the other matter, the sheep, the fellow is sticking to sheep, thank God."

But I am not so certain, just now, as to destroying the lamp. This is the result of a conversation with Annie Cochran, as I admitted her, armed with broom and pail, to the house this morning.

She represents, I imagine, the lowest grade of local intelligence, and I daresay she is responsible for much of the superstitious fear of the lamp. But after all, her attitude represents that of a part of the community, and if I destroy the lamp I shall undoubtedly be held responsible for any local tragedies for the next lifetime or two.

In a word, Annie Cochran not only believes that the lamp houses a demon; she believes that to smash the lamp will liberate that demon in perpetuity.

Incredible? Yet who am I to laugh at this, who went a-running to Lear with a double-exposure photograph, and have been secretly annoyed that little Pettingill has never asked me to one of his table-tipping seances? Or who have, in deference to Annie Cochran and her kind, most carefully locked away the red lamp in an attic closet of the other house, there to contain its devil unreleased. Or who am, at this moment, somewhat oppressed by a so-called spirit message I have just received, forwarded to me by Cameron's secretary.

It is a difference of degree, not of kind.

This is my first letter from the spirit world, and it comes via Salem, Ohio! I have had a curious message or two, witness the unknown correspondent who for several years at intervals sent me a playing card in an envelope, so that it was nothing unusual for me to receive the deuce of spades with my bacon and eggs, or the knave of diamonds for tea. But this one stands in a class by itself.

It has, in Mr. Cameron's absence, been forwarded to me by his secretary.

"My dear Mr. Porter:

"In Mr. Cameron's absence on his vacation I am forwarding the enclosed message at the request of the writer, who appears to have considerable faith in our ability to locate the person for whom it is intended!

"We have had no previous correspondence with the young lady. At least I can find none in our files. But I know you will not mind my saying, in Mr. Cameron's absence, that he has always regarded these ouija board communications as purely subconscious in origin; in other words, as unconscious fraud."

The enclosed note is very long, and fully detailed. Even the arrangement of the furniture in the room is described, and the lighting of it. How she came to omit a red lamp I cannot tell; I have somehow grown to expect one! But no amount of light handling of the matter on my part can alter the fact that I am not as comfortable about the thing as I might be. The damnable accuracy of it is in itself disconcerting. The name is right, even to my initial; I am living in a lodge, which even my own subconscious mind could hardly have anticipated a few days ago. And I am warned of danger, on a morning when I feel that danger is, as Edith would say, my middle name.

According to the writer, she and the other sitter, who she naively explains was her *fiancé*, received twice the name, William A. Porter. Assured then that they had it accurately, the "control" spelled out as follows:

"Advise you and Jane to go elsewhere. Lodge dangerous."

It sounds, I admit, like a telegraphic message, with one word to spare. One rather looks for the word "love," so often added to get full value for one's money. But it is a definite warning for all that.

So the Lodge is dangerous, and Jane and I advised to go elsewhere. Heaven knows I'd like nothing better. . . .

Our love story goes on, and I am as helpless there as in other directions; Edith proffering herself simply and sweetly, in a thousand small coquetries and as many unstudied allurements, and young Halliday gravely adoring her, and holding back.

To-day, along with the rest of the summer colony, they made a pilgrimage in the car to the scenes of the various meadow tragedies, ending up with the stone altar, and I suspect matters came very nearly to a head between them, for Edith was very talkative on their return, and Halliday very quiet and a trifle pale.

And to-night, sitting on the verandah of the boat-house, while the boy set off Roman candles and sky-rockets over the water, Edith asked me how I thought she could earn some money.

"Earn money?" I said. "What on earth for? I've never known you to think about money before."

"Well, I'm thinking about it now," she said briefly,

and relapsed into silence, from which she roused in a moment or so to state that money was a pest, and if she were making a world she'd have none in it.

I found my position slightly delicate, but I ventured to suggest that no man worth his salt would care to have his wife support him. She ignored that completely, however, and said she was thinking of writing a book. A book, she said, would bring in a great deal of money, and "nobody would need to worry about anything."

"And you could get it published, Father William," she said. "Everybody knows who you are. And you could correct the spelling, couldn't you? That's the only thing that's really worrying me."

And I honestly believe the child is trying it. Her light is still going to-night as I can see under her door.

July 5th.

THE Sheriff has offered a thousand dollars reward for the apprehension and conviction of the sheep-killer. A notice to that effect is neatly tacked on a post outside our gates, and must rather appeal to Greenough's sense of humor, if he has any. I understand Livingstone is privately offering another five hundred.

Mr. Bethel and his secretary arrive to-morrow, and the house is about ready for them, in spite of the fact that Annie Cochran moves about it, unoccupied as it is, like a scared rabbit. I shall see him at once on his arrival.

Halliday will finish the float to-day, and I understand intends then to start on the sloop. He has found a way to address me, instead of the formal "sir" of the first day or two, and now calls me skipper.

He is visibly more cheerful since yesterday. However hopeless the future looks, he must, during that "show-down" yesterday, as Edith would undoubtedly call it, have been fairly assured of her love for him. To-day I overheard a conversation between him and Clara.

"Well, I must be getting on," he said. "It's my wash day."

"Wash day, is it?" she commented sceptically. "I'd like to see your clothes after *you* wash them."

"Who said anything about clothes?" he demanded. "It's my dish-washing day. I always do them every Monday morning."

I watched him go down the drive, his head virtuously erect and Jock, who adores him, bidding him a reluctant good-bye. He will not follow him in that direction.

The boy wheedles Clara out of food, too, while Jane stands by and smiles. Passing the pantry window yesterday I saw him stop abruptly, and stare at the table inside.

"I beg your pardon, Clara," he said, "but are those *custard* pies?"

"They are. And you needn't be thinking——"

"Real, honest-to-goodness custard pies?"

"That's what the cook-book calls them."

"Would you mind if I came a little closer, Clara?" he inquired. "I have heard of them, but it is so long since I have seen one, let alone tasted it——!"

"They're too fresh to cut," said Clara, weakening, one could see, by inches.

"But I could come back," he said gently. "I could go and sit in my lonely boat-house, surrounded by the cans I live out of, and think about them. And later I could come back, you know."

And although he did not come back, a half hour later I saw Clara carrying one down to him, neatly covered with a napkin.

To-day, for the first time, I have taken him fully into

my confidence. I had been half way debating it, but the matter of the dressing gown decided it.

(Note: I find that in the original Journal I made no note of this incident. The facts are as follows):

At Jane's suggestion I proceeded to the main house, to remove such of Uncle Horace's clothing as remained in the closets and so on, to a trunk in the attic. Since the night of her experience in the pantry she had not entered the house. Armed with a package of moth-preventive, I was on my way when I met Halliday, and he returned with me.

We worked quietly, for there is something depressing in the emptiness of such garments, and in their mute reminder that sooner or later we must all shed the clothing that we call the flesh.

I said something of this and the boy gave me rather a twisted smile.

"It can't be so bad," he said. "Not worse than things are here sometimes, anyhow. And as Burroughs said—wasn't it Burroughs?—'the dead do not lie in the grave, lamenting there is no immortality.'"

"Then you don't believe in immortality?"

"I don't know what I believe," he replied. "I know it isn't any use telling us we're going to be happy in the next world, to make up for our being darned miserable in this."

It was shortly after this that I located the dressing gown which poor old Horace was wearing when he was found, and discovered that there were blood-stains on it near the hem.

"I'm going to ask you something," I said to Halliday. "A man dies of heart failure, and as he falls strikes his head, so that it bleeds. He lies there, from some time in the evening until seven o'clock in the morning. There wouldn't be much blood, would there?"

"Hardly any, I should say."

"And none in this location, I imagine."

I showed it to him, and he looked at me curiously.

"I'm afraid I don't get it, Skipper," he said. "You mean, he moved, afterwards?"

"If you want to know exactly what I mean, I believe the poor old chap was knocked down, that he got up and managed to dispose of something he had in his hand, something he didn't want seen, and that *after that* his heart failed."

He picked up the dressing gown and carried it to the window.

"Tell me about it," he said quietly.

As neither one of us knows anything about the heart, or what occurs when a fatal seizure attacks it, it is possible Halliday is right. That is, that feeling ill he got up, crumpled the letter in his hand, turned out the desk light, and then fell. But that he recovered himself and managed to drag himself to his feet again, when the full force of the seizure came, and he fell once more, not to rise.

"There is no real reason to believe that he was not alone," he said. "Nor even that he 'saw something,' as Mrs. Livingstone intimates."

But the letter I had found in the drawer interests him. He has made a copy of it, and taken it home to study.

"I appeal to you to consider the enormity of the idea. Your failure to comprehend my own attitude to it, however, makes me believe that you may be tempted to go on with it. In that case I shall feel it my duty, not only to go to the police but to warn society in general.

"I realize fully the unpleasantness of my own situation; even, if you are consistent, its danger. But——"

"But—what?" said Halliday. "'But I shall do what I have threatened, if *you go on with it.*'" He glanced up

at me. "It doesn't sound like sheep-killing, does it?"
"No," I was obliged to admit. "It does not."

July 6th.

I AM in a fair way to go to jail if things keep on as
they have been going! And not only for sheep-killing.
If we have not had a tragedy here, certainly to-day there
is every indication of it. And with the fatality which has
attended me for the past week or so, I have managed
to get myself involved in it.

Last night a youth named Carroway, sworn in by
Starr a few days ago as deputy constable, was assigned
the highroad behind our property as his beat. He was
armed against the sheep-killer with a 30-30 Winchester,
which was found this morning in the hedge not far from
our gates.

Nothing is known of his movements from nine o'clock,
when he went on duty, until a few minutes after midnight,
when he appeared breathless on the town slip, minus his
rifle, and jumping into a motor launch moored at the
float, started off into the bay.

Peter Geiss, an old fisherman, was smoking his pipe
on the slip at the time, but Peter is deaf, and although
Carroway shouted something the old man did not hear
it. There is, however, an intermediate clue here, for on
his way Carroway had run into the Bennett House, and
told the night clerk there to awaken Greenough and get
him to our float; that the sheep-killer had taken a boat
there and was somewhere out on the water.

The deputy's idea was probably to drive the fugitive
back to the shore, and as there are, due to the marshes,
but few landing places there, he seems so far as I can
make out to have figured that the unknown would be
forced back to our slip.

Greenough appears to have lost no time. He threw an overcoat over his pajamas, took his revolver, and commandeering a car in the street, was on our pier before Carroway had been on the water ten minutes. And here, with that fatality which has recently pursued me, he found me returning from the float!

There are times when misfortune apparently picks up some hapless individual as her victim and, perhaps for the good of his soul, hammers him on this side and on that until he himself begins to think he has deserved it. He is guilty of something; he knows not what.

I was a guilty man as I faced Greenough! And yet the scene must have had its elements of humor. I, rather shaken already with the night air, my teeth rattling, and this ghostly figure suddenly appearing on the run-way above me and turning my knees to water; a terror which only changed in quality when this ghost instructed me to put up my hands.

But I knew the voice, and I managed as debonair a manner as was possible under the circumstances.

"Nothing in them but a flash-light," I said. "However, if you insist——"

He seemed to hesitate. Then he laughed a little, not too pleasantly, and came down the run-way to me.

"Out rather late, aren't you, Mr. Porter?" he asked.

It was my turn to hesitate.

"I came down to pull the canoe up onto the float," I said finally. "Mrs. Porter thought the sea was rising."

"Sounds quiet enough to me," he retorted and turning on his flash, he ran it over the surface of the water, which was as still as a mill-pond, and onto the canoe, which lay bottom-up and still dripping, on the float.

It is indicative of the whole situation, I think, that he lighted the flash. He was no longer lurking in the dark, waiting for the motor boat to drive the marauder ashore.

That marauder, in the shape of a shivering professor of English literature, slightly unbalanced mentally, was before him.

Then he seemed to be listening, and knowing the story this morning, I daresay he was listening, for the beat of the motor engine. There was no sound, and this I imagine puzzled him, as it is puzzling the entire community to-day. I am myself not particularly observant, and any testimony I might give would, under the circumstances, be discredited in advance. But my own impression is that there was the sound of an engine from somewhere on the bay as I crossed the lawn, and that it had ceased before I reached the water's edge.

Greenough was frankly puzzled. He had, one perceives, a problem on his hands. He wanted Carroway to come in and identify me, for without that identification he was helpless. And somewhere out on the water was Carroway, possibly with a stalled engine. He put his hands to his mouth and called:

"Hi! Bob!" he yelled. *"Bob."*

But there was no answer, except that Halliday came running out and asked what the trouble was. Greenough was thoroughly irritated; he lapsed into a sulky, watchful silence, and offered no objection when I shiveringly suggested that I go back to my bed. I left them both there, Halliday preparing to row out and locate the launch if possible, and came back to the Lodge.

This morning I learn that Carroway's boat was found by Greenough who had a fast launch with a searchlight, at one o'clock this morning, drifting out with the tide and about two miles from land. It was empty, and no sign of young Carroway was found. As it trailed no dory, our mystery has apparently become a tragedy.

And I am under suspicion. I have put that down, and sitting back have stared at it. It is true. And suppose what I am expecting at any moment takes place, and Greenough comes into the drive, to confront me with the damnable mass of evidence he has put together, the circle enclosing the triangle; the fact that the sheep-killing did not commence until after our arrival at the Lodge; the night Morrison, driving his truck-load of produce, saw me on the road; and most of all, with last night!

Suppose I tell him the actual fact? That my wife has some curious power, and that in obedience to it she last night roused me from a virtuous sleep, to tell me she had clairvoyantly seen a man taking a boat from our float, and that I must immediately go down; that there was, she felt, something terribly wrong? Suppose I told him that, which is exactly the fact? And also that, once there, I found that Edith had left the canoe in the water, and that I had, like the careful individual I am, drawn it up out of harm's way? Will he believe that? I wonder——

Quite aside from my unwillingness to drag Jane into this, particularly as the possessor of a faculty which she herself only reluctantly reveals even to me, is my conviction that such a story, soberly told, would only increase Greenough's suspicion of my sanity.

And as if to add to the precariousness of the situation, Halliday himself in all innocence has added another damning factor; gave it, indeed, to the detective last night.

Yesterday, it appears, in repairing the float, he found a new and razor-sharp knife between the top of one of the barrels and the planks which made the flooring.

"I didn't tell you, Skipper," he says, "because I was afraid of alarming you. And, of course, there might have been some simple explanation. Starr might have dropped it, during his carpentering."

He was first amused and then infuriated by the web which seems to be closing around me.

"Of course they can't do anything," he says, "unless they catch you in the act."

But the unconscious humor of that statement set me laughing, and after a moment he saw it and grinned sheepishly. "You know what I mean," he said. "And in one way, if you can stand it, it's not a bad thing."

Pressed for an explanation, it appears that he had been thinking of going after the reward himself, and that this matter of Carroway has decided him.

"Reward or no reward," he said, quietly, "I've had a bit of training; they put me in the Intelligence in Germany, during the occupation. And of course the way to catch a criminal is to keep him from knowing who's after him. Then again, if he learns the police are watching you—and he may—he's watching *them,* you know—it may make him a bit reckless. You never can tell."

But he has a third reason, although he has not mentioned it. He is chivalrously determined to protect me, and through me, Edith.

July 7th.

ANOTHER day has gone by, and I am still at large. Free, I suppose in order that I may eventually again sally forth, some dark night, with my piece of chalk and another knife—for has not Greenough my original one?—to kill more sheep; if indeed there be any remaining for slaughter; or to stab and throw overboard another hapless boatman.

To save my life, I cannot prevent my absurd situation from coloring my actions. I constantly remind myself of the centipede which, on being asked how it used its many legs, became suddenly conscious of them and fell over into the ditch.

For example, at breakfast this morning I gravely poured some coffee into Jock's saucer, instead of the left-over cream from the breakfast table. And Edith caught me in the act.

"Nobody home," she announced. "Poor old dear, so nice and once so intelligent! It is sad," she said to Jane, "to see his mind failing him by inches. But his heart is all right. If the worst comes to the worst——"

"Don't talk about my mind," I snapped, and then was sorry for it. "I don't feel humorous at breakfast, my dear," I said. "I'm sorry."

But the plain truth is that I am sadly upset. Even what before seemed a plain and obvious duty, to go to the other house to-night and tell Mr. Bethel on his arrival the exact situation, has been all day a matter for most anxious thought. It had seemed quite simple before. I would say to him: "Sir, I have rented you this house. True, I warned your secretary of certain unpleasant qualities it is supposed to have, but I must also warn you. The building is reported to be haunted. I do not believe this, nor I daresay will you, but I feel that I must tell you."

Or again:

"There is also a popular—or unpopular—idea that some recent sheep-killings around the vicinity are somehow connected with this haunting. The police do not think so, but the more ignorant of the natives do. If this alarms you, I am prepared to pay back your money to you."

Not quite in this fashion but with a similar candor, I have been prepared to clarify my relations with my new tenant. But now what happens? Will Greenough, for instance, credit my entire disinterestedness? Will he not rather believe that I have given but one more evidence of my essential lunacy? Would I not myself, only a few weeks ago, have distrusted any individual who came to me with such a tale?

After all, I have told young Gordon. At least I have that to my comfort if anything happens. But what am I writing? What can happen? "It is sad," says Edith cheerfully, "to see his mind failing him by inches." Perhaps it is. . . .

I have seen Bethel, and I have not told him. He gives me every impression, in spite of his infirmity, of being able to look after himself, and after to-night's experience he is welcome to do so. Let him have his raps and his footsteps; let him find his tea-kettle on the floor, and his faces in the pantry. Let him freeze in cold airs or stew in his own juice. I have done my part.

His car drove in at eight-thirty, and I followed it along the drive. True to her agreement, Annie Cochran had only waited until seven and then had taken a firm departure, and I daresay this threw him into the execrable temper in which I found him. The secretary had assisted him into the house, and I found him in the library, with only one lamp going, huddled in a chair among a clutter of wraps, and introduced myself. He barely acknowledged it.

"Where the devil's the servant?" he barked at me. "I thought there was a woman, or somebody."

"There is a very good woman," I said, "but she goes home before dark. That is," I corrected myself, "she leaves early. I told your secretary that."

"Do you suppose she's left a fire? Gordon!" he called. "Go and see if there's a fire. I want some hot water."

He fumbled in a pocket and brought out what I fancy was a beef cube or some similar concoction, and sat with it in his hand.

"Which way does the house face?" he asked, suddenly.

"East. Toward the bay."

"Then I want a back room. Don't like the morning sun. Don't like anything in the morning," he added, and peered up at me through his spectacles.

Young Gordon returned then with a cup of hot water and a spoon, and Mr. Bethel favored me with little or no further attention. He has but one usable hand, and the secretary held the cup while he stirred the tablet in it. Only once did he favor me with direct speech during this proceeding. He glanced up as I stood—he had not asked me to sit down—and said:

"Been having some sheep-killing around here lately, haven't you?"

I may have flushed slightly, but I doubt if he could see it, although his eyes were on me. "Yes," I admitted.

"Saw it in the papers," he said, and went back to his broth.

Then if ever was my time to plunge, but to save my life I could not do it. That truculent, childish old man, one leg stretched out before him in the relaxation of partial paralysis, one hand contracted in his lap with the tonic spasm of his condition, taking soup under the direction of a pasty-faced boy who grinned at me above his white head, was no recipient of such information as I had to give. And he allowed me no further opportunity; the cup empty, he indicated that he wished to go upstairs, and with a nod in my direction he shuffled out, Gordon supporting him on the infirm side.

I had had some notion of offering my assistance, but I felt that this recognition of his condition would only annoy him; obvious as it was, he had not mentioned it to me, and I guessed that it was a cross borne not only without fortitude, but with a continuing resentment. I followed them to the foot of the stairs however, and part way up, pausing for breath, he must have suspected my presence there for he turned and looked down.

"What do you think is behind this sheep-killing?" he said. Just that. Not good-night. Nothing whatever about the house; nothing about my presence or my approaching departure. "Who's killed them?" he rasped.

"Some maniac, probably."

"A maniac!" he barked, and steadying himself by Gordon, twisted around so he could see me the better. "Religious tomfoolery, eh? The Blood of the Lamb!"

He cackled drily, staring down at me. Then he turned, without another word, and went on up and out of my sight.

July 8th.

ON Halliday's advice I am not leaving the property, and whenever it is humanly possible, I am in sight of Thomas. Thus to-day I have been weeding Jane's flower beds for her, and with the garage doors open have been ostentatiously oiling the car. To-night, too, I have drawn the table in my room to the window and am there making this day's entry, in full view of any observer who chances to take any interest in my movements.

I am, I am convinced, under espionage. Old Thomas is too frequently in view, as he patters around his daylight tasks, and to-night I have a distinct impression that some observer who takes an interest in my movements is outside, watching my window. Jock believes this also. He is restless, moving from the passage into my room and back again, and twice, standing near me, the short ruff on the back of his neck has risen. . . .

Halliday brought me to-day further details about Carroway's disappearance:

"The hotel clerk ran down to the piers," he says, "and

he heard the engine going for some time. The boat didn't
start up the beach, but out into the bay, as if Carroway
felt the other man had a good start of him, and was trying to cross the bay. Then he either lost the sound of the
engine, or it stopped.

"He waited on the slip for a half hour or so and then
went back to the hotel. Greenough came in about that
time and called up Starr, and they went together to the
town slip. But Carroway hadn't shown up, and after
a time Greenough decided to go out after him.

"They found the boat pretty well out in the bay—the
tide was going out—and empty. They looked around, as
well as they could, then Starr got into it and brought
it back. But here's the part they're not telling: Peter
Geiss says Greenough got some waste and wiped something off the top of the engine box."

"He didn't see what it was?"

"They wouldn't let him near the boat, but he says it
was the circle again."

Of any other details there are apparently none. Bob
Carroway has apparently gone the way of all flesh, poor
lad. And while Greenough or some emissary of his
watches me from my own drive, the murderer is perhaps
concocting some further deviltry.

In the meantime a veritable panic has, according to
Halliday, seized the country-side, and of this we have
certain evidence ourselves. The road beyond the Lodge
gates, usually a procession of twin lights, is to-night dark
and silent. No motor boats with returning picnic parties rumble across the water, throwing us now and then a
bit of song. The fishermen, starting out at three in the
morning, are going armed and in fear of their lives.
And each man suspects the other.

My own position is as unpleasant as possible. To-day
Jane said to me:

"I wish you would get a meat knife in Oakville to-day, William."

"What do you mean by a meat knife?"

"Just a good sharp knife," she said, "with a long blade."

"My dear," I said, "anyone buying such a knife in Oakville to-day would be put into jail at once. Personally, I need razor blades, but I shall grow a beard like the sloop's before I purchase any."

"You could send for one, in town."

And I could not tell her that such a proceeding would be even worse than the other.

Jane's own attitude these days is curious. She is quite convinced, for instance, that she had a premonition of Carroway's death the night she sent me to the slip. As she has no idea that this premonition of hers may be most unpleasant in its consequences to me, to-day I got her to talk about it.

"Just how did it come?"

"I don't know. I had been asleep, I think. Yes, I know I had. I wakened, anyhow, and I seemed to be looking at the slip. There was somebody there, kneeling."

"Kneeling? Saying his prayers, you mean?" with a recollection of the altar.

"I think he was feeling for something, under the float."

There is a certain circumstantial quality to this, one must admit. He had been seen and was being followed, and his knife for some reason was still where he had left it. Or rather, it was not there, since Halliday had that day found it and taken it away. Had it not been for that, poor Carroway might have met his end there on our slip, and not later. But the knife was gone, and there was nothing left but flight.

Just where that flight began no one can say. It seems incredible that he had left his boat moored directly below our boat-house, with Halliday so close at hand. It seems more likely that he ran up the beach a way, and that— well, *de mortuis nil nisi bonum.* Perhaps I am wrong, but it seems to me that Carroway could more easily have followed him by one of the row-boats from our slip, than follow the method he did, with the loss of time involved.

Still, I myself would not have started out unarmed after a killer, even of sheep, unless I had first raised the alarm and was fairly sure of assistance to follow.

"But I don't see," I said to Jane, "why you felt that there was anything ominous in this dream of yours, or whatever it was."

"I never have them without a reason."

"But that night when you so unjustly accused me of holding up the chapel wall——"

"There was a reason there," she said, coldly. "I thought it quite likely I might have to go and get you."

There may be one comfort to the superstitious in all this; not once, since the night when we lighted the red lamp in the pantry, has it——

Midnight: I have just had rather a curious experience, and I am still considerably shaken.

I had no more than written the above words when I glanced out the window, and distinctly saw a small red light through the window of the den in the main house.

My first thought, so certain was I that the lamp was carefully hidden in the attic, was of fire. Long before I had seen Mr. Bethel's light, in the room above it, go out, and soon after that young Gordon's had been likewise extinguished.

I went quickly to my window and leaned out. So dark is the night that it hangs outside like an opaque curtain, and as the light almost immediately disappeared, I was left staring into this void, when suddenly Jock on the staircase landing gave vent to an unearthly howl.

The next moment I heard, under the trees and toward the house, the short dry cough of cardiac asthma, and smelled the queer unmistakable odor of Uncle Horace's herbal cigarette.

I have reasoned with myself for the last ten minutes or so. All the evidence is against me; Greenough may be watching me, or having me watched, and some poor devil out under the trees is suffering from the night air. Or old Mr. Bethel, unable to sleep, has somehow dragged himself out for a midnight airing under the trees.

But I saw the lamp. And it is locked in the attic. I myself put it there, and at this moment have the key.

July 9th.

I MADE an excuse this morning to Annie Cochran, and she slipped me up the kitchen staircase of the other house and so to the attic. The lamp was as I had left it and the closet locked, and to-day I am asking myself whether, with that curious lack of perspective one finds at night, I did not see instead of the lamp far away, the lighted end of a cigar close at hand.

Annie's report on my tenants is satisfactory on the whole. She doesn't much care for the secretary, but the old man's "bark is worse than his bite." He comes down in the morning, or is helped down, to his breakfast, and she cuts his food for him—he seems to dislike the boy's doing it—reads the paper and then goes to work.

"To work?" I asked. "What sort of work?"

"He's writing a book."

But it appears that he is writing it only in the non-literal sense. He is dictating a book. And it also appears that he has chosen this place because of its isolation, and Annie's orders are that he receives no visitors.

But it also appears that young Gordon is perhaps not as courageous as he made out to me when he came to look over the house, and that he has been "hearing things."

"What sort of things?"

"He didn't say. But he asked me this morning if I'd been in the house last night. 'If you find me here at night, it'll be because I'm paralyzed and can't move,' I said, 'and if you take my advice, you'll not go round hunting if you hear anything.'"

"That must have cheered him considerably."

"I don't know about that. He just looked at me and said, 'What's the game, anyhow? I'll bet a dollar you're in on it.'"

Edith has sprung a surprise on us all. I have noticed for a day or two that she has been taking a keen interest in the mail; yet Edith's mail, with Halliday here, is largely a matter of delicate paper and the large square hand-writing of the modern young woman, and has dealt this summer largely with reports on house-parties, summer resorts, and various young men who seem recognizable to her under such cognomens as Chick, Bud and Curley.

This morning, however, her mail included a business-like envelope, and she flung the white, rose and mauve heap aside and pounced on it. A moment later she got up and coming around the table to me, gravely kissed that portion of my head which is gradually emerging, like a shore on an ebb tide, from my hair.

"As one literary artist to another," she said, "I salute you." And placed before me a check for twenty dollars.

She has written a feature article on our sheep-killing, and has sold it.

"And it took me only two hours," she says triumphantly. After that she was rather silent, computing I dare say how much she can earn, giving four hours a day to it for six days a week. At the rate, then, of ten thousand a year!

"Considerably more than I receive, Edith," I said gravely, and I saw I had been right by the way she started.

She set off at once for the boat-house, but came back later considerably crestfallen, and poured out her troubles to me.

"If he had anything he would give it to me," she wailed. "If I can write and make money——"

"You can't fight the masculine instinct, my dear, to support its woman; not be kept by her."

"And wait for years and years to do it!" she said. "The best years of our lives going by, and—nothing."

"Besides, have you considered this? You will not always find subjects as salable as this one has been."

"Subjects!" she said scornfully. "Why, this place is full of them."

The result of which has been on my part all day an uneasy apprehension as to what she will choose next. Nor am I made easier by a question she asked me just before dinner.

"What became of the Riggs woman?" she asked. "Do you suppose she's still around here?"

"I imagine not. Why?"

"I just wondered," she said, and wandered to that particular corner of the verandah from which she has a distant but apparently satisfactory view of the boat-house. . . .

Perhaps Halliday is right. (Note: In his suggestion that Jane and I take the sloop and go down the coast for a few days.) If any sheep are killed in my absence, or anything more serious should happen, it will serve to rout Greenough's absurd determination to involve me, and provide a complete alibi. At the same time, it will be rest and recreation for Jane, and it may put me in a better frame of mind.

Peter Geiss, he thinks, would go with us as captain and bunk under a pup tent, leaving the cabin to Jane and myself.

(On board the sloop) July 10th.

A MAZING, the celerity with which youth thinks and acts. To-night Jane and I—and Peter Geiss—are rolling gently to our anchor in Bass Cove, close enough in to be quiet and far enough out to escape the mosquitos. And yet only yesterday the plan was an amorphous thing, floating in the air between Halliday and myself, a mere ghost of an idea, without material substance.

I am glad to sit in my wicker chair, this Journal on my knee, and rest my body. I have indeed earned my night's repose. Now and then I reach out a languid hand and touch a fishing line, one end of which is tied to the arm of my chair, the other extending into those mysterious depths from which I hope to lure to-morrow's breakfast.

The sloop is tidy. Is even fairly sea-worthy. Her bottom has to-day been scrubbed with a broom, and her sails, slightly mildewed, still present from a distance a certain impressiveness.

"What," I shout at Peter Geiss, "is that small sail in front? Forward, I mean."

"How's that?"

"The sail there, what's its name?" I say, pointing. *"Name?"*

"I'll say it's a shame," he says. "Canvas on this boat cost the old gentleman a lot of money."

By and by, however, I learn the jib and the flying
jib. Also that sea-water is an unsatisfactory cleansing
medium, as witness the supper dishes.

"Why," I demand of Jane, "did Nausicaä wash her
garments in the sea, when there was a river at hand?"

"I haven't an idea," she says absently, her eyes on
her alcohol cooking stove. "They weren't overly clean
in those days, were they?"

But I think my dear Jane is exceedingly uncertain as to
just what days were those of Nausicaä.

We have a small cabin, with four bunks in it, and two
of these are now neatly and geometrically made up,
ready for the night. In Jane's small closet there is food
of all sorts, neat rows of tins and wax-paper packages.
If we are washed out to sea we can, I imagine, live
indefinitely on deviled ham, sardines and cheese. And I
have always my fishing line.

Ah! a tug at it!

July 11th.

I HAVE been playing solitaire to-day, as a cover for my
thoughts. For this, I take it, is the great virtue of
solitaire, that it insures against frivolous interruption,
while at the same time leaving the mind free to wander
where it will.

My worries are dropping from me. Helena Lear is
with Edith, and no doubt Halliday is camped on their
doorstep, as vigilant as a watch dog, and certainly more
dependable than Jock. I can see, too, with better perspective how absurd my anxiety has been as to Greenough. It is his business to believe every man guilty until
he has proved himself innocent. And am I not now
in the act of proving my innocence?

But my problem remains. And trying to solve it is

like playing solitaire with a card missing. I have, we will say, lost the knave of clubs out of my pack, and without it the game cannot go on.

Halliday, I know, believes that there is a possible connection between the killer and Uncle Horace's letter. He believes, in other words, that some curious and perhaps monstrous idea lies behind the sheep-killing, and that it may be the same idea to which the letter refers.

"There is something behind it," he asserts. "Something so vital to the man who believes it that he is ready to kill—has killed certainly once and possibly twice —to protect it."

But the nature of the idea, or conviction, he nobly evades.

"And this monstrous idea was to kill sheep, and build a stone altar?"

"How do we know that isn't merely a propitiatory sacrifice, Skipper? A sort of preliminary to the real thing?"

"And what is to be the real thing?"

"What is the wickedest crime you can name, against society?"

"The taking of human life."

"Exactly."

But this, as he says, is as far as he goes. He is, however, careful to say that his theory has got him somewhere; that is, that there is a definite idea behind what has been happening.

"An insane one, then."

"Not necessarily," he objects. "Your Uncle Horace didn't write that letter to a man he considered in-sane." . . .

Peter Geiss has his own theory about poor Carroway's death. Carroway, he says, probably located the boat; he could do that by cutting off his engine and listening for the oars. Then, in black darkness, he steered toward it, probably with the idea of driving the fellow back. But Peter does not think that Carroway would have closed in on the murderer, unarmed as he was.

"The chances are," he said to-day, "that the fellow crept up on him, quiet-like, and leaped into the launch."

"But he was unarmed, too," I said remembering the knife under our slip.

It seemed to me that Peter not only heard that with surprising distinctness, but that he shot a stealthy glance at me.

"He had an oar," he said, and fell back into his customary taciturnity.

The nights are wonderful. I have brought my mattress out of the cabin, and shall sleep to-night face up to the stars. We are anchored in Pirate Harbor, that small enclosed anchorage the shore of which has been so frequently dug for treasure that it is pitted like a pockmarked face.

In our fore-rigging hangs our riding light. It should be white, but as in a burst of energy this evening I scraped a supper plate over the side, I also scraped off the lantern. So it is red, our red sailing light. It reminds me of the lamp at home. I think about light in general. What do I know about light, anyhow? That it is a wave, a vibration, and that only within a certain fixed range can it be perceived by my human sensorium; that, below the infra-red, and above the ultra-violet, are waves our human eye cannot perceive. Then, all around us are things to which our human senses do not react. How far dare I extend that? From invisible things to invisible beings is not so far, I dare say.

What is reality and what is not? Only what we can see, hear, touch or taste? But that is absurd. Thought is a reality; perhaps the only reality.

But can thought exist independent of the body? The

spiritists believe it can. And undoubtedly the universe
is full of unheard sounds; all the noises in the world go
echoing around our unhearing ears for centuries, and
then comes the radio and begins to pick them up for
us.

But the radio requires a peculiar sort of receiving instrument, and so with the sights and sounds beyond our
normal ken. Jane may be such an instrument. So for all
I know may be Peter Geiss, snoring in his pup tent.
Even myself——

(Note: I fell asleep here, and the entry is incomplete.)

July 12th.

JUST what did Peter Geiss see last night?
If I were asked to name, in order of their psychic
quality, the three persons on this boat, I would put
Jane first and Peter last.

He is a materialist. Not for him the interesting ab-
stractions, the controversial problems of the universe.
The life of the mind, the questions of the soul, are hidden
from him. His food, his tobacco, the direction of the
wind, the state of the tide, these cover the field of his
speculations and anxieties. And yet—Peter saw something last night.

It was about one o'clock in the morning, and he had
wakened and crawled out of his pup tent, with, according
to him "the feeling that we were in for a blow. There
was a cold wind across my feet."

So he rose, and he saw that our red lantern was burning low, and gingerly stepping across me, reached into
a locker for the oil can. When he straightened up he
saw a shadowy figure standing in the bow of the boat,
directly under the lantern.

He thought at first that it was I, but the next moment

he had stumbled across me as I lay supine, and the oil can fell and went a-rolling. The noise did not disturb the figure, and Peter gave a long look at it before he howled like a hyena and brought me up all standing.

It was only then that it disappeared. "Just blew to windward," according to Peter. I never saw it at all.

Peter did not go to bed again all night, but sat huddled by the wheel, staring forward, a queer old figure of terror without hope. And I admit I was not much better.

For Peter says that it was that of a man in a dressing gown, and that "it looked like the old gentleman." By which he means my Uncle Horace.

July 13th.

ELLIS Landing.

We have had bad news, and are preparing to land and take a motor back.

Edith wires that Halliday has been hurt. She gives no details.

July 14th.

HALLIDAY'S condition is not critical, thank God. We found him (Note: in my bedroom here at the Lodge) with Edith and Helena fussing over him, and with his collar bone broken, the result, not of the attack but of his ditching the car.

For he is the indirect victim of an attack.

On the evening of the 12th he was on his way to the station at Oakville to meet Helena Lear and Edith, who were in town on some mysterious feminine errand which detained them until the late train.

At eleven o'clock, then, he took the car and started off, and as he was early took the longer route through the back country. The one by Sanger's Mill and the

Livingstone place. It was near the drive into Livingstones' that a man carrying a sawed-off shot-gun stopped
the car and asked for a lift into town. He was, he said,
one of Starr's special deputies, watching for the sheep-
killer.

It was very dark, and he could only see the outlines of
the deputy. But as, all along, he had come across men
similarly armed—"The fence corners were full of them,"
he says—he thought nothing of it, and told the fellow
to jump in.

"I hadn't seen him," he said, "but I got an impression
of him. You know what I mean. A heavy square
type, and he got into the car like that, slowly and deliberately. I think he had a cigar in his mouth, not lighted;
he talked like it, anyhow."

Once in the car the man was taciturn. Halliday
spoke once or twice, and got only a sort of grunt in reply,
and finally he began to be uneasy. He had, he says, the
feeling that the fellow's whole body was taut, and that
his silence was covering some sort of stealthy motion,
"or something," he adds, rather vaguely.

"And of course he had his gun. Lying across his
knees as well as I could make out."

They had gone about a mile by that time, and then
Halliday began to smell a queer odor.

"He was not trying to anaesthetize me," he is certain. "He'd had it in his pocket, and something had
gone wrong; the cork came out, perhaps. Anyhow, all at
once it struck me that ether was a queer thing for one of
Starr's deputies to be carrying, and I felt I was in for
trouble."

He took his left hand quietly from the steering wheel,
and began to fumble in the left hand pocket of the car,
where he had put his revolver. And although he is confident he made no sound, the fellow must have had

ears like a bat, for just then Halliday saw him raise the gun, and as he ducked forward the barrel of it hit the seat back behind him with a sickening thud.

But he had somehow turned the wheel of the car, and the next moment it had left the road. Halliday made a clutch at it, but it was too late; he saw, as the car swung, the lights of another car ahead and coming toward them; then they struck a fence, and the machine turned over.

He had been found, by the people in the other car, unconscious in the wreckage, and brought to the Lodge. No sign of the other man was discovered.

But this story, curious and ominous as it is, is as nothing to my sensations to-day when I visited my small garage, where my car is awaiting insurance adjustment before undergoing repairs.

The point of the matter is this: Greenough has already been to see our invalid, and has assured him that he has been the victim of an ordinary attempt at a hold-up.

"Only difference is," he told Halliday, "that our men around with weapons gave the fellow a chance to carry his gun openly. Gave him a good excuse for a lift, too. Most people around here now aren't stopping their cars for anything or anybody. But of course they'd pick up a deputy."

"I'm not as familiar with crime as you are," Halliday had responded. "But is ether part of the modern hold-up outfit?"

"It's pretty hard to name off-hand anything they don't use," said Greenough, imperturbably. "From silk stockings up."

Which was, I imagine, a bit of unconscious humor.

So Greenough dismisses the possibility of any connection between Halliday's trouble and the unknown malefactor; in a word, my absence has probably not altered his suspicion of me a particle. Or had not, for within the next half hour I propose to show him that an absolute connection exists between the two.

On the right-hand cushion of my car, which during the salvaging of it was thrown upside down into the rear, there is marked an infinitesimal circle in chalk, enclosing a crude triangle. I have sent for Green-ough. . . .

Later: Truly the way of the innocent is hard.

Dr. Hayward was making his afternoon call on Halli-day when the detective came, and as I feel confident that the doctor is in Greenough's confidence I was glad to spring my little bombshell on them both at the same time. But to-night I am feeling much like Bunyan's Man in an Iron Cage. "I am now a man of despair, and am shut up in it."

Edith was on the verandah when the detective came, and young Gordon was with her. During our absence he has struck up with her an acquaintance of sorts, but she dislikes him extremely. She has, Jane tells me, nick-named him Shifty.

As Hayward was still upstairs, I sparred politely with Greenough for a few minutes. We had had good weather for the trip; fishing was only fair. It was too bad to be brought back as we were. Yes, but if things like that were going on, it was better to be on the ground. "What sort of things?" he asked.

"We have had two murderous attacks, haven't we? One successful, and one not."

"So you class this little affair of young Halliday's with the other?"

"Don't you?"

"Not until I've got something that ties them together, Mr. Porter."

Hayward had come in and stood inside the doorway, gnawing at his fingers and listening.

"But if you found something *did* tie them together?"

"For instance?"

"I'm going to ask you something. Was there or was there not something drawn on the top of the engine box of the boat from which Carroway disappeared?"

"How do you know that?" he shot at me. And like a fool I said, thinking to protect Peter Geiss: "That doesn't matter, does it? It's the fact I'm after."

"Suppose there were. What would that prove?"

"And suppose I can show you another, and similar mark on my car, made there by Halliday's assailant before he struck at him?"

It was then that Greenough smiled horribly, damnably.

"It's there, is it?" he said, and looked up at Hayward.

"It is there."

He got up, the remains of that smile still plastered on his face, and confronted me.

"That's curious," he said. "I examined that car in the ditch, before they moved it, Mr. Porter. And I've been over it here with the doctor, since. If there's anything there of the sort you describe, it's been put there since yesterday afternoon."

And then I saw where I stood. They believed that, finding Halliday assaulted during my absence, I was attempting to link that assault with the sheep-killing and with Carroway's death, and turn it to my own advantage. In other words, to prove that the reign of terror had gone on in my absence!

A drowning man, swimming exhaustedly toward a log which sinks when he touches it, must have much the same sensation that I had, as I stood there facing Greenough's vile smile and the doctor's searching gaze.

"You can go out and look," I said feebly. "It's there."

I did not go with them. I heard Edith and Gordon follow them out, and then I sat down and faced my situation.

And indeed it has passed the point of philosophical endurance. Even if Carroway's body is not found and no charge of murder can be brought, it is not hard to see what power lies in this detective's hands, backed by his conviction of my guilt. He may not imprison me, but he can cost me my reputation, even my position in the university. He can hound me out of the only life I know and am fitted for, the warm place behind the drain pipe.

It is well enough for Halliday to say that we can assume a counter-offensive. When? With him temporarily crippled, and every act of mine watched and questioned? And, even with all other things equal, how?

Nor do I see, as he does, any possible clue in young Gordon finding the chalk with which the drawing was done, behind the lawn-roller in the garage, a fact which Edith reported after Hayward and Greenough had gone, or in the scrap of paper in which it was wrapped when found. For one thing, Edith's memory as to what was on the paper may be at fault. Naturally, not knowing my situation, she would observe it only casually.

According to Clara, the only persons visiting the car after it was brought back yesterday morning were Annie Cochran and Thomas, who were there when it was returned; Greenough, who spent some time there while the doctor made his call on Halliday; the doctor himself, who wandered in later to look at it; young Gordon, who she says showed particular interest in it and a sort of ghoulish amusement, and the Livingstones. Or rather, Livingstone only, who appears to have stood in the doorway smoking and surveying it while his wife carried up to the invalid a jar of jellied broth.

But as the garage door was unlocked all night, such speculation is purely futile.

Edith suggests malicious mischief.

"The village children are chalking up circles with triangles all over the fences," she says, "and old Starr came out here yesterday with one between his shoulders. He almost had a stroke when I told him."

Her explanation of the paper found about the chalk and what was on it is equally simple. That in itself, she concludes, proves her contention: "It looked as if children had been playing with a typewriter," she says. And she has reproduced it from memory, as nearly as possible, Greenough having carried it off with him.

It was done, she says, on a typewriter in a curious jumble of capitals and small letters, and the paper was perforated at the side, as if it were from a loose-leaf note-book. Also, it had been torn, so that only a portion of the typing remained.

This portion was, according to her, as follows:
GeLTr, K. 28.

(Note: As will be seen, Edith's memory was extremely good. She made only one error in the cipher. The final number, 28, should, of course, have been 24.)

To-night I have had a long talk with Halliday. It appears that the time of Peter Geiss's apparition almost exactly coincides with the attack. This, however, does not impress Halliday as it does me.

"You have to remember, Skipper," he says, "that old Geiss has been scared almost out of his wits the last few weeks. And the Carroway affair has carried the terror right out onto his domain, which is the water."

"Then why didn't he see Carroway?"

"Search me," he said, with a shrug that set him wincing. "What's bothering me is why doesn't anybody see Carroway? Eight days, and no body found yet."

When I left him a few minutes ago, he had Edith's memory copy of the paper found in the garage, and was propped up in bed with a pencil.

"If we had the original we'd be better off," he said. "It oughtn't to be hard to find the typewriter in the vicinity that wrote it. And if Greenough isn't crazy with the heat he's looking for it now."

I glanced at my own portable machine, sitting on the table, and he followed my eyes and smiled.

"You've got your best alibi right there," he said, "if this turns out to be a cipher. And I think it is."

He has, it appears, some small knowledge of ciphers, and from the mixture of capitals and small letters he believes he recognizes this one. But it requires a key word, or two key words.

"Even without it," he says, "it could be solved, possibly, if I had enough of it. But with only this scrap—! And I don't get the number added to it."

The idea of this type of cipher, I gather, is to take a word, or two words, containing thirteen letters of the alphabet, no one used twice. Written first in small or lower case size these letters represent the first thirteen letters of the alphabet. The same word or words repeated in capitals becomes the second half of the alphabet.

Thus the words "subnormal diet" become a key in this fashion:

s u b n o r m a l d i e t   S U B N O R M A L D I E T
a b c d e f g h i j k l m   n o p q r s t u v w x y z

But as "subnormal diet" was the only key phrase we could think of, and as it obviously did not fit, I left him still biting the end of his pencil, and came to complete this record. . . .

Renan said that the man who has time to keep a private diary has never understood the immensity of the universe. But I reply to Renan that the man in my position, who does not keep a private diary and thus let off his surplus thoughts, is liable to burst into minute fragments and scatter over the said immensity of the universe!

Sunday, July 15th.

THE one pleasure that never palls is the pleasure of not going to church. . . .

Again, as I recorded once before, a quiet morning and I am still at large. Jane has gone. Sometimes I suspect Jane of throwing a sop to Providence in this matter of church-going; almost, one might say, of bargaining with the Almighty. "I will do thus and so," says Jane to herself, "and in return I have a right to ask thus and so."

Yet she asks little enough; a quiet life, peace, and if not active happiness, that resignation which after the hot days of youth are over, passes for contentment. And as she went out this morning, demurely dressed in the Sabbatical restraint which is a part of her bargain, I felt rather than said a small prayer for her; that she who asks so little may keep what she has.

And Jane is worried. She knows nothing, but she suspects everything. By that, I mean that she is somehow aware, after her own curious fashion, that there is something wrong with her world. She watches me, when I am not looking at her. She has an odd, rather furtive, dislike of Doctor Hayward. And she is almost criminally forwarding Edith's love affair.

Since Halliday was brought here Jane and I have shared her bedroom, and this morning, buttoning my collar, I said:

"The sooner that boy goes back to the boat-house, the better."

"Why?" she demanded, almost militantly.

"Well, if you can't see what's going on under your eyes, my dear——"

"I don't see why it shouldn't go on. There's not too much love in the world."

"Nor enough bread and cheese."

"We didn't have very much when we started, William," she said, looking up at me wistfully.

"And we haven't much more now," I said, and kissed her.

But the plain truth is that Jane's nerves are shaken. She wants Edith settled; she would like nothing better than a speedy marriage, if that would take us back to the city at once. All her old hatred and distrust of this place have been steadily reviving, and the attack on Halliday has about eaten away her resistance.

All life is the resistance of an undiscoverable principle against unceasing forces. And my poor Jane, after years of protected life, is only discovering those unceasing forces. . . .

Later: Poor Carroway's body has been found. The tide was unusually low at two this afternoon and a yawl from Bass Cove, crossing the bay, saw it floating face down, and recovered it, not without difficulty. The poor lad had been tied with the end of an anchor rope, and the anchor thrown over with him. Thus for days the body has been only a few feet beneath the surface, floating at the end of its tragic tether.

From the doctor, making his afternoon call here, we heard the details. He was summoned as soon as the body was brought in, and made a hasty examination. From that it appears that Carroway was beaten over the head first and then thrown into the sea.

"He was probably dead before he touched the water," is Hayward's opinion. "Of course the autopsy will tell that. If there is no water in the middle ear or the lungs, we can be certain."

But from Peter Geiss, who wandered in this afternoon after salvaging certain of his personal possessions from the sloop, we learned other facts. Thus, Peter declares that the man who killed Carroway was a sailor, or at least knew how to use a rope, sailor-fashion.

And as Halliday said to me, aside, this was cheering news, for my best friend could not accuse me of any nautical knowledge.

The body, it seems, was tied with two half-hitches around the wrists; from there the rope extended to the ankle, with similar half-hitches, and to these ends, again, the anchor had been affixed. To my query as to whether such a proceeding would not take considerable time Peter says not.

"Two half-hitches is about the quickest and easiest tie there is," he assures me, "and the best to hold. If it slips one way it holds another."

There is, it seems to me, a certain relish in Peter's account of these gruesome details; a gusto in the telling. Like the ancient Greeks, Peter's literature is purely oral, and he has by accident stumbled on an epic.

But the recovery of the body has roused the neighborhood to fever heat. There have been those, up to now, who have half-believed that Carroway had been the victim of an accident; had somehow stumbled and fallen overboard, and to prove this they brought out the fact that, like many of the men on the waterside, he could not swim.

There were others, too, who still inclined to the belief that some supernatural influence had been at work; that Carroway, indeed, had been the victim of some other-world foul play. But even these superstitious folk cannot now blame the red lamp. Carroway has been murdered, by hands which wielded the oar that struck him, and which tied the half-hitches which "if they slipped one way, held the other."

The anchor presents the only possible clue, and that is a feeble one. There was no anchor in the boat Carroway took out. On the other hand, there is a sort of half-hearted recognition of it by Doctor Hayward as one stolen from his small knock-about sometime late in June.

"Of course, all these anchors are as like as peas," he said this afternoon, "but the boys down at the wharf say it's mine, and they can tell two fish-hooks apart, same size and same kind." . . .

The county authorities have finally roused themselves and the Sheriff, Benchley, is in Oakville. Under the excuse of examining our float Greenough brought him out, and Halliday dressed and went with them, to show where he had found the knife. On their return they stopped in and looked at my car.

When Halliday came back he was grave and quiet. In vain did Edith try to coax him into his usual light-heartedness. While I have no idea as to what happened, I can make a fair guess, for he announced at supper that he was through playing the invalid.

"It's time for me to be up and about," he said.

Benchley has increased the County's reward to twenty-five hundred dollars, and this with Livingstone's makes three thousand. As a result, until twilight frightened them back to their hearths, the vicinity was filled this afternoon with amateur detectives. According to Annie Cochran, one of them was skulking around the hedge of the main house when Mr. Bethel saw him and drove him off.

Just what that irritable and exclusive gentleman makes of the situation, I do not know. He must have learned, through Gordon, of our trouble here, but he makes no sign. Now and then, but not often, I see him on the terrace, and if he acknowledges my finger to my cap, I do not see it.

He is so consistently unpleasant that one must respect it, as consistency of any sort is respected. . . .

My own position is rather strengthened than weakened by to-day's developments, and I imagine Greenough himself is somewhat at sea. Not only am I no sailor, and obviously no sailor, but I am not a physically muscular man. In the pursuit of English literature the wear and tear is on trouser seats rather than on muscles; in ten years my one annual physical orgy has been putting up the fly-screens each April.

I could no more strangle a man than I could bull-dog a steer.

And, unless Greenough is more beset with prejudices and theory than I think he is, he must know this. He has, in addition, a slowly growing list of qualifications, all of which the murderer must possess, and few of which are mine. Thus:

The murderer is physically strong. I am not. The murderer (or at least Halliday's assailant) wore a soft dark hat, well pulled down. I have here in the country a golf cap and a summer straw. No other. The murderer had a sailor's knowledge of a rope. I haven't the slightest knowledge of a rope, except that it is used on Mondays to hang out the washing.

On only two points do I plead guilty, and there with reservations. For the murderer shows a knowledge of the country-side, not only equal to my own, but better. And Halliday says he got into the car as would a man of middle life, rather than youth. I am middle-aged,— if that be not the next period just ahead and never quite reached, until some day we waken to find that we have passed it in the night and are now old, and taking an ingenuous pride in that age.

July 16th.

I AM facing an unusual quandary, which is: shall I or shall I not attend poor Carroway's funeral to-morrow? What is the customary etiquette under the circumstances? Does the suspected agent of the death remain decorously absent, the only one in the entire neighborhood so missing? Or does he go, with a countenance carefully set to show exactly the polite amount of concern, and be suspected as the dog returning to his vomit?

There is an old theory—I would like to question Greenough about it, if I dared—that your true murderer has an avid curiosity as to the work of his hands; that, against all prudence, he returns to it. Under these circumstances, what shall I do?

Compromise, probably, send more flowers than I can afford, and stay at home. The same sort of compromise which I effected with my soul yesterday, when I gave Jane a rather larger amount than usual for the collection plate. . . .

One of the reporters who has been hanging around the vicinity since the recovery of the body approached me to-day on a possible connection between the murder and the attack on Halliday. I found him coming out of the garage, but as Greenough had carefully erased the symbol on the seat cushion, I doubt if he had found anything valuable.

He pried me with polite questions, but I evaded him as well as I could.

"But don't you, personally, believe there is some connection?" he insisted.

"I should have to have some proof of such a connection."

"And you have none?" he asked, eyeing me closely.

"I imagine you know at least as much about it as I do. Have you found any?"

Perhaps my attitude had annoyed him, or perhaps he merely had the discoverer's pride in achievement, for he put away the handful of yellow paper, on which he had made no notes, and smiled.

"I haven't found any connection," he said. "But I have found something your detectives missed, Mr. Porter. I have found where the fellow hid after the crash, when the other car was rescuing Mr. Halliday."

But the odd part of that discovery to my mind is not that hiding place, nor Greenough's failure to locate it. As a matter of fact, I doubt if Greenough has ever looked for it. He seems to have taken for granted that Halliday's assailant merely escaped the wreck and made off in the dark.

No. The point that strikes me, and struck Halliday when I told him is the intimate knowledge of that location shown, and the quickness with which he took advantage of it.

(Note: In view of what we now know, I imagine this is an error. The chances seem to be that he was thrown near the mouth of the culvert, and that the lights of the on-coming car showed it to him.)

Crossing the road, according to the reporter, and about fifteen feet from where the car was ditched, is a small culvert. Hardly a culvert, either, but a largish clay pipe designed to carry the drainage of the higher fields on one side to the lower on the other.

"Have you searched this pipe?" I asked.

"I looked in. If I'd had a pair of overalls I'd have gone in. But as the only clothes I have with me are on me—" he smiled again. "It's a good job for a ferret," he said.

He gave me up reluctantly, at last, and prepared to go. "So you think it's only an ordinary case of hold-up?" he asked.

"I think it's a damned unpleasant case of hold-up," I replied, and he went away. But I have been thinking of his phrase since his departure.

How much of the present world disorganization lies in that very use of the word "ordinary!" Time was when no hold-up was ordinary, and an act of physical violence or a murder caused a shock that swept us all. Is it true, then, that one cannot turn the minds of a people to killing, as in the recent war, and then expect them at once, when the crisis is over, to regard life as precious? And is this the reason Greenough spoke of its being a "queer time in the world?"

Is every criminal then merely seeking escape from reality?

But why the word "criminal"? Was not I myself seeking to escape it, when on June 16th I wrote in this very Journal:

"Yet what is it that I want? My little rut is comfortable; so long have I lain in it that now my very body has conformed." . . .

For the rest of this afternoon, I have made my will! "To my dearly beloved wife, Jane Porter, I bequeath, etc."

There is something strangely comforting in making a will; it is as if one has completed the last rites, and now, with such complacence as may be, faces whatever is to come. Like Ishmael in "Moby Dick," I survive myself; my death and burial are locked up in my desk. I am "like a quiet ghost with a clear conscience, sitting inside the bars of a snug family vault."

A ghost, too, I begin to feel, among other ghosts. . . .
Ignore it as I will, there is a certain weight in the
slowly accumulating mass of evidence at my disposal,
a weight and a consistency which have commenced to
influence me. I am bound to admit that, if I were able to
conceive of the survival of intelligence beyond death, I
could also conceive that poor old Horace has been on
hand during some of our recent experiences.

Not Thomas's "George," the spirit evoked by Mrs.
Riggs and still surviving in the lamp; not some malicious
demon, frightening honest folk by ringing bells and
pinching women in the dark. But a mind like my own,
only greater in its wider knowledge, and painfully trying
in its bodiless state to communicate that knowledge to me.

The sum total of evidence is rather startling.

(a) Jane's photograph, taken on Class Day.

(b) Jock's refusal to enter the main house, persisted in to this time.

(c) My own curious telepathic message, relative to
the letter.

(d) Jane's experience under the red lamp in the
pantry. (Doubtful.)

(e) Halliday's lights over the marsh. (Again
doubtful. It may have been the unknown, finding the
boat-house occupied and seeking a way to the beach.)

(f) My own experience in hearing Uncle Horace's
peculiar cough and smelling the odor of his asthmatic
pastilles, or cigarettes.

(g) Jock's peculiar conduct at the same time.

(h) Peter Geiss's vision on the sloop, and his identification of it. (Yet Peter is a staunch supporter of
"George." Had he been looking for such a visitation
would he not naturally have seen George?)

(i) And the fact that this vision corresponds in
time with the attack on Halliday.

In this attempt to refresh my memory I have not included Jane's premonition the night Carroway was murdered, or her dislike and distrust of the house. Nor have I included the vague stories of haunting told by Mrs. Livingstone, Annie Cochran or Thomas. Of the latter, they are not only beyond my personal experience or contact, but they are, if the word may be used in such a connection, apparently without motive.

With Jane, too, I feel that a faculty which enabled her to rise in the morning without seeing her clock, may be extended further without touching the supernatural. I grant her a strange power, possessed doubtless by many criminals and a few human beings, of being able to see and hear what cannot be seen and heard by normal eyes and ears. But as I grant this same faculty to Jock, it seems to me to be rather a question of ordinary limitations than of a peep-hole, as I may put it, into another world.

On the other hand, I must not disregard the fact that Jane seems an essential part of the phenomena which I have recorded. On the two occasions when I have had the strongest impression of some disembodied presence, she has been asleep nearby. In the case of the photograph, it was Jane who operated the camera; in the pantry of the main house, it was Jane who saw the face behind her, reflected in the window. And so on.

I am driven to wondering if, in some states, Jane herself does not provide the medium for these manifestations. Whether she does not throw off some excess of vital matter, in which the poor naked and disembodied intelligence may clothe itself.

But that is to accept the whole theory of spiritism, and I am not prepared to do that; to travel with Cameron and little Pettingill, weighing the dying with the one and claiming that the purely chemical loss of weight is the weight of the soul; and sitting in the dark with the other, asking non-physical intelligences to commit various physical acts! Putting their belief in eternity into the grasping hands of a paid medium, and seeing God in the pulling of a black thread.

Which reminds me of an amusing conversation at luncheon to-day, Halliday's last meal with us before returning to the boat-house.

"What becomes of all the mediums?" Edith asked suddenly, apropos of nothing at all.

"What becomes of all the hairpins, and dead birds?" I asked, not too originally.

"But it is queer," she persisted. "These women come and make a *furore*. Then all at once they disappear."

"They get discovered and then quit," Halliday said. "And of course, even a medium must die in time. Not that they actually die, of course. They simply go into the fourth dimension."

"And what's the fourth dimension?"

"Why, don't you know?" he asked. "The simplest thing in the world. It's the cube of a cube. And once you get into it you can turn yourself inside out like a glove. Not that I see any particular use in that, but it might be interesting."

Edith, it appears, intends to write an article on mediums!

July 17th.

I DO not like young Gordon. He has little enough time to himself—only, I gather, an hour or so after luncheon, while Mr. Bethel sleeps—but he spends that here, if possible.

Edith snubs him, but he is as thick-skinned as one of the porpoises which rolls itself in the bay.

"Why, if you're so clever," I overheard her to-day,

"don't you go out and do something? Use your brains."

"It takes brains to do what I'm doing," he said, "and don't you forget it."

But as to what he is doing he is discreetly silent. There is a book under way, but he parries any attempt to discuss it. Also, he seems to delight in investing Mr. Bethel with a considerable amount of mystery.

"The Boss is having one of his fits to-day," he will say.

"What sort of fits?"

"That would be telling," he says craftily, and ostentatiously changes the subject.

Edith, who has a very feminine curiosity, has questioned Annie Cochran but without much result. The "fit" days, so far as we can make out, are merely days when the invalid is less well than others, and mostly keeps his bed. Annie Cochran, however, has her own explanation of them; she believes that those days follow nights when "George" has been particularly active, and when presumably Mr. Bethel has not been sleeping on his good ear.

And as proof of this, she produces the fact that twice now, having left her tea-kettle empty on top of the stove, she has found it full in the morning. As Mr. Bethel cannot get downstairs unassisted, and as the secretary has always stoutly maintained that he has not left his room all night, Annie Cochran falls back on "George"; and, one must admit, not without reason. . . .

Poor Carroway was laid away yesterday, after the largest funeral in the history of these parts. And so ends one chapter in our drama. Ends, that is, for him. What is to come after no one can say.

One thing has tended somewhat to relieve the local strain. No sheep have been killed for eighteen days, and the altar in the field still remains without oblation. There are, I believe, one or two summer people who still make it the objective of an early morning excursion, hoping to find on it who knows what horrid sacrifice. But they have only their walk for their pains.

Maggie Morrison, who passes it every morning in her truck, makes a daily report of it to Clara, and so it filters to the family.

"Clara says the altar is still empty."

"I suspect her of longing to lay a chicken on it, herself. There is something pantheistic about her."

Jane—or Edith, as it may be—is silent, reflecting on the meaning of pantheistic.

It is Maggie, too, who brings us much of our local news. To-day, for instance, she informs us that the detective has gone away, "bag and baggage," from the hotel, and probably this accounts for the lighter tone of this entry. I am reprieved, at least until some other sheep are killed. . . .

Later: Halliday and I, late this afternoon, made an examination of the culvert, or pipe, in which our unknown hid after the accident. We chose a late hour, in order to avoid the procession of cars which winds along our back roads—the further back the better—during the afternoons.

In this we were successful, for although, like my own, the general sentiment is one of reprieve, there are few still who will trust themselves out after twilight. Mr. Logan, the rector of the Oakville Episcopal church, Saint Jude's, had an experience in point the other night: Calling late on a dying parishioner he ran out of gasoline on the main road, some six miles from home. He endeavored to stop various cars as they flew past, but in the general terror no one would pick him up, and after being fired at by one excited motorist he gave it up and walked back to the rectory.

We must have presented a curious study for any observer, working with guilty haste, and I in particular emerging from the pipe covered with mud and a heterogeneous collection of leaves and grasses. Not only was Halliday too broad in the shoulders for easy access, but his injury forbade the necessary gymnastics. There was a time when, half in and half out of the pipe, I could hear him laughing consumedly.

But I found nothing, save that undoubtedly someone had preceded me into it. A man skilled in such matters might have read a story into the various marks and depressions, but they were not for me.

I retreated, inch by inch, and was again free as to my legs but a prisoner as to the remainder of my body, when Halliday called that a car was coming. I had three choices; one was to remain in my present shameful state; another was to emerge and face the public eye, looking as though I had been tarred and feathered; and the third was to retire into my burrow.

I retired. With that peculiar venom with which fate has been pursuing me, the car stopped over me, and Starr spoke.

"Looking over the scene of your trouble?" he said.

"Looking for the clues you fellows can't find," Halliday retorted, easily.

I could hear Starr snort, and then chuckle drily as he let in his clutch again. "I'll give you a dollar for every clue you find," he called, and the car moved on.

When Halliday gave me the signal I emerged feebly into the open air, and stood upright. "That was a narrow squeak," I said.

But he was looking after the disappearing car. "Yes," he said. "But I think it was a mistake. I should have told him you were there."

The net result of the search was not encouraging. True, Halliday picked up, outside the pipe, half of the lens of an eye-glass, but there is no proof that it belonged to his assailant. On the other hand, I myself had made a discovery of a certain amount of importance. Halliday had said that the man he had picked up had seemed to be a heavy man, broadly and squarely built.

But my experience showed me that no very heavy man could have entered the pipe. We have, in effect, to recast our picture of the murderer; a man of medium size, we will say, compactly if muscularly built.

To-night, sitting down to make this entry, I have missed my fountain pen, and as it has my initials on it we must recover it to-morrow if possible. It would be extremely unpleasant under the circumstances for Starr, for instance, in a burst of zeal to find it in the pipe.

True, Peter Geiss could swear that, at the moment Halliday was attacked he and I were looking for a ghost in the fore-rigging of the sloop. But I am at this disadvantage, that they give me no opportunity to defend myself, for they make no accusation. Their method is that damnable one of watchful waiting; Greenough's psychological idea that, given enough rope a criminal will hang himself.

July 18th.

EDITH and Halliday went this morning to recover my fountain pen, Edith in spite of our protests determined to crawl into the pipe for it. To this end she put on my mechanic's overall in which I oil and grease my car, and very sweet indeed she looked in it.

But the pen was not there. She found the cap of it, embedded in the mud, but not the pen itself. It looks as though Starr has lost no time!

Edith, I believe, suspects something. There is a growing gravity and maturity in her; she tries to show me, by small caresses and attentions, that she believes in me and loves me. But she knows that there is something wrong.

And she has, I think, quarreled with Halliday. There was nothing on the surface to show it, on their return to-day, but he declined her invitation to luncheon and went off, whistling rather ostentatiously, to his bacon and beans at the boat-house. This afternoon, while Mr. Bethel slept, she accepted young Gordon's invitation to go canoeing, and had the audacity to take the canoe, so to speak, from under poor Halliday's nose. According to Jane, she needs a good shaking.

There is, I understand, no definite engagement between them.

"Much as I—care for her," Halliday said to me, while he was still invalided here, "and I guess you know how it is with me, Skipper—I'm not going to tie her down until I've something to offer her beside myself. She's young, and I'm not going to take that advantage of her."

"But you do care for her?"

"Care for her? Oh, my God!" he said, and groaned, poor lad.

Three years, he has figured, maybe four. "Three with luck." And what Edith cannot understand is that he does not dare trust himself for that length of time. The urge that is in him is so different from hers; sentiment and attachment on her side, and strong young passion on his. Heigh-ho!

When one thinks that a mere ten thousand dollars or so would stop all these heart-aches, and that there are men to whom ten thousand dollars is only a new car, well—heigh-ho again! . . .

I must not forget to enter that Halliday last night believes he saw the red lamp burning, in the den behind the library of the main house. He told me the details this morning as he waited for Edith to don my overalls.

It was his first night, after his accident, at the boat-house, and he could not sleep.

"I had a good bit of pain," he said, "and at one o'clock I got up and went outside. There was a sort of dull red light coming from the windows of the library of the other house, and I watched it for awhile. It was extremely faint, and at first I thought it might be a fire; then, as it didn't grow any, I saw it must be a light of some sort."

He knew the stories of the red lamp, but he also knew I had locked it away, so after a time he started up toward the house. He was about half way up the lawn when it went out, suddenly, and left him staring.

But he was curious, and he went on. He made a complete circuit of the building, but there was no movement or sound from within, and so he turned and went back again. He believes the light was in the den, not the library, for he saw only a diffused reddish glare, as though it came from behind. He could not, through any of the three long French windows which open onto the terrace, see the source of that glare.

Here, then, is corroboration of my own impression of some few nights ago, but with a difference. For I saw the light itself, a momentary flash as though a breeze had for an instant pushed open the heavy curtains at the den windows, and then had let them fall again.

I am convinced that young Gordon has never seen the light, or he would have spoken of it. He is fluent enough about what he calls the "spooky" quality of the house. It is unlikely that Mr. Bethel, imprisoned in his upper room, can have any knowledge of it. Yet here we have two dispassionate observers, seeing at different times and under different circumstances, a light apparently of spontaneous origin and no known cause.

Cameron says (Note: "Experiments in Psychical Phenomena," a book I had sent for some days before.) that the production of lights is very common; he quotes the appearance of bluish-green lights in the experiments with Mary Outland, the brilliant star-like white lights of Mrs. Riggs, and the luminous effulgence which was frequently seen hanging over the head of the Polish medium, Markowitz.

But in no case is the production of red light mentioned, and in every instance this spontaneous production of light is in the presence of a medium.

In the case of Markowitz, for instance, I find on referring to him:

"Following the appearance of the effulgence, usually came the materialization. Sometimes there emerged from between the curtains of the cabinet, while the medium was in sight and securely held,—a large white face; again it would be a small hand and arm which apparently came, not from between the curtains, but through the material itself."

But this is no field of conjecture for a man about to go to bed. My nerves are not at their best, anyhow, and in spite of myself, I find that from behind the slight breeze which is waving my curtains, I am expecting something extremely unpleasant to appear.

July 19th.

A SUDDEN and terrifying storm outside. Above the howling of the wind I can hear the surf beating against the shore. Halliday reports, over the telephone, that the float is in danger and that the run-way has broken loose. But there is nothing to do. I have just been out, and I do not propose to be soaked again.

(Note: The approach of the storm had made Jane very nervous, and I had driven in to Doctor Hayward's for a sleeping medicine for her.)

Jock is as bad as Jane, and should have a narcotic also! He is moving uneasily from place to place, now and then emitting a dismal howl, and Clara is sitting forlornly at the foot of the staircase, under the impression that it is the only place free from metal in the house, and thus less likely to attract the lightning.

It is indeed a night for dark deeds. And for dark thoughts. . . .

I wonder if I have any justification for my suspicions? Why should Hayward, preparing to go out to an obstetric case, start me along a new and probably unjustified line of thought? Surely, of all men in the world, he has the best right to carry ether. I must be careful not to do as Greenough has done, allow my necessity for finding the guilty man to run away with my judgment.

And yet, in spite of myself, I cannot help feeling that Hayward fulfills many of the requirements. He alone, of all the people hereabout, is free to move about the country at night without suspicion. He knew Uncle Horace "as well as anybody." He is—and God forgive me if I am wrong—enough of a sailor to know and use the half-hitch.

There are other points, also. He is about my age, if anything older, but he is a muscular man. And he is, like all general practitioners in the country, by way of being a surgeon also. He would know how to find the jugular vein of a sheep. . . .

I have re-read this. Possibly Greenough is right after all, and I am a trifle mad. For why sheep? Sheep and a stone altar! And only an hour or so ago he was saying to me, in his professional voice: "Tell her to take plenty of water with it, and not to be impatient. These things take an hour or so to get in their work."

"In all earnestness I appeal to you to consider the enormity of the idea," wrote poor old Horace, more than a year ago. But while killing sheep is unpleasant, even sad, there is no particular enormity in it. I pass by a leg of spring-time lamb without considering that a tragedy lies behind it. The murder of Carroway, too, cannot come under the strictures of that letter; it was done as a matter of protection.

Nearest of all to the possibilities suggested by the letter comes the attack on Halliday, and if the sheep-killer did that, why not have put his devilish symbol on the car during that silent ride of a mile before he prepared to strike?

Why have crept in later and done it?

But here again—the doctor had access to the car, after Greenough had examined it. He went in alone, according to Clara, and was there some time.

Was it, then, the doctor's typewriter which wrote the cipher over which Halliday has been puzzling? The GeLTr, K. 28?

July 20th.

MAGGIE MORRISON disappeared last night; disappeared as completely as though she had been wiped from the face of the earth by the storm.

Livingstone telephoned me the facts at seven this morning, and Halliday and I took the car and went over. We have been out with the searching party all day, but without result.

After luncheon young Gordon joined us, sent by Mr. Bethel, who had not heard the news until that hour. It was all we three could do to keep Edith from starting out also, but it was not work for a woman.

To-night the search is still going on. Starr has sworn in more deputies, and the entire country-side is aroused.

Jane has been ill all day, and has kept her bed.

July 21st.

NO trace of the unfortunate girl to-night, and all hope of finding her alive is slowly being abandoned. . . .

I can now record such facts as we know, relative to the mystery.

The girl went in to Oakville yesterday to do some shopping, and remained for dinner with Thomas and his wife. In spite of Thomas's prophecy of a storm she insisted on staying over for a moving picture, and it was therefore ten-thirty when, alone in the farm truck, she started out of town.

Nothing more is known of her movements, save that she got as far as the Hilburn Road, about two hundred yards beyond the Livingstones' gate. The truck was found there yesterday morning at daylight by an early laborer on the Morrison farm, who however thought that she had abandoned it there during the storm the night before, and neglected to report it.

At the farm house itself there was no uneasiness, as the family supposed the girl had remained in town. But when the hour came for her to start out with her milk delivery, and she had not arrived, inquiries were set on foot.

The truck shows no signs of any struggle, and that robbery was not the motive of whatever has happened is shown by the fact that the missing girl's pocketbook was found behind the seat of the truck, where she usually placed it.

Greenough and the Sheriff were on the ground when we got there, as well as a small knot of country folk, kept at a distance by a deputy or two, and already a small posse, hastily recruited, was beating the wood nearby. Such clues as there may have been, however, had been obliterated by the storm. There is no trace of the dreaded symbol in chalk.   .   .   .

Halliday has reconstructed the story, in view of his own experience.

"The fellow was waiting," he said, "and hailed her, as he hailed me. He knew nobody would pass a man caught out in a storm like that. He got in, and closed the storm curtains, and of course she hadn't a chance in the world."

He does not therefore agree with the general conviction, that we are dealing with a sexual crime. And that word "general" does not include all of the population; there are many, I understand, among the more ignorant who have put together the almost uncanny violence of the elements that night, a night indeed for demons, and the complete disappearance of the unfortunate girl, and are building out of it and their own superstitious fears a theory that the girl's body will never be found; that she has been, indeed, spirited away.

It has its elements of strangeness, at that. Possibly five hundred men and boys have been searching steadily since yesterday morning; the back country, where it happened, is fairly open; the sea, with its salt marshes, both of which would give unlimited opportunity for concealment, is fully six miles by road from where the truck was found.   .   .   .

Much talk is going around as to a story from the light-house on the extreme tip of Robinson's Point to-day. As is to be expected, the superstitious are making considerable capital of it. And I myself am not disposed to dismiss it without considerable thought.

The story is as follows:

On the night of the tragedy, a flying night bird of some sort broke one of those windows of the light-house which protect the light itself. The keeper and the second keeper repaired it as best they could, but the terrific gusts of the wind made them uneasy, and they remained on watch.

(Note: In light-houses of a certain type there is a small aperture, running down through the successive floors of the building, and through which, as the light revolves, the weights of the clock-work mechanism of the lamp slowly descend.

It should also be said that the Robinson Point light is a red flash, timed at ten seconds.)

They sat, high in the air, in the room just beneath the light, now and then glancing up to see that all was well. The storm increased in violence, and as the sea came up the surf beat on the rocks below with a crashing only equalled by the thunder itself. As is usual in the high tide of the full moon, the low portion of the point to landward, and the keeper's houses, the engine shed, boat-house and oil storage tank were soon cut off from the mainland by a strip of angry ocean.

Nevertheless, they were comfortable enough, and the under-keeper had actually fallen asleep, at eleven o'clock, when there came a sudden lull in the storm. It was that time, which I well remember, when there came one of those ominous and quivering pauses in the attack which seem, not a promise of peace, but a gathering together of all the powers of wind, sea and sky for one final and tremendous effort.

And in that pause Ward, the light-keeper, heard something below in the tower. He touched his assistant on the shoulder and he sat up. Both of them then distinctly heard footsteps on the lowest flight of stairs, five floors below.

They were alone in the tower; cut off from the mainland by a rushing strip of tide, and no boat could have landed through the surf. And outside was that unearthly quiet which was more sinister than the storm itself. Neither one of them moved or spoke, but the keeper remembers that, as the steps came on inexorably, a cold air began to eddy around the small circular room, and that he looked up at the red light apprehensively.

The act, one sees, was the habit of a life-time. Even then, with his body fairly frozen with terror of what was on the staircase, he looked up.

At the top of the second flight the steps paused, and both keepers drew a breath. Then they heard a small dry cough, and the steps recommenced on the third level.

Up and up. The stairs curved round the inside wall of the tower, and they knew they would not see what was climbing until it was fairly on them. They sat there, their eyes glued to the door, and heard the steps coming up the last round. Whatever it was, it was on them. It reached the top, and the next step would bring it into view.

Then the storm burst again, in an explosion that fairly set the tower rocking, and simultaneously the electric lights in the room went out.

It was then that the assistant keeper swears that something touched him; something cold; but there seems to be no doubt, whether that is true or not, that the whole room was filled with the cold eddying wind referred to before.

I prefer to trust the head-keeper's statement. Ward is an unemotional type, and this is what he says:

"I was scared enough, but when the lights went out I looked up at the lamp. It's an oil burner, and it was all right. Old Faithful, we call it. Well, you have to understand that we weren't entirely in the dark, even then; some of the red light from above came down, and I could see where Jim was standing. I couldn't see him, y'understand, but I could see where he was. And there was a third party in the room, over near the stair-door. That is, he was there one minute; the next he was gone."

They did not make an immediate investigation. True to their type, they ran up and inspected the lamp, but it was "sitting pretty," as Ward says. They had candles, for it was not unusual for storms to put the Oakville light company out of service, and keeping close together they went down through the successive floors of the tower. They found nothing, and the outer door was still closed and bolted.

In view of so detailed and corroborative a statement, the final support of my early scepticism has had a severe blow. . . .

What would be the change, should we enter another world, with the same faculties we have now, but no limi-tations in their use? For after all, it is the brain that sees, and the human eye is only a faulty window, which shows us but a tiny portion of the universe; the ear hears only a modicum of sound. To carry with us that strange thing of which the brain is only an instrument for our poor physical use, and thus to hear all things, see all things, perhaps even know all things.

And thus equipped with limitless faculties, who would dare to leave out the emotions? To sorrow, then, to love, even perhaps to hate. And who shall laugh at the poor ghost who, knowing and suffering all things, makes its desperate attempt to avert a wickedness? To convey, through the thick mantle of the flesh, a knowledge that is not conveyable. To stand by, wringing its pale amor-phous hands, while crimes go on and unnecessary wretch-edness inhabits the earth?

Nothing bodily accounts for personality. Back of

everything physical, and greater than anything physical, is the mind. And mind is not an attribute of matter.

July 22nd.

THE body has not been found, and the Sheriff has raised the reward to five thousand dollars. This with Livingstone's original five hundred for the sheep-killer, which is to go to the finder of the murderer as being in all probability the same individual, raises the reward to fifty-five hundred dollars.

To-day, however, certain information acquired by Halliday has shifted the scene of the search to the salt marshes and the bay, and to-night, as I glance from my window I can see lanterns moving in the marsh beyond the main house, and up and down the shore. Jane has made coffee, and those of the searchers who come up this way from the beach have been stopping in.

Every bit of woodland in the county, according to the Sheriff, has been beaten without result, and to-morrow they will drag the bay.

We get a curious reaction from the men who are searching. The police, of course, see in it nothing unusual, and are prosecuting the case with vigor. But the fishermen, always a superstitious crowd, seem to me only half-hearted in the search.

The story from the light-house has convinced them once more of the diabolical nature of whatever is at work among us, and there is current also a tale from some passing motorist that the red lamp was burning in the main house at midnight the night of the 19th.

Coming up from our salt marsh, there is more than one who has made a wide detour to avoid the other house. . . .

Halliday's discovery, made to-day, is as follows: He calculated just how far the truck would have to go after it was hailed, before it stopped, and went back to that point, which was not far from the entrance to the Livingstone drive. Already the crowd of searchers and sensation hunters had pretty well destroyed any clue that might have been left, but about twenty yards from the gates he found marks in the mud indicating that, not only had the truck been backed to that point, but it had been turned there and headed back toward Oakville and the bay.

Just where it left the road again, if at all, is a question. I believe Halliday has taken a scraping from the wheels and proposes to have it analyzed. He finds something suspicious in it. I cannot say what.

I have spent to-day reorganizing my household. None of the women, including Clara, are to leave it after nightfall unaccompanied, and although no entrance into any house has yet been attempted, Halliday and I have spent the late afternoon tightening window locks and adding new bolts where they are necessary.

I took advantage of the opportunity to tell Halliday my suspicions about the doctor. He was so astonished that he let go of a window sash, dropping it on my fingers.

"The doctor!" he said. "Never in this world, Skipper."

And when I had put forth all my evidence he was still sceptical.

"I admit, of course, that the weight of it is rather startling," he said slowly. "But it wasn't the doctor I picked up. I'd know him, even in the dark."

"I'm not so certain of that, Halliday. But I think Maggie Morrison would have."

"Meaning——?"

"That I don't believe she would have stopped that truck at night for anyone she didn't know. You have to consider the character of the girl; she was as timid as a rabbit about some things. Superstitious, too. I say she would have gone by, after your experience, unless she had had a particular reason for stopping. And I still think she recognized this man, possibly by the lightning, which was practically incessant, and so she stopped."

"You're right in one thing, probably," he said. "She had a reason for stopping."

Edith has been recalcitrant about not leaving the house in the evening, but has finally agreed to it.

"I can write," she says resignedly. "I haven't really buckled down to it yet."

But nothing is more clear than that Edith's dreams of opulence are slowly fading. Her article on "The Beach at Low Tide" has been returned to her, and the Morrison mystery is being covered as spot news by those who are doing it as a part of the day's work, and on a salary basis.

Jane has entirely recovered, and has to-day resumed work on her tapestry, with us a barometer of normality. She has even agreed to dine at the Livingstones to-night, not particularly to my delight.

"Come over and dine," Mrs. Livingstone telephoned, "and let's have a little bridge. I've had the horrors for three days."

"You don't object to my wearing my revolver, as a part of my evening outfit?"

"Everybody's doing it," she said. "This house has been turned into an arsenal."

But in the midst of death we are in life. Clara, going to turn down my bed last night, saw two feet projecting from beneath it, and let out a series of wild shrieks.

Needless to say, they were my boots, hastily discarded for a pair of dry ones. . . .

Later: Doctor Hayward stopped in this evening for a final professional visit to Jane, and on an impulse

I showed him Uncle Horace's letter. I may be mistaken, but it seemed to me that, under pretense of reading it a second time, he was playing for time.

"Curious!" he said, when he passed it back to me. "What do you make of it?"

"The last part of it is fairly clear. He was in danger, and knew it."

"But the rest of it?" he said. "What does he say?, The wickedness of the idea. What idea?"

"You haven't any opinion on that yourself?"

"No," he said slowly. "I can't say that I have."

The tension, or whatever it was, seemed to relax then. "As a matter of fact," he said, "I thought it was addressed to me, when I commenced it. We'd had a long argument not long before his death, on euthanasia. I believed in putting the unfit out of the world; he didn't. But of course the end of it settles that."

He laughed again, bit the end of a thumb, hesitated, and then got his hat.

"Danger!" he said. "And the police! No, that wasn't for me."

"And you still believe he died of heart disease?"

"It was his heart, all right," he said, and going out, climbed heavily into his car. He seemed abstracted, and made no reply to my good-night.

I can read into this what I like. His manner was not that of a guilty man; on the other hand, it was not entirely natural, either. He was both watchful and self-conscious. And I do not believe he read the letter twice. . . .

One of the evening newspapers to-night prints a photostatic copy of the cipher found in our garage, and offers a prize for its solution.

Edith's memory is shown to have been faulty in only one particular. The cipher, as published reads:

GeLTr, K. *24*.

July 23rd.

MRS. LIVINGSTONE has given me something to think about. . . .

The dinner went off very well. A trifle too much food and service, according to Jane, for a meal *en famille* in the country.

"One can see they have not always had money," says Jane, with the calm superiority of one who has never had it.

But the bridge was irritating. It is always a mistake to seat four people at a table, and place cards before them, when their minds are full of another and totally different matter. Thus: I would deal and bid a spade, for example, and wait patiently for Livingstone to sort his cards. In the pause, conversation between the women would be going on. Finally Livingstone would say:

"Who dealt?"

"I did," I reply, as patiently as possible. "And bid a spade."

"A heart," from him.

"You'll have to say two hearts."

"All right," he assents reluctantly. "Two hearts."

Then we wait. Mrs. Livingstone finishes what she is saying and picks up her cards.

"Let's see," she says, "did anybody do anything?"

"I dealt," I say, "and bid——"

"It wasn't your deal, was it? I'm perfectly sure I dealt that last hand."

"We have the blue cards," I explain. "Now I have bid a spade, and Mr. Livingstone has bid two hearts. If you want to declare anything——"

"I don't," she says promptly, and starts laying out the dummy. We restrain her by main force, and Jane looks bewildered.

"I'm afraid I'm a little mixed," she says. "You bid two spades, Mr. Livingstone?"

After two hours of that sort of thing last night I was ready to go out and bite a hole in one of the porch pillars. But Jane at that point tactfully ended the game and saved my reason.

Nevertheless, the evening was not without a peculiar interest of its own. While Mr. Livingstone took Jane to see his hot-houses I had a few moments alone with his wife, and I received what is to me a new angle on the whole mysterious business.

We were in the library, and I was wandering around looking at Livingstone's books. They were the usual uncut editions a man thinks he should have on his shelves, but reserves for his old age to read; Darwin, Huxley and Haeckel, de Maupassant (in English), Tennyson, Wordsworth and Shelley, and of course, Emerson, among others.

In one corner, however, was a large and well-worn collection of books of an entirely different character. They were, as a matter of fact, books on psychic subjects, and as I glanced up from them Mrs. Livingstone was watching me, gravely.

"If you do not know what you believe on these matters," I said, "you must certainly know the opinions of others."

"And you?" she said. "Are you still a cynic? A carrion crow?"

I turned and faced her.

"I don't know what I am."

"Ah! You have heard the light-house story?"

"Yes."

She said nothing for a moment, then:

"What about your new tenant? Your Mr. Bethel? Has he made any complaint?"

"Not yet. As a matter of fact I have talked to him only once."

"And that was——?"

"Mostly about hot water and a beef cube," I admitted. "And the direction in which the house faces. He struck me as an extremely irritable and material type."

" 'Irritable and material,' " she repeated thoughtfully. "And yet I suppose you know they are saying that he is using the red lamp."

"The red lamp is locked away. So far as I know, he doesn't even suspect its existence."

For some reason or other that puzzled her.

"But it's been seen burning," she protested, after a blank pause.

"It is locked in a closet on the upper floor, Mrs. Livingstone, and I have the key. What is more, I heard that story some time ago, and investigated. So far as I can tell, it has not been disturbed since I put it there. Of course, he may have brought another similar lamp, but that's going rather far, isn't it?"

"Annie Cochran would know."

"I'll ask her, if you like. But privately, I believe that if she so much as saw such a lamp, she would run shrieking from the place."

She picked up some knitting at her elbow and worked at it thoughtfully.

"You have changed since I last talked to you," she said at last. "What has brought about that change, Mr. Porter?"

"A good bit has happened since then."

She looked up at me searchingly.

"Including the light-house."

"Including the light-house," I agreed, soberly. It was then she put down her knitting.

"Why has he come back?" she asked, watching me intently. "Why is he earth-bound? Have you no idea?"

"I haven't an idea what you mean by earth-bound."

"Just what I appear to mean, and you know it," she said.

But after a moment, during which she continued her curiously searching gaze at me, she picked up her work again, with a smile.

"There is always a reason," she said. "You can laugh if you like; Liv does. But I know what I know. There is always a reason when they come back like this. A very good reason."

But beyond that she refused to go. Whether she has an inkling of this "reason" to which she attributes what she refers to as his "coming back" I have no idea.

The conversation, as I record it, seems as extraordinary as the entire situation; two intelligent people, a man and a woman, discussing the return of a spirit to earth, much as they might that of a friend from Europe:

"What brought him back?"

"Goodness knows! Some sort of business, perhaps."

Some of the humor of the thing occurred to me on the way home and, with no disrespect, I chuckled.

"What in the world are you laughing at?" Jane demanded.

"Sheer relief that that's over," I said.

It was then that Jane made the remark about the Livingstones not always having had money.

July 24th.

THE truck, according to Halliday's analysis, had been driven through heavy leaf mould. But a second drenching rain toward morning, and still continuing, discourages him. Into the bargain, the cars of searchers and summer tourists alike have made it practically impossible to identify any trail.

He has given his information and the result of the report to Greenough, but that gentleman appears to think he requires no assistance.

"If you amateurs would keep out," he grumbled, "we would get somewhere with this case. Some day one of you is going to be missing, and I'll have more trouble on my hands."

From which one may gather that Mr. Greenough feels that we are not through with the situation.

Greenough himself is frankly puzzled. Whether his espionage of me assures him that my single excursion the night of the tragedy was to Doctor Hayward's office and back again, or whether he believes that this new catastrophe bears no relation to the sheep-killing, I do not know.

But the fact remains that, when we met to-day, he showed me more civility than he has shown in our casual encounters recently. But I have reason to believe that I am still being carefully watched, especially at night, and that his vigilance has increased since the loss of my fountain pen.

He has, in his mind, definitely connected me with Carroway and it is, I daresay, only needed to establish some connection between this recent mystery and the ones that have preceded it, to set him at my heels again.

As a matter of fact, until the body is found or some such connection is established, he has no case in law against anybody, according to Halliday.

"There can be no murder without a body," says Halliday. "The law of *corpus delicti,* you know. He either has to find the Morrison girl, or failing that, pin his case to Carroway."

He (Halliday) and Edith have taken the car and gone out this evening. Jane is very uneasy, but I feel that they will be safe enough.

The best time to travel is immediately after a railroad accident.

July 25th.

A ND now where are we?

We can no longer doubt that the same hand which throttled Carroway and attacked Halliday, has brought about the disappearance and almost certain murder of Maggie Morrison.

Halliday knows it. Edith knows it. I know it. But what use are we to make of our knowledge? What effect, for instance, will it have on my own serio-comic position? Could Greenough arrest me on suspicion? Although Halliday laughs at that, he is, I think, a trifle uncertain. He feels, as I do, that before long Greenough will have to satisfy the public by an arrest of some sort, and that I am the only person against whom he has the shadow of a case.

We held a three-cornered conference at the boat-house this afternoon, while Jane slept after luncheon, and for the first time Edith was taken fully into our confidence. She went a trifle pale, but she slipped a hand into mine as a vote of confidence.

"You," she said, "the gentlest soul on earth, hiding a knife under that float there, and going out at night in a boat to kill somebody! Why, you can't even row a boat, properly!"

The small laugh which followed helped us all.

What developed last night is as follows: Halliday got out of the car at the spot where the truck was found, and had Edith go back and approach slowly, along the road from town. Approximately, the conditions were the same as those of the night of the disappearance, save that no rain was falling.

Halliday, it appears, was searching for that spot, back among the trees, where the unknown had waited, secure from observation but still able to see the truck's lights far enough away to be able to run out and hail it before it had passed.

After two or three experiments he found the proper location, and there commenced a sort of intensive search with the pocket flash, with Edith in the car, to warn him of any approach, and the lights out.

(Note: Perhaps it is as well, to record here a conversation with Halliday, which took place a day or so before.

In that, I recall, he stated that the first man who takes a case blazes the trail for any others who may come after. The situation more or less crystallizes under his handling of it. This he claims is the weakness of the French system which follows one direction until it ends in a blind alley, before it takes up another, and the strength of Scotland Yard, where into a central office is brought from varying sources all collectible material, which is there assorted and clarified.

"Greenough's mistake here," he said, "is that he has directed all his efforts toward finding the body, under the impression that that will yield the necessary clues. That's all well enough, but time is going by, has gone by, and he has nobody. And in the meantime rain is wiping out some possible clues, and the murderer himself is free to pick up the others."

He insisted that there would be clues, of one sort or another.

"There is no such thing as a perfect crime," he said, "and of course the general idea that a clue is some mysterious phenomenon which it requires super-human powers to understand, is all bosh. Clues are practically always trivial, because it is only the trivial things the criminal overlooks. He takes care of the big ones."

It may be as well to add, too, that the reason he did not make this investigation earlier was that, until the search shifted to the sea and the marshes, the vicinity where the truck was found was still the focal point, and was rarely without its constable, or its group of curious on-lookers.)

Not under the tree he had selected, but perhaps a dozen feet away from it, he found, well trampled into the ground, a small screw cap, made of tin; exactly similar, he tells me, to those used on the cans of certain makes of ether, and underneath which there is a cork.

"In my case, he was unlucky," he explains. "He went through the same procedure, and took the cap off before he hailed me, but the cork came out. He had better luck this last time."

As to his discovery of the murderer's infernal symbol, he is more reticent. He had some sort of a "hunch" to examine the trees themselves, he says simply.

"What do you mean by a 'hunch'?"

"I don't know. Just an idea, I suppose."

"You thought there might be something on a tree?"

"I don't know that I thought about it at all, Skipper. I just turned the flash up, and there it was."

Perhaps I am wrong, but his explanation does not quite satisfy me, nor, I think, does it satisfy himself. With all his keen intelligence he is strictly conventional; I think he believes it would somehow invalidate his manhood to confess that his "hunch" might have been a guidance by some unseen source.

But the triangle enclosed in a circle was there, on a tree only thirty feet back from the road.

July 26th.

A NNIE COCHRAN says absolutely that there is neither a red lamp nor a red lantern in the other house.

I stopped her this morning and asked her. . . .

The day has brought no developments in the Morrison case, which has settled down more or less into a routine. The searchers are fewer each day; the fishermen have gone back to their nets and trawls, and to-day will probably see the last of the attempts to drag likely spots on the bay.

There are many now who believe that this time the anchor rope is shorter, and that the body, securely anchored to the ooze at the bottom of the bay, will not be uncovered by the lowest tide.

But if the day has brought no developments outside, it has brought one or two to us here.

For one thing, the morning mail returned to me through the dead letter office my letter of thanks to the young woman in Salem, Ohio, an event which would puzzle me more, did I not suspect the lady of using a fictitious name, for all her apparent frankness.

For another, Jane has at last unbosomed herself. She maintains that on the night of the nineteenth she saw Maggie Morrison, clairvoyantly. Rather, on the morning of the twentieth, for granted that she has actually had another of her curious psychic experiences, there is a discrepancy in time here as marked as the interval between Uncle Horace's death and her vision of him lying on the library floor.

Maggie Morrison disappeared presumably at eleven o'clock the night of the 19th; Jane's vision occurred at three the morning of the 20th, or four hours later. . . .

This morning, at eleven o'clock, Jane left the cottage

for the first time in days, giving as an excuse that she meant to look over Warren Halliday's clothing and bring back such as required mending.

"I need a little attention of that sort myself," I observed. "I don't mind competing with a tapestry—after all, that is art, and what am I to art?—but I resent competing with a younger and handsomer man."

She gave me the smile with which every wife greets an old familiar jocularity of every husband, and left me to my reading.

When an hour, however, had gone by and she had not returned, I began to grow uneasy. Halliday, I knew, was out on the bay, and in such times as these any small deviation from the normal is upsetting. I started after her, therefore, and was startled not to find her in the living quarters or on the verandah. But when I called she answered from below, and going down I found her among the boats.

"Well!" I said. "And are you going fishing?"

"I was just wandering about," she said. "There's another boat, isn't there?"

"Halliday's out in it. Why?"

But she pretended not to hear me, and went up the steps again. Even then she made various excuses not to leave at once. She went inside, and I could hear her straightening the small living room. When there was nothing more to do she came out again.

"I don't think he has cooked a thing since it happened," she said. "Suppose we wait for him, and take him back to luncheon?"

She is no actress, is Jane, and it began to dawn on me that she was determined to wait for Halliday's return, and that she had one of her hidden reasons for it. It was there, sitting on the boat-house verandah, that she finally told her story, which is detailed in the extreme.

"You remember," she said, "the night of Maggie's disappearance, that a storm was threatening, and that I was nervous. I felt queer—I can't describe it, William. I had a sort of premonition, I think, anyhow, I didn't want to go to bed, and when I told you that you started off to Doctor Hayward's for a powder."

"You had meant deliberately to stay awake?"

"Yes. Once in awhile something terrifies me, and I am afraid even to wink for fear something happens while my eyes are closed. It was like that.

"Edith was writing something or other, shut in her room, and after you had gone the storm began to come up, and I felt queer and jumpy. I went around the windows downstairs, and then went into the living room and sat down to wait for you."

"Let's see. What time was that?"

"It must have been ten o'clock; maybe a little later. Then—I hate to tell you this, William. It sounds so silly."

"I've been thinking some pretty foolish things myself, lately, my dear," I said, gravely. "Go ahead."

"Jock was very strange, from the moment we went in there. He sat and stared at that old parlor organ. I——"

"At the parlor organ! What in the world——"

"At the parlor organ," she said positively. "Or rather, above and behind it, where it sits across the corner. And after awhile, I thought I saw something there."

"What sort of 'something'?"

"I can't tell you," she said, and shivered. "That is it wasn't really anything. It was like a mist. I could just tell there was something there, and then Jock lifted up his head and howled at it, and—I don't even remember getting upstairs, William."

Now, so far, this runs fairly true to form; the usual strange combination of the grotesque—witness the parlor organ!—overstrained nerves due to the approach of an electrical storm, and Jock, absently staring at nothing at all and preparing to give the storm howl for howl.

It is the remainder of Jane's story which seems worthy of consideration, in view of her previous average of hits.

She went to sleep, sinking fathoms deep into unconsciousness, but at three o'clock she wakened, suddenly and fully, and sat up in her bed. But she was not in a bed at all. She was in a boat, and Maggie Morrison also was in it, lying at her feet. After a time—she has no idea how long—the vision faded, and she was still sitting up in her bed.

Such details as I can draw from her are as follows:

"Did you see Uncle Horace in the same way?"

"Wakening out of a sleep? Yes."

"Was there the same sort of light?"

"Not a light exactly. It doesn't come from anywhere. I can't describe it exactly; the things I see are luminous."

She has, however, her strict limitations; she speaks of a boat, but whether it was quiet or in motion she has no idea; asked if she and the girl were alone, she thinks not, but can give no reason for so thinking. Asked as to why she believed the girl was dead, she says: "I *felt* that she was dead," and then qualifies that by adding: "Besides, I never have these visions unless some one has died."

This, like most broad statements, is an error, but in this case the general developments bear her out. I myself believe that, if she saw the Morrison girl at all, she saw her dead, as she says.

She saw no rope on the body or in the boat, and there was no sign of injury on the girl.

"She looked very peaceful," says Jane, and sets me to shuddering.

On one point, however, she is entirely definite. She maintains that there were pieces of cloth tied around the oar-locks of the boat. "White cloth," she adds, as an after thought.

"Why cloth?"

"To keep the oars from making a noise," says my Jane, who has been in a row-boat perhaps a half dozen times in all her life! . . .

We sat on the verandah while Halliday came in with the boat; he had been out, I daresay, on some scouting business of his own, and I confess to a sort of terror that by some unlucky chance we might find the oar-locks of this very boat, wrapped with white cloth, "to keep the oars from making a noise." But they showed no stigma of crime.

"Why," I said to Jane, as Halliday tied his boat and came with his splendid stride up the run-way, "why did you come down here to look at *our* boats, my dear?"

She showed a faint distress.

"I don't know, William. I just had a feeling that I had to come."

I have not asked her why she has suppressed this experience for so long. Carrying it down with her to pour my breakfast coffee, going with it through the day, and at night mounting the stairs with it and so to bed. Brushing her hair meticulously, and settling Jock for the night; going in to kiss Edith and tuck her into her fresh white bed, and then closing her door and shutting herself away with it for the night. And always with the guilty feeling that she was withholding that which should be known.

For she no more doubts that Maggie Morrison was killed and thrown into the sea from a boat with muffled oar-locks, than she doubts her own existence. But coupled with that certainty has been her dread of possible publicity, and that ever present feeling of hers that whatever power she has is somehow shameful.

My poor Jane.

July 27th.

THE blow has fallen again, and this time almost at our very door. That it is not murder is not due to any lack of intention, but to weakness in execution. I have spent a large portion of the day in urging Edith and Jane to go back to town, but without result.

"Not unless you go," Jane said firmly, and Edith and I exchanged glances.

As a matter of fact, last night's events have left me in a more precarious position than before, and I feel that any move on my part would only precipitate matters. Greenough has given out a statement to the reporters that an early arrest may be expected, and I do not for the life of me understand why he has not pounced already.

I imagine the only thing that has saved me, so far, has been the single fact that Peter Geiss knows I was on the sloop the night and hour when Halliday was attacked. That puzzles him. . . .

To record last night's strange affair in sequence:

I could not sleep, a condition which is growing chronic with me lately, and at or about midnight I went downstairs and outside. The night was extremely dark; I paced back and forward along the drive, keeping at first close to the Lodge, but gradually extending my steps as I grew accustomed to the darkness.

After twenty minutes or so of this, and at the extreme of my swing toward the other house, I heard some sort of movement in that direction, and stopped to listen. It was a cautious disturbance of the shrubbery, and I swung in among the trees and stood listening. It was not repeated, however, and I turned to go back.

I had, however, lost my way, and for some brief time I floundered about. At last I found the sun-dial, by striking against it, and thus orienting myself, turned about and struck back toward the Lodge.

I had not gone ten feet before I heard the bell ringing.

(Note: A large bell on the kitchen porch of the main house and used in times before the telephone was installed, to summon the gardener. It is rung by pulling a rope attached to it.)

It rang sharply twice and then abruptly stopped, and the sudden silence seemed somehow ominous, like the stillness after a shriek.

There were no lights in the main house, and no further sounds came from it. I daresay at such times one does not think; one acts automatically. Someone has said, "With the spinal cord. Not the brain." I do not recall thinking at all, but I do recall trying to feel my way through the trees, and that I ran into one and was partially stunned for an instant.

The house was still completely dark and silent. I felt my way with more caution, skirted the shrubbery, and at last found the railing leading up the steps to the kitchen. Here I was on safer ground, and I crossed the small porch to the door with increased confidence, only to stumble over something and almost fall. I knew at once what it was, and I felt suddenly ill, although my brain was as active as ever in my life. "In the pit of his stomach man is always a coward." But I found some matches in my dressing gown pocket, and striking one bent over a figure lying prone at my feet. It was young Gordon, unconscious and bleeding from a blow on the head, and securely tied with a rope. I was still stooping over him, fumbling for another match, when a flash-light shone in my face, fairly blinding me. It played on me for a moment, and then on the boy stretched on the floor and now slightly moving.

"What's happened?" said a voice from behind it, and with relief I recognized it as the doctor's.

"He's hurt," I said, rising dizzily. "Struck on the head, I think."

"Open the door there and turn on the lights. I'll carry him in."

I did as he told me, being still somewhat unsteady, and as he laid the boy on the floor and straightened I was aware that his eyes, as they rested on me, were hostile and suspicious.

Immediately, however, he went to work on the boy, examining him first and then removing the rope.

"He's only stunned," he said, and leaving him lying as he was, began to move about the room. Just inside the door was the poker from the kitchen range, and this, with the rope, he laid aside carefully. Then he went outside, and with his flash examined the bell.

"Just where were you, Porter, when this happened?" he asked.

"In the grounds, by the sun-dial. I couldn't sleep. When I heard the bell I came on a run."

"It was the boy who pulled the bell?"

"I haven't an idea."

He went back to his patient, and examined the wound in the scalp more carefully. After that he dressed it, the boy by that time moving about and groaning, but still only partially conscious. I gave such help as I could, getting water and so on, and when the dressing was done the doctor disappeared and returned with a cushion. Keeping the boy supine, he slipped it under his head. Then he straightened.

"You'd better notify the old man," he said. "I'll stay here, if you don't mind."

And from the look he gave me, I gathered that he had no intention of leaving me with the boy.

I made my way upstairs to the room over the den, and knocked for some time before I was heard. Then Mr. Bethel called out, startled, and I asked if I could come in. I heard him making heavy work of getting out of bed, and finally he shot the bolt and opening the door an inch or two glared out at me.

"What the devil's the matter?"

"Nothing serious," I said. "There's been a little trouble downstairs, and we thought you'd better be told."

"A fire!"

"Not a fire," I reassured him, and gave him a brief account of what had occurred.

He was not particularly gracious; demanded to know what the boy was doing outside at that hour, and seemed to feel that, with a doctor already in the house, his responsibility was ended. As there was actually nothing he could do, I helped him back to his bed and left him sitting on the side, an unpleasant but helpless figure.

As I went out he asked me to bring him a cup of hot water!

The boy was conscious when I went back to the kitchen, staring around him, and particularly concentrating on the doctor and myself. He put his hand to his head and felt the bandage.

"Where'd I get that?" he asked thickly.

After a time he tried to get up, and the doctor put him into a chair.

"Now, Gordon," he said, "what happened to you? Try and think."

"He hit me," he said finally. "The dirty devil!"

"Who hit you?"

But he was still too dazed for coherent thought. He improved rapidly after that, however, although he complained of severe headache. He became garrulous, too, as happens after concussion, but out of his maunderings we were able to secure a fairly connected story.

He had been unable to sleep, because of certain noises in his room. He glanced at me. "You were right, old dear," he said elegantly, "when you said the place has an unpleasant reputation. I'll tell the world it's unpleasant."

He had got up, and gone down to the kitchen for something to eat. After that, reluctant to go up to his room again, he had wandered out onto the kitchen steps and sat there. It was then that he heard someone stealthily approaching the house.

He listened, and finally he heard a window of the old gun room next to the laundry being raised. He stared that way, and insists he saw a dark figure there. The next moment it was gone, and he was certain there was someone in the house.

He had, apparently, turned to enter the house and head off the intruder, but was struck down in the doorway. On the matter of ringing the bell he was rather vague at first, not remembering that he had done so, but later saying he had had his hand on the rope, when the blow came.

Hayward listened to this intently. Then he turned to me.

"And you were where, Porter?"

"By the sun-dial. On the other side of it. I had started toward home."

"Do you mean to say that, after that bell rang, this man Gordon speaks of had time to tie him and escape, before you got here?"

"I've told you the facts. It isn't a simple matter to get here from the sun-dial, in the dark."

I remembered the hot water then, and finding some in the tea-kettle carried it up to Mr. Bethel. He showed me more civility this time, inquired after the boy, and even offered his pocket flask, lying on his bedside table. There was revolver beside it, and he saw me glance at it and smiled grimly.

"What with the sounds inside your house, and the things that are happening outside, I think it best to be prepared for anything."

So, in spite of young Gordon's prophecy, he too has been hearing things. . . .

In spite of the doctor's attitude and my own fears, I cannot see to-day that a dispassionate examination of the evidence would really involve me.

Gordon saw a man enter the gun room window, and was attacked from the kitchen by that man. It must be perfectly evident to Greenough, on hearing the doctor's story, that had I for any reason desired to make some nefarious entrance into the house, I need not have resorted to a window. I have keys to every door, and can produce them.

Thomas, however, who seems to have his own methods of acquiring information, to-day tells a fact which, in my ignorance of such matters, I had not noticed last night. He states that the doctor reports the boy as having been tied in the same manner as poor Carroway; in two half-hitches around the wrists, a turn or two about the body and arms, and ending in two half-hitches at the ankle.

The rope, it appears, was not brought for the purpose, but had been left lying on the top of Annie Cochran's laundry basket in the kitchen, when she went home last night.

Later: Greenough and Doctor Hayward have driven

past, on their way to the main house. I have telephoned to Halliday, and he is on his way here. I may need him.

July 28th.

AFTER all, things passed off yesterday better than I had hoped. The detective concedes that, while in daylight it is a simple matter to reach the main house from the sun-dial, it is not an easy one at night. And I think he was puzzled when I said:

"After all, the real mystery to me is how Doctor Hayward, who says he was passing on the main road in his car, could reach the house so soon after I did."

"He had his car."

"But he didn't drive in. You left it outside the Lodge gates, doctor, didn't you?"

"I didn't know just where the bell was ringing."

"But you knew there was such a bell on the main house. Everyone around here knows that. Even at that, you made very good time. I had only had time to light one match and see the boy, when you turned your flash-light on me."

I imagine, and Halliday agrees with me, that whatever Greenough had in mind when he came, the new element thus introduced caused him to hesitate. And to add to his hesitation, the doctor, from the breezy unctuousness of his entrance, took to twitching and gnawing his finger tips.

"I don't suppose you are intimating that I knocked the boy down, Porter," he said, "but it sounds like it. As a matter of fact, I didn't even know him; never saw him, to my knowledge, until last night."

"I'm not intimating anything. I'm in a peculiar position; that's all. And you have been considerably more than intimating that I was where I had no business to be last night. I had, you see, exactly as much reason to be there as you had. Rather more, I imagine."

I was perhaps a trifle excited, but heaven knows I had a right to be.

"I know what you have in your mind, Mr. Greenough, and I'm glad to have this chance to lay my cards on the table. Ask my wife why I was on the float, the night Carroway was killed in the bay. She'll tell you I was in bed, until she roused me and sent me down to the beach. Ask Peter Geiss where I was at the hour when Halliday was attacked; he can tell you. Ask the newspaper reporter who told me, right here, about that culvert under the road where Halliday's car overturned; and ask Halliday himself about our excursion to examine it, and my losing my fountain pen there. And then ask yourself if I would open the gun room window of the main house to make an entrance when I have in this desk a key to every door in the place."

Greenough smiled drily.

"That's a pretty strong defense, considering that you haven't been accused," he said. "As a matter of fact, we hadn't found your fountain pen, Mr. Porter. I'm afraid we overlooked something there!" . . .

Since they have gone, I feel, although he has not said so, that Halliday believes I have made a tactical error. And I dare say, in one way, I may have. I have given my defense to the opposition, and not only that; I realize that my list of witnesses is painfully weak; my wife, my niece's lover, and Peter Geiss!

And Peter Geiss, by local repute, is, like some of the weak sisters of the world, to be bought with a price. . . .

Nevertheless, I feel a great sense of relief. I have at least made a hole in that web of circumstantial evidence which has seemed to be closing around me, and sent the detective scurrying back to the center of it again, to spin such new threads as he is able.

July 29th.

TO-DAY has been quiet. Those constant reminders of the latest tragedy, the boats dragging the bay, have disappeared, and once more we see gay little picnic parties, chugging across the water to Robinson's Point or thereabouts, laden with hampers and, I dare say, with flasks.

Edith came down to luncheon in her best pink frock, with a hat to match, and made shameless eyes at me during that meal. The cause of this sudden attention developed later, when she took the car—and Halliday— and went to the light-house. Over the purpose behind this unexpected display of interest in our coast-guard service she draws a discreet veil.

For the rest of the day, there is nothing to record. Jane and I took a brief walk this afternoon, and noticed a man clearing the woods on Nylie's farm, across the road. We stopped and watched him for a time, and he seemed curiously inexpert at the job. But perhaps I am too ready to suspect Greenough's fine hand in everything I see.

I confess, however, to a certain unholy joy when Jock made a most ungentlemanly attack on him, and was only called off with real difficulty. . . .

Young Gordon, although still confined to his room, is up and about again.

To-day I asked Hayward, who had been to see him, if I might visit him, but he shook his head.

"He is still in an excitable condition," he said. "Better give him a day or two more."

As, however, Annie Cochran reports him in excellent

shape, although moody and irritable, I can only feel that the doctor has his own reasons for keeping me away from him. At the same time, I must be careful not to allow suspicion to carry me too far. Mr. Bethel states flatly that the boy has no idea of who attacked him and himself suggests Thomas! . . .

My talk with Mr. Bethel last night was interesting and not without an unusual quality of its own. He chose to be civil, and rather more than that. I felt that the alarm of my entrance once over, he not only greeted me with a sense of relief, but kept me as long as possible. And he voiced something of the sort before I left.

"My infirmity cuts me off from my kind," he said. "I am dependent on the indulgence of others, and that is a poor thing."

As it was the first time he had referred to his condition, I ventured to ask how he managed without Gordon. It seemed to me that the small laugh he gave was ironical.

"Paid solicitude!" he said. "I can manage without it. I make heavy weather of it, but I manage." My offer to assist him upstairs before I left, however, met with a decided negative. He was not going up yet; when he did, it would be a slow process, but he had done it the last night or so, "somehow." My last impression of him is of a helpless and yet indefinably militant figure in a dimly lighted room, sitting upright in its chair, one withered hand palm upwards, on his knee, and the other not too far from the revolver. . . .

I am puzzled over that picture, as I am over the one which I saw from the terrace window, as I approached. He gave the same impression then as he did when I left, of a man waiting for something.

As I looked in at him, he was facing toward the hall and the dining room door, directly across, with a concentration so great that my light tap at first did not reach his ears. And during the entire conversation which followed, every now and again I was conscious of a sudden abstraction on his part, an intent listening, that made me nervous in spite of myself.

But the conversation was both interesting and enlightening. He was, through the secretary and Annie Cochran, acquainted with the general outline of what has been going on, and even of the stories current about the house itself, especially as to the red lamp.

"I dare say my statement that the red lamp is locked away," he said whimsically, "would not greatly assist the situation. As I understand it, they would simply say that this was some further evidence of its abnormal powers."

I gather that, like young Gordon, he has heard certain sounds in the house at night, but does not intend to be stampeded by them, to use his own words. He has some theory of a disturbance of molecular activity, by some undiscovered natural law, which I could not follow closely. But in the discussion of superstition in general which followed, I was a trifle disconcerted to find him laying much of it to the Christian religion; that our present theology had given birth to the wide-spread belief in evil spirits and in sorcery. He went even further, and classed the adoration of saints as polytheism, and the worship of sacred relics as fetichism.

Strangely enough, I had at that moment one of those curious sensations which I have heard referred to as a failure of the two sides of the brain to synchronize.

(Note: Lear, who has read this, advises me that this is now an exploded idea, and that only one side of the human brain functions at all.)

I had the feeling that sometime, somewhere, eons ago, I had sat in a dimly lighted room and heard those same words. And that I had had the same instinctive revolt from them.

But the impression was fleeting, and seeing perhaps that our views did not coincide, he added that I must not believe that he disregarded the spiritual side of the individual, or of the universe. And he quoted Virgil's *Spiritus inter alit* with a certain unction.

"Soul animating matter!" he said. "It is a great thought, Mr. Porter. And I have reached that time in life when what is to come is assuming more importance than that which has gone."

Then he dismissed the subject, and went back again to the local situation, this time taking up the crimes themselves. He sees no necessary connection between the disappearance of Maggie Morrison and the tragedy of Carroway, and on this I did not enlighten him. On his saying, however, that in my place he would not feel safe in keeping Jane and Edith here, I told him at some length of my own involvement, and this brought about a discussion of Greenough and his methods.

He smiled drily over my account of the detective's psychological attitude.

"Psychology," he said, "the study of men and motives, is a science in itself. With all due respect to the gentleman in question, I imagine that his chief psychological resource would be that portion of the third degree which consists in knocking a man unconscious, and then obtaining his confession before he has entirely recovered his senses. I would rather trust your young friend at the boat-house. At least he appears to be using a certain independence of thought."

He broke off there, as he had once or twice before, and seemed again to be listening. But in a moment he picked up the talk again. The mention of unconsciousness had brought Gordon to my mind, and his first words on recovering. It was then that I inquired if the secretary had recognized, or thought he recognized, his assailant that night, and that Mr. Bethel replied in the negative.

"At least," he said, "he has not said so to me. But he is a queer boy; moody and sometimes sullen. A good secretary, but an indifferent companion."

As to the strange affair of the attack on Gordon, he himself with Annie Cochran's assistance, examined the gun room the next morning. The lock of the window was broken, but he fancied that was a matter of old standing. He was having it repaired.

"The boy's story seems to be borne out by the facts," he said. "There were indications, as you probably know, that someone had entered by the window. But what strikes me as strange is that whoever did so should have known his way so well. Gordon says no light was turned on, yet this fellow puts his hand on the only weapon about, the poker, without difficulty." He turned and glanced at me. "How long have you known Thomas, the gardener?" he asked.

"Too long to think he would do a thing like that," I said, rather warmly.

"I dare say. And, although I think Thomas is not fond of Gordon, that would be carrying a distaste rather far, I imagine."

He has no anxiety for himself, or at least so he said; I am personally not so certain. For as I looked back from the terrace on my way out, he was once more facing toward the hall, and—I somehow felt—watching it.

July 30th.

I HAVE to-day borrowed some of Mrs. Livingstone's books on psychic research, and intend to go into them thoroughly. If there is any proof in a mass of evidence, it is certainly here.

On the other hand, one must remember that the hope of survival is the strongest desire of the human heart. How many, if they felt that this life was all, would care to go on with it?

Analyzing my last night's experience, however, I can find nothing in my mind before I went to sleep, to account for it. I ate a light dinner, and spent the evening after Jane retired, with this Journal. The night was quiet, and my last waking thought was concerning the wood-cutter across the road, who seems so singularly inactive except when someone leaves the Lodge, or appears at one of its windows.

One thing I have traced, however. It is distinctly possible that the herbal, aromatic odor I noticed at the end of the experience was due to the leaves he collected yesterday, and which I find have smouldered throughout the night. . . .

It was after midnight when, just as I was dozing off, Jane came to my door and asked me if I would mind sleeping in her room.

"I can fix you a bed on the couch," she said, avoiding my eyes. "I'm nervous to-night, for some reason."

I went at once, trailing my bedding with me, and while she prepared the couch I observed her. She was very white, and I saw that her hands were shaking, but she refused my offer of some brandy with her usual evasive answer.

"I'm all right," she said. "I just don't like being alone."

She fell asleep almost at once, like one exhausted, but the change of beds had fully roused me, and I lay for some time staring into the darkness. I do not know when it was that I began to have the feeling that we were not alone in the room, but I imagine fully half an hour had passed.

I saw nothing, but I had the sensation of being stealthily watched, and with it something of horror rather than of fear. I was rigid with it. Then something seemed to tug at my coverings, and the next moment they had slid to the floor. Almost immediately after that there came a rush of air through the room, a curtain billowed over my face, and the door into the hall swung open. Then all was silent, save for a low whine from Jock, outside in the hall.

How much of this to-day to allot to my nerves I do not know. Undoubtedly Jane's nervousness had affected me; equally undoubtedly bed clothing has a tendency to slip from a couch. I have quietly experimented to-day. A gale of wind would blow out a curtain and open an unlatched door.

On the other hand, I am as certain to-day as I have been certain of anything recently, that I had bolted the door when I entered the room. But it was not bolted in the morning.

If I have indeed actually had a psychic experience, it seems singularly purposeless. Up to this time I have imagined, correctly or not, that these inexplicable occurrences have had a concealed but definite objective, if such a phrase may be used. But in this case there is apparently nothing.

Otherwise the night was quiet, without new developments. Greenough continues his work, handicapped by the usual difficulty besetting a detective in the country, that his every move is known and watched. Jane herself wakened this morning, after a quiet sleep, and although she is languid, the present intense heat may easily account for that.

We have had, however, a development of our own, and this from Edith!

It appears that this morning, seeing Doctor Hayward pass on his round of morning calls, she went to his office and, on his housekeeper reporting him out, asked permission to go into his office and there leave him a note.

"A note?" I inquired. "What sort of a note?"

"Any sort of note," said Edith. "As it happens, I asked him to tea to-morrow. It was all I could think of."

But what she really did was to type a few lines on his typewriter, tear the paper out and put it in the small vanity case which is as much a part of her as the nose she powders from it.

(As a net result of which audacious performance Halliday now informs me that the cipher words were not written on the doctor's machine.)

A careful comparison under a magnifying glass shows this so that even I can recognize it. So there we are again.

If we are to believe that the chalk which marked my car was brought in that paper, we must grant that the doctor did not mark the car. Or in other words, that our contra-offensive is not to be launched, as yet, and that our only course is to continue rather ignominiously in our trenches.

July 31st.

HALLIDAY has found the boat.
At least he has found a boat which answers Jane's description. To-day he took me to see it.

It lies in the small creek which extends through the marsh half a mile north of the boat-house, and just beyond Robinson's Point.

(Note: This creek is really a narrow estuary from

the bay, almost entirely overgrown and its entrance hidden by reeds, and is only a few hundred feet in length. At its upper end, where the boat lay, the swamp ends and woodland commences. Although on another estate, the woodland is a continuation of our own.)

The boat, evidently an old and abandoned one, gives some evidence of recent use. That is, although it contains some water, there is very little, whereas, as Halliday says, after the recent rains it might well be full.

The oar-locks are wrapped with dingy white cotton cloth, and to prevent their being stolen, or the boat taken away, the oars had been skillfully hidden in the marsh. Halliday located them but left them as they were; but with his pen-knife he cut away a small bit of the muffling on the oar-lock, for later possible identification.

During the search for the Morrison girl undoubtedly this boat was discovered and examined; there are numerous foot prints on the bank which effectually prevent any clue being discovered among them. But the discovery of an entirely sea-worthy boat, in so remote a location, with only the light-house in sight and that at a considerable distance, is in itself suspicious.

It was in this boat, Halliday believes, that the murderer fled onto the bay from our slip the night Carroway discovered him, and from it too that he later climbed into Carroway's launch and attacked him.

Small wonder that the boy's face set hard as he examined it.

Yet, for one must find some humor nowadays or go mad, there was something humorous in the careful indirection by which we reached it. We made rather ostentatious preparations to go fishing, Halliday working with hooks and sinkers, and I hopelessly entangled in coils of line.

Later, we rowed across the bay and anchored by the

whistle buoy, where we fished assiduously for some time. Our approach to the mouth of the creek was therefore of a most desultory sort, but once around Robinson's Point, we abandoned caution and rowed rapidly.

The mouth of the creek was well closed with water weeds, but we poled the boat through them and over a shoal, into the deeper water beyond. Then, with a look around, we settled to the oars again.

Had Greenough been able to see us, from start to finish, he would have had some basis for his suspicions of me.

Whether Halliday's later discovery has any significance or not we are not certain. Believing that, on the night of the girl's murder she was brought in the truck to the water front, and coupling this with the finding of the boat, he left me sheltered from observation in the woodland and started through it toward the main road.

In a half hour or so he came back again, and reported that he had found the track of wheels driven through the woods, and that in one place a barbed wire fence had been taken down and boards placed over it, to permit the passage of a car across it.

This is, I imagine, fair presumptive evidence, although it brings us no nearer the identity of the criminal than we were before. And it has this disadvantage, that the villagers have always exerted a right of pre-emption over the fallen timber in the woods hereabout, as I know to my cost, and that the trail may be nothing more nor less than that of some thrifty individual, seeking fuel for his cooking stove.

One thing, however, may be valuable. Edith, who knows a number of unsuspected housewifely things, insists that the strips which wrapped the oar-locks are of a fine grade of material.

"Look for somebody," she says, "who uses linen sheets

on his bed, and doesn't care that they cost twenty-five dollars a pair nowadays."

From which I gather, among other things, that our little Edith has been pricing the equipment of a home. . . .

To-night that old sea-chest which in the boat-house holds on its top the law books which were to occupy Halliday's leisure this summer, and which so far seem to be used chiefly to hold open his doors on windy days—the old sea-chest contains to date the four clues which are our sole ammunition in the putative expedition against Greenough. They are:

(a)   Half of a broken lens from a pair of eye-glasses.

(b)   A scrap of paper, containing a cryptic bit of typing in large and small letters.

(c)   The small cap of an ether can.

(d)   A fragment of white cloth.

Had it not been for Halliday's unwittingly placing a weapon in the enemy's hands we should also have had:

(e)   A very sharp knife, with a plain wooden handle and a blade approximately six inches long.

August 1st.

I AM now convinced that any attempt to solve these crimes by the discovery of an underlying motive is a mistake. Nor will Greenough's study of psychology help him here, unless he be expert in its psychopathic developments.

One cannot piece together into a rational whole the fragmentary impulses of a lunatic. . . .

An incendiary fire was started beneath the boat-house last night, or rather toward morning. An assortment of what was apparently oil-soaked waste was placed in one of the pails from the sloop, and a candle lighted and placed in it. Over this was laid such lumber as was left from the repair of the pier.

Had Halliday been asleep the entire building might have burned. As it happened, he had been in the woods near where we found the boat, on a chance that its proprietor might pay it a visit. He discovered the fire from some distance and by hard running, reached it in time to extinguish it.

He notified Greenough early this morning, but that gentleman was extremely noncommittal. He stood with his hands in his pockets, kicking over the ashes of the fire.

"What's the big idea, Mr. Halliday?" he inquired.

"I don't get that," said Halliday, belligerently.

"Don't you?" said Greenough, and after kicking the ashes once more, took an unruffled departure.

The best we can make of that is that the detective believes the whole thing a clumsy but concerted plan, on Halliday's part and mine; that we have endeavored to show that, although his watchers would be able to testify that I had not left the house last night, the unknown is still at work.

Nor can I entirely blame him for that. Whoever built the fire knew that Halliday was out at the time. But Halliday could not so state without betraying his knowledge of the boat, a matter he wishes to keep to himself as long as possible.

Small wonder that the detective, estimating from its charred remains the amount of lumber heaped over the flame, was sceptical.

"You are a good sleeper, Mr. Halliday!" he observed. . . .

A new month begins to-day, and like Pepys, it behooves me to take stock of myself. In spite of my best endeavors, some of my anxiety has crept into this record during the last month; and not always anxiety for my-self. Alone, I could take off my coat and fight this thing out, but I am handicapped by Edith and Jane.

Edith will not go and leave Halliday; Jane will not consider abandoning me here, although she has no idea of the true situation.

"If you want to go back to town," she says, "I'll go too, of course. But if you are talking about staying here alone, for some silly reason, I won't even consider it. You wouldn't have a clean shirt, after the first week."

But, even if I felt that no action would be precipitated by the police, in case of such a move, I have a responsi-bility I cannot evade. The responsibility to my tenant.

I have, by a reduced rent and an alluring advertise-ment, brought here an elderly paralytic and his young secretary. And, evade the issue as I may, the fact re-mains that the last two acts of violence have been on my property. From the beginning, indeed, the most casual survey of the the situation shows me that Twin Hollows has been a sort of focal point. It was on this property that Nylie saw the sheep-killer hunt sanctuary; not on it, but adjacent to it, is still hidden the boat, and it was from my own float that he first escaped from Carroway and later killed him; it was even very possibly his flash-light that Halliday saw, the night of his arrival when, finding the boat-house occupied, he worked his way through the salt marsh toward the sea.

More recently the radius of his activity has been nar-rowed to the property itself. The secretary sees him outside a window; he enters the house and attacks him from within. And a few days later, possibly having overseen Halliday's discovery of his boat, he attempts to drive him away by setting fire to the boat-house. . . .

I am tempted to ask Mr. Bethel to cancel his lease;

to return him his money, entire, and relieve me of responsibility.

What would he say, I wonder?

August 2nd.

I WRITE and read, and now and then make a fugitive excursion into Jane's room, from behind her curtains to watch my watcher at work. In spite of himself he has achieved something, and will doubtless go back to the city somewhat the better for an unexpectedly athletic summer.

I have been reading Mrs. Livingstone's books, and a pretty lot of nonsense I find them. If there is anything in this question of survival, surely we cannot expect to find it in physical phenomena. Why not better accept that the nervous force which actuates the body may, in certain individuals, extend beyond the periphery of that body?

Nevertheless, it is as well that I brought away from the other house the book I found there on the desk, on "Eugenia Riggs and the Oakville Phenomena." It is no reading for Mr. Bethel, under the circumstances.

One finds, for instance, that the small panelled room which we call the den was used for her seances. That panelling in itself sounds suspicious. But stop! It was not panelled at that time; I recall when poor old Horace found that oak panelling and gleefully installed it in what had been the old kitchen of the original farm house.

An investigation, made just now, has supplemented my memory. The photograph (Note: Plate I, "Eugenia Riggs and the Oakville Phenomena") shows a plastered wall, and one or two crude water colors on it. Possibly the spirit paintings of the text.

It also shows that the cabinet, so called, was not a

cabinet at all, but a dark curtain on a heavy pole, which extends across a blank corner. In the picture these curtains are thrown back, showing a small stand on which are the stage properties of "George," a bell, a pan of something, a glass, and a small bunch of flowers. On the floor, ready for his ghostly hand, is a guitar. The wall is certainly plastered.

An inset shows the pan, set on its edge to allow photography, and with the title: "Imprint of hand in putty. Dec. 2nd 1902. Notice lack of usual whorls and ridges." But in spite of this rather militant caption, I find I am unimpressed. Rather am I wondering whether somewhere in the back-ground there was not a Mr. Riggs, with a short broad thumb and a bent little finger, who was not ignorant of the lack of the usual whorls and ridges in a pair of rubber gloves.

But it is no book for Mr. Bethel. Mrs. Riggs meets Markowitz on his own ground and fairly beats him. True, he produces a broad face and an arm which comes through the soiled stuff of the curtain. But she does that, and more; she shows, under very dim red light —and anyone who has tried to see by it knows how negligible that is—hands which may be touched and held.

"The hand," says one witness, "came out from the cabinet and advanced toward me. I could see no body, but the billowing of the curtain indicated some unearthly presence behind it. I asked permission to touch it and the medium agreed, provided I did it without force. I then took the hand and held it for a perceptible moment, when it seemed to dissolve away and slip from my grasp."

One may be sure it dissolved away! And that as speedily as possible.

But, considering that plastered wall, the entire evidence in the book, gathered together, forms a surprising whole. One must take off one's hat to the Riggs family, provided there were two of them, or to whomsoever assisted the lady. Especially since the windows were "shuttered and bolted, and small strings of bells, which would ring at the slightest touch, were hung across them."

One does not wonder, since Annie Cochran probably had access to the book, that she found her tea-kettle moved about, and had her bed clothing shamelessly taken from her.

August 3rd.

HALLIDAY, who is an early riser, burst in on us this morning at the breakfast table, fairly bristling with excitement.

"Good morning, everybody!" he sang out. "And how about a picnic to-day? Ginger ale and fried chicken, I to provide the ginger ale?"

"Sit down, man, and pull yourself together," Edith said, eyeing him. "William, fetch the aromatic spirits of ammonia. He will be all right presently."

"What do I receive for a piece of very cheering news?" he demanded.

"Who's to judge whether it's cheering or not?"

"Well, I leave it to all of you," he said. "Greenough's gone. Benchley came over yesterday and threw him off the case. At least, that's what they say at the post-office. Thirteen days he's been fooling around, and he couldn't get over the hump."

"If only he had stayed a little longer," Edith said regretfully, "and somebody had killed him! It's rotten bad luck, that's all."

The conversation had little or no meaning for Jane. She was, I could see, puzzled by our excitement and unable to understand our relief. "Surely they have

left somebody," she said. "We ought not to be left
without protection. Who knows when something will
break out again, and then where are we?"

"Where indeed?" said Halliday, and he and Edith
two-stepped into the living room, where Edith sat down
at the organ and played execrably a few bars of "Shall
We Gather at the River?"

"Latest song hit," she called. "Words and music
here, twenty-five cents."

"I think you are all a trifle mad," Jane said, and
went out to do her morning ordering. . . .

The move is a totally unexpected one. Yesterday, as
Halliday said, the Sheriff came over to the hotel and was
closeted for an hour or two with Greenough. A bell
boy reports that, on carrying some cracked ice to the
room, he found Greenough sitting morosely by a table,
and Benchley at the window, staring out. Half an hour
later the Sheriff left, passing out of the hotel without so
much as a nod to anyone, and within the hour Greenough was paying his bill in the lobby and ordering a car
to take him to the train.

Our own relief is enormous, but there is much
grumbling among the summer folk as well as the natives.
Starr is the usual variety of small-town constable, and
it seems extraordinary that the case should be left in
his care. It is of course possible that another man is
to be sent in Greenough's place, but if so we have no
intimation of it. . . .

Later: Incredible, the rapidity with which news cir-
culates here. The immediate result of Greenough's
departure has been rather to revive the interest in the
situation than otherwise. I dare say as long as the police
were on the case the people more or less lay back and
depended on them; now they are thrown once more onto
their own resources, and a variety of opinions and even

of clues are being exchanged at that central clearing house, the post-office. Thus:

This morning the cows of a man named Vaughan were found huddled in a corner of the field, giving every evidence of having been run to death during the night.

(To the common sense suggestion of a dog being the culprit, pitying glances.)

A stranger three days ago tried to buy a large knife in the hardware store.

(Later shown to be the Livingstone's new butler seeking a carving knife.)

The second keeper at the light-house has resigned, declaring the tower is haunted.

(This is true, so far as the resignation goes. He has, it appears, asked to be transferred. But Ward says there has been no repetition of the strange affair the night of the storm.)

A car driven recklessly and without lights has been seen twice near the Hilburn Road, both times after midnight.

(There seems a certain authenticity in this; the car, however, shows its lights until fairly close to another car, when it shuts them off entirely. There may be, of course, some defect in the dimmers.) . . .

My own relief is beyond words. Looking in my shaving mirror to-day, I am startled at the change in me the last few weeks. The Lears are coming out to dinner to-night. More power to them.

August 4th.

THE party last night was a great success. Lear had brought me out a bottle of claret, and with candles on the table and six wine glasses, hastily borrowed from Annie Cochran at the main house, we took on quite a festive air. Lear looked a trifle puzzled when, at Edith's suggestion, she, Halliday and myself drank to "the absent one!" But otherwise all was well.

We divided after the meal, Jane and Helena to talk, Edith and Halliday for the boat-house and a canoe, and Lear and I to pace the drive with our cigars.

Lear's quiet face and general dependability, and perhaps the need of a fresh mind on the conditions here, impelled me to tell my story, to which he listened without interruption.

His opinion is that we have to do with a homicidal maniac, and that the sheep-killing was preliminary to the rest, "a propitiation," he puts it.

"Of course, I am no psychiatrist," he said, "but what other explanation have you?"

"None at all," I admitted. "Of course, if I meant to commit a series of crimes, I might find it useful to establish my insanity first. I doubt if any jury, once convinced that the murderer and the sheep-killer are the same, would doubt his essential lunacy."

"On the other hand," Lear said, in his cold academic voice, "the man who sets out to commit such a series of crimes as this *is* unbalanced. He doesn't have to kill sheep to make a plea of that sort. He may present an entirely rational face to the world, but something has slipped, you can depend on it."

The supernatural angle of the case he put aside with a gesture.

"I won't even argue it," he said. "There may be something to it; I'm not denying that. But it's not stuff to be meddled with; when the Lord means to open that veil he will do it. And I am no peeping Tom."

He said further that Helena has taken up the ouija board, and sits for hours "with anyone she can entrap," getting absurd messages which sound well and mean nothing.

"In your place," he said, "I would forget it. If you get really to the point where you think you have something, send for Cameron and let him look into it. But keep out of it yourself, Porter. It's bad medicine."

I took them to the eleven o'clock train, and have only just returned. But I think it would amuse Lear, in spite of his hands-off attitude, to know that as I drove into the garage and shut off the lights and the engine, in the very act of getting out of the car I heard once more that peculiar dry cough, the faint slow footfall, and smelled again that curious herbal odor which I shall, all the days of my life, associate with my Uncle Horace.

So unexpected was it, coming on top of the happiest evening of the summer, that I stood for a moment immovable. Then I leaped from the terrifying darkness of the garage out into the moonlight, and there confronted young Gordon, standing outside and quietly smoking.

"Hello!" I said, when I could speak. "Out again, I see."

"Yes. That place gets my goat," he replied. "I guess I'm jumpy, since the other night."

He looked badly, and I asked him if he cared to sit down before starting back. But he refused.

"I'll get hell if he finds I've left the house," he said elegantly.

I turned and walked back with him toward the house, and seeing him secretly amused about something, asked him what it was, whereupon he said that he was thinking of the way I had shot out of the garage.

"Put something over on you there, didn't I?"

"You startled me. What do you mean?"

"I guess you know," he said, with his side-long glance. "That cough."

"You mean, the light-house story?"

He fell again into one of his secret convulsions of mirth.

"No, I don't mean the light-house," he said, and turning abruptly, struck off through the trees.

I can take from this as much or as little as I will. Is it possible that Gordon has heard the cough in the house, and associates it with the other sounds of which he has complained to Annie Cochran? Or has he merely been told of it, and with his perverted idea of humor, been deliberately alarming me with it?

If I am to believe my recent reading, according to tradition the discarnate frequently do, after death, the things they did most frequently in life; your hunter returns on horse-back, and is seen alone on country roads; ladies of ancient time who lighted themselves to bed with candles seem to go on perennially retiring to God knows what unearthly couch, with the same everlasting candle in their hands.

But to record, in all seriousness, the possibility that they carry with them, without the flesh, the weaknesses of that flesh, is beyond my power of credulity.

August 5th.

I RETURNED the wine glasses to Annie Cochran this morning, and as a result have been attempting ever since to reconcile what she says with the facts as we know them. . . .

Annie Cochran declares that young Gordon has been in the habit of slipping out of the house at night; that he commenced to do it shortly after his arrival, and has done it ever since; that, indeed, he was not sitting on the kitchen steps before he was attacked, but had been out in the car, and was trying to get back into the house.

She also believes that Mr. Bethel suspects it, and has been on the alert, especially since the night of the attack.

"There's been bad blood between them, ever since that night," she said. "They talk a bit when I'm in the dining room, but once I'm out of it, they're as glum as oysters."

She also suspects Mr. Bethel of being afraid of Gordon. On the nights when she assisted him upstairs, while the secretary was still invalided, she always heard him bolt his door as soon as he was inside.

"And the nights he stayed down," she added, "he had me bring down that revolver of his. He laid it to the fellow who got in by the gun room window, but I've got my own ideas about it."

Her reasons for not telling the detective are peculiarly feminine. He had antagonized her early by some high-handed method of his own, and "he was getting paid for finding things out. I wasn't."

But her other reason is curious, and shows a depth of loyalty to me which is unexpected and rather touching.

"I didn't see the use of dragging this place in," she says. "It's got a bad enough name already. And there's a lot of talk going on; some of it makes me sick."

From the way she avoided my eyes and rattled at her stove, I am left to conjecture that my wood-cutter —who by the way is missing to-day—has not passed unnoticed, and that possibly either Starr or Nylie has been talking. Probably Nylie. In any event, Annie Cochran, and very likely the entire vicinity, has evidently known that I have been under surveillance; a miserable thought, only relieved by Annie's loyalty.

"What makes you think he had been off the place, the night he was hurt?"

"He said he couldn't sleep, didn't he? And he got up and went downstairs to get something to eat, and then went outside?"

"So he said."

"Well, as far as I can make out, he was dressed from top to toe. He didn't need to do that to get down to the pantry."

And we had missed that! Hayward, Greenough and I had checked up that story, according to our several abilities, and had never noticed that discrepancy. "I sent his clothes to be cleaned the next day," she said, "and I noticed it then."

But her real contribution, if I may call it that, lay in the garage, and after tip-toeing to the hall and listening to the sound of Mr. Bethel's dictation from within, she drew me outside.

(Note: The small garage for the main house sits behind the kitchen, and not far from the kitchen door. There are two methods of access to it, one by the drive past the Lodge, which curves around the house, and the other by what we knew as "the lane," a dirt road leading through the woodland, which extends toward Robinson's Point, and which strikes the macadam highway further along.)

"So far as I know," she said, "that car's only been out twice since they came, and that was to take Thomas home one time, and me another, the night of the storm. But it's been out, just the same."

"Wouldn't the old man hear it?"

"He might and he mightn't. Suppose it was rolled along the lane and started? He wouldn't hear it there, would he?"

To support her contention she showed me a number of

marks in the lane, certainly suspicious but by no means evidential. It is nothing unusual for motorists to strike into the woodland along the lane, under the impression that it is a public road, and to be brought up all standing at the house.

But against all this, at least as pointing to young Gordon as our possible criminal, is what is to me an insuperable obstacle. We know that the crimes are connected with the killing of the sheep. It is not possible to doubt this. And the sheep were killed and the altar built before Mr. Bethel brought Gordon into the neighborhood. Annie Cochran has a certain support for her contention, but not enough.

And she dislikes the boy extremely. Probably she unwittingly revealed the reason for her attack on him just before I left.

"There's something wrong about him," she said. "When a man's dishonest he thinks everybody else is."

"Surely he doesn't say that about you."

"Well, he's taken to locking his room and carrying the key about with him. I never took a thing of anybody else's in my life."

As Halliday went to town early to-day, taking the scrap of paper with the cipher to an expert he knows there, I have not been able to discuss this new angle with him. Quite aside from the discrepancy in dates, however, Gordon not arriving until after the reign of terror was well under way, the chief stumbling block is the attack on the boy himself. . . .

Suppose the boy does slip out at night, and take the car? He is young, and I imagine pretty much a prisoner all day. He takes dictation all morning, types after luncheon while Mr. Bethel sleeps, and at four o'clock again is ready with his book and pencil. The few moments he has spent with Edith now and then are plainly stolen.

August 6th.

HALLIDAY'S expert was not particularly helpful, I gather. We have this to our advantage, however, if advantage it be; the typing was done on a Remington machine.

As I had expected, he does not take Annie Cochran's story very seriously, but he bases his scepticism rather on the beginning of the terror before the boy came, than on the attack on the boy himself.

"After all," he says, "how do we know that it wasn't the old man himself who knocked him out? I imagine he has considerable strength in that one arm of his."

"It's difficult, but I'll suppose it."

"Suppose the old chap heard him outside," he went on, "trying to get back into the house, and thought it was somebody else. The killer, we'll say. He'd be pretty well justified in banging him on the head with a poker."

"Granting he could have got there, which I doubt, how could he have tied him?"

"One point for you!" he said. "And one more theory hanged with its own rope. Still, you'll admit it's a nice idea to play with; Mr. Bethel kills a burglar with a poker, sees it is his secretary, rings the bell and calls help, and then gets up to his room and pretends to be asleep."

"It was Gordon who rang the bell."

"Oh well, have it your own way!" he said disgustedly, "But it was a pretty thing while it lasted. And it's my opinion still that there is more in it than meets the eye." . . .

Aside from this blind alley, up which Annie Cochran

started us, we are all more nearly normal than we have been since the early days of the summer. I rise, shave and bathe and go to my breakfast, no longer with the feeling that it may be, figuratively speaking, my last.

Jane is at the table, fresh in the crisp ginghams she affects, and which in their turn are no crisper than the bacon. She must have been sadly puzzled the last few weeks; she shows such evident relief now. Sometime during the meal Edith, who has been awaiting her turn at our solitary tub, breezes into the room surrounded by her usual aura, pats Jock, kisses Jane and takes from me the society portion of the morning paper, after a casual glance at the mail. Any step outside, Thomas preparing to wash the verandah, or the boy who has taken poor Maggie's place, brings a faint color to her face. But in case it turns out to be Halliday, she is cavalier in the extreme.

"Morning," she says airily, and it may be adds: "Where on earth did you get that shirt?"

"What's the matter with this shirt?"

"Nothing at all," she says, resuming her breakfast. "I just thought maybe someone had given it to you. It isn't exactly the sort of shirt one buys, is it?"

Her glance appeals to me; I am for a moment the arbiter between them.

"It is a perfectly good shirt," I say with decision, and am accused of sex solidarity and poor taste, both apparently equal sins in Edith's eyes.

It is the apotheosis of the trivial; small things once more make up our lives, and we find pleasure in them. Clara brings in more bacon, catches a reflection of our morning cheerfulness and smiles with us, and even Jock, hearing unaccustomed laughter, joins in with sharp staccato barks.

We are not worried by the uncertainty of the prospect

before us; the long period ahead of Edith and Halliday before they can marry; that next year, and the year after that, and God knows how many years to come, I shall be pouring the priceless treasures of the English language into ears that will not hear; that my vacation is more than half over, and that its net result so far is a loss to me of some odd pounds of weight.

We are once more safely behind the drain pipe.

August 7th.

EDITH has to-day received the large sum of ten dollars for the light-house story. While she is still far from the opulence she has anticipated, there has been great excitement here to-day, on receipt of the check.

She has kept a carbon copy, and has let me read it. It is well enough done, in her breezy fashion, but I find she has used the story of the so-called ghost at Twin Hollows as a basis to work from, and that she uses my name as the owner of the property. Quite aside from a distaste for seeing my name in print, I feel that the mere fact of its publication will give it a substantiality it has hitherto lacked.

It is characteristic of the average mind often to question what it hears, but to believe whole-heartedly what it reads. . . .

I find that Halliday has been quietly working along the lines opened up by Annie Cochran. He is convinced that Gordon has been going out at nights, clandestinely, and using the car to do so.

"I don't blame him for that," he said to-day. "The car's there, and not being used. And—I'm not keen about Gordon—but from such views as I have had of Mr. Bethel, a little of him would go a long way.

Gordon's disconnected the speedometer, by the way. But there's something else."

He thinks it was Gordon who set fire to the boat-house. He found a bit of waste outside the garage, hanging on a limb of blue spruce there, and a similar scrap on the raised walk over the marsh to the boat-house.

"Of course that isn't evidence, Skipper," he said, "except as a trout in the milk might be. But the stuff's there, and it needs some thinking about."

"But why?" I asked. "There has to be a reason."

"I can go a long way for one," he said thoughtfully, "and imagine he knows I've been working on the case and wants to get rid of me. But I grant that's not good. Burning me out wouldn't do that, unless he hoped I was inside! But that is to imply that he is guilty of the crimes, and I don't believe it."

But he added, as an after thought:

"There's one curious thing, though. That is, it may be curious; I'm not sure. The machine he's using is a Remington."

August 8th.

THIS has been a nerve-racking day. I for one am willing to cry quits, to compromise with crime, and to say, in effect, that if the murderer leaves us alone we will not disturb him.

And yet the reason for my moral surrender does not lie in any event to-day on which I can place my hand. I cannot say that for this reason, or for that, I am through. Discouraged. Ready to go to the mountains and come back from a walk with a withered bunch of wild flowers held in my clenched hand, or to sit on some piazza with my after-dinner cigar and talk politics in the presence of the universe. Or to go back to town and help Jane select a new wall-paper for my study.

My condition probably arises from sheer confusion. For the life of me I cannot see where the results of Halliday's search can lead us, nor I think does he. . . .

Edith this morning, at Halliday's request, telephoned to Gordon and asked him to lunch with us. He accepted, after a brief hesitation, and promptly at one o'clock came down the drive, clad in white flannels and with an additional dose of pomade on his hair.

Whether he was suspicious or not we cannot tell. I know that, watching him from a window, part way down the drive he came to a dead stop and then turned, as if he had some idea of going back on some pretext or other. But he evidently thought better of it, looked at his watch, and came on again.

He made a poor impression on us, furtively watching Jane's choice of fork or spoon and otherwise bestowing most of his attention on Edith. Such attention, that is, as he bestowed on anybody at the beginning. He was what a novelist loves to call *distrait*, although any question about himself roused him to a faint enthusiasm. He has, I suspect, an inordinate vanity.

"I'm a sort of wanderer," he said once, apropos of some question or statement of mine. "I stay in a place long enough to look about me and then I get the itch to move on. Restless," he added.

And restless he was. From where he sat he had his back to the windows, but more than once he managed to turn and look out. I had the feeling that the small room enclosed him too much; that he felt somehow trapped. And more than once I found his eyes on me, and felt that he suspected me of some purpose he was attempting to discover.

His nervousness finally infected me, and even Jane began to show signs of distress. The small lunch party, for some reason she could not understand, was going badly. Only Edith played up well; she pushed back her plate at last, and with her elbows on the table and her chin in her hands, said:

"And now, tell us about the night you were hurt."

He was lighting a cigarette at the moment, and he halted, the match held in mid-air, and glanced from her to me.

"I'll do that," he said, with his twisted smile, "if Mr. Porter will tell me how he and the doctor both happened to be such Johnnies on the spot."

But he carried that no further, and although the covert insolence of the speech brought the color to Edith's face, she continued to smile.

"There isn't much to tell," he went on. "The fellow got into the house all right; I turned to go in by the door and head him off, and that's all I remember."

"But you rang the bell first, didn't you?"

Whether because he hated to acknowledge that call for help, or for some reason none of us can determine to-night, he hesitated.

"Yes," he said finally. "I was pretty well excited, but I suppose I did."

On the subject of the house itself he was more fluent, showing a considerable curiosity as to its history, and inquiring with more particularity than delicacy as to the circumstances surrounding Uncle Horace's death.

"The Cochran woman has a line of talk about it," he gave as his explanation. "Seems to think he was done in, or something."

I told him of the doctor's verdict of heart failure, and he seemed to be considering that. But almost immediately he asked me if I had tried hearing the bell as far away as the highroad, "with a motor engine going."

"I don't believe it could be done," he said, with his sideways glance at me. "He's got good ears, the doctor."

He said something before he left about looking for another job, as this one was too confining, and the old man not easy to live with. "I only took it for the summer," he said, "and I'm about fed up with it. It's too confining. And he'd let that car of his rot before he'd let me take it out."

With which clumsy attempt to alibi himself regarding the car, he took his departure. Edith believes that in some manner he knows that the car has been examined, and she may be right. . . .

Halliday's investigation of his room during his absence proceeded without difficulty. With my keys and Annie Cochran's connivance he made an easy entry, Mr. Bethel having retired for his after-luncheon siesta.

At first glance the room offered nothing, and leaving Annie Cochran on guard outside, under pretense of cleaning the passage, Halliday made a more intensive search. The bed disclosed nothing, nor did the closet; his suitcase was locked, and over it Halliday spent more time than was entirely safe.

"Toward the end," he says, "I was pretty shaky. I kept thinking I heard him, and of course the more I hurried the more I bungled the thing."

He got it open at last without breaking the lock, and found in it the note-book.

(Note: I find I have given no description of the note-book in the original Journal. As it played a considerable part in the approaching tragedy, it deserves some attention.

It was a small compact volume of the loose-leaf type, a sort of diary, but not regularly kept. Most of the entries, due to the complication of the cipher, were very brief.   One or two, however, occupied almost a page, and all of them had been typed.

Needless to say, the cipher was the one we had found on the scrap of paper picked up in my garage.)

The discovery of the note-book with its cipher sent his excitement to fever pitch.   He ran through it for the code word, but was unable to find it.   Then, replacing the book and leaving the suitcase as he had found it, he set to work more carefully on the room itself.

The coil of rope and the knife were behind a row of books on the bookshelf, a packet of typing paper and a box of carbon sheets thrown over them with apparent casualness, to conceal them still further.

So closely had he calculated the time that he had barely restored them to their places when Gordon slammed the entrance door downstairs, and he says:

"If he had come straight up we'd have been caught.   I could have got out, but I don't believe I could have locked the door.   But he stopped there a second or two, and I just made it."

He had not time to make the back staircase, however. Annie Cochran opened the linen-closet door, and he bolted in there.   He heard Gordon unlock his room and enter it, and almost immediately re-appear and demand of Annie Cochran if she had been in it during his absence.   An angry dispute followed, within a foot or two of the linen-closet, not the less acrimonious because of its lowered voices, and of an almost hysterical quality in Gordon's.

Every particle of his veneer had dropped from him, and the threats he made if he should find she had been in his room are not even to be recorded here.   .   .   .

And now, once again, where are we?   We have, as against Gordon:

(a)   The knife and the coil of rope.

(b) Our belief that he uses the car, clandestinely, at night.

(c) At least an indication that he set the fire under the boat-house.

(d) The cipher, found in my garage.

(e) The note-book, in the same cipher. A man does not record his thoughts in this manner, unless he wishes to keep them hidden.

(f) The linen strips muffling the oar-locks, and suggested to Halliday to-day by his place of concealment. The inventory of the main house shows a certain number of linen sheets. If one is missing it will prove a strong factor in connecting him with the boat.

(g) The locking of his bedroom.

(h) Last and not least, an unpleasant personality. Halliday uses the word "degenerate," but I am not prepared to go so far.

As against all this, however, we have:

(a) The attack on him at the kitchen door, and the manner in which he was tied, corresponding to the rope about Carroway.

(b) The sheep-killing and murder of Carroway, taking place as they did before his arrival.

(c) The fact that Halliday cannot identify him as the man he picked up in his car.

(d) The distinguishing mark by which the criminal has signed his crimes, so to speak, is the circle and triangle, drawn in chalk; while this is not vital, Halliday found no chalk in the room. . . .

I have put to Halliday the boy's veiled inquiry about the doctor. It is impossible for us to experiment with the bell, but he thinks it could be distinctly heard from the main road.

On the other hand, the arrival of Hayward on the scene almost as soon as I had got there is extremely puzzling. We have to-night paced off the distance, in view of my statement that I had lighted only one match when the doctor's flash-light was turned on me.

There seems to be no doubt that Hayward was on the property that night. But I do not accept the possibility, suggested by Halliday, that as he was in Greenough's confidence he had been watching me. A man does not, I imagine, go out on such an errand with his medical bag in his hand, and the doctor had carried his bag. I recall distinctly his taking from it the dressings for Gordon's head.

August 9th.

L EONARDO DA VINCI said: "Patience serves as a protection against wrongs as clothes do against cold. For if you put on more cloth as the cold increases it will have no power to hurt you."

But I have put on all the extra patience I can find in my mental closet, and I am still uncomfortable.

Whether Jane has noticed our ostracism I do not know, but I have, and so I think has Edith. So marked has it become that to-day I greeted Mrs. Livingstone with a warmth that slightly puzzled her.

Nothing else new to-day. Halliday watched the main house last night, but no one left it. Annie Cochran reports that Mr. Bethel is suspicious of Gordon, and that the feud between them still continues. He declines the secretary's assistance as much as possible.

That he is not certain, however, is shown by the care with which he now has the house locked up at night.

"He waits in the library," she says, "until I've locked all the doors and windows. Then I bring him the keys, except the one to the kitchen door. He lets me have that to get in with in the morning."

He is showing considerable courage, to my mind. . . .

Mrs. Livingstone was slightly ruffled on her arrival. It appears she had tried to leave her cards and Livingstone's on the old gentleman at the main house, but was finally compelled to put them under the door, although she could hear voices in the library.

But she recovered sufficiently to tell us a new story, illustrative of the general state of the local mind. She says that three nights ago Hadly, who keeps the hardware store in Oakville, when passing the cemetery where Carroway is buried, saw a figure walking slowly past the grave. It stopped, looked at the mound and then moved on, fading into nothing at the clump of evergreens beyond it.

Hadly seems to have made no further investigation!

It is unfortunate, however, that Edith's story appeared to-day, evidently syndicated and receiving wide publicity. The confirmation is sufficient to send off most of the summer visitors, looking back over their shoulders, like Hadly, as they run.

August 10th.

A T midnight last night Halliday wakened me by throwing pebbles against the screen of my window. He was standing close underneath, and asked me to put on something and work my way quietly toward the other house.

"What's wrong?" I asked.

"He's getting ready to go out, I think. He put his light out at eleven, and turned it on again a few minutes ago."

Halliday moved away, and as quickly as possible I dressed and followed him. He was under the trees, waiting, when I joined him, and together we worked quietly across the garden and toward the garage, coming out beyond it, toward the lane. Here, while concealed ourselves, we had a full view of the house, but the light was out again and for a time it looked as though nothing more were to happen.

Halliday's plan was as follows: In case Gordon took the car, I was to follow it on foot at a safe distance as he went along the lane, while Halliday himself ran for my car. He would meet me at the fork of the road, and I would be able to tell him which of the two roads Gordon had taken.

We stood together, well hidden in the shrubbery, for some time. A slight wind had come up, and we could hear small waves lapping against the piles of the pier, and the monotonous wail of the whistling buoy beyond Robinson's Point, always an eerie sound. Halliday, who has not had much sleep for a night or two, fell to yawning, and I was not much better off, when I heard some sort of stealthy movement in the woodland to our left. I touched Halliday on the arm, to find him rigid and bending forward, staring toward the house.

"He's coming," he said. "Quiet!" The boy was raising his window screen, with all possible caution. Even when it was accomplished he stood so long, probably listening and watching, that I began to think he had changed his mind and gone back to bed, but as events showed, he had done nothing of the sort.

Up to this moment I had not suspected the use of the rope, although I believe Halliday had. I know my gaze was fixed on the kitchen door, with now and then a glance at the windows of the laundry and the gun room; or rather, in their direction. The darkness was extreme. But now I heard a faint scraping against the wall of the house itself and realized that he was coming down by means of the rope.

His coming was as stealthy as the preliminaries had

been. He was probably half way down, coming hand over hand, before I had interpreted the sound.

I was not even aware that he had reached the ground, when I saw him, a blacker shadow among other shadows, near at hand. But he did not come directly toward the garage; he walked along under the walls of the west wing to the gun room window and stood there. Then, with extreme caution, he raised it an inch or two, as if to reassure himself that it had been unlocked from within, and closed it again.

From there, with somewhat less caution, he moved to the corner of the house and seemed to be surveying the water front and the boat-house. We had our only real view of him then, as he stood silhouetted on the top of the rise. (Note: The main house stands, as I think I have already recorded, rather higher than the remainder of the property.) But suddenly something alarmed him. Neither Halliday nor I saw or heard anything, but evidently he did, and realized too his exposed position.

He dropped to the ground. So unexpected was his sudden disappearance, that I gasped; it was not until I heard him creeping along the ground that I understood his manœuvre. He lost no time in his retreat, nor did he attempt to use the rope again. He raised the unlocked window, crept over the sill, and closed it again, all with surprising rapidity and silence, and sooner than we could have expected we heard him drawing up the rope from his room overhead. . . .

No interpretation of this is possible without taking into consideration the really horrible stealth of the boy's manner. He was engaged on some nefarious business of his own, whether we can connect that with the crimes or not.

As to the extremely dramatic manner in which he chose to escape from the house, when he had already unlocked the gun room window, Halliday is divided between two theories, of which he himself favors the second.

"He may be merely dramatizing himself; you'll find a certain type of degenerate mind which is always acting for its own benefit. Or—and this is more likely—our old friend Bethel is suspicious and is watching him. The old man's door commands his. He locks his door from the inside, uses his rope, and is free to go where he pleases.

"But," he added, after a pause, "he unlocks the gun room window, too, so he can beat a retreat if he has to. That's the best I can do, and if it isn't correct it ought to be!" . . .

To-day I am convinced beyond doubt that Gordon is our criminal, and I think even Halliday is shaken. I am no detective, but it seems to me that the boy, coming here during the height of the excitement about the sheep-killer and young Carroway, found the way already paved for a career of secret crime, and adopting the methods and the symbol of some still undiscovered religious maniac, has carried on, one may say, under his banner.

My psychiatric friends have discussed with me the neurotic aftermath of the war; the search for the sensational, the wooing of fugitive and secret pleasures, often brutal and violent; and the apotheosis of the criminal. They quote, too, von Krafft-Ebing's theory that the instinct to kill is purely a legacy from the past, atavistic and more or less non-deliberate. In other words, that killing is inherent in all of us, and that to the ill-balanced the destruction of the artificial inhibition, from any cause, turns them loose on the world, hereditary slayers and doers of violence.

It would, accepting that, be possible to see in young Gordon the heir, not only to his own past, but to the crimes which preceded his arrival here; to see also that gradual process of identification by which he assumed his predecessor's attributes and even the symbol by which he signed his deeds. I believe that in such cases the mental degeneration sometimes continues to the point of complete loss of personality; in that case, accepting this theory, it may even be that the boy now believes that he killed Carroway, and takes a secret and gloating pleasure in it.

A theory which I shall be happy to place at Greenough's disposal, if the opportunity arrives. It should be one after his own heart.

Certainly one fact at least supports the idea. Halliday may be right, and the attack on him not have been made by Gordon. But there seems no reason to doubt that, some time on the day before we got back, he crept into my garage and put the infernal symbol where we found it.

We have discussed to-day at some length the desirability of notifying the police once more. But our recent experience with them is not reassuring. On the other hand, I feel strongly that Mr. Bethel should be warned. But Halliday argues against it.

"He knows something already," he says. "He is on guard, and the boy knows it. Then you have to remember that the game, so far, has been to strike in the dark, and run. That is, if you are correct, Skipper, and it *is* a game, without motive."

Probably he is right. There would be little chance for him if he attacked the old man; he is too well known to be on bad terms with him. Such a warning, also, might alarm Mr. Bethel to the point of getting rid of him, and after all the only chance we have is to let him go a certain length, and then, with our proofs, call in the police.

But I am very uneasy to-night as I make this entry. I have not Halliday's easy optimism that he "won't get away with anything without our knowing it."

August 11th.

TO-DAY is bright and sunny, and I am in a better mood. Edith came down this morning to an enormous stack of mail, and stared at it incredulously.

"Great heavens," she said, "not *bills!*"

As it turned out, however, they were not bills. Her article has brought out a curious fact; almost everybody has a ghost-story, and is anxious to tell it to somebody else; even the most incredulous of us, apparently, has some incident stored in his memory not capable of explanation. And a visible percentage of these victims of thrills and shivers have written to her about the ghost in the light tower.

She and Halliday are reading them on the verandah at this moment. Each has a heap of them, and such bits as this are to be heard:

"Here's a wonder," says Halliday. "Hold my hand, won't you, while I read it to you? There's some ghostly thing touching my neck at this minute."

"It's a spider," says Edith, coolly. "You can wait. Listen to this!" And so on. . . .

Which reminds me that I had a visit last night from "Cuckoo" Hadly, our village Don Juan, who sells hardware over his counter to pretty village matrons, and who was dubbed "Cuckoo" some years ago by a summer visitor who saw a resemblance to Byron in him, and evidently knew the quotation.

(Note: "The cuckoo shows melancholia, not madness. Like Byron, he goes about wailing his sad lot, and now and then dropping an egg into someone else's nest.")

Hadly was slightly sheepish. He knows, and he knows

I know, that his road home at night lies nowhere near the cemetery. At the same time, he had something to tell me, and was determined to go through with it.

"I guess you've heard the story, Mr. Porter," he said. "I don't suppose I'll ever hear the last of it. But there's a mistake being made, and I thought if Miss Edith was going to write it up, we'd better have it straight."

It appears, then, that it was not near Carroway's grave that Hadly saw the figure, but in the old part of the cemetery, and that there are some facts which he has not given out.

The cemetery is surrounded by a white fence, and inside it is shrubbery. Hadly, it seems, was not alone, but was standing in the road, "talking to a friend." If, as I imagine, the friend was a woman, it was surely a safe place for a rendezvous!

It was the "friend" who saw the light, and who accounts for the suppression of this portion of the tale. It shone through the shrubbery, a small blue-white light about two feet from the ground, and directly in front of the headstone of one George Pierce, who died in the late seventeen hundreds.

Hadly did not see the light, but the "friend" persisting, he crept through the shrubbery to take a look around. It was then that he saw the figure, moving slowly and deliberately toward the trees.

He seems to have no doubt that he saw an apparition, or that the information belongs to me, the reason he gives for the latter being that George Pierce is the gentleman who was, according to local tradition, shot and killed while attempting to escape the Excise in the old farm house which is now a part of Twin Hollows.

I have entered this here, because the day seems given over to the supernatural. We have breakfasted with the spirit world, and seem about to lunch with it.

Everything continues quiet at the other house.   .   .   .
Jane and I to-day returned the Livingstones' call. Although it seems absurd, I have never quite abandoned the hope of finding, in Uncle Horace's unfinished letter, a clue to the present mystery.

I therefore took it with me, hoping for an opportunity to show it to Mrs. Livingstone. But none came. Dr. Hayward was there when we arrived and remained after we left. Perhaps, because my own world is awry, I think the universe is so.

But it seemed to me that we were shown in to what almost amounted to a situation; that Livingstone, usually dapper and calm, was flushed, and that Mrs. Livingstone was on the verge of tears. The doctor, standing by the window, hardly acknowledged our entrance, and remained standing, glowering and biting his fingers, until we left.

He is, I understand, soon to leave for a holiday.

August 12th.

(No entry.)

August 13th.

(No entry.)

August 14th.

TO-MORROW Hayward says I shall be able to see Greenough; the first intimation I have had that he is back in the neighborhood.

But I feel that my consciousness of my own innocence will be as nothing against Greenough's sheer determination to prove me guilty. And yet, guilty of what? Of a bullet buried in the floor of my own house, and a broken window! We have had no further crime. Nothing is altered, save my own feeling that a net is closing around me, and that some malignant fate is sitting spider fashion in the center of it, waiting to pounce on me and destroy me.

Yesterday, being allowed to read, I found that with the single exception of the red light, my experience is fairly true to type in such matters; thousands of people have apparently gone through the same sort of thing, and have been neither the better nor the worse for it afterwards.

They saw, they believed, and then dismissed it, to be dug up out of their memories later to assist somebody to write a book, or to entertain a dinner table. But in my case, what?

My only hope, apparently, is to convince Greenough that I saw this thing; to show him the steps by which I was led to fire the shot; to put him, if I can, in my place for an hour or two.

Suppose, like a lawyer preparing a brief, I make my statement here, and to-morrow read it to him? At least I can make this entry full and explicit. It passes the time, and he may be willing to listen. . . .

This is the 14th. It was, then, the early evening of the 11th, when Annie Cochran stopped at the Lodge on her way home and asked to see me at the kitchen door.

"I'm leaving, Mr. Porter," she said. "I don't like to make trouble for you, but I can't stand that secretary."

"What has he done, Annie?"

"Done!" she said, and sniffed. "He's watching me, for one thing. I never go upstairs but he's at my heels. But that's not all. He's going to make trouble for Mr. Bethel. You mark my words. And Mr. Bethel knows it; he's scared to-night."

There had been a quarrel, she said, at dinner, carefully camouflaged while she was in the room, but breaking out again the moment she left it. So far as she could make out, it had to do with the secretary's leaving the house at night, and his insistence that he go out when and how he liked. But there was something beneath that, she thought. "That wasn't enough for the fuss they were making," she said. "There was murder in that boy's face, Mr. Porter."

Mr. Bethel, she thought, was trying to quiet him, but he refused to be quieted. Finally Gordon got up and flung open the pantry door, finding her inside it, and he said, according to her: "Listening, are you? Well, you'd better watch out, or you'll get something you don't expect." Then he went into the hall, got his hat and slammed out of the house, leaving the paralytic sunk in his chair.

"He's gone? Where?"

"He didn't say. He just took the car and went."

She was uneasy; she had construed what he said as a threat against her of a serious sort, and I drove her into Oakville myself. On the way I tried to persuade her to return to her employment for a time at least, on the ground that we might need her, and she finally agreed.

It was perhaps nine o'clock when I returned, to find the rector and his wife calling, and to sit through an hour and a half of gently unctuous conversation, while my uneasiness constantly increased, and my sense of guilt and responsibility. If we had warned the old man he would have been at least prepared to take care of himself in an emergency, but we had foolishly kept our knowledge to ourselves, and even allowing for exaggeration on Annie Cochran's part, there seemed no doubt that such an emergency might be at hand.

At 10:30 our visitors took their departure, and leaving

Jane prepared to retire and Edith to answer some of her letters, I wandered with apparent aimlessness down to the boat-house. Halliday was not there, and as the dory was missing I knew he was somewhere out on the water. After waiting until eleven, my restlessness was extreme and I walked up and around the main house, to find the garage doors open and the car still out.

Had there been any indication ot life in the building, I think I would have wakened Mr. Bethel and warned him; stayed with him, perhaps, until that murderous young devil was safely settled for the night. But his room was dark and his windows closed, so I thought better of it. But I did ascertain that the gun room windows were locked, and that if the boy effected an entrance at all, it would be by some less surreptitious method.

Thus reassured, I went back to the boat-house, and soon after Halliday rowed quietly in and tied the dory. He had rowed up, he said, to see if the boat was still there. It had not been disturbed, so far as he could tell.

I told him my story, but he was less anxious than I had expected.

"It's not the game," he said. "If Gordon is the killer, we've got to consider that he doesn't kill out of anger. That's different. He's cool and deliberate; he plans his stuff ahead and goes through with it. I don't even think he gets any thrill out of crime itself; the real secret joy is in baffling discovery. And he knows this: after the quarrel to-night, if old Bethel fell down the stairs and broke his neck, he would be blamed for it."

But he thrust his army automatic in his pocket nevertheless, and we started toward the house, with no particular plan in mind, but a fixed determination to protect Mr. Bethel "in case of any trouble," as Halliday put it.

We had almost reached the end of the walk over the

marsh when he halted suddenly and stared to the right.

"There was a light over there," he said. "In the woods. Wait a minute; maybe it will show again."

It did show, above the head of Robinson's Point apparently, in that lonely strip of woodland which leads to the hiding place of the boat.

(Note: In explanation of our conclusion, that we had seen one of the lights of the car as Gordon drove down through the trees, I can only give again the difficulty of distinguishing at night a small light comparatively close at hand from a large one some distance away.)

Halliday watched it, and then passed his revolver to me, first taking off the safety catch.

"Don't fall over anything," he warned me. "And don't shoot until you see the whites of his eyes! I'm going over there, Skipper."

He set off on a steady lope, heading for the light but obliged to make a long detour around the marsh. I myself, holding the revolver gingerly, started on to the house.

I was feeling, comparatively speaking, relaxed. I felt, as did Halliday, that Gordon was near Robinson's Point; my duty, as I saw it, was simply to stand guard until Halliday returned and we could make some plan; in case of trouble later to get into the house, if possible.

This thought, that we might want to get into the house, bothered me. My keys were at the Lodge, and I could hardly hope to secure them without disturbing Jane. I made, as a result, another round of the windows, and was brought up short by the fact that one of the gun room windows, certainly closed and locked before, now stood open.

It was the more startling, because I had but that moment ascertained that the garage doors still stood wide, and that the car was still missing.

I daresay every man has occasional doubts of his physical courage; I know that, after the sinking of the Titanic, I was obsessed with the fear that I might have fought like a demon to get into a lifeboat. But I daresay too that every man has a sort of spare reservoir of courage, on which he can draw in the emergency, when it comes. Yet I shall not pretend, even to myself, that I pulled up my shoulders, examined my weapon, and then boldly entered that window.

I crawled in, with knees that shook under me and a definite nausea in the pit of my stomach. And to make matters worse there was a slow footstep somewhere near, which I was a second or so in identifying as a drip from the old shower next door.

I had no doubt whatever that Gordon had returned, and the very fact that he had come without the car made that return sinister. I groped for the door into the passage and stood there listening, but there was no sound whatever, save the leak of the tap; I remember that as I passed the open door of the shower room I looked in, and a gleaming eye nearly lost me my equilibrium, until I remembered Edith's piece of phosphorescent wood. All this, it must be noted, was in complete darkness.

I reached the dining room without incident, and there a new thought struck me. Annie Cochran had represented the old gentleman as distinctly alarmed, and I myself had seen him some time before, more or less on guard, with a revolver. Suppose he saw a strange figure emerge from his dining room and start up the staircase? It seemed to me that he would have every right to shoot me first and investigate me afterwards.

It was while I hesitated there, near the sideboard, that I was first conscious of a cold air blowing around me. So distinct was it that my first thought was that some stealthy movement had opened the door to the passage behind me. Almost immediately on that there was a tremendous crash as though some heavy object had struck the dining room table, and following that the door into the hall burst open, slamming back against the wall outside. This was followed by complete silence.

So shaken were my nerves by all this that my next consecutive thinking found me once more in the gun room, ready to beat a retreat. But here I managed somehow to pull myself together, and to return to my original errand in the house. Convinced that the slamming of the door would have roused Mr. Bethel—if indeed anything were to rouse him again; and by this time, shaken as I was, I was prepared for the worst—the main staircase was not feasible.

I made my way, therefore, into the passage again to the servants' staircase and crept up it, one stair at a time, with the revolver clutched in my hand.

I have no idea how long all this took. Possibly ten minutes from the time I entered the house. Perhaps even more. I was subconsciously aware, I know, that it was too soon to look for Halliday's return, and in a way I was playing for time.

At the top of the kitchen staircase was a door, opening onto the main hall, and this I cautiously opened.

Save for the ticking of the tall clock on the staircase landing the house was entirely silent. The silence and the closed door gave me back my ebbing courage, and I advanced a step or two along the hall. Here I was close to Gordon's room, and I felt for and tried the knob carefully. It was locked, and listening outside I could hear no movement from within. The relief I gathered from this was enormous, and although my position was still unpleasant enough. the fear of tragedy began to leave me.

There remained, I figured, merely to ascertain that Mr. Bethel's door was closed and locked, and I could beat a retreat which I felt was by no means ignominious. I made my way, therefore, to his door and tried it. It was fastened also, and I heard him move within; the heavy creak of his bed-spring, no doubt as he lay uneasily awake, waiting for the boy's return.

I hesitated there, wondering whether to call to him and tell him he was not alone and helpless, or to retire, satisfied that he was awake and prepared for any trouble that might come. But there were no further sounds from beyond the door, and I turned away and prepared to retrace my steps.

It was then that I became conscious of a light somewhere below. Not a light, rather, but where before had been absolute darkness there was now something else; a faint illumination which outlined the staircase well, and which was reddish in color.

(Note: It is worthy of consideration that when, later on, Halliday and I made our experiment with the red lamp, lighting it in the den and opening the door into the corridor, we secured much the same effect, save that in the experiment the resulting glow seemed stronger than the one recorded here.)

And I will swear that a figure was standing at the foot of the stairs, apparently facing toward me and looking up. Or rather, not a figure, but a face; the light was so faint that no portions of the body were visible. I will swear that it moved, not toward the dining room and a possible exit by the window of the gun room, as Halliday suggests, but still upturned, toward the library, and that within a foot or two of that door it disappeared.

I will swear that the red glow persisted for a moment or so after that disappeared and then slowly faded away.

And I will also swear that I had no more intention of firing my revolver at that figure than I had of leaping down the staircase after it. Mr. Greenough would have done no less, in my situation, and might very possibly have done considerably more. The first knowledge that I had pulled the trigger came with the sound of the shot itself. I was certainly not aiming at the figure. If Mr. Greenough examines the mark left by the bullet, he will find, as Halliday and I did, that my bullet went almost directly down, and is embedded in the base-board of the hall, near the den door. . . .

As a matter of fact, the whole sequence of events, ending with the shot, had stunned me. I heard Mr. Bethel in his room, calling out, and someone outside shouting from the terrace. Almost immediately there was a crash of breaking glass in the library, as Halliday smashed a window with a porch chair, and the next moment was in the house and fumbling for the light switch inside the library door.

When he ran into the hall I told him what had happened, and he immediately set about his search. As Mr. Bethel was still demanding, beyond his door, to know what was wrong, I went back to reassure him, but it required some time to induce him to unlock the door. Thus it was Halliday who made the first investigation downstairs.

He is confident no one escaped from the library, unless in that brief time while he was feeling for a light. But it is to be remembered that the floor near the window was covered with broken glass; no escape by that method could have been noiseless. At the same time, any theory of departure by the windows of the den is impossible, since we found all these windows closed and locked on the inside.

I am convinced that the intruder was not the secretary.

As a matter of fact, he drove in a half hour later, saw the lights in the house and hammered for admission, and surveyed our group in the hall with an amazement which, under any other circumstances, would be humorous. And I am also convinced that it was not the doctor. Mr. Bethel showing signs of collapse, Halliday telephoned to Hayward. He replied at once. Had he been at the house that night, he could not have made it. . . .

I have no explanation whatever of the fact that Halliday and Hayward later on found the gun room window closed and locked, save that the intruder may have entered by it while I was working my way into the dining room; and that the cold air, the crash at the table, and the bursting open of the door in the hall, which so alarmed me, may have marked his passage through the room.

At the same time, no statement of the situation that night should fail to point out, loath as I am to believe in the supernatural, that for many years this house has had a reputation for similar phenomena; the bursting open of the door and the cold wind are merely repetitions of many similar unexplained occurrences. So also is the reddish color of the light I saw.

The disappearance of the figure and the blank darkness which followed that disappearance are difficult to account for, under any natural law at present known. I am not a spiritist, but it is to be remembered that only a second or so elapsed between Mr. Halliday's entrance by the broken window and his turning on of the lights.

Neither he nor I heard in that interval any movement; yet an escape over the broken glass of the window would certainly have made some sound. As I have said, the windows in the den were found to be closed and locked on the inside.

(End of memorandum for Mr. Greenough.)

August 15th.

UP to-day, but not allowed out of my room. Jock spends most of his time with me, whether from devotion or interest in the appetizing trays Jane sends up, I am slightly uncertain.

Edith suspects the latter, and has taken to calling him old dog Tray. She reproaches me bitterly for my faculty of getting myself into difficult situations, and quoted to me to-day those immortal words of Lewis Carroll, with a small amendment of her own:

" 'You are old, Father William,' his young niece said.

'And your hair has become very white.

'And yet you incessantly stand on your head.

'Do you think, at your age, it is right?' "

In preparation for the detective's visit she has laid out my best silk pajamas, and her reason for doing so sounds like her:

"No man is really at his best without his trousers," she observed. "But there's a sort of moral support about silk pajamas. It puts you out of the house-breaking class, anyhow."

"Not at all," I retorted. "Only our best house-breakers can afford them, these days."

But it shows her strength and my weakness, that I am now wearing them. . . .

Greenough has come and gone. What he thinks of things now I cannot say, but at least I am, as I have had occasion more than once to record here, still at liberty. The fact that the revolver I used was Halliday's, and Halliday's supporting statement, no doubt are in my favor.

At the same time, it is clear that, although he listened carefully to my preliminary statement relative to our suspicions against Gordon, he was not greatly impressed by it.

"How did you and Mr. Halliday reconcile that theory with the sheep-killing?" he asked, when I had finished. "He wasn't here, then, was he?"

"No, that has puzzled us, of course."

"Then again," he went on, eyeing me, "he himself was knocked down and tied. I don't suppose you accuse him of that, too?"

"I've told you," I said impatiently, "that we haven't a case; it's a theory. That's all. Take for instance that rope—"

"Oh, come now, Mr. Porter! I've slipped out of my room at night over a wood-shed; so have you, probably."

Coming down to the night of the 11th, he listened to my written statement without comment, save that he smiled somewhat over what he called my "ingenious conclusion." He also passed lightly over my picture of what followed; of Halliday's entrance, of Bethel brought down and sitting huddled in a chair in the library, somewhat dazed and showing signs of collapse. And of Gordon's return and our sudden realization of my predicament.

"Just what predicament?"

"I was in the house because I knew Gordon had a rope and a knife in his room. If we let him up there, and he did away with them, it left me in pretty poor shape."

"So you kept him downstairs! By force, he says."

"I wouldn't call it force. But we were three to his one, of course."

"In other words, you telephoned to the doctor, but you didn't telephone to Starr until Gordon came in and found you there."

"If you want to put it that way, yes."

"You broke into the house and found somebody there

who had no business there. But you didn't think of calling on the police."

"What I felt we needed was not a policeman, but a medium."

He condescended to smile at that, but he was back to the matter again like a needle to the pole.

"Gordon says that Hayward and Halliday went off somewhere, after telephoning Starr, and that you held the gun on him. Is that correct?"

"I still had the revolver. I didn't point it at him, if that's what you mean. As for Halliday and Hayward, they were going through the house. That's all."

"And they found the gun room window closed and locked?"

"So they say. I wasn't present."

"How do you account for that, if that's the way you entered?"

"I don't account for it."

"I suppose you have keys to the house?"

"I have."

"But you entered by this window?"

"Great heavens, man!" I said impatiently. "I don't carry those keys with me. I wasn't trying to get into the house. I went in because the window was open. And if you think I liked doing it, I'm here to tell you I didn't."

"You can't account for the window being locked, later?"

"I cannot. Why should I have locked it, if that's what you are trying to intimate? I had to get out again."

He abandoned that for the time.

"The point is this, Mr. Porter," he said. "You and Halliday have laid considerable emphasis on that knife. It was because Gordon had it that you were in the house, I understand."

"Had it and might use it," I amended.

"It was, in your opinion, either on him or in the room upstairs. But as it turned out, it was neither on him nor in his room. He denies ever owning such a knife."

"Halliday saw it. He's lying."

"It's your belief, then, that on this murderous errand of his, which was to end up at the house, he disposed of the very weapon which you had expected him to use?"

"I haven't said that, but I think it probable."

"Why? Why should he? He could have had no idea the house was to be entered, or his room searched. He came back, smoking a cigarette I understand, to find you and Halliday in the hall, a window broken and a bullet imbedded in the floor. That doesn't sound like a man who has been out hiding the evidences of his crimes."

He asked me abruptly after that how long I had known Halliday, and his relationship to the family. Then he attacked Halliday's statement that he thought he had seen the lights of a car by Robinson's Point, and had started for that.

"Mr. Halliday," he said, "says that he believed that this car was Mr. Bethel's and started toward it, giving you his revolver and leaving you alone; that he found no car there, and turned back. To support this statement, he says that a boat, lying in the creek there, had excited his suspicions because the oar-locks were wrapped. Muffled oar-locks are not uncommon things."

"The position of the boat was suspicious."

"Perhaps," he said. "But that was a matter for me to determine, not Mr. Halliday. As to the strips he maintains were wrapped around the oar-locks, I am not saying they were not there; but I am saying that they were gone when I went over the next morning to examine the boat."

What he had hoped to gain by that I do not know. He

shifted rapidly, perhaps in the hope of somehow trapping me; our reasons for hoping to connect Gordon with the crimes, since one of them had taken place before his arrival; when I had first missed my fountain pen; exactly where I was standing when the revolver was fired; when I had taken off the safety catch; where I was when Halliday broke the window. And from that, without a pause, back to the gun room window and had me repeat my story about finding it open, and entering by it.

"Yet you thought," he said, "that this boy, whom you consider a degenerate and a murderer, was inside. In a few minutes you expected Halliday back, but you did not wait for him. Is that right?"

"It is."

"Then you thought, in all probability, that the boy had this knife with him."

"I didn't think about it at all," I said. "If I had, I'm not sure I would have gone in."

"But later on the boy returns, and you won't let him upstairs, because the knife is there. Is that right?"

Looking back over the interview, he seemed to be anxious to break down my story, rather than to be following any idea of his own. Halliday stated it fairly well when I reported the examination to him.

"He's got nothing," he said. "Nothing but you. And that's where his system breaks down; it might work, if you were guilty, but it isn't worth a tinker's dam, since you're not."

One rather curious thing he added, however, in view of Greenough's questions about the knife.

(Note: I was not present when Starr followed by Gordon, Halliday and Doctor Hayward, went upstairs to examine Gordon's room.

During the interval of waiting for the constable I

had been conscious of an approaching nervous chill, the beginning of the illness which laid me up for the following three days.)

"Gordon was as surprised as I was," he says, "when Starr didn't find the knife. It was too good to be true; he could hardly believe it."

August 16th.

D OWNSTAIRS to-day for the first time.
As I had expected, Mr. Bethel intends to give up the house. He has so notified Thomas and Annie Cochran, and has sent me a note asking me to see him to-night.

The note was left by Gordon, and as I happened to be in the hall, it was I who received it.

He stiffened when he saw me, it being our first encounter since the other night.

"Mr. Bethel sent this," he said briefly, and started to go. On the verandah, however, he stooped and turned around. "Pretty dirty work the other night," he said, watching me. "And I'm not forgetting it."

He waited, apparently expecting a reply. On receiving none he stood studying me for a moment,—a most uncomfortable moment for me. Then he smiled, his curious sneering smile.

"I'm not afraid, you know," he said. "I can take care of myself. I'm not worrying."

He thrust his hands into his pockets and turned, not toward the other house, but toward the road. Near the gates he began to whistle, and thus theatrically assuring me that he was at his ease, started toward Oakville.

I have learned to-day that he is leaving Mr. Bethel, and has gone to the city to look for another position.

The boy puzzles me. Here I am, more or less a

specialist in boys; for more years than I care to remember I have known them, collectively and individually, but here is a new type.

He is weak; compared to that prognathous portion of Halliday's face, for instance, he has no lower jaw. He completely lacks personality; he could, according to somebody's description of a similar type, be stood up against a whitewashed wall and erased with a good rubber. He is, one would say, almost too weak to be vicious.

But nature apparently gives to these otherwise defenseless creatures of hers a sort of low cunning with which to protect themselves. He has that cunning.

He is not in love with Edith, I think, although that vain young woman probably believes that he is. He is interested in her, as the only young and feminine creature within his present *milieu;* for the same reason he hates Halliday, quite apart from the other night, as representing what he is not and would like to be. At the same time, he hates the world, because he feels himself incapable of coping with it.

But just how far does he carry this secret longing of his to escape his own inferiority? To the length of crime? Granted the desire so to escape it, has he the ability? Can he make his possible dream of being a master criminal come true? I think not. . . .

Other things go on much as before. Greenough after three days of no further discoveries has gone again. The situation at the main house the other night has, thank God, not reached the press. The boat, with the mufflings gone from the oar-locks, still lies in the creek beyond Robinson's Point, and the sole proof of such muffling, if the point is even brought up again, lies in the boat-house along with the broken lens, the bit of Gordon's cipher and the small screw cap of an ether can.

Our lovers move about their ordinary duties with an

eye out, as one may say, each for the other. Vague as the future is, they have each other, and only this morning I saw Edith with a basket of mending, from which looked forth what greatly resembled a masculine undergarment in need of buttons. Shades of twenty years ago, when each sex politely assumed that the other went, so to speak, undergarmentless!

They cannot turn the clock on. But there are times when there is a sort of despair in Halliday's face, and sometimes I see Edith sitting alone, her hands folded, looking three or four years ahead with a sort of tragic patience. So much, she seems to think, may happen in three or four years.

She asked him, the other day, out of a clear sky, if he had been gone over by a doctor recently.

And the reward, on which she had so blithely counted, seems as far away as ever. As far away as her dreams of earning a fortune with her pen. She has had another rejection or two, and the heart has gone out of her.

But she has had her moment. Mail still continues to come in. Which reminds me that she received a curious letter yesterday. Because it may be construed to have a bearing on our situation I record it here, but as a matter of fact, one must make certain allowances; Edith's articles used my name in full, and a small amount of investigation by the professional mediumistic under-ground would supply some of the remainder. The Jane, for example, is quite easily accounted for.

But the remainder leaves me considerably puzzled. The boat, for instance. And that strange condition of Mr.— at the end, a heart which is normal apparently failing him, so that he would have fallen had he not been caught. For all the world as though—but I must pull myself together. The letter from Salem was not authentic; why should I believe this?

Evanston, Illinois.
August 12, 1922.

"Dear Madam:

"I have read with great interest your account of the strange occurrence at the light-house at Robinson's Point, and would like to tell you of something which occurred here that same night and, allowing for the difference in time, at about the same hour.

"I am not a spiritualist, but following a small dinner here, it was suggested that we try table levitation, and against my husband's protests, this was arranged for.

"My husband, I may say, is not psychic in any way, and was greatly bored with the proceeding. We were not surprised, therefore, when after sitting in darkness for ten minutes or so, he fell asleep and began to breathe heavily.

"I tried to rouse him but was unable to, when the opinion was given that he was in a trance state. As none of us were familiar with that condition, and as he began to groan heavily, I was greatly alarmed. There was a doctor in the party, however, and on his saying that his pulse was all right, we sat quiet and waited.

"He then said 'Jane, *Jane*' in an agonized voice, and as my name is not Jane there was some amusement, especially when he added: 'She is asleep. I cannot rouse her.' Almost immediately after that, however, he said 'Robinson's Point,' and something about a boat there. (We think now that the allusion may have been to the light-house you mention.) After that he was quiet for a time and I begged to be allowed to waken him, but just as we had turned on the lights again he got up, with his eyes still closed, and leaning over the table, seemed to be staring at the gentleman across from him. (A Mr.

Lewis, a very nice man, with whom my husband plays golf a great deal.)

" 'I have not changed my attitude,' he said, in a really terrible voice. 'I repudiate you and all your works. I am not afraid of you. The thing is monstrous, and society should be warned against you.'

"I have forgotten to say that he had kept his right hand closed, as though he had something in it. He made a gesture as though he threw this something away, and then looked at Mr. Lewis again and said: 'I have warned you; I shall tell the police.'

"He seemed to be in a state of great excitement, and hardly able to breathe. He fell back into the chair, and our doctor friend reached over and felt his pulse. He says now that, although his heart is perfectly sound, it had almost stopped. Indeed, he would have fallen had the doctor not caught him. In a short time he came around and seemed to think he had been asleep. He felt, however, very wretched the next day.

"This may not interest you, but the mention of Robinson's Point in your article, and the similarity in time, has struck me as a strange coincidence. I am signing this in full, as an evidence of good faith, but I must ask you not to use it for publication."

(Note: I have since secured the writer's consent to the use of this letter, on condition that I withhold the signature.) . . .

"An element which works beyond our guess; Soul, the unsounded sea," says Browning. A poet's idea only, perhaps, but wasn't it Montaigne who said that all our philosophy is but sophisticated poetry?

What a joyous time little Pettingill would have with all this! Trotting about, a note-book in hand, adding up a glimpse here, a look there, until he had a complete panoramic view of all eternity. But the real question is, what would Cameron say? Not for him the amorous Hadly in the churchyard—a spot by the way, if our spiritists are right, not quite so exclusive as Hadly seems to have considered it—nor a tea-kettle moving about. His the coldly scientific method; the medium in a box, tied hand and foot; scales of weighing; cameras; notebooks; witnesses.

Not for him Pettingill's wide view into eternity, but a narrow slit, guarded by little bells on strings, through which the poor ghost must creep if he come at all.

I wonder what would happen if I could induce him to come here?

August 17th.

ONE lives and learns.

Mr. Bethel last night lifted a small corner of the mystery and showed me a few of the wheels within. With the net result that we are where we were before. . . .

He telephoned me at nine o'clock last night, the first time I have known him to use the telephone, and asked me to see him.

(Note: I have, I think, not mentioned in the Journal that the three buildings, the Lodge, main house and boathouse, are on one telephone. As this fact plays an important part later, it requires explanation.)

I found him alone in the library, but with certain changes from the last time I had seen him thus. The windows were closed and locked, and the heavy curtains drawn across them; both the rear and front doors in the hall were bolted, and when I was finally obliged to ring, I could hear the old man dragging himself slowly into the hall and there stopping.

"Who is it?" he called.

"Porter."

I was on the terrace, and he opened that door for me, working laboriously with his single useful hand. Once inside, he left me to close it for myself, and went back into the library. When I followed him it was to find him seated, with the revolver close at hand as before. He was a strange, half-sinister figure as he sat there, but when he spoke it was as the querulous invalid of our first meeting.

"I don't like your house, Mr. Porter," he barked at me, without preliminary.

"I don't like it myself," I admitted. "I am thinking of adding to the insurance and then setting a match to it. After you are out, of course," I added.

That brought a sort of dry chuckle from him, but the next moment he was back to the attack. He supposed he was responsible for the balance of the rent, but wasn't I morally responsible if he couldn't live there? I had known the stories about the house, and yet had let it to him. There was a question there.

"There is no question," I said. "I have no idea of holding you up for the balance of the rent."

It seemed to me, however, that he hardly heard me. He was listening again, as he had before, and when he spoke it was on a totally different matter.

"You find me rather on guard," he said. "I am alone in the house."

"Where's Gordon?"

"He went into the city this morning. He has not come back."

And there was something in the way he made the statement that caused me to look at him quickly.

"You mean that he has gone for good?"

"No. I wish to God he had."

There was fear in that, and I realized then that all the place showed fear, the locked and bolted house, the dim light—only one lamp going, and that on the desk— the revolver, and the old man's twisted body, crouched and watchful.

"I am afraid of him, Mr. Porter," he said. "I think he means to kill me."

"Nonsense!"

"I wish it were."

"Can't you get rid of him?"

"Don't you suppose I've tried?"

His story, if story it can be called, that rambling discourse broken into by his fits of listening, even once of sending me out to take a look around, is as follows:

He had picked the boy up in the city, knowing little or nothing about him, and from the time they arrived he had not quite trusted him. After a time, too, he began to suspect that he was getting out of the house at night, and possibly using the car.

"Not guilty in itself, perhaps," he said, "but it left me alone, for one thing. And it is not a house in which one cares to be alone." He glanced at me. "And for another,—well, I needn't tell *you* what has been going on."

But he was not, at first, really suspicious of these night excursions, save for his resentment at being left there, alone and helpless, with a killer loose in the neighborhood. He kept a watch, therefore, not so much over the boy as over the house and himself in his absence.

"If he left a door or window open," he said, "I was at the mercy of anybody who chose to enter."

And this, he says, was the situation on the night of the 26th of July. He had gone to the boy's room and found it empty, and had after some debate decided to work his way downstairs and lock him out.

"And myself in," he said.

It took him a long time to do it; he says too that he was very nervous; there were sounds, especially in the dining room. Nothing he could account for, but they upset him still further, and by the time he reached the kitchen he was in a bad way. He had to sit down there.

It was while he was sitting there that he heard sounds on the porch, and somebody at the door knob. From that on he says he was beyond coherent thinking, but he had no doubt in the world, because of the stealthiness of the movement, that the thing he had feared was happening. It seems never to have occurred to him that it was Gordon.

He dragged himself to the stove, found the poker, and as the door opened struck with all his strength.

"It was only when he made a leap for the bell that I knew what I had done."

He was stricken. He felt the boy's pulse and knew he was not dead, but off somewhere near the sun-dial he heard some one moving, and that alarmed him still more.

"A man never knows his cowardice," he said wryly, "until he is put to the test. I have very little idea of what I did next; my only clear recollection is of finding myself in my room. I don't remember getting there."

But—and this is the point—the boy suspected him. He was sure of it. There had been a complete change in his attitude since that time. And watching that change, studying Gordon as he had felt obliged to, he had felt that something underlay all this. In other words, gradually he had begun to associate the boy with the other crimes.

"He is weak," he said, "weak and vicious. And there is that curious mental state called identification; the weak see the crimes committed by the strong, admire them, admire the criminal. Then they begin to ape them, as Gordon may have aped your sheep-killer, finally even identifying himself with this unknown, adopting his symbol, or whatever one chooses to call it."

I listened carefully, trying to fit this new light on Gordon's injury with the evidence as I knew it. True, the weak link in our chain against him had been that he himself had been attacked. And this was now solved in a perfectly matter-of-fact manner. But there was some discrepancy there, something which eluded me until I had gone over in my mind the events of the night of the 26th in their sequence. Then I found it.

"But what about the man the boy saw enter by the gun room window?"

"Pure invention, I feel certain. Had he accused me he knew the matter of his night excursions would come out. That was the last thing he wanted."

It was my next remark, however, which has left us, as I wrote at the beginning of this entry, just where we were before.

"You haven't said anything about the rope, Mr. Bethel. That has always——"

"Rope!" he said slowly. "What rope?"

"He was tied hand and foot when I found him."

He glanced at me, and then down at his helpless hand.

"It's a very long time since I have been able to tie a rope, Mr. Porter," he said quietly.

I remained with him until an hour or so after the last train from the city had arrived, but there was no sign of Gordon. I offered to remain for the night with him, but he declined. He would not go to bed, however, and I left him there at last, his revolver within reach. . . .

Of that later talk there is one matter of real importance to record.

I have a strange picture in my mind, bearing on the relations of these two, the old man and the boy, and leading up to it; each watching the other, the old man terrified, the boy deadly. And on the surface, before Annie Cochran, all well enough between them; dictation taken, and the book growing. Small surface differences, perhaps, but underneath suspicion on one side and revenge and hatred on the other.

Then Gordon took to locking his room. It was Annie Cochran who told Bethel, and from that time on that locked room played its own part between them; the old man asking himself what was hidden in it, the secretary with his sneering smile quietly carrying the key. It grew, I gathered, to have a peculiar place in the old man's imagination; he wandered down the passage to it more than once; finally Annie Cochran caught him there, trying the knob, and he had made some excuse and gone away.

But the night young Gordon flung out of the house, the same night I saw the figure at the foot of the stairs, Annie Cochran had come to him before leaving, with a key in her hand.

"I thought you might like this, sir," she said. "I find it fits Mr. Gordon's door."

Then she had gone, and he went to the room and entered it. The knife and the rope were there, and *he took them.*

"What was I to say that night, when the constable came down and reported nothing there? In ten minutes, or an hour, you were going to leave me here with him. He was watching me; he knew."

And I daresay he was right. No matter what statement had been made relative to the rope and the knife, there was no reason for Gordon's arrest that night. In ten minutes, or an hour, they would have been left together. and who knows what might have happened?

August 18th.

GORDON came back early this morning. I invented an errand to the house soon after breakfast, but found that Mr. Bethel was still sleeping—as well he might—and that preparations for to-morrow's departure were well under way.

While Gordon was busy on the lower floor, Thomas and I made a tour of the house, with a view to closing it. I have instructed him to paint and put up the window boards which close the windows on the lower floor; I shall know no peace until the place is sealed, and left to its demons or its ghosts.

But I took advantage of my legitimate presence on the upper floor to examine the locked closet in which I had stored the red lamp. It is still there, and apparently has not been disturbed. . . .

Halliday to-day advised for me a period of masterly inactivity. Not that he calls it so, but that is what he means.

"I have an idea, Skipper," he said, "that this calling Greenough off the case was sheer bluff. Every move he made was being watched, and unless I miss my guess you'll find he's at Bass Cove, or some place nearby, under another name. I thought I saw his Ford a night or so ago."

What I finally gathered is that Halliday wants to eliminate me from the case, for my own sake.

"Just now," he said, "you are sitting very pretty. But one more bit of bad luck and he's ready to jump."

Although he smiled, I have an idea that he is deadly serious; that he knows Greenough is not far away, and that for some unknown reason he expects another bit of bad luck. His face is thin and haggard these days, and from the fact that he sleeps a great deal in the day time,

I am inclined to think that he sleeps very little at night.

Between him and Edith, too, I surmise some sort of mysterious understanding. At the same time, there is a noticeable absence of those three-angled conferences in which, some little time ago, we were free to air our various theories.

Willy nilly, I am consigned to innocuous desuetude.

Hayward started yesterday on his vacation.

August 20th.

4:00 A.M. Mr. Bethel was murdered between eleven o'clock and midnight last night. Gordon has escaped. . . .

7:00 A.M. Jane is at last asleep, and I have had some coffee. Perhaps if I record the events of the night it will quiet me. After all, one cannot forget such things; the only possible course is to bring them to the surface, to face them.

But I will not face that room.

Murder. The very word is evil. But no one has ever known how evil until he has seen it. Such things cannot be written; they should not be seen. They should not be.

We have had this murder. We have gone over, inch by inch, the scene of it. We have been spared no shock; the evidence of the struggle is on the walls, the floor, the furniture; we have the very knife with which it was committed. We have even gone further than that. We have followed it outside, along the drive to the garage, and from there by the car to the salt marsh beyond Robinson's Point.

And yet, according to Halliday, until we have gone still further, we have had no murder, according to the law.

Ever since daylight, I have been struggling to see the

justice of a law where, when Gordon is found—and Greenough believes he will be found—we cannot convict him unless we also find that bit of old flesh and blood and bone which was once Simon Bethel.

Is it only necessary, to escape justice, that a criminal artfully dispose of his crime?

And by how narrow a margin he did escape it! A matter of minutes. Between my calling Halliday on the telephone and my meeting him at the terrace; perhaps even between that and our entrance into that wrecked room. A matter of minutes.

In one thing only did he make an error, and even that may not have been an error. He may coolly have abandoned his suitcase, packed and hidden in the shrubbery; may have stood there a second or so, considering it, and then decided to let it lie.

The most grievous thing to me is that I should have given him the warning. And the most terrible picture I have is that, when I called Halliday, he stood listening in at the telephone, craftily calculating: "Can I make it? Can I not?" With *that* behind him. . . .

Crafty. As old in crime as crime is old, for all his youth. Out on the bay disposing of his horrible freight, and watching the lanterns as they searched for the boat; seeing them scatter, looking for other boats with which to follow him out onto the water, and then quietly heading back, into the creek again, and escaping through the wood.

Crafty, beyond words.

August 21st.

THE excitement is still intense. I have hardly seen Halliday since our trouble; he is working with the police, of which a number have come to assist Greenough. Curious crowds stand outside our gates, which we have been obliged to close and lock. A few of the more adventurous, gaining admission by the lane, are turned back there by guards who are on duty day and night.

Thomas, standing at the gate, has orders to admit only the detectives and duly accredited members of the press.

On the bay we have once more the familiar crowd of searching boats. Off the Point, dragging has been going on, but with no result. Owing to the fact that no guards were placed by the boat, a large portion of it has already been taken away by morbid individuals who will place their trophies, I daresay, on tables or mantel-pieces, and thereafter gloat over them.

Truly, just as the lunatic always insists that he is sane, so do the sane often demonstrate that they are mad.

And so far, nothing.

Nothing, that is, which leads to Gordon's apprehension. From the time he turned back in the boat and landing, made his escape into the woods above Robinson's Point, he disappeared entirely. Here and there a clue has turned up, to end in disappointment. Greenough believes that he will be found, that he cannot escape the police drag-net, but I am not so sure. . . .

Although almost forty-eight hours have passed Jane has not yet opened up the subject of the telephone, and because of her morbid reserve on such matters, I have not told the police.

Asked how I had happened to be at the telephone and thus receive the alarm, I have replied that the bell rang, that I went to the instrument, and was immediately aware that one of the receivers was down, either at Halliday's or at the main house; that I heard a crash over the wire, followed by a second and nearer one, and after that a silence; that following that I heard, near the receiver, the sobbing breath of exhaustion, and that immediately after that the receiver went up, and I called Halliday frantically; and that, on his replying, I told him my suspicion that something was wrong at the main house, and to meet me there at once.

But there is a discrepancy here which may cause me trouble if they come back to it. A telephone such as ours does not ring if one of the receivers is down. And the plain fact is that our telephone did not ring at all that night.

As I have not yet recorded the events of that tragic evening in their sequence, I shall do so now.

Halliday had dined with us, and had been more like himself than for some time past. The news that the house was to be given up had seemed to relieve him, for some strange reason, and I remember he said something which puzzled me at the time.

"After all," he said, "we can't undo what has been done. And it may be the end."

After dinner he and Edith sat on the verandah, and going to lower a shade I saw that she was holding a match while he drew something on a bit of paper. But the match went out almost at once, and I would have thought no more of it, had I not heard Edith say:

"And the cabinet was there?"

"In the corner," he replied.

I am no eaves-dropper, so I drew the shade and turned away.

He left at something after ten, and Edith joined us. She was very quiet, and sat watching me play solitaire while Jane sewed industriously. At half past ten or thereabouts, Jane suddenly said:

"The telephone is ringing."

Both Edith and I looked up in amazement; the instrument was in the small hall, not ten feet from where I sat; it would have been impossible for it to ring without our hearing it, and we had heard nothing.

"You've been asleep, Jane!" Edith accused her. But I glanced at her, and I remember that she was oddly relaxed in her chair; her face looked white and her eyes were slightly fixed.

"It is ringing," she said, thickly.

And that is how I happened to be at the telephone that night. And how, too, I gave the alarm which enabled the murderer to escape, by calling Halliday.

"Get your revolver and meet me at the main house," I said. "There's something wrong there."

I know that had I not rung the telephone, had I gone for Halliday instead, we would have caught the criminal. But to ring the one house was to ring the other; he may still have been standing there gasping. He had, for all he knew up to that time, the rest of the night in which to finish his deadly work; to dispose of the body, to gather up his suitcase, waiting outside, and get away.

But I called Halliday, and he listened. He knew then that instead of hours he had only minutes. He must have worked fast, in that ghastly shambles of a room; the car was probably already out, in the lane. He may even have stood there, at the corner of the lane, the engine turning over quietly, and watched Halliday running up toward the house. And perhaps he laughed, that secret laugh of his which had always rather chilled me.

Then—he simply got into the car and drove away. Cool and crafty to the last. No body, no murder. He made for the boat.

He left behind him only two real clues; the knife, which Annie Cochran identifies as one taken from the kitchen, and his packed suitcase. Not intentional, this last. He must have needed clean linen. And certainly that diary of his, in cipher—he would not want that in the hands of the police. But what would the diary matter, after all, if he himself escaped?

August 22nd.

AS time goes on the case is complicated with the eagerness of all sorts of people to bring in extraneous circumstances which they consider important.

For instance, Livingstone's butler, the one who bought the knife in Oakville and caused so much excitement by so doing, has been over to get a description of Gordon, preserving an air of mystery which under other circumstances would be vastly entertaining.

Another story concerns a middle-aged man of highly respectable appearance and of a square and heavy build, who was seen walking uncertainly along the main road near the Livingstone place at 1:00 A.M. the night of the murder. A passing car, seeing his state, stopped and asked if he was in trouble.

He replied that he had been struck by a car an hour or so before, and had been lying by the road ever since. His condition bore this out, as he was stained with blood and dirt. He accepted the offer of a lift, and was left at the railroad station at Martin's Ferry to catch the express there for the city.

There have been many similar ones; an innumerable number of people are convinced that they have seen Gordon, and apparently almost any dapper youth of twenty or so, with what Edith calls patent leather hair and an inveterate cigarette habit, is likely at any time to be tapped on the shoulder and taken to a police station. . . .

Of clues of other and lesser sorts there has been almost an embarrassment. Both the library and that portion of the hall near the telephone have furnished finger prints. But as Greenough says:

"Finger prints do not discover criminals; they identify them."

Nevertheless, great pains have been taken to preserve them. On the white marble mantel a very distinct imprint in blood was photographed without difficulty; others, less clear, were dusted with black powder before the camera was used. Detailed pictures were made of the library and hall, before any attempt to put them back to order was permitted, and these prints have been enlarged and carefully studied. One of them with a strange result.

Greenough, handing it to me to-day, said:

"This print is defective. You can keep it, if you care to."

But I wonder if it *is* defective. There is what Greenough calls a light streak in the lower corner, but it requires very little imagination to give to this misty outline the semblance of a form, and to the lower portion of it the faint but recognizable appearance of brocade.

I have said nothing. What can I say? . . .

One thing which puzzles the police is the violence of the battle; it seems incredible that Bethel could have made the fight for life which he evidently did. At the same time, they have two problems to solve which repeated searching of the house and wide publicity have not yet answered.

One is the disappearance of the manuscript on which Bethel had worked all summer. Annie Cochran has testified that this manuscript was kept locked in a drawer in the library desk; when Halliday and I entered the house this drawer was standing open and the manuscript was missing. It has not yet been located.

But perhaps the most surprising is the failure of any

friend or relative of Simon Bethel to interest himself in the case. Cameron's note to Larkin before Bethel rented the house expressly disclaims any previous knowledge of him.

"Here is a possible tenant for Mr. Porter's house," he wrote, "of which he spoke to me some time ago. I have no acquaintance with Mr. Bethel, save that he called on me a day or so ago, in reference to a statement in a book of mine. I imagine, however, that he would be a quiet and not troublesome tenant."

Halliday brought up this curious situation yesterday, in one of the rare moments he has given us since the murder.

"Has it occurred to you, Skipper," he said, "that it is strange that no one belonging to Mr. Bethel has turned up?"

"I dare say a man can outlive most of his contemporaries and most of his friends."

"He wasn't as old as all that." And he asked, apparently irrelevantly a moment later: "The two evenings you saw him and talked to him, how did he impress you? I mean, his state of mind?"

"The last time, of course, he was frankly frightened. He said as much."

"And before that?"

"He didn't say so, but he was more or less on guard. He had his revolver. Of course, those were rather parlous times."

As a matter of fact, the case is anything but a clear one against Gordon, as it develops. Greenough has been, all along, as convinced of Gordon's guilt as he had previously been of mine. But Benchley is more open to conviction, and a conversation between Halliday and him this morning, on the lawn near the terrace, is still running in my mind.

Halliday had been protesting against Greenough's method of "following a single idea until it went up a blind alley and died there."

"Of course," he said quietly, "you can make a case against Gordon; it's all here. But you'll have something left over that you won't know what to do with. We know that it was Mr. Bethel who hit Gordon and knocked him out some time ago, but who tied him? Where's the boy's own story about seeing a man at the gun room window? Mr. Porter here later on finds that same window open, and sees a man in the lower hall. Who was that? The same hand tied the boy that tied Carroway, and Gordon hadn't even seen this place at that time. What are you going to do with that?"

"Then where's Gordon now?" Benchley asked, practically enough.

"I don't know. Dead, maybe."

Benchley stood thinking.

"I think I get the idea," he said. "The fight, you think, was between Mr. Bethel and this unknown of yours; the boy either saw it and got mixed up in it, or knew he'd be suspected and beat it. Is that it?"

"Well, I would say that a man about to commit such a crime doesn't pack his suitcase, with the idea of escaping with it."

A thought which, I admit, had never occurred to me until that moment.

As a result of this conversation, Benchley has advanced a theory of his own which accounts at least for the failure of any relatives to make inquiry. This is that the old man was in hiding under an assumed name; hiding, in the most secluded spot he could find, from some implacable enemy who had finally caught up with him.

How he reconciles this with the Carroway murder

and the disappearance of Maggie Morrison I do not know, but certain facts seem to bear out this idea. He, was, in one sense, a man of mystery. His accounts were paid in cash; the automobile in which he arrived had been bought at second hand a few days before, by the secretary and in the same manner. And all identifying marks had been carefully removed from his clothing.

In addition to all this, there is the puzzling report on the knife itself. Examination under the microscope shows fibers of linen as well as fragments of cellular tissue. But it also reveals minute particles of tobacco leaf, showing it had gone through a pocket.

But Mr. Bethel was not a smoker.

At some one time, then, Bethel clearly secured the knife and wounded his assailant. Not seriously, evidently, since after that he was able to do what he did do, but sufficiently to turn the minds of the police toward the man who claimed to have been struck by an automobile.

This clue, however, has developed nothing. The night was dark, and his rescuers have no description of him, save of a heavy-set figure and a dazed manner of speech. They carried him to Martin's Ferry, but the conductor of the night express remembers carrying no such passenger. . . .

Greenough to-day showed me Gordon's diary, rescued from the suitcase. It has at some time been dropped into water, and certain pages are not legible. If indeed that word may be used where nothing is legible; where each page presents such jumbles of large and small letters as the following sentence, which I have copied as a matter of interest:

"Trn g.K. GTRgg UnMT aot LmGT MotrT."

The record is not a daily one, but apparently was used for jotting down odd thoughts or ideas. It continues, however, at intervals, for the entire period of his stay at Twin Hollows, the last entry having been made on August 17th.

Certain entries are neat and methodical. The one on July 27th, however, after his injury, is by hand, and shows certain erasures and changes. Once or twice in August the record is long, covering more than a page, while the July entries are all brief. On the last page, however, and without comment, he has drawn in, rather carefully, a small circle enclosing a triangle.

Greenough, while attaching a certain interest to it, has not yet sent it to be deciphered by the code experts of his department. As a matter of fact, I suspect him of holding it out, with the idea of being able to claim the reward if he finds Gordon.

Which reward, by the way, now stands at ten thousand dollars.

August 23rd.

HALLIDAY saw a red light in the house the night Bethel was killed. He has just told me.

He ran out, after I telephoned him, and from the foot of the lawn he saw it. It was gone almost at once.

He has asked me to experiment with him to-night, using the lamp from the attic closet. I have given him the keys. Apparently what he wishes to discover is the approximate location of such a light. I have no idea of his purpose. . . .

I understand that the guards who have been watching the house at night have been withdrawn, and that hereafter only such watch will be kept as will suffice to keep away the curious crowds that still throng here in daylight hours.

To-day Annie Cochran and Thomas have been putting the house in order, preparatory to its final closing. I shall never open it again. Thomas has already painted the window boards and put some of them in place. Let us pray that they keep inside what should be inside, and outside what should be out!

August 24th.

THE strings of small bells, fastened across the closed and shuttered windows, frequently vibrated as though a hand had been drawn across them."

(From "Eugenia Riggs and Her Phenomena.")

Any coherent record of our last night's experiment is difficult to-day; not only do last night's alarms always seem absurd in to-day's sunshine, but I am not at all certain now that I did not build up, out of my recent reading and what I knew about the house, a bugaboo of my own.

And yet—what a night!

A man is a fool who, preparing to spend a night in a haunted house, where a terrible crime has been recently committed, reads during the early evening the idiotic imaginings which other men have conjured out of their own disordered fancies. Or out of their disordered digestions, according to the newest theory.

Isn't it Wells who has the dyspeptic Mr. Polly sitting on a stile between two thread-bare looking fields, and hating the world in general and his own home in particular, after a meal of pork, suet pudding, treacle, cheese, beer and pickles? And Fraser Harris who attributes "the transcendent nonsense of the post-impressionists" to the absinthe in their blood?

So, last night, I must needs poison my mental digestion in advance; pick up a book which should be suppressed, or sold only to large ladies of a lymphatic type,

to read with a box of caramels. And with it fill myself with elementals, hideous masses of matter given
temporary life and strange forms; demons, summoned
by the diabolical rites of the Black Mass; and ghosts of
foul crimes, come to seek revenge on their slayers!

Even before I started the untimely ringing of Clara's
alarm clock, upstairs, set my nerves to jangling. And
there was a certain psychological preparation for me in
the very steps I was obliged to take in order to get
out of the house. For a man of my age to put on his
pajama coat, and retire into his bed otherwise fully
dressed, was an act of deception nerve-racking enough
in itself. But when Jane came in after I had retired,
tardily remembering a missing button, and demanded
the shirt I was still wearing, I broke into a cold sweat.

It was with difficulty that I got her away, shirt-
less, and settled down to wait until the house was
quiet. . . .

Halliday had opened the main house, and the red lamp
was already in the den. Owing to the fact that the
windows were boarded from the outside, we had no
scruples about lighting it; but although it was better
than complete darkness it added very little to the general
gaiety. Halliday was quiet and somewhat strained, the
house itself hot and airless, and with all outside sounds
cut off, depressingly still. I lighted a match and glanced
into the library; it was a ghost of a room, the floor bare,
the furniture and pictures once more swathed in white.

Only the prisms of the glass chandelier reflected the
light and seemed, as it flickered, to be quietly in motion.

Halliday had little to say.

"I would like," he explained, "to reproduce conditions as nearly as they were the night you saw the figure
here." He smiled. "I don't suppose you really want to

go and stand at the head of that staircase, Skipper, but I'm going to ask you to, just the same."

I looked up the staircase nervously.

"If you are going to reproduce the previous conditions," I protested, "you may recall that I had a revolver at that time!"

"I also seem to remember that you fired it," he said, and grinned at me. "It will answer every purpose, and be considerably safer, if you will merely point your finger at me and say 'crash!'"

But no amount of lightness on his part or mine could do more than temporarily lift the gloom; the shadow of tragedy hung over everything at which we looked. Halliday felt it, and suggested that "we get to work and then get out."

The question in his mind, he said, was this: I had said that, a second or so after the shot and the disappearance of the figure, the red light had died out in the den. If, as he believed was possible, this glow came from the lamp upstairs, brought down for some reason, or from a similar lamp, this required that the man I saw had time to go into the den, extinguish the lamp and conceal it, (since it wasn't in evidence later on) get back to the library, and be ready to leave by the broken window before he, Halliday, had turned on the light.

"It's a matter of time," he said. "I was by the terrace when I heard the shot. I figure it took me ten seconds to pick up the chair, run to the window and smash it."

It was nervous work going up the staircase, but I managed it and took up my position. He stood below.

I fired—theoretically—and he did what the figure had done; moved toward the door, still facing me, turned and went into the library. I heard him moving about and the light went out. Then in the darkness he ran into the library again, where he struck a match.

"Twenty seconds," he called.

His voice trailed off; his shadow extended through the den doorway into the hall, and as I watched it, it shows the condition of my nerves that it did not seem to be his shadow at all, but something quite different. For all the world like an old man in a dressing gown. Then the match went out and I heard him coming out into the hall again.

"Did you move a minute ago?" he asked.

"Move!" I said. "I wouldn't move for a million dollars. Strike a light."

"Funny," he said. "I thought I heard something."

He groped his way back to the den, and the red lamp looked actually cheerful after the complete darkness. I heard him go into the library again and apparently stand there and listen, and very shortly after he reappeared and asked me to change places with him.

"See how you can make it, Skipper," he said.

I came down rather more rapidly than I had gone up, and Halliday took my former position. I had never had any particular stomach for the business, and now my one idea was to get it over. I did as Halliday had done, moved to the library door, turned and then, more or less holding my breath, dived into the library and through it to the den. I brought up there, close to the red lamp, caught my foot in the cord and jerked it from the socket. Instantly we were in darkness again, and in absolute silence. Halliday, I believe, was still leaning over the stair-rail, waiting for me to complete the movement, and the sudden plunge into darkness had startled me more than I care to remember.

But I do remember that in a sort of panic I got down on my knees to feel for the connection, and that at that moment, whether due to overstrained nerves or not I cannot say, I distinctly heard a soft movement in the library. Trying to analyze that movement to-day I find it difficult. It was as though the linen coverings in the library had been set in motion, a soft and quiet motion, like that perhaps of a woman with a fan, and above that the faint clink of the prisms on the chandelier, like the ringing of small bells. But whatever had caused it, it was dying away when I noticed it. As if somehow the extinction of the light had taken away its source of power.

(Note: It is to be observed that we secured this phenomenon later, during the seances. As no explanation of it has ever been given, it remains a portion of that unsolved factor in our equation to which I have referred previously.)

I knelt there, my face covered with a cold sweat, staring in the direction of the library door. I felt that if I looked away, if I were to lower my guard for an instant, something would come through that door.

I was, in effect, holding it back with my eyes!

And Halliday had made no sound. He too, I now know, was listening.

This, as accurately as I can record it, was the situation last night when the next move came. The house was absolutely silent again. Halliday was up-stairs, and I was watching the door into the library, when the location of the sounds changed. Protected by my eyes, in front, I was attacked from the rear, so to speak. At the window above and behind me, something was trying to get in. I could hear its hands sliding slimily over the wood of the shutter, keeping on that blind and dreadful groping, until finally some sort of hold was secured and the shutter was shaken.

And with that every last ounce of my self-control

left me, and I leaped into the hall as if I had been fired
out of a gun.

"Halliday!" I shouted. *"Halliday!"*

He came downstairs; rather he leaped down the
stairs. He says he found me in a corner, gibbering,
and I dare say he did, but I must have told him my
story with sufficient clearness, at that, for he left me
alone again in that damnable place and ran outside. And
as I had no intention whatever of being left alone again
for the remainder of my life, I ran also. There was
nobody outside the window, but the fresh green paint was
the thing that, according to Halliday, saved me from
being sent to-day to some sanctuary for the mentally
deranged.

It showed unmistakable signs of entirely human investigation. At least a hand with the usual equipment
of thumb and fingers has left more than one impression
on it. . . .

Later: And now where are we? I am willing, even
anxious, to accept Halliday's verdict, that the sounds
we both heard in the library were due to an east wind
blowing down the chimney, plus the settling and creaking
of the old portion of the house.

But we have just returned from an inspection, in
broad day, of the marks outside the boarded-up window
of the den.

There is a complete imprint of the hand on it, and
it shows a broad short thumb and a curved little finger.
What is more, there is a complete absence of the usual
whorls and ridges of the ordinary hand. One could
take this imprint and put it side by side with the one
in the bowl of putty. They are identical.

Halliday seems to have seen a great light from somewhere, but to me the situation is as absurd as it is
maddening. It is as outrageous as that, out of some

forgotten corner of my memory, I should have dug up a triangle within a circle, to find it cropping up soon after as the signature to a crime.

August 25th.

FIVE days have passed since the murder, and we are apparently as far from its solution as ever.

What work is being done is now centering about the county detective bureau in the city. A deputy constable keeps up a more or less casual surveillance of the property during the day, but is careful to depart before twilight. The dragging of the bay has once more been stopped, and Benchley's idea of an unknown enemy of Bethel's has apparently been abandoned in favor of Gordon as the killer.

At the same time we are not without developments, of a sort.

Although he is reticent on the subject, Halliday seems to feel that the experiment the other night, incomplete as it was, negatives the theory that the man I saw escaped by the broken window in the library.

"Then where did he go?" I asked.

"That's the point," he said. "Where did he go? When we've answered that we'll have answered a number of things."

But he tells me, surprisingly enough, that he has taken up a sort of temporary residence in the house.

"Whoever tried to get in the other night may come back again," he says. And assures me that the place isn't so bad "when one gets used to it."

"I read Kant," he says, as if that explains something.

I have offered to stay with him, but not, I dare say, with any enthusiasm. But he declines with a smile.

"You are too psychic, Skipper!" he says.

But it is perfectly evident that he does not want me.

This morning, going unexpectedly into the boat-house, where this conversation took place, I found him sitting by his table, and spread out before him the bit of linen, the cipher, the broken lens and the top of the ether can which constituted our various exhibits before I was gently eliminated from the case. But he also had a box of figs and a hand mirror before him, and when I entered unexpectedly he was studying himself in the glass.

As he immediately asked me if I cared to go fishing, which I did not, I saw that he was not prepared to make any explanation. . . .

The other development, although it does not solve the crime, or touch on it, came to me through Lear to-day, and throws a new and interesting light on poor old Bethel himself.

Lear did not like his errand; he prefers a presumptuous scepticism to an irrational credulity, and knows no middle ground. Those things which lie beyond his understanding he refers to as "poppycock," a favorite word of his. And to-day he prefaced his business with a small lecture to me, taking me into the drive to deliver it.

"You don't look like a man who has been on a vacation," he began, surveying me. "I know you've had a bad time, but after all, it's no possible responsibility of yours."

"I rented him the house. And I knew I had no business to rent it to anybody."

"Poppycock!" he said, and cleared his throat.

He had fallen into step with me, but at that he stopped and faced me.

"Now see here, Porter," he said, "there's a good bit of talk going around. Some of your friends are saying that you and Jane are laying the blame on some damn fool nonsense about the house itself. That's poor hearing, and it's ridiculous into the bargain. The Morrison girl was not killed in the house."

"I'm not so sure she wasn't. At any rate, *he* was. And I believe the same hand killed them both."

"But a human hand, of course? You're not going to say——"

"Oh, I admit that," I said. "But there are a lot of curious things. If you think the house is normal, spend a night there and see."

"Normal!" he snapped. "Of course the house is normal. It's the people in it who aren't." And warming to his subject: "You and Cameron should be locked up together. And Pettingill," he added.

Which brought him to Cameron, and his errand. . . .

Immediately on Cameron's return from the Adirondacks he had gone to bed with an infected hand, which had been torn by a fish-hook, and had been too ill to look at the accumulation of mail. But the day before, although still very weak, he had gone through his letters, and there found one from Mr. Bethel, dated late in July.

In this letter Bethel recited various "abnormal conditions" in the Twin Hollows house, and asked Cameron, at the earliest possible moment, to go out and investigate them.

"And he wants to come?" I asked Lear.

"I tell you he's been sick," Lear said impatiently. "He wants to know about showing it to the police. He doesn't want to be dragged in, if he can help it."

"You've seen it?"

"Yes. There's nothing in it except what I've told you."

"He doesn't describe these abnormal conditions?"

"No. But he said he had made some experiments

of his own, and was anxious to have his results verified."

"Experiments? Using a red light?"

"He didn't say," Lear said, with some asperity. "A red light! What in heaven's name has a red light to do with the immortal soul?"

He enlarged on that, savagely. Helena, he said, had been off in a corner saying "om, om" to herself half the summer, and when she dozed off in so doing, would waken to claim that her astral body had been off on some excursion or other.

"I can't appeal to her reason," he said, with a shrug of his thin shoulders, "but I have appealed to her decency. I've asked her if it is fair to intrude on the privacy every human individual is entitled to at times. But it's no good. She keeps a record, and I'm convinced it would jail her."

The only advice I could send Cameron was to use his own judgment concerning the letter. Personally, I do not see what value it has, save to corroborate my own ideas concerning the house. But it has suggested to me the advisability of asking Cameron to come here quietly and look the place over.

I rather think he wants to do so.

August 26th.

ALL along, I have been impressed by the attitude of at least the summer public to our tragedies; as each one came it brought with it its temporary thrill; for a moment, one might say, the dancing stopped and a bit of drama was enacted on the stage. Then the curtain fell, the band struck up, and the whirl began again, with some inconsiderable of the dancers missing.

Poor Carroway's widow is working at one of the shore hotels, and has bobbed her hair. And a small boy with adenoids delivers our milk and chickens; I caught

him this morning chalking up a triangle within a circle
on one of the pillars of the gate.

The main house shut and empty, a new assistant keeper
at the light-house, and perhaps a closed room and grief
at the Morrison farm house,—these are the only apparent scars left, to mark our summer's wounding.

I saw Larkin this morning. He believes that we may
be able to sell the property as a hotel site; as this would
ensure destroying the house, it seems the best thing.

But one other change I have not recorded.

Watching Halliday as I do, affectionately and not too
openly, I can see a very considerable change in him. He
is like a man lit from within by some flame, of vengeance
perhaps, of resolution certainly. And he is moody at
times; his old gaiety is gone. He has put me out of
his confidence, not because he does not trust me, but
because for some reason he is afraid for me. And the
same, I think, is largely true of Edith in the last day
or two.

It is as though he said, in effect:

"Keep out. It is dangerous. I am willing to take a
chance, but I want to know that the rest of you are
safe."

Now and then, however, I gather something. Thus
yesterday he said: "You have to remember this; we
are not dealing with a criminal, but with an idea."

Again, he has asked me for Uncle Horace's letter,
and has been apparently making a study of it.

Only along the lines of what I call the super-normal
phenomena of the summer does he show his old open-
ness, and there he is frankly puzzled. My decision not
to call in Cameron has, I think, disappointed him. But
my reasons are sound. Cameron's coming might result
in unpleasant press publicity for us, and more than that,

puts me where I do not intend to be placed, among the believers in spiritism.

He accepted that decision to-day, however, without comment. But shortly after he asked Edith for the letter from Evanston, and sat thinking over it for some time.

"Of course, with a little imagination," he said, "you might figure that these people were somehow let in on what happened here last year. But why Evanston?" And after a pause, following a train of thought:

"Of course I suppose, if you grant a spirit world, you have to grant that where time and space do not exist and only vibration counts—whatever that may mean—you could tune in Evanston as well as—well, as easily as you can on the radio."

But he got up soon after, saying that we were all crazy and he himself was the maddest of the lot, and went away.

August 27th.

LIVINGSTONE is a curious chap; dapper, fastidious and taciturn. He is almost too much of a gentleman; I have had the feeling, and I think Jane has also, that a part of his reticence is caution, that he is always watchful, subconsciously at least, lest the veneer crack, and something secretly vulgar be exposed.

I am still wondering why he came to see me to-day; he was sitting, gloved and spatted, in our small living room when Clara brought his card to me in the garage and I hurried in. Sitting, too, staring at our ridiculous parlor organ, with an odd look on his face.

"Haven't seen one for years," he said, in his clipped and yet deliberate manner. "Where'd you happen on that one?"

"It was here when we came," I explained.

He gave it another glance before we sat down, and then apparently dismissed it. But not entirely. Now and then he looked toward it, and once I thought I saw a slight smile, as though back in his mind was some equally faint humorous memory. But he came to the point with a certain directness.

"You're a man of sense," he said. "I came because you've got a head on you."

"I used to have," I admitted modestly. "Lately, of course——"

He bent forward.

"Use it," he said. "Don't let this spirit bunk get you. Easiest stuff in the world to fake."

"I don't intend to let it get me."

He brushed that aside, and glanced once more at the organ.

"You take a thing like that," he said, "and start it in the dark. It gets you creepy in no time. They all use it; it used to be organs like that; now it's phonographs. They say it starts the vibrations! Well, I'll tell you what it does; it gets you worked up. Sometimes it covers something the medium wants to do."

"So I imagine," I agreed.

His volubility suddenly left him then, and he seemed rather at a loss.

"Let it alone," he said. "Let well enough alone." After a pause: "There may be something, but let it alone."

And that, so far as I can make out, was the purpose of his visit. He showed a certain relief, as if he had got rid of something momentous to him, and soon after he took an abrupt departure. Being careful to remove his glove, which he had absently put on again, before shaking hands!

Thomas tells me that another attempt was made to get into the house last night. He had left his pruning ladder outside under a tree, and found it upright against Gordon's window this morning. . . .

Later: Halliday corroborates Thomas's story, with further details. He was on the lower floor, reading, when he was disturbed by the crash of a pane of glass above. He ran upstairs, but was evidently heard. There was no one on the ladder when he got there, and a thorough search showed no one in the house.

The window was the one through which we had watched Gordon leave the house by the rope.

August 28th.

IT is impossible for me to-night to draw any conclusion from last evening's discovery; I have not my old faith in circumstantial evidence. I can only ask myself if an innocent man hides in his own house. . . .

Jane had one of her bad headaches last night, and at eleven o'clock I took the car and went in to the village pharmacy. It was closed, however, and I was at a loss to know what to do. In the emergency I thought of Hayward's office; like most country doctors he keeps a medicine cabinet and fills many of his own prescriptions. I went there, therefore, and rang the bell.

It took some time and several rings to rouse the housekeeper, an elderly and taciturn woman, and when she finally opened the door it was to say that the doctor was away, and to attempt to close it again. I prevented this, however, and managed to get past her and into the hall.

"I only want to get some medicine," I explained. "The cabinet is in the back office, isn't it?"

"I'm not allowed to let anybody into the office."

"Nonsense!" I said sharply. "Anyhow, you are not allowing me. I'm going."

She seemed completely at a loss, and I thought too that she was listening. With my hand on the knob of the waiting room, I caught the attentive look on her face, and found myself listening also. It seemed to me that there was somebody moving in the back office, and immediately after I caught the stealthy closing of a door somewhere. With that she appeared to relax.

"You are sure you know what you want?" she asked.

"Quite sure," I said, and went through the waiting room to the consulting office. She followed me and turned on the light, and stood there watching me intently. The room was filled with tobacco smoke, and she saw that I noticed it, for she said:

"My husband was sitting in here. I'd be glad if you don't say anything about it."

I am not suspicious, and the confession satisfied my faint feeling that something was not quite right in the house. I got the tablets from the cabinet, and being nervous about unlabelled bottles went to the desk; there, neatly piled up, were the month's bills for Hayward's professional services, written in his own untidy hand, and one not finished on the pad.

The woman was still watching me, and I managed to write my label, glue it to the bottle, and make my departure without, I think, showing that I had made any discovery whatever.

But nothing can alter my conviction that Hayward is hiding in his own house, and that he was in that back room when I rang the door-bell at something before midnight. Not even Halliday's opinion that, since Hayward is officially at home to-day, he had the right to be "not at home" last night.

"After all," he said, "give the poor devil his due,

Skipper. He works hard, and why shouldn't he get back a day earlier than he is expected and steal a few hours to get out his bills? He has to live."

But he seems to me to be a trifle too casual about it. I admit that he puzzles me, these days.

August 31st.

A FTER all, one can find the mysterious where it does not exist. I may not yet know why Halliday considers it necessary to watch the main house at night. But I do know the reason for Livingstone's extraordinary visit.

Mrs. Livingstone, sitting with Jane during her convalescence, read the letter from Evanston, and is eager to form a similar circle, to sit in the house itself. And poor Livingstone is opposing it and is making, for some reason or other, quite a business of it.

"After all, why not?" she urged to-day. "It can be quite secret."

She was supported in this by Edith, and even, half-heartedly, by Jane herself. A change of front which astonishes me. Mrs. Livingstone has apparently some absurd idea that we may receive "a clue, or something," as she vaguely puts it; and on my firm refusal departed, indignantly convinced that I have lost a great opportunity to solve our mystery. . . .

Later: Halliday wants the seance! Nothing has so surprised me in years as his willingness to join the table-tippers. But I suspect in him some purpose not far removed from Mrs. Livingstone's, although just what he hopes to discover baffles me entirely.

"Why not?" he said, when I told him. "After all, we have to keep an open mind on this thing, and we've had enough already to make something of a case for the other side."

"The other side of what?"

"The other side of the veil," he explained gravely, and then, seeing my face, was obliged to laugh.

" 'There is a pleasure in being mad, which none but madmen know,'" he quoted at me. "I've heard you say that Descartes advises us to seek for truth, freed from all preconceived ideas. Who are we, to stand in the way of truth?"

"And we are to search for it, sitting around a table in the dark?"

"Precisely that, Skipper," he said, with sudden gravity, and has left me to make what I can of it. . . .

Twelve days have now elapsed since the murder here, and the police know no more than they did on the morning of the 20th.

Now and then a car stops outside the gate, but our curious crowds are gone. Save that some nocturnal relic-hunter has chipped a corner off the sun-dial, the place is much as it was before. All this water over the dam, and it has brought us nothing.

September 1st.

I DARE say there is no type of investigation in which the grave—no pun here—is so mixed with the gay, as in this particular psychic search on which we are at present engaged. For, let Halliday use it for such purposes as he will, to Jane, Edith and Mrs. Livingstone it is a deadly serious matter.

Their reactions are peculiar. Jane accepts it stoically and without surprise; it is almost as though, from the beginning she has known that it was to happen. But she is nervous; she has eaten almost nothing all day.

Edith shows a peculiar and rather set-faced intensity. Whether she knows that something quite different lies behind it, or only suspects it, I do not know.

Halliday, also, is grave and quiet. He is less interested, however, in the manner of the sitting than in its *dramatis personæ*. The list he has made out himself; Hayward, the two Livingstones, Jane, Edith and himself. On my pointing out a slight omission, namely, myself, he told me cheerfully that I belonged among the Scribes and Pharisees.

"The Scribes, anyhow," he said. "You are to sit by the red lamp and make notes. I am particularly anxious to have notes," he added.

On the other hand, Mrs. Livingstone has entered into it with extraordinary zest. She appeared this afternoon, slightly wheezy with the heat, carrying a black curtain of some heavy material and demanding a hammer and assistance before she was fairly out of her car. As it was apparently up to me to furnish both I did so, but anything less conducive to a spiritual state of mind than the preparations which followed at the main house it would be hard to find.

To stand on a ladder in the heat and darkness of the den, and to nail up that curtain across a corner with no more ritual than if I had been hanging a picture; to place inside it a small table and a bell on it, while beside it leaned an old guitar, resurrected from the attic and minus two strings, struck me as poor psychological preparation for confronting the unknown.

But we are curious creatures. The sun was low before we had finished, and as we sat resting from our labors dusk began to creep into the house. And with it came —self-created, of course—a sort of awe of that cabinet I had myself just made; it took on mystery; behind its heavy folds almost anything might happen. It brooded over the room, tall and menacing, with folds that seemed to sway with some unseen life behind them.

I left Mrs. Livingstone placing chairs about a small table and went out into the air!

The arrangements are now complete. Mrs. Livingstone has brought over a phonograph, with a collection of what appear to be most lugubrious records; she also promises Livingstone, alive or dead.

"I left him sulking," she said. "But he will feel better after he's had his dinner."

And to this frivolous measure we start the night's proceedings.

NOTES MADE DURING FIRST SEANCE

Sept. 1st; 11:15 P.M. Present: Jane, Edith, Hayward, the two Livingstones, Halliday and myself. Livingstone and Edith examining house. All outside doors locked and windows boarded. The red lamp on small stand in corner diagonally opposite cabinet and my chair beside it.

11:30 P.M. All is ready. Mrs. Livingstone at end of table, next to cabinet. On her left Jane, Hayward and Mr. Livingstone. On her right, Halliday and Edith. A red silk handkerchief over lamp makes light very faint. I have started the phonograph, according to instructions. I was right about it; it is playing: "Shall We Gather at the River?"

11:45 Small raps on the table, and one strong one, like the blow of a doubled fist.

11:47 The table is moving, twisting about. It ceases and the knocks come again.

11:50 The curtain of the cabinet seems to be moving. No one else has apparently noticed it. I have stopped the phonograph.

11:55 The curtain has blown out as far as Mrs. Livingstone's shoulder. All see it. Edith says something has touched her on the right arm. To my inquiry if any one has relaxed his grasp of the hand he is holding, no one has done so.

12:00 The bell inside the cabinet has been knocked from the table, with such violence that it rolls out into the room.

12:10 Nothing since the bell fell. Livingstone has asked if less light is required, and by knocks the reply is "Yes." I have put out lamp.

(The following notes were made in the dark and are not very distinct. I have supplemented them from memory.)

All quiet since the last entry. There is a mouse apparently playing about in the library. Edith says that Jane seems to be in a sort of trance. She is breathing heavily. More raps, apparently on door frame into library. I am cold, but probably nerves.

There is a sense of soft movement in the library; the covers are rustling; the prisms of the chandelier can be heard.

Edith says her chair is being slowly lifted. It has crashed to the floor. A hand has apparently run over the guitar strings. All complain of cold. I am alarmed about Jane.

I notice the herbal odor again; no one else has, apparently.

(Note: At this point, Jane's breathing continuing labored, and my apprehension growing, I insisted on terminating the seance.)

September 2nd.

JANE shows no ill-effect from last night, and indeed appears to have no knowledge of the later phenomena.

"I think I must have fallen asleep," she said this morning. "How silly of me!"

She has no idea of her entranced condition and I have not told her.

She accepts the idea of a second sitting to-night, without enthusiasm, but apparently with the fatalistic idea that what must be must be. She took a little tea and toast this morning. . . .

As to what Halliday had hoped to discover, I am as completely in the dark as ever. On my decision to end the seance, and on turning on the lights as I did without warning, the group was seen to be as it had been at the beginning, except that Mrs. Livingstone's chair appeared to have been pushed back, and was somewhat nearer the cabinet than before.

Hayward, so far as I can tell, had not changed his position. His attitude throughout seemed to me to be one of polite but rather uneasy scepticism. Livingstone, on the other hand, showed strong nervous excitement from first to last, but certainly never left the table.

He is ill to-day, which is not surprising, but I understand the intention is to carry on the experiment without him to-night. . . .

. . . . Regarding the phenomena themselves, what can I do but accept them? Certainly they showed no connection with what Mrs. Livingstone likes to call the spirit world; on the other hand, either they were genuine, or they showed an experience in trickery utterly beyond any member of our small group.

And who would trick us? And why?

Livingstone was right, however, as to the psychological effect of the preliminaries; in spite of myself they influenced me. The music, the low light followed by darkness, the strange and fearful expectancy of something beyond our ken, all added to the history of the house itself and its recent tragedy, had prepared us for anything.

The billowing of the cabinet curtain was particularly terrible. Sceptic as I am, I had the feeling of some dreadful *thing* behind it; something one should not see, and yet somehow might see. . . .

Both Crawford and Cameron believe that certain individuals have the ability to project from their bodies rod-like structures of energy, invisible to the naked eye but capable of producing levitations, raps and other phenomena. They believe that these structures are utilized by outside spirits, or "controls." My own conviction is, that if such powers exist, they are not directed from outside, but by the medium's subconscious mind. In that case, of course, it is possible that Jane was the innocent author of last night's entertainment.

Mrs. Livingstone suggests that if we secure anything of interest to-night, I consult Cameron with a view to his joining us later on. . . .

NOTES OF SEANCE HELD ON EVENING OF

Sept. 2nd; 1:00 A.M. Largely from memory, since all the later part was held without light, but made immediately following seance. Present: Jane, Edith, Hayward, Halliday, Mrs. Livingstone and myself. Livingstone absent.

I have moved lamp out from corner, and am now near door into hall.

Doors from den and library into hall closed. Door into library open.

11:10 Table moves almost immediately. Edith says is rising from floor. It has risen, but one leg remains on floor.

11:15 All remove hands, and table settles down.

11:20 Loud raps on table. Construed as demand for less light. Handkerchief thrown over lamp. Curtain of cabinet billows into room. Guitar overturned inside cabinet. All quiet now.

No phenomena whatever for about ten minutes. Jane very quiet. Hayward feels her pulse; is fast but strong. Mrs. Livingstone asks if too much light, and rap replies "yes." I have put out the lamp.

(Note: From here on I was able only to jot down a word or two in long hand, the previous night's experiment of making stenographic notes in darkness having shown its practical impossibility. The following record I have since elaborated from memory.)

The bell in cabinet rings violently and is flung across room, striking door into hall.

A small light, bluish-white, about a foot above Jane's head. It shines for a moment and then disappears.

It has flashed again, near the fireplace.

A fine but steady tattoo is being beaten, apparently outside of the door to hall. A tap or two on metal, possibly the fender. Silence.

Jane apparently in trance.

The sounds extend into the library, and there is movement there. The covers seem to be in motion as before. The prisms of chandelier tinkle like small bells. From where I sit I can see a small light over bookcase in library. It is gone.

The herbal odor again.

Jane is groaning and moving in her chair. Mrs. Livingstone and Hayward having trouble holding her hands. She calls: "Here! Here!" sharply.

Hayward says something has touched him on the shoulder. "Something floated by me just now," he says, "on the left. It touched my shoulder."

A crash on the table. I notice the herbal odor once more. Silence again.

Something is in the hall. It is groping its way along. It is at the door beside me. . . .

My notes end here. I had reached the limit of my endurance and, as the switch was beside me, I turned on the lights. As before, Mrs. Livingstone's chair seemed somewhat nearer the cabinet; no other changes in position, except that Halliday had gone out to search hall and lower floor. The bell was on floor near door into hall, and lying on table, "Smyth's Everyday Essays."

To the best of my knowledge this book was in the library at the beginning of the seance.

No signs of disturbance in library or hall, to account for sounds I heard. But an unfortunate situation has arisen, owing to Mrs. Livingstone's failure to lock door from hall to drive. She had pushed the bolt, but as the door was not entirely closed, it had not engaged. We found this door standing open.

This, however, although Hayward seems uneasy, hardly invalidates the extraordinary phenomena secured to-night.

Jane exhausted, and Edith with her.

September 3rd.

I HAVE seen Cameron, and he will come out. He has evidently been seriously ill, but it shows the dominance of the mental over the physical that he brushed aside my apologies and went directly to the matter in hand.

But it is a curious thing to reflect that, a short time ago, it would have been I who was the sceptic and Cameron who would have been ranged on the other side. To-day it was I who was excited. And Cameron who was to be convinced!

"This Edith, of whom you speak," he said, "how old is she?"

"Twenty."

"A nervous type?"

"Yes, and no. Not hysterical, if that's what you mean."

Certain of the phenomena, too, seem to puzzle him. The table levitation, the lights and other manifestations were not unusual, he said, with a strong physical medium present, and this he imagined Jane to be. The book, however, particularly attracted his interest. Over my notes on that he sat thinking for some time.

"You say it crashed onto the table?"

"At the last, yes. But Doctor Hayward, who was nearest the library door, says that after my wife called, 'Here!' he felt something pass his shoulder. Float past, is the way he puts it. He thinks it was the book, and that it dropped onto the table after that."

"About what you heard in the hall; was this hall dark?"

"Yes. There were no lights anywhere in the house."

"You heard footsteps?"

"No. It was like something feeling its way along. You know what I mean." . . .

Toward the end of the conference he leaned back and studied me through his glasses.

"What started you on this, Porter?" he said.

He did not remind me, although he might well have done so, that my previous attitude, to him and his kind, had been one of a sort of indifferent contempt; that, during his entire time at the university, I had never so much as set foot in his rooms, nor asked him into my house; that on the two or three times only when we had met, I had taken no pains to hide my rejection of him and all that he stood for.

But it was implied in his question, and I dare say I

colored. I told him, however, as best I could, and he smiled.

"I rather imagine," he said, "that when we pass over, our interest in this plane of existence is impersonal; we may hope to educate it as to what is beyond. But we hardly carry our desires for revenge with us."

Of all that I had told him, however, the Evanston matter interested him most. Over the letter he sat for a long time, his heavy, almost hairless head sunk forward as he read and re-read it.

"Curious," he said. "What do you make out of it?"

"A great deal," I told him, and detailed my discovery of the letter behind the drawer of the desk, and my theory as to old Horace Porter's death. I had brought that letter also, and he studied it as carefully as he had the other.

" 'The enormity of the idea,' " he repeated. "That's a strong phrase. And he threatens to call in the police! Have you any notion as to what this idea may have been?"

"Not the slightest," I said frankly.

"I would like to keep this for a while, if you don't mind," he said at last. "I have a medium here in town —but I forget. You don't believe in such things!"

"I don't know what I believe. But you are welcome to it, of course."

It was only after this matter of the letter that he finally agreed to come out the day after to-morrow.

September 4th.

THE words "making trouble," lightly underscored on page 24 of "Smyth's Everyday Essays," are the key to Gordon's cipher. The entire sentence is: "It is often the ingenuous rather than the malicious who go about the world making trouble."

In a few hours, then, we shall have solved our mystery, or at least such portion of it as is locked in the diary. Read with this key we have already translated the sentence I recorded here on the 22nd of August. Although we cannot interpret it without the context, it becomes:

"The G. P. stuff went big last night."

In the same way the scrap of paper found in my garage is now discovered to read, "Smyth, P. 24." Edith's single error lying in the number, which she had remembered as 28.

Halliday suggests that the G.P. above may refer to George Pierce, but makes no attempt to explain the reference. . . .

Halliday's story of his discovery is interesting; certain portions of the two seances he apparently accepts without comment save: "It was the usual stuff," and lets it go at that. Although "usual" is hardly the word I should myself use in that connection. But the book was, as I gather it, not the usual stuff.

"There was something about the way it came, that night of the seance," he says, and makes a gesture. "Mrs. Porter called it, and it came. Like a dog," he says, and watches me to be sure I am not laughing at him.

However that may be, the book and the strange manner of its arrival in our midst had interested him, and he had spent some time over it. Thus, he found where it belonged in the library, and tried to discover some significance in that. But there was none.

"I drew a blank there," he says. "I examined the wall behind, but there was nothing. You see, it couldn't have been *thrown* in; it wasn't possible. And when Hayward said it touched him, both his hands were being held. In other words, he didn't put it there."

All the time, I gather, he was feeling extremely foolish. He would pause now and then, in order to assure me that he felt "a bit silly." He didn't believe in such things; when there was a natural phenomenon there was a natural law to account for it. Maybe telekinesis, or whatever they called it.

"But there had to be some *reason* for that book," he says. "I just sat down and went through it."

He has taken the key words to the city, and has just telephoned (2 P.M.) that the detective bureau has put a staff to work on it.

"It will be several hours," he said. "It's slow work. But I'll be out with the sheets as soon as they've finished."

September 5th.

TOO much exhausted to-day to make any coherent record. The four hours last night in the District Attorney's office have worn me out. I have called off Cameron to-night, for the same reason.

The mystery seems to be increased, rather than solved, by the diary. By such portions, at least, as were read to me. And I do not understand the conditions under which I was questioned, nor the questions themselves. Good God, are they suspecting me again? Halliday is still in town. . . .

Later:

Edith has removed my anxiety as to Halliday's return. He has telephoned, and she has just brought me the message.

"He says you are not to worry," she reports. "He is working with them on the case. And you will not be disturbed again."

She looks pale, does Edith, and Jane is not much better. I have told Jane the whole matter; my absence last night had possibly prepared her, but the very confession that I had been subjected to what amounted to the third degree has roused her to a fury of indignation.

"How can they dare such a thing!" she said. "How can they even think it?"

"It's their business to believe a man guilty until he proves his innocence," I reminded her. "And Gordon thought it; you must remember that."

For nothing is more clear to me to-day than that this diary of Gordon's, which Halliday himself carried to the police, has somehow incriminated me.

September 6th.

HALLIDAY is still in town. I can do nothing but wait here, eating my heart out with anxiety, and allowing my imagination to run away with me in a thousand ways.

My women-folk support me according to their kind. Jane serves me sweetbreads for luncheon, and Edith sits by, giving me an occasional almost furtive caress as an evidence of her faith in me.

But Edith is curiously lifeless; that small but burning flame in her which we call optimism, for want of a better word, seems definitely quenched. She is silent and apathetic, and has been so since yesterday.

She seems to resent our having sent in the key to the diary.

"If only you hadn't done that," she said to-day.

"What else could we do? We have to get at the bottom of this thing."

"I don't see that it has got you anywhere. It has only mussed things up."

What she has in her mind I do not know, unless, poor child, she has been building a future on Halliday's solving the crime, and that now that prospect is gone. She tells me that Starr has been on guard at the main house, quietly, for the two nights Halliday has been in town.

But if she knows any explanation of his presence she does not give it.

"He's afraid to go inside," she said, scornfully. "He just sits out on the terrace and smokes. If anybody said boo behind him he'd jump into the bay and drown himself."

She has apparently implicit faith in Halliday's ability to keep me from further indignity. But I am not so certain. The sound of a car on the highway sets my pulse to beating like a riveting machine; at the arrival of the Morrison truck a few minutes ago with some belated buttermilk I got up and buttoned my coat.

My place in my little world behind the drain pipe is neither large nor important, but it is difficult for me to imagine it without me.

"Suppose the worst to happen," said Matthew Arnold to the portly jeweler from Cheapside; "suppose even yourself to be the victim; *il n'y a pas d'homme nécessaire.* . . . The great mundane movement would still go on, the gravel walks of your villa would still be rolled, dividends would still be paid at the bank, omnibuses would still run, there would be the same old crush at the corner of Fenchurch Street." . . .

This is the sixth. It was on the fourth, then, a few hours after Halliday had gone to the city, that a taxi stopped here, and Greenough got out. There seemed to me to be a trifle more than his usual ponderousness in his manner, and a distinct concentration in the way he looked at me as I came down the staircase. At the same time, he was civility itself, and he stated his errand matter-of-factly. They had a staff working on the diary, and he knew I would like to be present when it was finished.

"It's a long job," he said. "But we've split it into a

half dozen parts, and it ought to be ready by eight, or half past."

It was six then, and as our early dinner was almost ready, I asked him to stay. We ate cheerfully enough, took the seven-fifteen express from Oakville, and were in town and at the county building at something before ten. I was surprised but not startled to find Benchley, the Sheriff, there, and three or four other men, including Hemingway, the District Attorney. Hemingway held some typed sheets in his hand when we entered, and was reading them carefully. Halliday was standing by a window staring out into the square, and the first indication I had that anything was wrong was the expression on his face as he turned and saw me.

The second was a polite invitation to Halliday to leave the room, and his manner of receiving it.

"I'm staying," he said flatly. "If there's any objection to that, I shall advise Mr. Porter to make no statement and to answer no questions, until he can be properly protected."

"Protected?" I asked. "Protected from what?"

"From this strong-arm outfit," said Halliday, and surveyed the room with his jaw thrust forward.

"I am under arrest?"

Hemingway put down the papers and took off his glasses.

"Certainly not," he said. "Your young friend is being slightly dramatic. I know that you want this mystery solved as much as we do; more, since it directly concerns you. This is not a trap, Mr. Porter; we shall ask you some questions, and I hope you will answer them. That is all."

"I reserve the right to interfere in case of any trick," Halliday put in.

"We have framed no trick questions," Hemingway said quietly. "We want the facts, that's all."

He rang a bell, and a secretary came in. My mouth was dry and some one placed a glass of water before me. From that on, for four hours, I answered questions; at the end of that time I walked out, still free although slightly dizzy. . . .

(Note: Halliday has recently secured a copy of the stenographic notes of that night. As they would make a small volume in themselves, I give here only such portions as seem to forward the narrative.)

Q. Your name, please.

A. William Allen Porter.

Q. Age?

A. Forty-six.

Q. Your profession is——?

A. I am a professor of English literature at—— University.

Q. You own the property at Oakville, known as Twin Hollows?

A. I do. I inherited it something more than a year ago, on the death of my uncle, Horace Porter.

Q. Had you known that this property was to come to you on your Uncle's death?

A. It was always understood between us. He had no other heirs. . . .

Q. Had you any previous acquaintance with Mr. Bethel? I mean, before he took your house?

A. None whatever. I never saw him until he came out to take possession. His secretary inspected the house, and negotiations were carried on through my attorney.

Q. In any of your talks with Mr. Bethel, did you gather that he had known Mr. Horace Porter, previous to his death?

A. Never.

Q. When you rented the house, did you retain any keys to it?

A. I have a full set in my possession.

Q. You had access to the house, then?

A. I never used my keys, if that's what you mean.

Q. On the night of the 26th of July, Mr. Bethel's secretary was attacked outside the kitchen door of the house, and managed to ring the bell there before he fell unconscious. Just where were you, Mr. Porter, when that bell rang?

A. The police have my statement as to that. By the sun-dial.

Q. Doctor Hayward was on the road in his car; you were by the sun-dial, close to the house. Yet when he reached you, you had apparently only found this boy. Is that correct?

A. It seems to me that the question there might be, was Hayward on the main road that night, as he says, or nearer to the house than he admits. . . .

Q. You own a boat, I believe?

A. I inherited one with the property. A sloop.

Q. Do you sail the boat yourself?

A. I don't know one end of it from the other. . . .

Q. In your various conversations with Mr. Bethel, did he ever mention the character of the house? By that, I mean any curious quality in the house itself?

A. He recognized such a quality. Yes.

Q. Did he ever mention a letter written by him to a Mr. Cameron, here in the city? A member of the Society for Psychical Research? Relative to the house?

A. Never. But I know of the letter. Cameron sent me word of it a day or so ago.

Q. Are you a believer in spiritualism?

A. I never have been. Recently, however, I——

(Note: Here I caught a warning glance from Halliday and changed what I had intended to say.)

Recently I have been trying to preserve an open mind on the subject.

Q. Why recently?

A. For one thing, Mr. Bethel had found the house queer; so had the secretary. . . .

Q. On the day you asked the secretary to luncheon, the intention was to allow Mr. Bethel to go through his room?

A. Bethel? Certainly not.

Q. I shall read you this entry from Gordon's diary. (reads) "Porter asked me to lunch to-day, so B. could go through my room. They left the knife, but at least they know I have it."

A. That's a lie! I asked him to luncheon so Halliday could search his room. It was Halliday who found the knife. You can ask him.

Q. We'll let that go, just now, and come to the night you were found in the house, Mr. Porter, by Mr. Halliday.

A. I wasn't found in the house by Mr. Halliday. We had started for it together. The maid, Annie Cochran, had reported a quarrel between Mr. Bethel and Gordon, and that Gordon had gone away. You must remember that we suspected the boy of being the killer. I was anxious, and went for Halliday.

Q. What time did the maid tell you this?

A. About seven thirty, possibly eight o'clock.

Q. And when did you go for Mr. Halliday?

A. It was about eleven, I imagine.

Q. What did you do in the interval?

A. She was nervous, and I took her home. After that we had callers.

Q. Did you see Mr. Bethel, in that interval?

A. No.

Q. Had it occurred to you that Gordon might be going to see the police?

A. I never thought of it. Why should he be going to the police?

Q. Did Mr. Bethel think of it?

A. I've told you; I didn't see him.

Q. On the night of the murder in the house at Twin Hollows, what led you to your discovery of the crime?

A. My wife heard the telephone ring, and I went to it. All three buildings are on one line, and the receiver at the main house was down. I heard a crash, and heavy breathing near the telephone.

Q. That made you suspicious?

A. I had been expecting trouble between Mr. Bethel and Gordon.

Q. Why did you expect trouble?

A. I knew they had quarreled. Mr. Bethel had told me that it was he who had struck Gordon, mistaking him for a burglar, and that Gordon suspected it.

Q. When did he tell you that?

A. I don't know exactly. About three days before the murder, I think.

Q. Can you remember the burden of that conversation?

A. Very well. He said that he was suspicious of the boy; that he was weak and vicious, and possibly criminal. He knew he was going out at night. On the night of the 26th of July Gordon was out, and he dragged himself downstairs. When he heard him at the kitchen door he struck him. But he maintained that he had not tied him. I believe that, personally. He had one useless hand.

Q. Did you ever have any reason to believe that Mr. Bethel exaggerated his infirmity?

A. Exaggerated it? What do you mean?

Q. You believe he was as helpless as he appeared?

A. I can't imagine a man assuming such a thing. . . .

Q. Now, Mr. Porter, you have said that the telephone receiver at the main house was down, and you heard over it enough to alarm you?

A. Yes.

Q. It rang, and you went to it?

A. Yes.

Q. How could it ring, if the other receiver was down?

A. As a matter of fact, I didn't hear it. My wife said it had rung, and to satisfy her I went to it. . . .

Q. Did the secretary, Gordon, ever approach you on a matter of money?

A. Money? I don't understand the question.

Q. Did he ever ask you for money? Or intimate that he needed it?

A. Never. He said something once about giving up his position. . . .

Q. Where was he, the night you held the conversation with Mr. Bethel, relative to him?

A. Here in the city, I believe.

Q. And Mr. Bethel thought he might have gone to the police?

A. That's the second time you have intimated that Gordon had something to tell the police. I can't talk in the dark like this. If anybody wanted to avoid the police, it was this boy. . . .

Q. I am going back to the night Mr. Halliday found you in the house——

A. He didn't *find* me. We had started there together.

Q. You say you saw a figure at the foot of the stairs, and fired at it?

A. I didn't intend to fire.

Q. You didn't recognize this figure?

A. No.

Q. It was not Mr. Bethel?

A. Bethel? No. He was locked in his room. . . .

Q. You say you are not a spiritualist?

A. Certainly not.

Q. You have never made any experiments in spiritualism?

A. I have been present at one or two seances.

Q. When? Recently?

A. We have held two sittings in the main house within the last few days.

Q. When did you first hear of the symbol of a triangle inside a circle?

A. If you mean in connection with the crimes——

Q. Before that. You told Mr. Greenough, some time ago, that you had heard of it in some other connection.

A. I told him I had happened on it in an old book on Black Magic, and told a group of women about it. It was a purely facetious remark.

Q. Can you account for its use in connection with these crimes?

A. I have no official knowledge that it was used in connection with the crimes. Only with the sheep-killing.

Q. But you know it *was* so used?

A. I know that it was used once when Mr. Greenough did not find it.

Q. Where was that?

A. On a tree near where the Morrison truck was discovered. I have heard it was on Carroway's boat, but I don't know that. I know it was deliberately put on my car, after Mr. Halliday was hurt.

Q. You say, put on the car? Do you mean by that, Mr. Bethel did it?

A. Bethel? How could he? We have thought lately that Gordon was responsible. We found a piece of his cipher near by.

Q. You have felt all along that Gordon was guilty?

A. I won't say that. I would say that the burden of the evidence indicated that he was guilty. Mr. Halliday has had considerable doubt of his guilt.

Q. Have you ever considered that it might be Bethel who killed Gordon?

A. Never. He couldn't have done it.

Q. But if he had had assistance?

A. Are you telling me that Bethel *did* kill Gordon?

Q. I am telling you that somebody killed Gordon, Mr. Porter. His body was washed ashore at Bass Cove this morning.

September 7th.

HALLIDAY has saved me from arrest, by giving to the police the information which he has been gathering on the case all summer. Has made a quiet gesture, which is like him, and given me back to life, liberty, and the pursuit of literature.

He came out late last night, and I understand is still asleep. He has had very little sleep, poor lad, for a long time.

I myself collapsed this morning, and Hayward has put me back to bed. Edith, spreading my coverings neatly before Greenough came up, says I am now so thin that:

"You really make a hollow, William. If it were not for your feet, nobody would know you are there!" . . .

It is impossible to record in detail my conversation this afternoon with Greenough, covering as it did more than an hour. He came in, I thought, slightly uncomfortable and perhaps a little crestfallen, and I motioned him to a chair. He sat down and mopped his face with his handkerchief, and after that stooped and rather deliberately wiped his shoes with it. Then he straightened and looked at me.

"Well, professor," he said, "it's a darned queer world, there's no denying it."

"The world's all right. It's the people in it who mess things up."

"Like fleas on a dog," was his rather abstracted comment. He felt in his pocket, with much the same gesture as on that early visit of his when he had drawn the triangle within the circle on the back of an old envelope. Whether the movement was reminiscent to him, as it was to me, I cannot say. But he glanced at me quickly and then smiled.

"Sort of had me going, you did, there for a while!" he said. "But I was getting pretty close to the facts before this diary came along. Of course, it helped."

He had Gordon's diary in his hand.

"Naturally," he said, fingering the book, "your young friend's information was valuable; I'm not discounting that. The hand-print on the window board, for instance. I'd have found it sooner or later, but it saved time. And the young lady, too. She's done her bit, all right. I've been handicapped by being too well known around here. And Starr's a fool."

He snapped out this last statement, and I gathered that he was still smarting under the knowledge that, without Halliday and Edith, he would still be nowhere. It was, more or less, his defense.

"Of course," he said, "ever since we got hold of this diary of Gordon's, one thing's been pretty clear. Bethel wasn't working alone. According to what I saw of him it wasn't possible. He couldn't even have made a getaway without help. The only question was, who'd helped him."

"So you picked on me?"

"Well," he said wryly, "you'll have to admit that you've seemed to go out of your way all summer to get into trouble! As a matter of fact, *I* didn't pick on you; it was Gordon." He looked at my clock.

"I've only got an hour," he said. "Your niece is sitting on the stairs now, holding a stop-watch on me. I can't read you this thing, but I can tell you what's in it. And believe me, that's plenty." . . .

Briefly, then, the deciphering of the diary had left me in a very bad position. When they had finished it, it was Benchley's idea to arrest me at once. They had the boy's body, a fact they had kept to themselves, and I was within an ace of a charge of murder.

But Halliday had stayed.

"He seemed to feel there was trouble coming," Greenough said. "He hung around and drove us all crazy. He insisted, as he'd brought the key, on his right to read the stuff as it came through; and as it went on, he didn't know exactly what to do.

"Finally, seeing what was in the air, he made a trade with us. He was willing to have you brought in and interrogated, but on condition that if you weren't held he'd come over with something of his own. You get the point, of course. There's a reward involved, and he'd been holding out on us a bit." He waved his hand. "That's natural. We don't hold it against him. But the point is, he made his trade."

Coming to my examination, my answers had apparently impressed Hemingway satisfactorily. On the other hand, added to the diary's constant suspicion of me, was Greenough's own case against me. He passed over that rather airily.

"I wasn't trying to make out a case against you," he said. "As a matter of fact, you couldn't have been the man who attacked Halliday. You weren't here."

"Naturally," I agreed, gravely, "I wasn't here. Of course, if I *had* been here——!"

He glanced at me quickly, but went back to the night of the inquiry.

"The question was, whether to hold you or not. You may remember Hemingway going out, when it was over, and talking to Halliday outside? Well, it was then he made the trade."

Apparently the fact that Gordon had been the victim had not been the surprise to the police that it had been to me. For one thing, the microscope had shown one detail which the detective had not mentioned to me at the time. Caught between the handle of the knife and the blade had been a short piece of hair. The microscope showed this hair not only young, a matter readily determined, and the approximate color of Gordon's; it also showed it liberally coated with pomade. Poor Gordon's glistening, varnished hair!

But Greenough had been inclined at first to think that there had been two victims, instead of one.

"Dying and passing on," he says, "is not like taking your thumb out of a bowl of soup. It's bound to leave some sort of a hole."

And there had been no hole. If Bethel had died and passed on, no one apparently missed him. As time went on and no queries were received, the thing began to look ominous; as though Bethel himself had been hiding away, under an assumed name.

The idea that Bethel had had an enemy from whom he was hiding, and who had found him, began to intrude itself.

"But," he said, with engaging frankness, "that eliminated you. And you wouldn't be eliminated. You were like some people you've seen, when there's a camera-man about; always getting in front of the machine and into the picture."

" 'And the king will not be able to whip a cat, but I shall be at the tayle of it,' " I quoted. He looked rather bewildered.

Then came the diary, and Gordon brought me in unmistakably, and in a way they had not thought of. Not an enemy, but an accomplice; Bethel hiding there, with my connivance, and the two of us, he the brains presumably and I the hands, working out between us some sinister design which even the boy could not understand.

"Whatever it is," Gordon had written, shortly after the Morrison girl's disappearance, "he's got outside help." And he wonders if I am guilty. But he is not sure of that; he even suspects Bethel, in one entry, of being less helpless than he appeared, and possibly of "working on his own." He abandoned that idea, however, and there was a time when he suspected Thomas; even a time when he thought of bringing his suspicions to me.

But Bethel was beginning to be afraid of him. He thinks Bethel knows he has discovered the boat. He grows alarmed, and buys a knife; he records that "he can take care of himself." But there is bravado in it. Later on, he finds that he is occasionally stealthily locked in at night, for three or four hours, and he buys a rope and hides it in his room. After that matters moved rapidly.

He found the gun room window unlocked on certain nights, and set a watch on it. And on one such night Bethel tried to kill him.

"He tried to kill me last night," he writes on the 27th of July, and goes on to say that Bethel couldn't have tied him, and that "maybe it was Porter." From that time on he suspected me.

And Bethel was watching him. Nothing is so dramatic in all the diary as the situation unconsciously revealed between the paralytic and the boy; each watching the other; the guard up between them, while the servant is in the room, and then down again. The boy recklessly mocking, the old man grim and waiting.

And nothing said. The boy goes to the city and tries to buy a revolver, but there is a new law in effect, and he fails. He has the knife, and has to trust to that. He thinks of going to the police while he is in the city; the reward would be a big thing. He says: "I could go around the world on ten thousand." But his case isn't complete; he needs the outside man. He suspects me, but he "hasn't the goods" on me.

And there are times when he admits the possibility that I may not be the outside man. One night he hears the unknown in the house. There is a reddish glare and he sees a figure steal into the den. But it "did not look like Porter." And he is more puzzled than ever, for Bethel is in his room, asleep, and although the boy camps on the stairs until daylight, he does not see the figure again.

"At daylight examined den and library. All windows closed and locked. It beats me."

It is about this time, too, that he begins to believe that Bethel is not only watching him, but that he is expecting trouble from some other source. He tells Bethel he has seen a figure go into the den at night, and Bethel shows alarm.

"He and the other one have quarreled," he says. "And B.'s afraid of him."

But on the night when he came home, to find Starr, Halliday and myself in the house, his suspicions of me returned in full force. He decides that Bethel and I have had a quarrel, and that one of us has tried to shoot the other! But his knife has been taken; he steals one from the kitchen and carefully sharpens it; but he is not so frightened as he has been. Bethel and I have quarreled, and he "can handle the old man."

But matters were rapidly approaching a climax. Bethel was going to give up the house and let him go. He seems to have dared Bethel to discharge him, and to have more than hinted at what he suspects.

"I can talk for ten thousand," he writes, "or keep quiet for twenty. He can take his choice."

He has the upper hand, now. The other man is no longer in evidence; they have apparently quarreled, and Bethel is left to bear the situation alone. The boy lays various traps, but no one enters the house. "The murder pact" is broken, and the old man sits in his chair and broods.

"Blackmail is an ugly word," he says once.

"Not half so ugly as murder," retorts Gordon, and notes it with satisfaction in his diary.

"Murder" was the last word he wrote there. . . .

But, for all his apparent frankness, Greenough's errand was clearly only to relieve my anxieties concerning myself. He refused all further information.

"We have a suspect, all right," he said. "I don't mind saying that. But we haven't a case yet, and it's touch and go whether we get one. Until we do, we're not talking."

September 8th.

HALLIDAY'S attitude is very curious. He is taciturn in the extreme; he avoids any confidential talks with me, and Jane commented on it this morning.

"He worries me," she said, "and he is worrying Edith. If you go out now and look, you'll see him pacing the boat-house verandah, and he has been doing it for the last hour."

I admit that he puzzles me. It was Greenough's errand, so far as I can make out, to relieve my mind as to myself, but to treat Halliday's case, as given to the police, as entirely confidential.

"It's the outside man we are after," he said; "and the outside man we are going to get."

But on my mentioning my right to know who was under suspicion, he only repeated what the detective had said.

"You understand," he said, "there's no case in law yet. Knowing who did a thing, and proving who did it, are different things entirely."

But they would prove it, he was confident. So confident, indeed, that before he left he inquired the make and cost of my car. Evidently he has already mentally banked the reward.

On the other hand, certain things seem to me still to be far from clear.

Halliday, I understand, passed over to the police the following facts:

(a) A copy of the unfinished letter from Horace Porter to some unknown.

(b) A description of the print of a hand, left on the window board.

(c) A small illustration from the book "Eugenia Riggs and her Phenomena," and showing the same hand print.

(d) A sworn statement of the Livingstones' butler, the nature of which I do not know.

(e) An analysis of his own theory of the experiments referred to in the diary.

(f) And a letter to Edith from an anonymous correspondent. (To be referred to later.)

(g) The possibility that the two attempts to enter the main house are due to the fact that, in the haste of the escape, something was left there which is both identifying and incriminating.

But so far as I can discover, he has not told them that, from the time the guards were taken away from the house at night, he was on watch there.

In other words, from shortly after the murder he must have known that something incriminating had been left there, when Bethel and his accomplice, Gordon's "outside man," made their escape the night the secretary was murdered. He may even know what it is, and where. But he has not told Greenough.

Again, there is the fact that a statement by the Livingstones' butler was a portion of the evidence he submitted. Surely they are not endeavoring to incriminate Livingstone!

September 9th.

IT is Halliday's idea to hold another seance, using Cameron's coming as the excuse for it. I gather that he believes that, under cover of the seance, another attempt may be made to secure the incriminating evidence left in the house. Not that he says so, but his questions concerning the sounds I heard in the hall during the second seance point in that direction.

"This herbal odor you speak of, Skipper," he asked, "was that before you heard the movement outside?"

"Some time before. Yes. But the odor seemed to be *in* the room; the sounds were beyond the door."

"You don't connect them, then?"

"I hadn't thought about it, but I don't believe I do."

"Did you hear any footsteps?"

I had to consider that. "Not footsteps; there was a sort of scraping along the floor."

"And the moment you spoke this noise ceased?"

"Yes."

The whole situation is baffling in the extreme. I cannot ignore the fact that the seances were proposed by Mrs. Livingstone, that it was she who left the hall door unbolted at the second sitting, or that Livingstone himself was absent that second night, presumably ill. At the same time, it was Livingstone who indirectly advised me against the business.

"Let it alone," he warned me. "Let well enough alone."

So far as Halliday is concerned, it is clear that he does not like the idea of another seance, but feels that it is necessary. He assures me the police will be on hand, inside and outside the house, but he does not minimize the fact that there will be a certain risk, and that he dreads taking Jane and Edith into it.

"It's like this," he said to-day, feeling painfully for words. "In a sense, you and I are at the parting of the ways in this thing. We can let it go, and turn loose on the world a cruel and deadly idea which may go on claiming victims indefinitely." He made a small gesture. "Or—we put into the other side of the scale all we have in the world, and then——" He pulled himself up. "There's only possible danger," he said. "Unless things slip, there should be very little."

The same list of those present as before. There is an unconscious emphasis placed by Halliday on Hayward and Livingstone, but perhaps I am over-watchful.

I daresay, thus placed between my duty and my fears, I shall do my duty. I perceive that either Hayward or

Livingstone is once more to be allowed access to the house, and under conditions more or less favorable to what is to be done. But which one? . . .

Later: I have done my duty. I have telephoned Cameron, and he will come out to-morrow night.

September 10th.

H ALLIDAY has taken every possible precaution as to to-night. As it has been our custom to go over the house before each seance, and as Cameron may do this with unusual thoroughness, it has been decided not to place Greenough and his officers until after the sitting begins. Halliday has therefore to-day connected the bell from that room, which rings in the kitchen, to a temporary extension in the garage, with a buzzer. When the lights are lowered, he will touch the bell, and Greenough is then to smuggle his men in through the kitchen.

While no one can say what changes Cameron may suggest in our previous methods, Halliday imagines he will ask us at first to proceed as usual. In any event, I am to sit as near to the switch as possible, and when Halliday calls for lights, am to be ready to turn them on. . . .

8 : 30 Everything is ready. But I am concerned about Halliday. Has he some apprehension about his own safety to-night?

He came an hour or so too early to start with the car for Cameron, and borrowing pen and paper, wrote a long communication to Hemingway. What is in it I do not know, but he took it with him, to mail on his way to the station.

(END OF MR. PORTER'S JOURNAL)

CONCLUSION
CHAPTER I

THE Journal takes us up to the evening of September 10th, 1922. It was to the fourth and last tragedy of that summer, which filled the next day's papers, that little Pettingill referred, in the conversation recorded in the introduction of this Journal.

It was with this tragedy that, as Pettingill said aggrievedly, the story "quit" on them. And quit it did. We felt then that the best thing to do, under the circumstances, was to let it rest. Once more, *de mortuis nil nisi bonum*.

There was nothing to be gained by giving the story to the public, and much to be lost. At that time, it is to be remembered, a wave of spiritualism, or rather spiritism, was spreading over the country; it was still filled, too, with post-war psychopaths. The very nature of the experiment which had been tried was of the sort to seize on the neurotic imagination, and set it a-flame. It was not considered advisable to allow it publicity.

Now, of course, things are different. The search goes on, and perhaps some day, not by this method but by some legitimate and scientific one, survival may be proved. I do not know; I do not greatly care. After all, I am a Christian, and my faith is built on a life after death. But I accept that; I do not require proof of it. . . .

Picture us, then, that evening of September 10th, when the Journal ends, waiting for we knew not what; Jane picking up her tapestry and putting it down again; Edith powdering her nose with hands that shook in spite of her best efforts; Halliday at the railroad station with the car to meet Cameron; and off in the woodland, where the red lamp of the light-house flashed its danger signal every ten seconds from the end of Robinson's point, Greenough and a half dozen officers.

Picture us, too, when we had all gathered; Cameron, with his hand still bandaged, presented to the *dramatis personæ* of the play and eyeing each one in turn shrewdly; Mrs. Livingstone garrulous and uneasy; and Livingstone a sort of waxy white and with a nervous trembling I had never observed before. Of us all, only Halliday seemed natural. And Hayward, natural because he was never at ease.

What Cameron made of it I do not know. Very probably he saw in us only a group of sensation-seekers, excited by some small contact with a world beyond our knowledge, and if he felt surprise at all, it was that I had joined the ranks.

He himself did not appear to take the matter seriously. He made it plain that he had come in this manner at my request; that his own methods would be entirely different. When Edith, I think it was, asked him if he made any preparation for such affairs, he laughed and shook his head.

"Except that I sometimes take a cup of coffee to keep me awake!" he said.

On the way up the drive I walked with Livingstone. Why, I hardly know, except that he seemed to drift toward me. He never spoke but once, and it seemed to me that he was surveying the shrubbery and trees, like a man who suspected a trap. Once—he was on my left —I was aware that he had put his hand to his hip pocket, and I was so startled that I stumbled and almost fell. I knew, as confidently as I have ever known anything, that he had a revolver there.

"Careful, man," he said.

Those were his only words during our slow progress

toward the main house, and so tense were his nerves that they sounded like a curse.

Cameron and Edith were leading, and I could hear her talking, carrying on valiantly, although as it turned out she knew better than any of us, except Halliday, the terrible possibilities ahead. Hayward walked alone and behind us, his rubber soled shoes making no sound on the drive. It made me uneasy, somehow; that silent progress of his; it was stealthy and disconcerting. And I think Livingstone felt it so too, for he stopped once and turned around.

Yet, at the time, as between the two men, my suspicion that evening certainly pointed to Livingstone. Not to go into the cruelty of my ignorance, a cruelty which I now understand but then bitterly resented, I had had both men under close observation during the time we waited for Cameron. And it had seemed to me that Livingstone was the more uneasy of the two. Another thing which I regarded as highly significant was his asking for water just before we left the Lodge, and holding the glass with a trembling hand.

And, as it happens, it was that very glass of water which crystallized my suspicions. The glass and the hand which held it. For the hand was a small and wide one, with a short thumb and a bent little finger!

From that time on, my mind was focused on Livingstone. It milled about, seeking some explanation. I could see Livingstone in the case plainly enough; I could see him, pursuing with old Bethel the "sinister design" to which Gordon had referred, but to which I had no key. I could see him, with his knowledge of the country, using that knowledge in furtherance of that idea which my Uncle Horace had termed a menace to society in general. With the swiftness with which thought creates visions, I could even see him hailing poor Maggie Morrison in the storm, and her stopping her truck when she recognized him.

But I could not see him in connection with Eugenia Riggs and her bowl of putty. Strange that I did not; that it required Jane's smelling salts for me to find that connection. A small green glass bottle, in Edith's room, used as a temporary paper weight on her desk.

As I say, my suspicions were of Livingstone, during that strange walk up the drive. But I had by no means eliminated Hayward.

He was there, behind me, walking with a curious stealth, and with an uneasiness that somehow, without words, communicated itself to me.

All emotions are waves, I daresay. I caught the contagion of fear from him; desperate, deadly fear.

And once in the house, my suspicions of him increased rather than diminished. For one thing, he offered to take Cameron through the house, and on Halliday's ignoring that, and going off with Cameron himself, was distinctly surly. He remained in the hall at the foot of the stairs, apparently listening to their progress and gnawing at his fingers.

Watching him from the den, I saw him make a move to go up the stairs, but he caught my eye and abandoned the idea.

It was then that Jane felt faint, and I went back to the Lodge for her smelling salts. . . .

The letter, undoubtedly the letter which Halliday had shown to the police, was lying open on Edith's desk, under the green bottle, and as I lifted the salts it blew to the floor. I glanced at it as I picked it up.

Chapter II

IN recording the events leading up to the amazing *denouement* that night—the details of the seance—I am under certain difficulties.

Thus, I kept no notes. For the first time I found myself a part of the circle, sitting between Livingstone and Jane, and with Cameron near the lamp, prepared to make the notes of what should occur.

"Of course," he said, as we took our places, "we are not observing the usual precautions of what I would call a test seance. All we are attempting to do is to reproduce, as nearly as possible, the conditions existing at the other two sittings. And——" he glanced at me and smiled "——if Mr. Porter's admission to the circle proves to be disturbing, we can eliminate him."

He asked us to remain quiet, no matter what happened, and to be certain that no hand was freed without an immediate statement to that effect.

"Not that I expect fraud, of course," he added. "But it is customary, under the circumstances."

I am quite certain that nobody, except myself, saw Halliday touch the bell as the light was reduced to the faint glow of the red lamp.

It was not surprising, I daresay, that beyond certain movements of the table and fine raps on its surface, we got nothing at first! in fact, that we got anything at all was probably due solely to Jane's ignorance of the under-lying situation. Livingstone, next to me, was so nervous that his hands twitched on the table; across, Halliday was beside Hayward, and as my eyes grew accustomed to the semi-darkness, I could see him, forbidden recourse to his fingers, jerking his head savagely.

And, for the life of me, I could not see where all this was leading us. A breaking of the circle was, by Cameron's order, immediately to be announced. Even in complete darkness, when that came—as I felt it would —what was it that Halliday expected to happen?

But the table continued to move. It began to slide along the carpet; my grasp on Livingstone's hand was relaxed, and indeed, later, as it began to rock violently, it was all I could do to retain contact with the table at all. I began to see possibilities in this, but when it had quieted the circle remained as before.

Very soon after that came the signal for darkness, and Cameron extinguished the lamp. Soon Edith, near the cabinet, said the curtain had come out into the room, and was touching her. The next moment, as before, the bell fell from the stand inside the cabinet, and the guitar strings were lightly touched.

Without warning Cameron turned on the lamp; the curtain subsided and all sounds ceased. He was apparently satisfied, and after a few moments of experiment with the lamp on, resulting only in a creaking and knocking on the table, again extinguished it. On a repetition of the blowing out of the curtain, however, he left his chair for the first time, and with a pocket flash examined the cabinet thoroughly, even the wall coming in for close inspection.

When he had finished with that, however, I sensed a change in him. I believe now that he suspected fraud, but I am not certain. He said rather sharply that he was there in good faith and not to provide an evening's amusement, and that he hoped any suspicious movement would be reported.

"This is not a game," he said shortly.

Jane was very quiet, and now I heard again the heavy

breathing which I knew preceded the trance condition, or that auto-hypnotism which we know as trance.

"Who is that?" Cameron asked in a low tone.

"Mrs. Porter," Halliday said. "Quiet, everybody!"

The room was completely dark, and save for Jane's heavy breathing, entirely quiet. Strangely enough, for the moment I forgot our purpose there; forgot Greenough and his men, scattered through the house; I had a premonition, if I may call it that, that we were on the verge of some tremendous psychic experience. I cannot explain it; I do not know now what unseen forces were gathered there together. I even admit that probably I too, like Jane, had hypnotized myself.

And then two things were happening, and at the same time.

There was something moving in the library, a soft foot-fall with, it seemed to me, an irregularity. For all the world like the dragging of a partially useless foot, and —Livingstone was quietly releasing his grip of my hand.

I made a clutch at him, and he whispered savagely:

"Let go, you fool."

The next moment he had drawn his revolver, and was stealthily getting to his feet.

The dragging foot moved out into the hall. Livingstone, revolver in hand, was standing beside me, and there was a quiet movement across the table. Cameron was apparently listening also; he made no comment, however, and in the darkness and the silence the footsteps went into the hall, and there ceased.

I had no idea of the passage of time; ten seconds or an hour Livingstone may have stood beside me. Ten seconds or an hour, and then Greenough's voice at the top of the staircase:

"All right. Careful below."

Livingstone moved then. He made a wild dash for

the red lamp and turned it on. Hayward was not to be seen, and Halliday, revolver in hand, was starting for the cabinet.

"More light," he called. "Light! Quick!"

I had a confused impression of Halliday, jerking the curtains of the cabinet aside; of somebody else there with him, both on guard, as it were, at the wall; of some sort of rapid movement upstairs; of the door from the den into the hall being open where it had been closed before, and of a crash somewhere not far away, as of a falling body, followed by a sort of dreadful pause.

And all this is in the time it took me to get around the chairs and to the wall switch near the door. And it was then, in the shocked silence which followed the sound of that fall, in the instant between my finding the switch and turning it on, that I will swear that I saw once more by the glow of the red lamp the figure at the foot of the stairs, looking up.

Saw it and recognized it. Watched it turn toward me with fixed and staring eyes, felt the cold wind which suddenly eddied about me, and frantically turning on the light, saw it fade like smoke into the empty air. . . .

Behind the curtains of the cabinet somebody was working at the wall. Edith, very pale, was supporting Jane, who still remained in her strange auto-hypnotic condition. Livingstone's arm was about his wife.

And this was the picture when Greenough came running triumphantly down the stairs, the reward apparently in his pocket, and saw us there. He paid no attention to the rest of us, but stared at Livingstone with eyes which could not believe what they saw.

"Good God!" he said. "Then who is in there?"

He pointed to the wall behind the cabinet.

Chapter III

THE steps by which Halliday solved the murder at the main house, and with it the mystery which had preceded it, constitute an interesting story in themselves. So certain was he that, by the time we were ready for the third seance, his material was already in the hands of the District Attorney. And it was not the material he had given to Greenough.

For the solution of a portion of the mystery, then, one must go back to the main house, and consider the older part of it. It is well known that many houses of that period were provided with hidden passages, by which the owners hoped to escape the Excise. Such an attempt, many years ago, had cost George Pierce his life.

But the passage leading from the old kitchen, now the den, to a closet in the room above it, had been blocked up for many years. The builder was dead; by all the laws of chance time might have gone on and the passage remained undiscovered.

In 1899, however, Eugenia Riggs bought the property, and in making repairs the old passage was discovered. Although she denies using it for fraudulent purposes, neither Halliday nor I doubt that she did so. She points to the plastered wall as her defense, but Halliday assures me that a portion of the base-board, hinged to swing out, but locked from within, would have allowed easy access to the cabinet.

But Halliday had at the beginning no knowledge of this passage, with its ladder to the upper floor. He reached it by pure deduction.

"It had to be there," he says modestly. "And it was." . . .

Up to the time young Gordon was attacked at the kitchen door, however, Halliday was frankly at sea. That is, he had certain suspicions, but that was all. He had discovered, for instance, that the cipher found in my garage was written on the same sort of bond paper as that used by Gordon, by the simple expedient of having Annie Cochran get him a sheet of it, on some excuse or other.

But his actual case began, I believe, with that attack on Gordon. At least he began at that time definitely to associate the criminal with the house.

"There was something fishy about it," is the way he puts it.

And with Bethel's story to me, forced by his fear that the boy knew it was he who had attacked him, the belief that it was "fishy" gained ground.

"Gordon was knocked out," he says. "And that ought to have been enough. But it was not. He was tied, too, tied while he was still unconscious. Somebody wasn't taking a chance that he'd get back into the house very soon."

It was that "play for time," as he terms it, that made him suspicious.

All this time, of course, he was ignorant of any underlying motive; he makes it clear that he simply began, first to associate the crimes with the house, and then with Bethel. He kept going back to his copy of the unfinished letter, but:

"It didn't help much," he says quietly. "Only, there was murder indicated in it. And we were having murder."

He had three clues, two of them certain, one doubtful. The certain ones were the linen from the oar-lock of the boat, torn from a sheet belonging to the main house, and the small portion of the cipher. The one he was not certain about was the lens from an eyeglass, outside the culvert.

He began to watch the house; he "didn't get" Gordon in the situation at all; there was no situation there, really; nothing, that is, that he could lay his hand on. But on the night I called him and he started toward Robinson's Point, as he came back toward the house he saw the figure of a man, certainly not Gordon, enter the house by the gun room window. When he got there the window was closed and locked.

He was puzzled. He looked around for me, but I was not in sight. Still searching for me, he made a round of the house, and so was on the terrace when I fired the shot. From that time on he saw Bethel somehow connected with the mystery, but only as the brains.

"There was some devil's work afoot," he said. "But always I came up against that paralysis of his. He had to have outside help."

On the night in question, then, he was certain that this accomplice was still in the house through all that followed; through Hayward's arrival and Starr's. He was so certain by that time of Gordon's innocence that he very nearly took him into his confidence the next day. But he was afraid of the boy; he was not dependable; Halliday had an idea that "he was playing his own game."

But if this man was in the house that night, where was he?

He grew suspicious of the den, after that, and he found out through Starr the name of the builder who had put in the panelling in the den, for Uncle Horace. It was a long story, but in the end he learned something.

Tearing the old base-board prior to putting up the panels, the builder had happened on the old passage to the room overhead, and he had called Horace Porter's attention to it. It seems to have appealed to the poor old chap; it belonged, somehow, to the room, with the antique stuff he was putting into it. He built in a sliding panel; it was not a particularly skillful piece of work, but it answered. And he kept his secret, at least from me.

I doubt if he ever used it, until Prohibition came in. Then, no drinker himself, he put there a small and choice supply of liquors, some of which we found later on. And one bottle of which placed Halliday in peril of his life, a day or so after the night I had fired the shot into the hall.

He had borrowed Annie Cochran's key to the kitchen door, and after midnight entered the house and went to the den. Although he is reticent about this portion of it, I gather that the house was not all it should be that night.

"You know the sort of thing," he says.

But, pressed as to that, he admits that he was hearing small and inexplicable sounds from the library. Chairs seemed to move, and once he was certain that the curtain in the doorway behind him blew out into the room. When he looked back over his shoulder, however, it was hanging as before.

He had no trouble in finding the panel, and as carefully as he could he stepped inside. But he had touched one of the bottles and it fell over.

"It didn't make much noise," he says, "but it was enough. He was awake, and paralysis or no paralysis, I hadn't time to move before he was in the closet overhead, and opening the trap in the floor."

He had not had time to move, and even if he had, there were the infernal bottles all around him. So he stood without breathing, waiting for he knew not what.

"Things looked pretty poor," he says. "I didn't know

when he'd strike a match and see me. And it was good-night if he did!"

But Bethel had no match, evidently. He stood listening intently, and in the darkness below Halliday held his breath and waited. Then Bethel moved. He left the trap door above open and went for a light, and Halliday crawled out and closed the panel quietly.

From that time on, however, he knew Bethel was no more helpless than he was. He abandoned the idea of an accomplice, and concentrated on the man himself. . . .

Annie Cochran was working with him; that is, she did what he asked her, although she seems not to have known at any time the direction in which he was working. Her own mind was already made up; she believed Gordon to be guilty. She made no protest, however, when he asked her to break Mr. Bethel's spectacles one early morning, and give him the fragments. But she did it, pretending afterwards that she had thrown the pieces into the stove.

Bethel was watchful and suspicious by that time, and she had a bad time of it, but what is important here is that Halliday took the fragments into the city, and established beyond a doubt that they and the piece of a lens found near the culvert were made from the same prescription.

And he had no more than made his discovery, when Gordon, attempting at last the blackmail which he had been threatening, was put out of the way as quickly and ruthlessly as had been poor Peter Carroway.

"Twenty-four hours," Halliday says bitterly, "and we would have saved him."

But twenty-four hours later Bethel had made good his escape, and everything was apparently over.

But from that time Bethel as Bethel, ceased to exist for Halliday. . . .

He was not working alone, however. Very early, he had realized that he needed assistance, real assistance. Annie Cochran's help was always of the below-stairs order. And he found the help he wanted after the night Gordon was attacked, in Hayward. As a matter of fact, it was Hayward who went to him.

"He was worried about you, Skipper," Halliday says, with a grin. "He considered it quite possible that the attempt to wrangle English literature into too many brain corrals might have driven you slightly mad."

And breaks off to wonder, "by Jove," if that's where the English get their collegiate term of wrangler!

On the night, then, when Gordon was hurt, the doctor was impulsively on his way to Halliday and the boat-house.

"He came within an inch of having you locked up that night," says Halliday.

Later on, he did go to Halliday, and Halliday then and there enlisted him in his service. He was not shrewd, but he was willing and earnest, and from that time on he was useful. He had started, presumably, on his vacation but actually on a very different errand, when the murder at the main house occurred, and Halliday recalled him by wire.

But when he returned, it was, at Halliday's request, to hide in the Livingstone house. It was from there that he came, at night, to assist Halliday in guarding the main house. And to provide, by the way, that sworn statement of the Livingstones' butler, that after the murder they had concealed some one in the house, which threw Greenough so completely off the track.

One perceives, of course, that the Livingstones had been brought into the case. Dragged in, is the way

Halliday puts it. But after the first conference between the doctor and himself they were in it, willy nilly.

"Who," Halliday asked Hayward, referring to his copy of my Uncle Horace's letter, "were likely to have access to Horace Porter at night?"

"No one, so far as I know. The Livingstones, possibly."

"Then the man who came in while he was writing this letter might have been Livingstone?"

"He was ill that night. I was with him."

"Then Livingstone's out," said Halliday, and turned in a new direction.

"Some theory, some wickedness, was put up to him. And it horrified and alarmed him. A man doesn't present such a theory without leading up to it. Let's try this: what subject was most interesting Horace Porter during the last years, or months, of his life?"

"Spiritism, I imagine. I know he was working on it."

"Alone? A man doesn't work that sort of thing alone, as a rule."

'I'll ask Mrs. Livingstone, if you like. She may know."

And ask the Livingstones he did, with the result that Halliday got his first real clue, and elaborated the daring theory which culminated in that fatal fall from the ladder, in the secret passage on the tragic night of the 10th of September. . . .

All this time, of course, it remained only a theory. Hayward scouted it at first, but came to it later on; the Livingstones offered a more difficult problem.

"They didn't want to be involved," Halliday says. "But after Edith's letter came I more or less had them. And of course after he'd tried to get into the house, and left the print of his hand on the window board, they had to come in. They'd denied any knowledge of the

passage before that. But he knew it as well as I did, or
better, and that there was a chance old Bethel knew it too,
and had used it."

This letter of Edith's, to which I have already referred,
runs as follows:

"Dear Madam:

"I have read your article with great interest, and would
like to suggest that a good medium might be very useful
under the circumstances.

"You have one of the best in the country in your
vicinity. She has retired, and is now living under another
name somewhere in the vicinity of Oakville. I understand her husband has made considerable money, but she
may be willing to help in spite of that.

"When I knew her she was known as Eugenia Riggs,
but this was her maiden name, which she had retained.
Her husband's name is Livingstone; I do not know his
initials.

"She has abandoned the profession in which she made
so great a success, but I understand is still keenly interested."

The letter is not signed. . . .

Halliday did not require that knowledge; he had suspected it before. But it gave him a lever. One attempt
had already been made by Bethel to get back into the
house. Time was getting short; before long we would
have to go back to the city, and although he knew by
that time who and what Bethel was, he could prove
nothing. To go was to abandon the case.

He could not secure the arrest of a man because his
lens prescription was the same as the murderer's. Or
on the strength of an unsigned book manuscript left
behind the wall of the den. He could not prove that

Maggie Morrison had died in the process of the experiment Gordon had puzzled over, because the mud on the truck wheels corresponded with the red iron-clay of the lane into the main house. He could not prove his own interpretation of the abbreviations S. and G. T. so liberally scattered through the diary. And he could not prove that it was Bethel who, looking for the broken lens in or near the culvert, had found my fountain pen there. A fact which Gordon had noted in the Journal as follows: "I have them now, sure. W. P. was here last night and left his fountain pen."

But he could, through the Livingstones, take a chance on proving all these things. And, against Livingstone's protests and fears, prove it he did.

"As a matter of fact," he says, "they were in a bad position themselves, and they knew it. They had to come over again!" . . .

Things were, indeed, rather parlous for the Livingstones. The butler's story had turned the suspicions of the police toward them. And on the night of my threatened arrest Halliday deliberately used them to avert that catastrophe.

"As a matter of fact," he says cheerfully, "I gave the police a very pretty case against them. It was all there, according to Greenough. Even to the hand-print!"

But he held them off. He had done what he wanted, turned the police along a false trail and was free once more to travel along the true one. And in this he says, and I believe, that his purpose was not mercenary.

"The situation was peculiar," he says. "The slightest slip, the faintest suspicion, and he was off."

And he goes back again to the subtlety and wariness of the criminal himself; so watchful, so wary, that throughout it had even been necessary to keep me in ignorance.

"You had to carry on, Skipper," he says. "In a way, the whole thing hung on you. Even then, you nearly wrecked us once."

Which was, he tells me the night of the second seance, when the criminal actually fell into the trap and entered the house. Livingstone was on guard upstairs that night, and everything would have ended then probably.

"But you spilled the beans!" he accuses me.

From the first the seances were devised for a purpose, and I gather that some of the phenomena were deliberately faked, in pursuit of that purpose. On the other hand, Mrs. Livingstone has always been firm in her statement that "things happened" which she cannot explain. The sounds in the library, the lights and the arrival of the book on the table are among them.

But, trickery or genuine psychic manifestations, in the end they served their purpose. I called the third seance, and the mystery was solved. . . .

It is not surprising that my memory of those last few moments is a clouded one; I was, of all those present except the police, the only one in complete ignorance of the meaning of what was going on about me. Edith knew, and was bravely taking her risk with the others; even my dear Jane knew a little; no wonder she required her smelling salts.

Actually, out of the confusion, only two pictures remain in my mind:

One was of Greenough staring at Livingstone, and then jerking aside the curtains of the cabinet, where Halliday and Hayward had opened the panel and after turning on the red globe hanging there, were stooping over a body at the bottom of the ladder.

The other is of that figure at the foot of the stairs.

I know now that it could not have been there; that it was lying, dead of a broken neck, at the foot of the ladder.

I have heard all the theories, but I cannot reconcile them with the fact. How could I have imagined it? I did not know then who was inside the wall.

I am not a spiritist, but once in every man's life comes to him the one experience which he can explain by no law of nature as he understands them

To every man his ghost, and to me, mine.

In the dim light of the red lamp, dead though he was behind the panel, I will swear that I saw Cameron, *alias* Simon Bethel, standing at the foot of the stairs and looking up.

Chapter IV

WHO are we to judge him? If a man sincerely believes that there is no death, the taking of life to prove it must seem a trivial thing.

He may feel, and from his book manuscript hastily hidden behind the wall of the den we gather he did feel, that the security of the individual counted as nothing against the proof of survival to the human race.

But that he was entirely sane, in those last months, none of us can believe. Cruelty is a symptom of the borderland between sanity and madness; so too is the weakening of what we call the Herd instinct. It is well known at the University that for the year previous to his death he had been distinctly anti-social.

Certainly, too, he fulfilled the axiom that insanity is the exaggeration of one particular mental activity. And that he combined this single exaggeration with a high grade of intelligence only proves the close relation between madness and genius: Kant, unable to work unless gazing at a ruined tower; Hawthorne, cutting up his bits of paper; Wagner's periodical violences.

The very audacity of his disguise, the consistency with

which he lived the part he was playing, points to what I believe is called dissociation; toward the last there seems to have been a genuine duality of personality: during the day old Simon Bethel, dragging his helpless foot and without effort holding his withered hand to its spastic contraction; at night, the active Cameron, making his exits on his nocturnal adventures by the gun room window; wandering afoot incredible distances; watching the door of Gordon's room and locking him in; learning from me of Halliday's interest in the case, and trying to burn him out; very early realizing the embarrassment of my own presence at the Lodge, and warning me away by that letter from Salem, Ohio.

It seems clear that he had not expected me at the Lodge; Larkin apparently told Gordon, but Gordon neglected to inform him. Just what he felt, what terror and anger, when I greeted him at the house on his arrival will never be known. I remember now how he watched me, peering up at me through his disguising spectacles, with the beef cube in his hand, and waiting. Waiting.

But the disguise held. My own very slight acquaintance with him, my near-sightedness, my total lack of suspicion, all were in his favor. And of the perfection of the disguise itself, it is enough to say that Gordon apparently never suspected it. He did suspect the paralysis.

"He moved his arm to-day," he wrote once, in the diary. "He knows I saw it, and he has watched me ever since."

"It takes very little to change an appearance beyond casual recognition," Halliday tells me. "The idea is to take a few important points and substitute their opposites. Take a man with partial paralysis; one side of his face drops, you see. Well, he can't imitate that, but he can put a fig in the other cheek and raise it. Put hair

on a bald-headed man, and watch the change. And there
are other things; eyebrows now——"

Only once did I come anywhere near the truth, and
then it slipped past me, and I did not catch it. That was
on the night he sent for me, after he had struck Gordon
down. He was frightened that night, we know now.
Gordon was suspicious; might even have gone to the
police.

And that night he tested his disguise and me.

I have recorded the revolt I felt after his attack on
the Christian faith. And that I had the feeling of having
heard almost the same thing, eons ago. I *had* heard the
same thing, from Cameron, on the first occasion of my
meeting him. . . .

Much of the explanation of that tragic summer becomes mere surmise, naturally. There is no surmise,
however, necessary as regards Cameron's coming to the
third seance, at my invitation. So far as he knew, we
still believed that Simon Bethel was dead. That our circle,
so innocent in appearance, so naive, was a cleverly devised
trap seems not to have occurred to him. My frankness,
the product of my ignorance, would probably have reassured a man less driven by necessity than he was.

But even had he suspected something, I believe he
would have come. His other attempts, to enter the house
and secure the manuscript, had failed. And any day some
bit of mischance, a mouse behind a panel, a casual repair,
and this book of his, with its characteristic phrasing, its
references to his earlier works, would be in the hands
of the police.

With what secret eagerness he accepted my invitation
we can only guess. Halliday, carefully plotting, had
already discounted his acceptance in advance.

"I knew he would come, of course," he says. "He
wanted to get in. We offered him not only that, but

darkness to cover any move he wanted to make. It had to work out."

And here he explains the necessity of having the criminal caught *flagrante delictu*. It had to be shown, he says, not only that Cameron had written the manuscript, but that it was he who had hidden it where it lay.

"The case against him stood or fell by that," he says. . . .

But aside from this, much of the explanation of that tragic summer becomes pure guesswork. We have, however, elaborated the following as fulfilling our requirements as to the situation:

We know for instance that on old Horace Porter's developing interest in spiritism, Mrs. Livingstone referred him to Cameron. But we do not know why that interest developed.

Is it too much, I wonder, to say that the house itself led him to it? In this I know I am on dangerous ground, and it becomes still more dangerous if one grants that Mrs. Livingstone's gift of a red lamp led him to experimenting with it.

We do know, however, that after he had had this lamp for three months or so, he got in touch with Cameron, and it seems probable that such experiments as were made there at night with this lamp roused Cameron to fever heat.

Mrs. Livingstone believes there was a pact between them, the usual one of the first to "pass over" to come back if possible. We do not know that, but it seems plausible. Neither Halliday nor I believe, however, as she does, that Cameron killed the older man, in a fit of rage over the rejection of his proposal to carry their investigations to the criminal point.

What seems more probable is that Cameron had very early recognized the advantages of the house for the psychic and scientific experiments he had in mind, and that he finally submitted the idea to old Horace. With what growing horror and indignation they were received we know from his letter.

They turned a possible ally into an angry and dangerous enemy; the rejection of the proposition, with the threat which accompanied it, left Cameron stripped before the world as an enemy to society. He went home and brooded over it.

"But he couldn't let it rest at that," Halliday says. "He went back. And the old man was at his desk. There was danger in Cameron that night, and the poor old chap was frightened. We'll say he crumpled his letter up in his hand, and Cameron didn't see it. Maybe there was an argument, and Cameron knocked him down. But he got up again, and he managed to drop the letter into an open drawer; after that, his heart failed, and he fell for good."

We acquit him of that. Of the others—? . . .

We are, with regard to the underlying motive, the so-called experiments, again obliged to resort to surmise. We know, for instance, of Cameron's early experiments in weighing the body before and immediately after death. He has himself recorded them. But in the manuscript of his book he distinctly states his belief that the vital principle, whatever that may be, is weakened by long illness, and his belief that those who pass over suddenly out of full health, are more able to manifest themselves.

He quotes numerous instances of murdered men, whom tradition believes to have returned for motives of vengeance. But he himself believes that this ability to return is due to the strength of the unweakened vital principle. The *whole* spirit, he calls it. And although his manuscript in itself does not deal with any discoveries he may have made during the summer, there are accompanying it certain pages of figures which seem to prove that he made more than one experiment along those lines during his occupancy of the house.

What waifs and strays he picked up on those night journeys of his we do not know; poor wanderers, probably, with no place in the world from which they could be missed.

At the same time, Halliday feels that the experiments were not necessarily to be with life and death; he suggests that they were to lie, rather, in deep narcosis, pushed to the danger point, and that it was under this narcosis that Maggie Morrison, for one, succumbed.

Among Cameron's papers, later on, we found a curious document entitled, "The reality of the Soul through a study of the effects of Chloroform and Curari on the Animal Economy," with this note in Cameron's hand:

"The soul and the body are separated by the agency of anæsthesia. The soul is not a breath, but an entity."

Of the nature of the further tests made we have no idea. Halliday believes that, shown the space behind the wall by Horace Porter, he later utilized it to conceal such apparatus as he used in his experiments.

"It seemed to be full of stuff," he says, "the night I found it."

But later on, as the chase narrowed, he got rid of it bit by bit at night, probably throwing it into the bay. This is borne out by the fact that, late that following autumn, going back to Twin Hollows to look over the property with a real estate dealer, I found washed up on the beach the battered fragments of a camera.

Only a portion of the lens remained in the frame, but this lens had been of quartz. As nearly as I can discover, the theory of quartz used in such a manner is to photograph the ultra-violet. In other words, I daresay, to make visible that strange world which may lie beyond the spectrum and our normal vision.

Did he obtain anything? We shall never know.

But sometimes I wonder. Suppose a man to have done what he had done to prove the immortality of the soul; to have taken lives and have risked his own, to give to the world the survival after death it so pathetically craves. And he fails; there is nothing. His own conviction has not weakened, but his proofs are not there.

Then, in the twinkling of an eye, he himself breaks through the veil. With that idea dominant, he passes over to the other side, perhaps to the long sleep, perhaps not. But in that instant between waking and sleeping, to prove his point! To make good his contention! To justify his course!

I wonder.

And I wonder, too, if at that moment of realization the supreme irony of the situation could have occurred to him? That the wounded hand, the one injury poor Gordon had managed to inflict on him, was the factor which had shot him, head-foremost, into eternity? . . .

Was Cameron our sheep-killer? We believe so, with certain reservations. We know he was at Bass Cove, under an assumed name, at the time, probably looking over the ground.

At the same time, it seems unlikely that he killed the first lot of Nylie's sheep; that we believe was an act of revenge on the part of a man Nylie had recently discharged.

But that the idea seized on his imagination seems probable. He was planning that mad campaign of his, and it fell in well with what was to come. It prepared the neighborhood, in a sense, but it set them looking for a maniac with a religious mania. And it was an effective alibi for him, occurring before his arrival at the house.

Jane has always believed that he added the symbol in chalk deliberately to incriminate me. I do not. He added it, after Helena Lear had told him of it, as he added the stone altar, a madman's conception of a madman's act.

Carroway's murder was incidental to that preparation of his, but in view of all we know, we can reconstruct it fairly well.

Thus we have the boy, tiring of carrying his rifle, putting it away in the darkness and possibly dozing. We have the appearance of the killer, and Carroway unable to locate his rifle quickly, following him to the waterfront and reaching it too late.

Underneath our float the killer should have found his knife, but as we know, Halliday had taken it away. They were two unarmed men, then, who met that night on the quiet surface of the bay. And one of them, although nobody knew it, was not sane.

Unarmed only in one sense, however, for Cameron had an oar. And used it.

When it was over, he apparently rowed back quietly to the creek beyond Robinson's Point, left his boat there, and walked to Bass Cove.

The proprietor of the small hotel there seems never to have known that he was out at night.

"He was a very quiet gentleman," he says, "and always went to bed early." . . .

One thing which had puzzled us, in the Morrison case, was that the girl had stopped her truck, at a time when the nerves of the country-side were on edge. It seems probable, therefore, that on some nights, at least, it was not the square and muscular Cameron who went forth, but an old and crippled man.

Shown to her by the lightning flashes that night, age

and infirmity by the roadside and a storm going, what wonder that she stopped? The only marvel is that, this bait having proven successful, it does not appear to have been used again . . .

And now, postpone it as I may, I have come to that portion of our summer to which I have early referred as the X in our equation. We have solved our problem. We may say quite properly, *Quod erat demonstrandum.* But there remains still the unsolved factor.

Much that impressed me strongly at the time has lost its impression now. It is a curious fact that a man may see a ghost—and many believe that they have done so— without any lasting belief in so-called survival after death. And so it is with me.

On editing my Journal, however, I find myself confronting the same questions which confronted me during that terrible summer.

Have I a body, or is my body all there is of me? In other words, am I an intelligence served by certain physical organs? Or am I certain physical organs, actuated by an intelligence as temporary as they?

Frankly, I do not know.

But any careful analysis of the extra-normal phenomena of the summer seems to show, every so often, some other-world intelligence, struggling to get through to us. As though—

We have never had, as I have said, any explanation of the coming of the book during the second seance, nor of the sounds from the library. While much of the physical phenomena of the first two seances was deliberately engineered by Mrs. Livingstone, in pursuance of Halliday's plan to get Cameron into the house, these two things remain without explanation.

The same thing is true of my finding of the letter, of the light-house apparition, of the sitting at Evanston, and of Jane's clairvoyant visions. None of which, by the way, she has had since. And yet all of which had their part, large or small, in our solving and understanding of the crimes.

Peter Geiss, and the figure in the fore-rigging of the sloop, my own vision of Cameron at the foot of the stairs, when he lay dead behind the panel, what am I to say of these?

Am I to accept them as I do Jane's "vision without eyes" as no more extraordinary than the feats of somnambulists, who go through their curious nightly progress with closed eyelids?

Am I to accept them, refute them, or evade them? . . .

There are, however, certain incidents which, puzzling as they were at the time, lend themselves to very simple explanation. Among these are the cough I heard more than once, and Hadly's story of the materialization in the Oakville cemetery.

Throughout Gordon's diary, here and there, were the letters S. and G. T. There was also, in one place, a sentence which translated, became "The G. P. stuff went great last night."

Halliday believes that Gordon was what we know as a medium, and that it was in that capacity primarily that Cameron took him to the country. The S. he therefore translates as "sitting," and the G. T. as "genuine trance." After the G. T. there almost invariably follows the rather pathetic entry: "Feel rotten to-day," or "all in."

Hadly's ghost, then, in all probability was the secretary, securing data for the "sittings" which he so carefully differentiates from the nights when he went into genuine trance. Being honest with himself, poor boy, and honest nowhere else. And the same was no doubt true as to the dry cough which he practised on me, the night I was in the garage, almost to my undoing.

It was during those "sittings" too, almost certainly, that under pretended control from beyond he began to ferret out, with the cunning of his kind, the story underneath; to bring back Horace Porter, and watch the reaction; to mention the boat he had discovered, and see the man across from him, in the dim red light, twitch and tremble.

To play him, to fool him, and at the last to threaten and blackmail him. And, in the end, to die.

But there remain these things I cannot explain. One of the most curious is the herbal odor; that this was not a purely subjective impression is shown by the fact that both Hayward and Edith noticed it during the second seance. The scent of flowers is, I believe, not unusual during certain psychic experiments; Warren speaks of the impression of tube roses being waved before him in the dark by some ghostly hand.

Of this, as of the other inexplicable phenomena, I can only say that at the time I did not doubt them; living them again, as I prepare this manuscript, I accept them once more. But I do not explain them.

"You wish," said Cicero, "to have the explanation of these things? Very well . . . I might tell you that the magnet is a body which attracts iron and attaches itself to it; but because I could not give you the explanation of it, would you deny it?" . . .

In closing this record, I cannot do better than copy the following extract from my Journal, made the following June.

June 1st, 1923.

Our little Edith was married to-day. Heigh-ho. And again, heigh-ho.

I have done the proper thing; led her up the aisle to Halliday (and would as lief have knocked him down as not) stepped back out of the picture and her life, and feeling for my handkerchief, like the besotted old fool I am, pulled out a washcloth instead.

Fortunate, perhaps, as I was on the verge of loud and broken sobs!

How we begrudge the happiness of others when it is at our expense! How I hated Halliday when, once in the house, he put his arms around her and held her close. How I resented that calm air of possession with which he took his place in the line beside her, and shook hands smilingly with the hysterical crowd that kissed and blessed them, on the way to the dining room and food.

And yet—how happy they are, and how safe she is.

"My *wife*," he said. "Forever and ever. Amen."

Old glass and new glass; china, silver and linen; the Lears' candle-sticks; every corner of the house filled with guests and gifts—and Jock. And for the two of them nothing and nobody; just a space filled with shadows which smiled and passed; themselves the only reality.

And perhaps they are. Love at least is real; the one reality perhaps. "Love, thou art absolute; sole Lord of life and death." . . .

So they have gone, and to-night Jane and I are alone. Safe and quiet—and alone, alas, behind the drain pipe.

Heigh-ho!

THE END